The Oracle

The Sarah Weston Chronicles
Book III

D.J. Niko

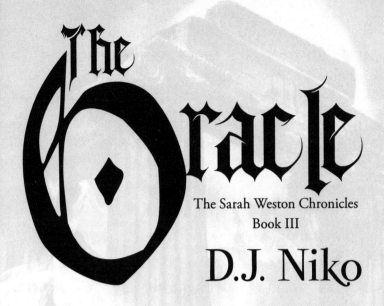

The Oracle

The Sarah Weston Chronicles
Book III

D.J. Niko

MEDALLION

Medallion Press, Inc.

Printed in USA

Published 2015 by Medallion Press, Inc.
4222 Meridian Parkway, Suite 110, Aurora, IL 60504

The MEDALLION PRESS LOGO
is a registered trademark of Medallion Press, Inc.

Cataloging-in-Publication Data is on file with the Library of Congress.

Typeset in Adobe Garamond Pro
Printed in the United States of America
ISBN 978-1605426-27-3

10 9 8 7 6 5 4 3 2 1
First Edition

For Yianni, my father
In memoriam

Tell the king the fair-built hall has fallen.

Apollo now has no house or oracular laurel or prophetic spring.

The water is silent.

—Message from the Delphians to
Julian the Apostate,
fourth century CE

One

Livadeia, central Greece,
393 CE

Like a beast being hunted, the priestess sprinted through the woods. The men who sought her were the worst kind of predators: they would skin her alive while chanting the hymns of the righteous.

The fallen leaves of the mother oaks lay in strata upon the forest floor, crumbling beneath her swift feet and revealing her position as she ran toward salvation. She felt the angry thump of her heartbeat in the pit of her stomach. The shadows that followed her gained ground.

She implored Apollo for a silver thread of moonlight. As she gasped for air to fill her constricted lungs, the pewter clouds parted and a beam flashed through the tree branches, illuminating patches of ground. There, along the hillside, beyond the barren oaks, was the stand of evergreens lining the path to the river Herkyna. Though she could not hear it over her own frantic breath, she imagined the murmur of the river's sacred waters, and it gave her strength.

Just a few more steps to the cave.

Would her brothers be waiting there? Or had they given up on her? It had been so long since she was abducted, dragged into the den of the savages who waved the banner of a new god. Had her tribe remained loyal to her, to their shared principles? Or had they suffered a similar fate and scattered to the four winds?

She would soon know the answer. She ignored her body's protests and commanded her legs to run faster.

Just a few more steps . . .

"Aristea of Delphi." The whisper of a male voice mocked her. Was he friend or foe? Without slowing her pace, she looked over her shoulder. No one was there.

He repeated her name, this time with a hiss that made the fine hairs on her arms stand on end. She felt a searing presence and saw in her mind's eye the red-hot iron they had used to brand her, as if she were the property of their despicable temple. The thought unnerved her.

Sucking at the cool air with great gasps, Aristea kept running toward the pines. Her hood caught on a low-hanging branch and was ripped off her head, exposing her shorn hair. The monk's habit she wore as a disguise was soaked through with perspiration, and the linen gauze of the tunic beneath clung to her skin.

None of that mattered. She sought only to escape from the madmen who hunted her, the ones who justified their atrocities by crouching behind a higher power. She knew they were capable of anything. She had been the recipient of their abomination.

"Aristea." Voices now taunted her from multiple

directions, as if they had surrounded her. "You cannot hide."

Again she glanced over her shoulder, and again she saw nothing. She faced forward in time to see the peeling bark of the evergreens coming fast toward her. The impact made her fall backward and land on her tailbone on top of a jagged piece of limestone. The pain shot up her spine like Zeus' thunderbolt.

A terrible laugh came from the shadows. Panting, Aristea stumbled to her feet. Her knees so trembled with fatigue she feared they would fail to support her. She gritted her teeth and told herself she was indomitable, the daughter of gods.

She was the oracle of Delphi.

The thought was a tonic to her spirit. She pushed forward, limping toward the entrance of the cave. She could see the brass spikes of the enclosure glinting in the moonlight.

Just a few . . . more . . . steps . . .

The voices quieted. Had she imagined them? No, this was no ordinary silence. It was the baring of the teeth before the attack. The gust of wind before the torrential rain.

Ignoring the pain, Aristea bounded over a tangle of fallen branches and landed on all fours in front of the brass obelisk that opened the gate. She knew what to do: she twisted the stake two turns to the right, then one to the left, and half back again.

The earth yawned open.

With shaking hands, she groped for the rope ladder.

Her heart leapt when her hand came across the gnarled jute. She unfurled the ladder and let it dangle in the lightless void. Before climbing down into the womb of Trophonius, she removed the obelisk so her pursuers would have no way of entering.

With the stake under her arm, she stepped onto the first rung and tried to find her balance on the unstable contraption. Her racing heart did not help. She took a deep breath and held it for several moments, a practice she had employed during captivity to manage her fear and focus on the possible.

Her breathing more even now, she stepped onto the second rung, then the third. Before stepping onto the fourth and final rung, she wiped the sweat from her brow and surveyed the ground below. It was too dark to judge depth. She threw the obelisk down and waited. Within seconds a series of clangs came as the stake hit the ground.

It was a leap of faith, but it was all she had. She treaded onto the last braid of jute and let go, dropping into the dark chasm.

Aristea landed hard on her side. She hurt, but she was safe. She looked up at the circular opening some ten cubits above. According to the tenders of the cave of Trophonius, the door was rigged to close when there was no pressure on the ladder and reopen when someone inside tugged at the rope.

That night, it did not.

Was she too light to trip the mechanism made for men? Had she been misinformed? Whatever the truth, she was at the bottom of an earthen womb, exposed and vulnerable.

Then she heard them.

"So it exists," one whispered. "The cave of demons."

A second man guffawed. "Two notches on the board. We will be paid well for this one."

Bounty hunters. Someone had hired them to capture her—and no doubt kill her. It was not enough that they had tortured and humiliated her over the course of so many moons she'd stopped counting; they wanted her blood.

She would take her own life before letting them win.

"A ladder. Let us see where it leads."

"You first. I will look out for beasts."

Aristea crawled to the side of the cave and crouched against a wall dressed with stones, like an oven. Somewhere there was a cavern that led to the inner sanctum. Trophonius himself, the great architect who'd built the sanctuary of Apollo at Delphi, had fashioned the passage in the most ingenious way, and only the faithful knew how to enter it.

Propelling herself on hands and knees around the perimeter, she groped for the opening whose breadth was said to be two spans—so small the uninitiated would miss it.

"The ladder does not reach all the way down."

"Jump, you fool."

There. Aristea's hand sank into the indentation. She lay on her back and pushed her bare feet into the groove: the prescribed method for entry. She regretted she had no cakes kneaded with honey to offer to the spirit of Trophonius, nor had she performed the ritual ablutions at the river. She prayed the gods would forgive her that once, recognizing in her plight the epic ruin that had befallen Greece.

The fugitive priestess was testament to the fact the Greeks were no longer free to worship as they wished. Their gods were mere whispers in the wind, spoken softly into one ear and another like secrets from the grave, abolished from the fecund earth and dispatched to a desolate hell.

With some effort, she pushed her legs farther into the tight opening. She heard a thud. Her assassin had landed.

Suppressing a grunt, she forced her knees into the hole. *Take me, Trophonius. Take me into your rapturous darkness.*

An unseen energy tugged at her legs. It was working. The force, akin to the vortices that swallowed ships in the Aegean, snatched her in earnest and sucked her in. The sleeve of the habit caught on something and, with a rip that resonated in Aristea's ears, was torn away.

The force propelled her down with a violent thrust. Cool, moist earth brushed against her bare arm as she slid on a chute toward the unknown. She should have been frightened, yet she felt safe. She trusted that whatever was down there, in the grave Trophonius had dug to facilitate the terrifying journey into one's true nature, was better than the fate that awaited her aboveground.

The chute expelled her into a void, and she fell into complete darkness, flailing her arms and legs in a futile attempt to gain purchase on something, anything. She closed her eyes and embraced the falling sensation.

Trust. Apollo will not abandon his chosen.

Aristea landed on her legs and tumbled thrice before the mass of her body slammed against the cave wall. Liquid trickled into her mouth. Her tongue registered a metallic tang: the taste of her own blood. She struggled to sit up. Her left leg was twisted beneath her and would not cooperate. As she willed her body to an upright position, a stabbing pain tore through her knee and up her torso until every cell in her body pulsed with the sensation.

She bit her lip to contain a scream and reached down to examine the immobile leg. Through broken skin, she felt the sharp edges of splintered bone. She gasped.

"Look at this." The men's voices were muffled, barely audible. She listened closely.

"Her robe. She must have escaped through another hole."

"We must look for the way out."

Silence.

Her heart hammered as she imagined them searching for the secret entrance to the cave's inner sanctum. She begged her patron god for redemption from the nightmare, not for the sake of her own trivial life but for the preservation of the secret.

"I don't see a passage."

"She is probably trapped underground, like a rat." He chuckled. "And there she will stay. Now let us make haste. We must seal this opening so the devil's work cannot be done."

"What about this?" There was a pause. "It's heavy."

The obelisk. Aristea's eyes widened.

"Take it. We will throw it into the river so that no one will enter this den of evil again."

The voices were reduced to a murmur, then ceased altogether. Aristea was alone, drenched with sweat and shivering in the blackness. Her own rapid, strained breath punctured the silence. Her mind amplified the sound, driving her mad.

She tried again to move her leg. It was no use. The injury was too grave to launch into a heroic escape. She leaned onto the earthen wall. The cold mud against her bare neck sent a quiver down her back.

She thought of her brothers, the priests who tended the sanctuary at her beloved Delphi and who had raised a woman to lead them in the adoration of the one who replaced darkness with light. For the first time, she allowed the possibility those good men had been exterminated, like so many others.

For the first time, hope had left her.

Hot tears streamed down her cheeks. She let herself collapse into soft sobs and succumbed to the icy embrace of despair.

Two

Thebes, Greece,
present day

The mobile phone vibrated against the glass top of the bedside table. Sarah Weston blinked awake, and the world slowly came into focus. The window of her one-room dormitory was embroidered with raindrops shimmering in the moon's pewter light.

She fumbled for the phone and tapped it on. "Weston here."

"Did I wake you?" The voice on the other end of the line sounded like it belonged to a chain smoker who hadn't slept all night.

She sat up. "Evan? What's happened?"

"I cannot go into detail. Meet me at the museum as soon as you can." He hung up.

In the two months she had worked with Evangelos "Evan" Rigas, she had come to appreciate his laconic style. The director of the ephorate of prehistoric and classical antiquities in Thebes was a man of few words. In Greece, he was known as the "lone wolf"—a hardened scientist with a certain disdain for the collaborative spirit and a particular suspicion of his colleagues from the West. It was obvious from his passive-aggressive stance that he resented the presence of Sarah and her partner, anthropologist Daniel Madigan, who were assigned as consultants to the archaeological digs overseen by the ephorate. But in a dismal monetary climate, Evan needed the funding granted by the British A.E. Thurlow Foundation, so he had no choice but to stomach the foundation's hired guns.

She dismissed her doubts and threw on dusty khakis and a well-worn chambray shirt. She pulled a messy tangle of blonde curls into a ponytail and reached for her Barbour coat as she bolted out the door.

At four o'clock on an early-February morning, daylight was still a couple of hours away. Sarah exhaled and watched her breath form a cloud of warmth that was quickly claimed by the winter frost. It reminded her of the long winters at her family manor in the English countryside and of happier times. She zipped up her coat and raised her hood before launching into the drizzle.

Normally, she would drive up to the top of the Cadmeia, the acropolis of ancient Thebes, but both the expedition jeeps were gone. She was irritated that neither Evan nor Daniel had waited for her. She didn't mind walking, even in the rain, but the half-mile slog uphill through muddy terrain would take longer than necessary.

At least she knew the path well. She made that trek daily but normally veered to the southeast, to a hillock where the little-studied sanctuary to Ismenian Apollo stood, its ruined marbled columns arranged like prehistoric henge among the overgrown grasses.

At first, Sarah had had reservations about taking an assignment in so obscure a location. But Daniel, enthused about Ismenion's reputation as one of ancient Greece's important, if long forgotten, oracular sites, had convinced her to give it a chance. She had agreed to support him but didn't share his conviction. She felt as if their particular talents could be put to better use elsewhere.

Looking on the bright side, she admitted the place was quiet, predictable, and devoid of controversy. After her last two assignments, where things had gotten a bit prickly, she looked forward to flying under the radar for a change.

As she rounded the corner to the peak on which the museum was perched, she considered she might have been dead wrong.

In the flickering light of a wall-mounted lantern half off its hinge, she noticed the red-and-white tape of Greek police surrounding the museum courtyard. Two cops stood outside beneath an overhang, chatting and smoking cigarettes. Sarah called out to them. "I'm Sarah Weston. I work with Professor Rigas. He's asked me here."

One of the men eyed her up and down. Without bothering to ask her to produce ID, he waved her in.

She ducked under the police tape and crossed the courtyard to the main entrance. The front door was open, and all the house lights were on. She looked past the cracked crystal of her Timex: 4:49.

She heard voices down a hallway and walked toward them. Evan was there, giving a statement to an investigator. Loath to intrude, she backed up and scanned the corridors. All was quiet. Where was Daniel? Had he not gotten the same call?

Something crunched beneath her well-worn leather hiking boots. It was the unmistakable dull crackle of broken glass.

A theft.

With her gaze, she followed the trail of glass shards to a flat case in Room B, where pottery and small objects were displayed. She checked over both shoulders to ensure she was alone and walked toward it.

Standing over it, she frowned. The case had been shattered and gutted. She read the display text, written in Greek: *Brass stake, unknown origin.*

That was odd. Usually, objects of unknown origin or chronology were not displayed until they could be studied further.

Sarah looked around. On the far side of the western wing, the same candy-cane-striped tape sectioned off an open doorway. She recalled that was the entrance to a storage room where the museum's archives were kept. She walked toward it.

She saw the papers first. Every box had been upturned, its contents strewn along the floor, on shelves, on a work table. The place had been ransacked.

Behind a stack of empty boxes, she saw a pair of feet. Sarah's face warmed as adrenaline surged through her. She stepped over the slack tape, just enough to get a better view without disturbing the crime scene.

She raised a hand to her mouth to contain a gasp. The night guard lay motionless in a corner, his hands tied with a computer cable and mouth sealed with black tape. His face was badly bruised and bloodied. A long line of raw skin cut across his neck, as if someone had tried to strangle him.

She felt a hand on her shoulder and jumped.

"Sorry to startle you."

Relieved to see Evan, she exhaled loudly. "It's all right. Care to fill me in?"

"It's what I'm told I have to do."

Sarah ignored his snarky remark.

"There was a break-in in the middle of the night." Though his English was flawless, his Greek accent came across in the trilled *r*.

"Who's the guard? I don't recall seeing him before."

"He was new. Not even a week on the job." He scanned the scene. "Looks like he put up quite a fight."

Sarah felt nauseated. In the twelve years she'd worked as an archaeologist, she had witnessed antiquities theft and violence over and over—and it never got any easier to process. "I don't understand. Didn't the alarm sound?"

"It did, but no one heard it—at least not in time." He shrugged. "Since the budget cuts, we were forced to do away with the monitoring."

Sarah grimaced, an outward expression of her contempt for the government's shortsightedness. She was well aware that the Ministry of Culture had suffered since the economic crisis, but failing to protect its national treasures was nothing less than criminal—particularly in light of all the opportunists who circled like vultures, waiting for the right time to strike.

"How did the police know to come here then?"

"I called them." He pushed his round, black-rimmed glasses up the bridge of his nose. "I was driving up to the lab to complete a report when I heard the alarm. I rushed to the museum, but it was too late."

She recalled the broken case. "What was taken?"

"Nothing, actually. The object had been removed."

"Removed . . . to where?"

Evan was quiet for a moment. He turned to her, his deep-set eyes obscured beneath a heavy black brow. "I can't say."

"Can't or won't?"

"The investigation is open. You know what that means." He turned toward the door. "Look, I have to go. They have more questions."

"Evan, wait." Her tone was sharper than she intended it to be. "Where's Daniel?"

"He had to go to Athens."

"Athens?" She tensed. "What for?"

"I can't talk now. They're expecting me."

Sarah watched Evan walk toward the men and wondered what he wasn't telling her. She considered the improbability of Daniel leaving in the middle of the night to go to Athens. What could be so urgent? And why not inform her? Something did not add up.

Her internal alarm tolling, she felt a bit numb. She gazed absently at the vandalized storage room and the motionless form of a man who a few hours prior was very much alive. Her thoughts raced across memories from her recent past: a monk knifed to death for keeping an ancient secret, a tribal warrior gored in sacrifice to a madman seeking biblical treasure, her father held hostage and nearly killed. She rubbed her eyes to shake the unwelcome visions of the violence that seemed to plague her assignments, tainting the thrill of archaeological discovery.

She decided not to linger. As she walked down the corridor toward the exit, she noticed tiny red droplets on the floor between the shards of glass. She followed the trail down the hall and to the front door. Near the threshold, a muddy footprint tinged with blood pointed toward the building. Though the impression was faint, she could make out the herringbone pattern of the sole.

Sarah pushed the door open slowly and scanned the courtyard but saw nothing. Any more traces of the intruder were surely washed away by the rain. She walked past the cops and out of the crime scene. At the edge of the museum complex she stood still for a moment, gazing at the slate sky that signaled the hour before dawn.

She reached into her pocket for her phone with the intention of calling Daniel. As she looked down, she noticed something odd. A small object attached to a black leather lace was half buried in the mud. She looked behind her at the guards; they were still smoking and guffawing.

She squatted for a closer look. She brushed away the wet soil with her hand, revealing a pendant, or perhaps an amulet, made of marble. The bottom edge was ragged and sharp, as if a piece was missing, and the leather chain had broken cleanly. She picked up the object. A glance at the veining and coloration placed the stone in an ancient context, but she could not be sure in the demilight.

Sarah turned it over. Her jaw tightened as she realized there was an inscription on the back. She rubbed the mud off and revealed a symbol she did not comprehend. Carved into the marble was a row of four evenly spaced dots.

Three

Daniel Madigan stood at the edge of the tarmac at the private jet port at Athens International, his gaze fixed on the refracted wing lights as the plane taxied toward him. The high-pitched whine of the engine seared his ears, adding to his unease.

The marshaller crossed a pair of fluorescent yellow light wands overhead to signal the plane to stop. The five minutes before the aircraft door opened seemed like hours. Daniel rubbed his eyes in an attempt to erase the fatigue. He couldn't remember when he last had a good night's sleep.

The man he was expecting stood at the top of the metal stairs and lifted the collar of his trench coat. He descended the stairs with a lively step that belied his portly figure.

Daniel walked toward him, meeting him halfway. He'd been given specific instructions: the meeting was to take place on the tarmac, where they could not be overheard.

"Madigan." James Langham, the chairman of the A.E. Thurlow Foundation, extended a puffy, short-fingered hand. "Thanks for meeting me on such short notice."

"Don't mention it, James." Daniel exaggerated his

Tennessee accent, as he often did when talking to high-born Brits. He also left out honorifics, in this case *Sir*, because he never could stomach the pretense.

"I trust no one knows you're here."

"No one. Just like you asked."

"Not even—?"

Daniel cut him off before he could say *Weston's daughter*. Hearing her name only added to his guilt over keeping secrets from her. "Look, I know the drill." He crossed his arms. "Let's just get to the point, all right?"

Langham put his hands in his pockets and exhaled a puff of mist. "There has been a complication. We need you to do more than originally agreed upon."

"Such as?"

"It seems the brass obelisk is more valuable than we'd thought. It appears to be the key to something."

Langham was referring to an object of mysterious origin, found a year ago in the bottom of a river in central Greece and turned over to the ephorate in Thebes. A collector whose identity was well protected had offered the Greeks a large sum in exchange for the artifact, but the foundation fathers used their political clout to block the transaction. The object had been displayed in the museum since.

There were reasons for this, and Daniel had been made aware of them. But as part of the deal he'd struck, he had to keep silent. Two months into this assignment, he felt as though he'd made a mistake. "A key. How do you know this?"

. "You know better than to ask this of a high-ranking officer of the British government. Simply assume our intelligence is accurate. We know two things"—he enumerated on those stout fingers—"one, the collector who offered to buy the obelisk is the man we have been seeking, and two, he's desperate to get his hands on it—or rather what it unlocks. To catch him, we must play a bit of cat and mouse." He nodded to Daniel. "This is where you come in."

Daniel felt the bite of a frosty gust on his lips. "That wasn't the deal we had. 'Get the information, and get out'—remember?"

"It seems you're the one who doesn't remember." Langham's voice took on an acerbic tone. "Need I remind you what we did for you a few months ago?"

Daniel resented being backed into a corner. But he had no choice: he'd given his word. "That won't be necessary. I will repay my debt to the British government, as I said I would."

"Good. Now, listen carefully. Things are heating up. There was a break-in at the museum"—he looked at his watch—"about an hour ago. Someone attempted to steal the obelisk."

His brow wrinkled as he thought of Sarah. "Was anyone hurt?"

"Things got a bit messy. Apparently, the guard put up

an unreasonable fight. For whatever reason, he defended the archives as if they were his own." Langham shook his head. "Silly sod. It cost him his life."

Daniel exhaled. His breath hung in the frigid air, dissipating in slow motion.

Langham went on. "There is good and bad news. The good: the obelisk was not in its appointed case. It appears Rigas had moved it to the vault just hours prior."

"What? How could he have known?"

"He says he didn't. He claims he moved it for further study. But something does not smell right to me."

"What's the bad news?"

"The papers cataloguing the obelisk have gone missing. They now have all known information on the object, including that pesky detail about its storage in the vault." He huffed. "They will be back."

"Let me guess. You have a plan."

He smiled sideways. "Indeed. But we must act quickly. This is what I need you to do."

four

On the morning following the heist, the stones at Ismenion Hill were particularly silent. Beneath a moody sky, Sarah worked alone on the site of a second millennium BCE Mycenaean tomb.

She brushed the dirt away from the lip of a funerary vessel, looking for solace in the fastidious act. She could not concentrate. In her mind she replayed the predawn events, trying to find an explanation.

It wasn't the break-in itself that baffled her. Museum thefts and ancient site lootings were rampant in crisis-stricken Greece. It was always the same story: the thieves plundered only a few objects and seldom the most charismatic ones. Rather than a large, identifiable cache, they consistently funneled small numbers of stolen antiquities into a vast black market, like drops that disappeared in a bucketful of water. It was akin to opening a wound a little at a time: the pain was not enough for people to care, and no one took note of the cumulative damage.

But this was different. The looters were after information, not artifacts. Though the local police were treating the incident as a botched theft, Sarah's instincts told her something big was percolating beneath the surface.

She reached into the small pocket sewn into the seam of her trousers and pulled out the marble amulet with the four dots. She ran a finger across the ragged edge. The sharp surface indicated it was broken rather recently, perhaps in the skirmish. Earlier that morning, after the investigators had left, she'd quietly returned to the site and scoured the ground for another piece of the amulet but found nothing. Either it had vanished, or it was never there in the first place. She closed her fist around it. There was more to this object than met the eye.

Sarah's thoughts turned to Daniel. His trip to Athens in the middle of the night was another straw in a pile of unexplained behavior. In the short time they had been in Thebes, he had been quiet and at times aloof. His laid-back style and signature wit had all but evaporated.

Her gaze wandered as she recalled a phone call Daniel had received the afternoon prior. He had looked down at his phone and frowned. He turned away to answer, saying only "I'll call you back." A moment later he excused himself from the lab, leaving Sarah and Evan in the midst of conversation. When he returned, five minutes later, he looked agitated.

"What's wrong?" Sarah asked.

He gave a rigid smile. "All good. Just a call from the foundation. Let's get back to work."

Sarah wondered now if that was the call summoning him to Athens. But why the secrecy? She wanted to give him the benefit of the doubt, to not accuse him of omitting the truth, but memory mocked her, reminding her of a history she had been trying hard to ignore.

She put the brush down and leaned back on the excavated bedrock. She slipped the bandana off her head, letting her hair tumble down her back, and wiped the grime from her face. In the leaden light of the overcast morning, the Italian cypress trees—slender spires sprouting from the rocky ground—displayed none of their usual majesty. The olive trees, with their gnarled old trunks and silver-green leaves, looked like denizens of a petrified forest.

Beyond the hill, tiny gray dots emerged from the mist like brushstrokes in a pointillist landscape. The city of Thebes, an arbitrary arrangement of tiny red-roofed houses and monolithic white buildings interrupted by patches of green, sprawled on the valley. It was hard to reconcile the unremarkable modern city with the Theban powerhouse of antiquity. It was in that valley and in the citadel that rose above it that ancient Thebes' mortal enemies, the Athenians, had been driven into the earth and the fateful alliance with Xerxes' Persians had been formed. And it was there that hubris led to ruin as the Sacred Band of Thebes fell spectacularly to Alexander the Great's long-speared armies.

She had always found solace in walking in the footsteps of ancient sages and fools, warriors and poets, great leaders and wicked traitors: the men who, with their blood or their tongues, shaped western civilization. Yet at that moment such comfort eluded her, like water escaping from a sieve.

Out of the gloom emerged a hunched figure. Sarah stood, thinking it was Daniel. She felt a tinge of disappointment when she realized Evan was walking toward her, his hands in his pockets and head bent as if to avoid a blustery wind.

She tucked the amulet back in her pocket and met him halfway. "Any news?"

Evan's face was tight to match his guarded posture. "Not much. Since nothing was taken, they're closing that part of the case. They're still investigating the murder, but that could take years. The cops here are a joke."

"How can you be certain nothing was taken from the archives?"

He shrugged. "Even if there was, they are not concerned about that. No antiquities are missing; that's the important thing."

"They may not be concerned, but we should be. Surely you've taken inventory. You must know whether some files are missing."

He looked away, obviously uncomfortable.

"Evan." She waited for him to look at her. "I can't

help you if I don't know."

He hesitated. Something in the way he scanned her face indicated he was framing his answer. "All right. They took the folders pertaining to the artifacts currently in storage."

"You think they are after something in the vault?"

"I doubt it. They're probably just fishing to see what we have. These petty criminals do things like this all the time."

Sarah stared at Evan. Was he really that naïve—or just acting the part? "Is the brass stake in the vault?"

"Yes. That, and a hundred other items we're studying."

"May I have a look?"

Evan shrugged. "Suit yourself. I'll be in the lab in about an hour. You can come by then." He squinted at the sky. Dark clouds crowded the western horizon. "Looks like more rain anyway."

Sarah nodded. "I will be there."

He started to walk away but stopped. He turned back to her. "About Daniel . . . He's been acting odd, hasn't he?"

"What do you mean?"

"The other day, I overheard him talking to someone on the phone about going back to the Middle East." He shrugged. "Well, you probably know about it."

She felt the familiar burning sensation in her abdomen. Fears she thought she'd buried were clawing their way to the surface.

A frigid breeze, the harbinger of the storm, whistled through the olive leaves. Evan raised his collar, put his hands back in his coat pockets, and disappeared into the gathering mist.

The green LED numbers on the alarm clock read 02:20. Sarah rolled onto her back and stared at the peeling plaster on the ceiling. Like naiads in the brooks of antiquity, thoughts swam through her mind, rendering her sleepless.

She had spent the afternoon in the lab, examining the brass stake and the other artifacts stored in the vault. She had pressed Evan for data on each of the objects, but he was only able to produce the original log. All other information had been taken from the archives.

According to the log, the obelisk-shaped stake was a chance discovery at the headwaters of the Herkyna river, just outside of the town of Livadeia. It was handed over to the ephorate about a year prior and was still being studied.

But there was another object of interest: an anthropomorphic pottery rhyton in the shape of a wolf's head. Like the obelisk, the ceremonial drinking vessel that looked to be late fifth- or early fourth-century BCE had very little information ascribed to it. It was apparently unearthed during the building of a church in Chaironeia, a village outside of Livadeia. It had been found in pieces and partially reconstructed.

A connection between the two objects didn't seem likely, but both were materially different from anything on display in the museum or in the storage facility. And they were found very near each other. That was as good a reason as any to start her research there.

Sarah willed herself to stop thinking about it—at least for the moment. She needed sleep. She got up from the bed and walked across the dark room to make a cup of chamomile tea. As the kettle heated, she gazed out the window. The soft pewter light of the waxing quarter moon outlined the canopy of the grove like a halo. A rogue breeze stirred the leaves of a chestnut tree outside her window. Then everything was still again.

The kettle whistled. As she poured hot water over a handful of dried chamomile flowers, in her peripheral vision she saw a flash of light. She stood at the edge of the window and surveyed the darkened landscape. She saw it again: a tiny stream of white light darting to and fro, as if someone was searching for something. It quickly disappeared.

Whoever was there did not want to be seen.

She watched the light turn on and off in short spurts as it traveled eastward across the hillside. When she realized where it was heading, she held her breath.

She threw her coat over her T-shirt and drawstring pants and slipped out the door. She skulked barefoot through the thicket of olive and chestnut trees, keeping herself hidden behind their ancient trunks.

The lab was two hundred yards away from the staff housing complex, a lone building in the midst of a grove. It was protected with a combination lock and an alarm, but it was unguarded. If someone wanted to break in, it wouldn't be impossible. Given the events of the night prior, Sarah had good reason to suspect this predawn foray was not official business.

Sarah heard nothing but the rise and fall of her own breath as she approached the building from the south side. The light grew larger and brighter, a profane presence in the dead stillness of the night. The intruders were almost there.

Her feet sank into the cold mud of the still-moist ground. She tried to pick up the pace, but exposed roots extending from the trees like gnarled fingers commanded her full attention. One misstep could slow her down and, worse, reveal her position.

The light pointed toward the grove. Her heart hammering, Sarah ducked inside the hollow of a massive olive tree. She was close enough to hear the voices of two men speaking Greek with the local Boeotian accent. They made no attempt to keep the volume down; they were either overly confident or foolhardy.

"Here it is. This is where it's kept."

"You sure you know how to get in?"

"Yes, you idiot. I have the code. Step aside."

A chill traveled down Sarah's spine. She fumbled inside her coat pockets for anything she could use to create a distraction.

Pieces of paper . . . loose change . . . her room key . . .

her mobile. She could use the phone to call police, but by the time anyone arrived these guys would be long gone, possibly with an archaeological treasure under their arms.

She stood slowly and peeked around the trunk. Ten yards away, the two men were bent over the keypad, punching in the sequence of six numbers. Both wore dark jackets and ski caps. One was short and heavyset. She could not see their faces or make out any more detail.

I have the code. Within moments, they would breach the building. Even if it meant risking her own safety, she could not sit back as that happened.

When she was sure they weren't looking, she slipped away from the tree and darted to the side of the building. She clung to the plaster and listened.

"What the devil?" The voice was barbed with frustration.

"What's going on?"

"It's not working."

"You're doing something wrong. Try again."

Sarah could hear the clicks as the intruder's fingers punched in the code. She bit her bottom lip. Should she do it?

He uttered a string of expletives, then kicked the door.

"Let me try. What's the code?"

"Forget it, fat guy. He trusted me with it, not you."

"Well, I'm not going to watch you fail. I want my reward. Understand?"

"Shut up!" His voice echoed across the grove. As if he

regretted the burst of anger, he dialed back to a whisper. "I'm going to try one more time."

Sarah saw their bickering as an opportunity. Her heart thrashed like a caged beast as she tiptoed toward the front of the building, preparing to confront the perpetrators.

"Wait," the leader said. "I think I've got it."

She felt a man's arm across her chest and a hand press against her mouth before she had a chance to gasp. A voice whispered in her ear: "Don't move."

Five

Delphi,

391 CE

Sunlight filtered through the clusters of almond blossoms, granting them a diaphanous pink hue that recalled the rose-lined clouds at dawn. The sun's kiss released the flowers' perfume. It was sweet like a lover's promise, an assurance that the winter frost had given way to spring, and the fair earth would soon erupt with life.

The arrival of spring meant more than this to Aristea. It marked the return of Apollo from the land of the Hyperboreans, where the sun god retreated at the first breath of winter. Apollo's arrival at Delphi meant his oracle would soon be called into duty.

In the sixteen years since she had been chosen to utter the god's word at his most sacred sanctuary, Aristea had always regarded this moment with a measure of excitement. It heralded the advent of a new crop of supplicants who would journey to Delphi, as their fathers had done before them, to hear the oracle proclaim their fate. It was a responsibility she did not take lightly, for the prophecies she dealt could change men's lives.

Or, indeed, history itself.

Aristea walked to the Castalian Spring and kneeled

on its edge. She looked inside the water, which was calm as glass, and her image gazed back at her with smoldering brown eyes. She lifted a hand to her cheek. She had the same olive skin as her ancestors, or so she had been told. She hailed from a long line of priestesses who descended from Themistoclea, teacher of the sage mathematician Pythagoras.

Like them, Aristea had guided countless souls and foretold the inevitable. Her prophecies were always pointed and true, like the nature of the god who whispered in her ear. Truth, however, was an enchantress, assuming different forms before different beholders. Men being what they were, they interpreted the oracle's words to suit them, sometimes with devastating results.

She ran a hand across the water, effacing her reflection.

It had happened the summer before last. An envoy from Alexandria had made the two-month journey to Delphi, by boat and on foot, to seek the counsel of the oracle.

On the night he was deemed worthy of receiving the word of Apollo, the Egyptian descended to the *adyton* behind two Delphic priests and was directed to stand behind the false wall.

Aristea sat upon the tripod of truth, gazing into a bowl filled with holy water from the spring of Kassotis. In her peripheral vision she could see the supplicant through a square window cut into the wall. His hands were clasped in front of him, and his head was bent toward the ground.

She inhaled and smelled the familiar sweetness, like

the nectar of honeybees that had feasted on orange blossoms. Apollo's sacred *pneuma* had permeated the *adyton*. She closed her eyes, let the spirit take her.

"What answer do you seek, Amenthes of Alexandria?" she heard one of the priests say.

"Is there salvation from the armies of Theodosius, who march now into Lower Egypt, or will they trample our kind into the ground?"

Our kind. Amenthes surely referred to the pagans of Alexandria, who for eons had practiced their rituals unquestioned. Theodosius, emperor of the eastern part of the Roman Empire and a newly minted Christian, had launched a campaign into Egypt in 388, vowing to smite the heresy of those who believed in a pantheon of gods.

Aristea breathed the *pneuma* deep into her lungs and waited. Her breath was even and steady, and her head felt light, as if hollow. Thoughts came and went unchecked until they passed out of consciousness. She was ready to receive.

"Come now, Apollo, and guide your instrument," she whispered under her breath. She wanted no one to hear, for the concord was solely between her and her god.

An image flashed into her mind's eye: A long hall illuminated by the trembling light of torches hanging from iron brackets, its marble floor stained by dark pools of liquid. At the far end was an altar. Her mind traveled to it and stopped upon a bloody knife. Next to it, flies buzzed around a pile of entrails.

A hand stained with blood reached for the knife, held it up. The knife bearer turned around and glared at her with obsidian eyes hard with hatred.

She twitched. The vision did not relent. She saw a field of ruins: marble columns toppled, pediments broken, a bust shattered into hundreds of pieces. On one of the felled columns was painted the sign of the cross.

She opened her eyes with a jolt. "Approach, Amenthes of Alexandria." Her mouth issued words without her willing it.

Amenthes came forth.

Head bent beneath a white veil, Aristea looked into the water. Ripples fanned out in concentric circles from a disturbance at its center. She felt the bowl vibrate ever so slightly against her hands.

"There are two kinds of men: those who believe with their hearts and those who loudly proclaim their truth. Both will enter the house Ptolemy built, but only one will come out. And justice will stand victorious among the ruins, wearing the white robes of mourning."

"The house Ptolemy built," the Egyptian repeated. "The Serapeum?"

"The oracle has spoken," said the priest. "The burden is upon you to understand her words and master your fate. Now, go in peace."

Aristea heard the shuffle of feet and the swishing of fabric as the Alexandrian envoy exited the *adyton*. She had seen his name on the Book of Souls. He would not survive the winter.

And so it was. Aristea splashed water from the Castalian Spring on her face. Having just trickled into the fountain from the snowmelt on the high slopes of Mount Parnassus, the water was ice-cold. It braced her but could not wash away the memory.

In the winter that passed, word had reached Delphi that Theodosius' armies, with the blessing of the Alexandrian bishop, Theophilus, sacked the temple of Dionysus under cover of night, setting fire to the altars of sacrifice and defiling the sacred caverns with their filth.

Pagan worshippers, who had been free since the dawn of the Egyptian state, spilled onto the streets to express their outrage and were confronted by Christians. The fighting continued for two days, with casualties on both sides, before Theodosius' armies descended with their weaponry and turned the civilian clash into bona fide war.

The pagans retreated to the Serapeum, taking Christian prisoners with them. But their barricades did not hold: with great logs the imperial armies broke down the doors and entered the temple with their spears and slingshots, stabbing and stoning the worshippers until none was left standing.

Blood stained the marble so indelibly that even the perpetrators could not look at it. They demolished the temple and deposited its bloodied ruins into the sea. The Serapeum, Ptolemy's storied work of art, was no more.

It was the first time Aristea had predicted a massacre. But she suspected it would not be the last.

Six

*S*arah knew that voice, knew the scent of his skin. Her body relaxed, a signal that she would follow his lead. He released his grip.

A grunt came from the front of the building. "I can't believe this. He must have given me the wrong code."

"I say it's user error. Let me—"

An alarm blared. The shrill sound, which she had never heard before, was coming from the building.

"Idiot. Now you've done it."

"Let's get out of here."

"What about the spike?"

"Forget it. Run!"

As the slapping of panicked feet against mud grew fainter, Sarah turned to face Daniel. He clicked the remote to shut off a portable alarm, put up a hand to stay her, and peeked around the corner.

"All right. They're gone."

She took a step toward him. "Why did you let them go? They should be behind bars."

"I hadn't planned to let them go." He pressed his lips together. "There was a complication."

"You don't mean—" She cut herself off as she realized she had gotten in the way of his scheme, whatever that was. She huffed.

"I didn't want you to get hurt, Sarah. They were armed."

"Maybe if you'd tell me what's going on, we could avoid such complications." The last word was heavy with disdain.

He exhaled loudly. "It's a tangle of thorns."

She stared at him. She knew her partner so well, she could read the subtle changes in his gaze. The usual quiet confidence in his eyes had turned into unease.

"I've got all night." She nodded toward the building. "Shall we?"

He punched in the correct code, and the door yielded with a soft click. He held it open for her, then entered behind her and shut the door. He didn't bother with the lights.

A shaft of pale moonlight entered through the narrow clerestory windows across the top of the building, casting a supernatural glow onto the objects lying in research troughs and on analysis tables. She crossed her arms. "Evan said you were in Athens. Why?"

"The head of the foundation called for a meeting," he said.

"In the middle of the night? Come on, Danny."

"These people are constantly on the move. He was in the Middle East and flew through Athens last night on his way to London. Don't make more of this than it is."

"Fair enough. What was the meeting about?"

He hesitated, and Sarah knew he was weighing his response. It wasn't like Daniel Madigan to be cagey. He was a straight shooter without regard for convention or political correctness. She had seen him act this way only once, when he was trying to protect her from something.

"They're concerned about this rash of thefts around Greece," he said. "They want me to be their eyes and ears on the ground. That's all."

"That's all." She was aware of the irony in her voice. "Well, you can tell this to your foundation consorts: whoever was here last night and tonight has nothing to do with these other thefts. These people are after something specific: a brass stake shaped as an obelisk."

He avoided her gaze.

A crease formed in her brow. "But you probably knew that."

He nodded feebly and put his hands in the pockets of his faded, threadbare jeans. His muscles tensed beneath a tight black T-shirt.

She took a step toward him. "What is it? Why are they after it?"

"I don't know." He sighed. "That's the truth."

"What if I help you figure it out?"

Daniel forced a smile, and the lines around his eyes deepened. His shoulder-length mahogany locks were windblown and tangled, as if he hadn't bothered with them in days. He looked tired, older than his forty-three years. Though she knew he was keeping things from her, Sarah sensed his evasiveness was not hostile; he was in some kind of trouble. Whether he would say it or not, she knew he needed her.

She patted his arm. "You look like you could use some sleep. We can look at this with fresh eyes in the morning."

"Thanks." He gave her a gentle hug but quickly stepped away. "Thanks for understanding."

She didn't understand. But she was determined to.

Seven

Though he had not slept in more than twenty-four hours, Daniel had no intention of resting. He looked at his watch: a quarter to five in the morning. He dreaded the phone call he had to make.

He locked the door to his room and turned on the faucet in the washbasin. He entered the passcode on his phone and texted: *I have intel. Call me.*

He knew Langham was an early riser, so he was not surprised when, moments later, the phone vibrated. The caller ID read *Blocked.*

"Morning, James. You're up bright and early."

"Starting the day with a bit of a run." He sounded winded. "My cardiologist says I have to lose weight. So, what have you got?"

"Well, you were right. They came back. There was an attempted break-in late last night."

"Brilliant. Do we know who they're working for?"

Daniel rubbed his forehead. Despite the cold, it was moist with perspiration. "No. They got away."

There was a moment of hesitation. "What?" A single word, calm but loaded.

"I'm sorry. I ran into some snags."

"The plan was foolproof, Madigan. Changing the code was meant to slow them down so you could confront them. How could you fail?"

He gritted his teeth. He could not tell Langham the whole truth. "I had to abort the plan. They were too heavily armed."

Langham caught his breath. "I'm gravely disappointed. This puts us behind. It's time we can ill afford to lose."

"Putting my life on the line wasn't part of the deal."

"Listen to me, Madigan. You have forty-eight hours to figure out what that obelisk is for. I am leaving today for Belgium. By the time I come back, I expect a full report."

The line went dead. Daniel threw the phone onto the bed and exhaled sharply. He wasn't used to having his back against the wall and felt a tinge of self-loathing for allowing himself to get into this situation. He told himself he had no choice: two months ago, he was desperate. He would have bargained anything to save her.

So he did. And now it was time for payback—though the toll was heavier than he'd ever imagined.

A rapid knock startled him. He turned off the faucet before opening the door.

Evan stood on the other side. Behind him, a violet-hued, cloudless sky heralded the arrival of a clear day, the first in weeks. "I heard the water running and figured you were inside." He looked over Daniel's shoulder into the room. "I hope I'm not disturbing."

Daniel's tone was clipped. "What can I do for you, Evan?"

"I have been trying to get into the lab, but the code does not work. Any idea why?"

"We had some unwanted visitors overnight. Probably the same goons who broke into the museum. I had to change the code."

Evan blinked rapidly. His raven eyes looked huge behind thick glasses. "Why wasn't I informed of this earlier?"

Daniel was careful what he said around Evan. It was obvious someone on the inside was feeding information to the looters. Until Daniel could determine who that was, he didn't trust anyone. "Well, I'm telling you now." He scribbled the new code on a piece of paper. "I'll meet you there in half an hour. I have some questions for you."

Evan started to say something but instead nodded and walked away.

Daniel locked the door and went into the bathroom to take a shower. The intensity of the last thirty-six hours was beginning to wear on him, and he needed to reboot. But even as he stood beneath the stream of warm water, there was no escaping his thoughts.

It began with a plane crash.

His recollection of that late-November day was indelible. Even now, the flashing red light from the cockpit—the first sign of trouble—replayed often in his mind, sometimes haunting his waking hours, other times jolting him from sleep. It appeared when he sensed danger, flooding his mind's eye with the color of blood. He could not shake it, nor could he forget the pilot's frantic calls of mayday as the controls failed.

He was the sole passenger on Sir Richard Weston's private plane, headed from London to New York City, when it fell out of the sky. The plane plunged nose-first into the gray waters of the North Atlantic with such speed he could feel the g-forces threatening to push his eyes out of their sockets. He recalled his vision blurring as gossamers of cloud whizzed past. At that surreal moment, he thought they were the wings of angels who had come to claim him.

He was certain he was going to die. But it wasn't the worst of it. He knew with all his conviction the plane had been sabotaged, and he knew who had done it. And Sarah, en route to Israel at the time, would likely be walking into a similar trap. He had no way of warning her, and he regretted that above anything else.

It was the first time he had prayed, struck a bargain with God. *If I make it out of this alive*, he vowed, *I will make sure Trent Ashworth and his piece-of-shit father are brought to justice for what they've done, even if I have to exact it myself.*

Great waves of frothy water battered his window, and the plane shook like a jackhammer hitting a slab of steel. He felt himself spinning in a gray vortex. His seat, with him still buckled in, dislodged from its base by the force of the impact and spun wildly through the metal tube, slamming against the front of the plane. Warm blood trickled into his eyes. His senses began to leave him. The last thing he saw was the heaving waters of the Atlantic enter the cabin through a gaping hole where the tail once was.

How he got onto the wing, he would never know. He recalled only awakening beneath a steely sky, his bones aching like he'd been crushed in a vise, his teeth rattling from the cold. He smelled scorched metal and jet fuel, an odor that would forever be branded onto his olfactory memory.

He was broken, but he was alive. Even if it took his last breath, he would make good on his promise.

Daniel pushed his wet hair back and let the warm water from the shower pelt his face. If only it could wash away the memories that tormented him, wipe away the guilt.

It was a miracle he'd survived. He was found by some English fishermen, good-natured blokes who didn't mind keeping a secret. They delivered him back on English shores, and he made his way to London. His first call was to Sir Richard.

Sarah's father, who at the time was on a diplomatic mission to Uzbekistan, was stunned to hear from him. "Good heavens, Madigan. We all thought you'd perished."

"Your plane didn't go down by accident, Richard. I know who's behind it. Does the name Trent Ashworth mean anything to you?"

"The new chap heading up Judah Oil and Gas. James Ashworth's son. He's a bit of a zealot, that one. We're monitoring the situation in Jerusalem."

"Trent and his father sabotaged your plane. I can prove it."

There was a long pause on the other end of the line. "I've had some messages from Sarah that sounded quite distraught. She said she was on her way to Jerusalem. Is she in some sort of danger?"

"Jesus." Daniel rubbed his burning eyes. "We have to move fast. I need access to the hangar video . . . and someone from the inside who can help me nail down a case of international conspiracy."

"You ought to call James Langham. We're on the Joint Intelligence Committee together. He's former MI5. He has means that you and I can only dream of. I shall alert him you will be ringing."

"Be careful what you say." Daniel lowered his voice to a whisper. "If this is going to work, no one can know I'm alive. Not even Sarah."

His first meeting with James Langham was in a nondescript mews flat in Islington, where government heavyweights held clandestine rendezvous. Langham did not fit the textbook image of a man of power. He was the height of a jockey with far too much flesh for his frame and a thatch of disheveled white hair. His suit looked as if he'd slept in it, and the top button of his shirt was loosened to make room for the pink rolls that sprouted beneath his chin.

But the glint in his hyperalert green eyes suggested he gloried in the hunt. And so it was.

Langham had already known about Trent Ashworth's dubious rise to the helm of Judah Oil and Gas and about his father's conspiracy to sell aircraft defense systems and intelligence to the Israelis, a move that could well have led to war in the region. It was a precarious situation on the verge of developing into a clear and present danger. So far, Joint Intelligence had nothing illegal to pin on the Ashworths, so Daniel's claim of proof of criminal activity was enough to cause Langham to cancel a day's worth of meetings and head to Islington.

Daniel played for Langham the hangar video that showed the bald, pale-blue-eyed technician working on Sir Richard's plane. It was the same man who had worked on Harry Ashworth's—Trent's brother—plane before its systems failed during a flight over Scotland. Daniel then told Langham about the witness who could corroborate his story and watched the portly man's lips curl into a tight smile.

"If what you say is true, you have just done a great service to the crown."

"Be that as it may, I have a different motivation. Richard Weston's daughter is in danger. She's in Israel, and she's being hunted by Trent Ashworth. I need your help getting to her before he does."

Langham sat back on a wingback chair and tapped his fingers together. "There may be something we can do." He studied Daniel's face for a long moment. "Tell me, Dr. Madigan, how far are you willing to go for your friends?"

Daniel sensed this would cost him. But whatever Langham's currency, he was prepared to pay it. "I'm here, aren't I?"

"Good." Langham sprang from his seat with more energy than he looked capable of. He walked to a filing cabinet and removed a folder. "Weston tells me you can be trusted with privileged information. I should like to show you something."

Daniel joined him at the dining room table. Langham opened the folder to reveal a set of photos of artifacts in storage. Daniel knew the objects well. "The Elgin marbles."

"Indeed. The Parthenon sculptures and friezes Lord Elgin brought back to England in the early 1800s—the subject of much controversy, as you no doubt know."

Daniel nodded. He was well aware of the Greeks' desire to repatriate the objects and believed they had every right to claim them. He decided to leave his own convictions out of the conversation, for the British were immovable on their position.

"A priceless collection, no doubt," Langham continued. "One the Greeks would like to have back. They claim, as do other critics within the international community, that Great Britain has no right to the sculptures because they were removed without permission." He turned to another photo. "This is an English interpretation of an official translation in Italian of the original firman issued by the acting grand visier of the Ottoman Empire, in 1801. As you know, this was what allowed Lord Elgin to legally buy the marbles on behalf of His Majesty King George III."

Daniel knew of the controversial document. Many scholars had doubted its authenticity because it was two steps removed. Worse yet, there were discrepancies between the English and Italian translations, casting an even greater shadow on the purchase. The English version included alterations convenient to the British—for example, it named Lord Elgin's secretary as the official expediter, while the Italian version did not—and was eventually accepted by the Parliament, legitimizing the crown's claim.

"Naturally, the Greeks claim this document is a fabrication. They are calling for a reexamination of both translations by an independent body, seeking inconsistencies that would allow them to bring the case before an international court." Langham pursed his lips. "It is preposterous."

"Preposterous or not, it's reality. Not much Britain can do to stop it."

"There is one thing that will put an end to this dispute once and for all: the original Turkish firman, signed by the grand vizier himself."

"But that has never been found." Daniel raised an eyebrow. "If it ever existed at all."

"Of course it existed. Britain acquired those treasures through legitimate means and has a right to them now. It is thought the firman was destroyed during the War of Independence, but we have reason to believe it was stolen by Greek fanatics and guarded for generations."

"I suppose you're going to tell me you know where it is."

"If only it were that simple. We've been seeking it for decades, and we are quite close—but not there yet. Allow me to explain." He reached inside the cabinet and pulled out another folder. "Our investigation has launched us down a rabbit hole that is rather deep. We have been tracking an antiquities ring that has allegedly amassed billions of dollars' worth of Greek and Ephesian artifacts, mostly through unlawful means."

"You mean theft."

"Quite right. And flagrant theft, indeed. Most of it is happening under the noses of the Greek authorities, who have neither the power nor the resources to stop it."

"What proof do you have of this?"

"Let me show you." Langham pulled a stack of photos out of the folder and tossed them onto the table.

Daniel looked through the images depicting crates sitting in a warehouse and close-ups of their contents—marble sculptures, classic black-figure pottery, bronze and gold jewelry. "Where were these taken?"

"In a south London warehouse hired by a prominent gallerist, an Egyptian chap named Ishaq Shammas. We were tipped off by one of our agents that the shipment contained a bust of Apollo stolen from the museum of Olympia some years prior. So we went in to investigate and eventually arrested Mr. Shammas for trafficking in stolen goods.

"But in the process, we discovered something very interesting. The shipment prior to this one contained a document of Turkish provenance dating to the time of the Ottoman occupation of Greece. According to the warehouse log, the document was signed by the Kaimakam—the grand vizier—of the Ottoman Empire."

Daniel rubbed his eyes. The headache that had been plaguing him since the crash had begun to intensify. "Are you saying this guy was in possession of the original firman?"

"That is exactly what I'm saying."

"So what happened to it?"

"That's what we don't know. Supposedly, it was delivered along with the rest of the shipment to a collector whose identity Mr. Shammas has refused to reveal, even under pain of incarceration. He has since been extradited to Egypt and is now serving time in a rather unsavory prison in Cairo."

"Where does that leave you?"

"We simply have to obtain the information another way. Which shouldn't be hard, considering the pillaging of Greek artifacts continues. There has been a rash of thefts in Greece and the Turkish coast, which we believe are related to Mr. Shammas and his star collector. We were led to this conclusion by something we found whilst searching the gallery computers." He removed a drawing from the folder. "This rendering was attached to an e-mail sent by Mr. Shammas to one of his brokers. It read simply, *Any price*. Trouble is, shortly after the arrest, that broker was found hanged in his flat."

Daniel studied the artist's sketch of a golden obelisk with a sharp end, like a stake. The lack of ornamentation made it difficult to peg to any era. He'd not seen anything like it and questioned whether it was ancient at all. "I don't get it. Why is this significant?"

"We don't know. But by a marvelous stroke of good fortune, we do know where it is. And we intend to use it as a linchpin to get to this collector—and to the document that rightfully belongs to the British government."

"Is this the part where you tell me what you want from me?"

Langham closed the folder and placed it back in the filing cabinet. He gestured to Daniel to follow him to the library. They sat opposite each other on red leather armchairs that smelled slightly of tobacco. Langham sucked on an unlit cigar and began. "In addition to my duties for Her Majesty's government, I also serve as chairman of the A.E. Thurlow Foundation. You may know of it."

He did know of it. It was one of the oldest British institutions, capitalized to the tune of two billion pounds, and a major funder of archaeological research worldwide. "Go on."

"When we researched this obelisk and discovered it was in custody in a small museum in Greece, we decided to extend a rather sizeable grant to the local ephorate. They were in dire straits, so they were elated at the news—and willing to do anything we asked. Our condition was that the object be kept in the museum under heavy security.

"Meanwhile, we would leak the information in a controlled fashion so that it got to the operatives of this antiquities ring whilst we set a trap. We haven't been able to execute on that, because we haven't got the right partner on the ground."

"Surely the director of the ephorate—"

"The Greeks are buffoons. They cannot be trusted." His eyes glinted as he stared at Daniel. "What we need, Dr. Madigan, is a very smart and capable archaeologist who's sympathetic to the crown—or at least owes us a favor—to execute the plan."

Daniel could see where this was going. "And what would that involve, exactly?"

"Studying the obelisk and publishing your findings

in the proper academic journals. And when the looters come—and they will come—working with an Interpol team to ensure they are in custody. We'll take it from there, and you'll be free to go."

Daniel rubbed his throbbing forehead but quickly withdrew his hand when he felt a sharp sting from a gash above his left eye. He exhaled.

"We can take care of your assignment papers straight-away—if you'll agree."

A wrinkle formed between Daniel's brows. "Do I have a choice?"

"Of course you have a choice. This isn't an autocracy." He placed a hand on his guest's shoulder. "You could choose to be on your own—at which point we would wish you luck with saving your partner's life."

Langham had driven the point home: if Daniel wanted their help, he would have to play their game. "Fine. I'll go to Greece. But she comes with me."

"You can bring along the Dalai Lama if you so choose. But no one can know about this assignment. No negotiation."

Daniel turned off the water and felt the chill in the room needle his wet body. Langham's plan had sounded simple enough, but it had gone wrong. Before Daniel had a chance to study the object and publish about it, the in-formation was leaked another way. As a result, the theft caught them unawares—and now they were scrambling for plan B. Daniel had thought about walking away and taking the consequences, but he had given his word. To him, that still meant something.

The only way out of his predicament was through it.

The image of Sarah's perplexed face, outlined in the chalky glow of moonlight, was branded onto his memory. If she ever caught wind of the deal he'd cut and the secret he'd kept, she surely would walk away—for good this time. He wouldn't blame her. But even if it meant losing her, his conscience was clear: he had done what was necessary to save her life.

He dried off and threw on his well-worn Rutgers hoodie and the dusty, ripped jeans he'd been wearing for a week. It was time to face the day.

Eight

Though she knew the looters were after the brass spike, Sarah had spent the early morning hours studying something altogether different. She had a hunch the wolf's head rhyton held some clues that would help them piece together a theory on the mysterious object no one could identify.

She examined the pottery specimen under the fluorescent lights. It was painted in the Corinthian black-figure tradition against a natural clay background. The technique was prevalent from the Peloponnese to central Greece starting in the seventh century BCE but eclipsed in the early fifth century BCE, when the Athenians introduced red-figure painting, which was considered far superior. In Sarah's opinion, early black-figure painting—the intricate carving out of detail on silhouetted figures before firing—was underappreciated.

This rhyton was a perfect representation of the technique at its height. The face of a she-wolf was frozen in a menacing snarl, its narrowed eyes delivering a warning to the beholder: *Partake of me at your own peril.*

The rhyton's lip, only part of which had been

reconstructed, was painted with a male figure kneeling before a deity Sarah could not identify. She turned the vessel around and noted another solitary male figure, naked and crouched, as if in shame.

She stared at the obscure imagery. What did this cup hold? And who drank of its contents?

She moved the rhyton to the ultraviolet light area and placed it against a black cloth. According to the log, Evan had put the object under the UV lamp but had found nothing out of the ordinary. She repeated the test, just in case he had missed something.

She dimmed the room lights and turned on the lamp. She scanned the rhyton, one square inch at a time. She stared at the iconography for a long while, hoping it would reveal something. But, as Evan had reported, there was nothing remarkable.

She considered the symbolism of the wolf in ancient times. The beast supposedly was sacred to Apollo, for the god's mother, Leto, was said to be the personification of a she-wolf. According to legend, the source of Apollo's strength and wisdom was the milk of a wolf-woman.

Wolf's milk. Could there be something to that?

Sarah thought she had heard of a plant that bore that name. She searched the database for botanicals relating to the wolf and found *Euphorbia characias wulfenii*—commonly known as wolf weed, or wolf's milk. It was an ornamental plant that grew in the Mediterranean region.

A wider search for its properties revealed that the black nectar of the flower glands was toxic, causing convulsions, hallucinations, and possibly death.

Perhaps she had been looking in the wrong place.

She repositioned the rhyton and trained the light on its throat. She had expected to find traces of sticky sap, perhaps the residue of some ancient mind-bending potion, but what she found was altogether different. As she moved the light around, she saw a letter. Then another, and another, trailing into the dark heart of the vessel. A single word, written in ancient Greek.

So that was the answer.

Sarah glanced out the clerestory window. It was already light out, meaning the others would be arriving at any moment. She turned off the UV light and carefully repacked the rhyton. She would have to continue her experiment later.

As if on cue, a clicking sound came from the other side of the door. Sarah turned on the lights and returned to her workstation. She had just enough time to minimize her screens before Evan walked in.

"You're here early." He took off his jacket and hung it on a hook by the door. "What are you working on?"

"Paperwork." She took a sip of cold coffee.

Evan's gaze darted around the room before settling on Sarah. "I saw Daniel this morning. He said there was an attempted break-in. Do you know about this?"

"It's true. I suspect it's the same people who ransacked the museum."

His nostrils flared. "I should not be the last to know about things like that. I'm still in charge here." He raised his voice a notch. "And Daniel changing the code . . . Who's giving him such orders?"

"I suppose you should ask him that."

"Ask me what?"

Sarah and Evan turned in unison. Daniel was standing at the door, his wet hair pulled back in a ponytail. Though he had showered and changed, he looked as tired as he had in the predawn hours. Sarah recognized on his face the toll of insomnia, for she had seen it many times on her own.

"I'm confused, Daniel." Evan's tone was barbed. "Who's calling the shots here?"

Daniel walked up to them and stared at his Greek colleague for a long moment. "The people who are paying your salary. Is there a problem?"

Evan crossed his arms and looked away.

"So now we know what they're after." Daniel nodded toward the vault. "A simple brass spike found by a shepherd on the bottom of a river. Rather unlikely, don't you think?"

Evan turned to Daniel, his upper lip raised in a snarl. "Sounds to me like you have it figured out. So why don't you tell me what all this means?"

Daniel leaned into his face. "I think you know."

"What are you insinuating?"

Sarah stepped between them. "Enough of this pissing match." She turned to Evan. "Would you excuse us, Evan?"

Evan kept his gaze fixed on Daniel. "Gladly." He brushed past him a bit too hard as he walked out of the lab.

When the door closed behind Evan, Sarah turned to her partner. "What are you doing, Danny?"

"I don't trust him. I think he's the one who's feeding information to the looters."

"Even so, you must keep your cool. Inflaming him doesn't serve us in any way." She sighed. "I'm a bit concerned about you."

He put a hand up. "Don't be. I'm perfectly fine."

She didn't want a fight, so she dropped it. "There's something I want to show you." He followed her to the back of the room, where the rhyton lay in its protective crate. She peeled back the polyethylene foam to uncover the object. "Do you know what this is?"

"Wolf's head rhyton, Corinthian black figure . . . looks like seventh, maybe sixth century." He glanced at her. "That about right?"

"Roughly. May be as late as fifth century. It hasn't been dated. They're still working on the reconstruction." She put on gloves and lifted it out of the crate. "There's nothing extraordinary about it, except one thing. There's an inscription inside."

Daniel looked down the vessel's throat. "Don't see it."

"You can under the black light. Come."

He turned off the lights and joined Sarah at the UV lamp. She shone the light into the belly of the rhyton, revealing the four tiny ancient Greek letters, and waited for his reaction.

Though she couldn't read his expression in the darkened room, she heard the excitement in his voice. "I'll be damned."

"There may be more to the inscription in the deep part of the vessel. I won't know until I make an impression. But this part is clear."

"Lethe. One of the five rivers of Hades."

"The river of oblivion. Where the dead had their memories erased."

"You think there's something to this?"

She turned off the lamp and flicked the lights back on. As she moved the rhyton back to its crate, she shared her theory. "I haven't had time to research it completely, but I do know of a few historical references to Lethe. Plato wrote about it in *The Republic*."

"True," he said. "End of book ten. The dead had to drink of its waters before they could be reborn."

"Right. Then there are the references to Lethe and its opposite, Mnemosyne, in orphism. The waters of the two rivers were central to the postmortem rites. In direct opposition to Plato's theory, the orphic soul was forbidden from drinking the waters of forgetfulness and was instead required to drink from Mnemosyne, the river of memory."

"Lethe and Mnemosyne . . . Where else have I heard that?" Absently rubbing the dark stubble that had crept along his jaw, Daniel looked away. After a long moment, he snapped his fingers and pointed to Sarah. "The oracle of Trophonius."

Sarah had to search her memory to recall the obscure myth. As sketchy details came to her, she felt a fire ignite in the pit of her stomach. Before making any declarations, she sat at the computer and called up the second volume of Pausanias' *Description of Greece* in the Cambridge digital library.

A search of the volume brought up the ancient Greek chronicler's narrative about the mysterious cave and its oracle. A wrinkle formed between Sarah's brows as she read the meticulous description. It was uncanny.

Daniel leaned over her chair. "It's been so long since I've read Pausanias. I'd forgotten how much detail he goes into."

"It goes on for pages. Here is what he says about Lethe and Mnemosyne: 'The priests do not lead the seeker to the oracle but to the sources of the river which are very near each other. And here he must drink of the water called Lethe, that he may forget all his former thoughts, and afterwards he must drink of the water of Memory, and then he remembers what he will see on his descent.'" Sarah looked up at Daniel. "The rhyton was found in Chaironeia, not far from Livadeia. According to

Pausanias, the cave of Trophonius was somewhere in that area, near the Herkyna River. Could this be the cup the seekers of Trophonius drank from?"

He stood straighter. "It's not impossible. But why the wolf's head? The only animal mentioned in the text is the sacrificial ram."

"I have a theory about that as well. I know it sounds far-fetched, but there is a toxic plant that grows in the Mediterranean region that could impact memory if consumed in a certain way. *Euphorbia characias wulfenii*— also known as wolf weed. Maybe it wasn't the river waters that made them forget."

"You think they made some wolf-weed concoction and served it in that rhyton?"

"Why not?"

"I suppose anything is possible." He crossed his arms. "Now if we could make some connection to the obelisk."

She scrolled through the text and pointed to the screen. "There it is."

Daniel read aloud. "'The oracle is above the grove on the mountain. And there is round it a circular wall of stone, the circumference of which is very small, and height rather less than two cubits.'" He paused as he read the next part to himself. He whispered, "Wow."

Sarah swiveled her chair around to face him and repeated Pausanias' words. "'And there are some brazen pillars and girders that connect them, and through them are doors.'"

"Brilliant girl." He looked up and exhaled. He spoke softly, as if to himself. "This could be the answer."

She stood. "The answer to what?"

"Uh . . ." He seemed to fumble for an answer. "I mean the reason. The reason the thieves are seeking the obelisk."

"So what do we do with this information?"

"Keep it quiet for now." He put a hand on her shoulder and leaned in. "Mention none of this to Evan."

She was surprised at his reaction. She'd expected him to be keen to report it to Interpol, or at least the local authorities. Or perhaps to ship the object to a higher-security facility. She couldn't shake the feeling that he had an agenda she knew nothing about.

Daniel looked at his watch. "I've got to run into town for an errand. Maybe you can work on that impression of the interior of the rhyton. If there is more to the inscription, that could be a valuable clue."

"I don't know how much time I'll have. Evan will probably be back any minute."

"Don't worry about Evan. He has some meetings." He winked.

Sarah knew there were no meetings. All it would take was a text from Daniel to the foundation bigs, who clearly thought more highly of him than they did of the head of the ephorate, to arrange appointments that would keep Evan distracted for a few hours. With Evan out of the way, she could get the job done. She nodded in recognition of the tactic.

Daniel smiled and turned to leave.

Sarah watched him walk away. Though she was desperate to know why he was going into town, she didn't question him. She stroked the Tibetan prayer beads he'd given her, now wrapped three times around her wrist, as if they held the answers to the questions that nagged her: why did Daniel keep disappearing? Who was he answering to? What was he holding back?

And the one she was loath to admit, even to herself: could she trust him?

Daniel turned the engine of the Land Rover and gunned the throttle, raising a plume of dust behind him. When the camp was a speck in the rearview mirror, he texted Langham.

I have what you want.

Seconds later, the phone rang. Langham did not bother with a greeting. "Talk fast. I'm about to go in with the prime minister."

"The obelisk may be part of the original structure surrounding the cave of Trophonius."

"I'm not familiar."

"It was an oracular center in ancient Greece. The rituals there were mysterious, even terrifying. The cave is described in great detail by a few ancient writers, but nothing that fits those descriptions has ever been found."

"The intel we have states the obelisk is a key."

"Right. It could be the key that opens the entrance to

that cave." Daniel looked in the rearview mirror to make sure he wasn't followed. He recognized in himself the instinct of the hunted. His heart beat a little faster. "And what could be in there is anyone's guess."

"Sounds as if you have a theory to test. I want you to take the obelisk to the site and find out if it can be used as a key. Do it today."

"Sarah knows. She's the one who figured it out."

"Damn it, Madigan. You were to keep her out of this." He exhaled sharply. "Whatever you do, do not involve her in the recon. It's for her own good."

"If everything that's been written about that cave is true, I'm not sure it's a good idea to do this alone."

"You must. It's not negotiable."

"You're not being reasonable—"

"Hang on." Langham's voice was muffled as he spoke to someone else. When he returned to the call, he sounded rushed. "They're ready for me. Remember: no mistakes."

"James—"

The line went dead.

Daniel lowered the window and felt the brisk air cool his brow. He was unsure whether his anxiety sprang from fear or anger, but either way it was unfamiliar ground. He took two deep breaths to calm his racing heart. When that didn't work, he fumbled inside his pocket for a little blue pill. He swallowed it dry and winced at the bitterness.

Suck it up, he told himself. *It's almost over.*

He kept driving without a destination, struggling to rein in his thoughts as he mapped out his next move.

Nine

Mount Parnassus,
392 CE

*T*he girls sat beneath the shade of the old platanus tree, giggling and whispering as they waited for their teacher.

Aware they could not see her as she came down the hillside from Delphi, Aristea smiled. It warmed her to know they were so eager to learn that they arrived to school before her.

When Aristea approached, a solemn silence fell over the group. Pointing with her index finger, she counted seven heads. They were all present.

"Greetings, girls." Though they were very young, ranging in age from six to twelve, she never called them children, for that term was reserved for boys.

"Greetings, teacher," they said in unison.

She bade them sit on the ground and took her own seat on a tree stump. She brought forward her waist-long braid, wrapped with strips of leather as was the custom for high-born women, and let it rest on her left side. She opened a codex to the marked page and set it on her lap.

"Now, who can give us a synopsis of yesterday's lesson?" Seven hands went up. She pointed to a fair-haired girl with round eyes, like those of a frightened doe. "Thalia."

The seven-year-old daughter of Thracycles, treasurer of Delphi, stood. "We learned about moderation. All excess, even that of virtue, is anathema for the soul."

"Well spoken, Thalia. Let us repeat the doctrine by which we must live our lives."

"We must avoid with our utmost endeavor and amputate with fire and sword and by all other means"—the chorus of female voices echoed down the mountain—"from the body, sickness; from the soul, ignorance; from the belly, luxury; from a city, sedition; from a family, discord; and from all things, excess."

Aristea gave a satisfied nod to her pupils. They were extraordinary girls, each of them destined to lead. It was why she had taken it upon herself to give them a proper education, just as she had received from the strong women of her family. Without the school beneath the platanus, Greek females would be confined to the traditional lessons of cookery, housekeeping, embroidery, and tending to men, without being seen.

It wasn't Aristea's intent to undermine men, for she had the utmost respect for many of them, but to stand as their equal.

She leafed through the codex until she came to the page on which was pasted a piece of papyrus inscribed with Υ. She removed it and held it up. "Who can tell me what this is?"

Erasmia, the youngest of the group, raised a bashful hand.

With a nod, the teacher granted her permission to speak.

"Ypsilon, the twentieth letter of our alphabet."

"It is true." Aristea smiled to reward the girl's participation. "And yet it isn't." She shifted her gaze to the rest of the group, meeting every set of eyes to ensure she had their attention. "Sometimes things are not as they seem. Let me tell you a story.

"A long time ago, a young man walked upon a path for many days, searching for his fortune. As he sat to rest and take water from a spring, he was approached by two women. The first woman wore robes of white and had draped a gossamer veil over her face. She invited the young man to come work at her temple and learn the ways of her people.

"The second woman wore a purple gown cinched at the waist with a golden thread. From her neck hung strands of lapis lazuli from the East and turquoise from the Persian Empire. She held a silver tray piled high with grapes. She picked up a bunch and offered it to the young man.

"Now, he had not eaten in many days, so he took the grapes and devoured them greedily. Seeing his hunger, she beckoned him into the chambers of her temple with promises of plenty." She paused for emphasis. "What do you think the young man did?"

Themis, the orphan who served as a sweeper at the sanctuary, spoke. "He went to the temple of the woman with the grapes."

"Why?"

"Because he didn't want to be hungry."

Aristea nodded. "That's correct. He followed the woman who promised plenty and shunned the woman who offered work. And what do you think became of him?"

"He became fat and lazy," Themis offered.

"And ignorant," added Thalia.

The teacher shared the ending of the story. "He stopped working and seeking, because everything was made ready for him. He gave in to indulgences of the flesh and forgot about the inquiries of the mind. And when war came to his country and his patroness was killed, he was old and unconscious. He had no industry to fall back on, no knowledge of universal truths, no strength of mind. Eventually, he perished without honor at the hands of the enemy."

Seven sets of eyes gazed at Aristea as if the fountain of life sprang from her mouth. She knew they would carry this lesson with them always. "I tell you this story to remind you that life is about choices. Do not be fooled by riches or false promises, for they are like vessels with holes: they can never be filled. Opt instead for the way of industry and virtue, for knowledge and understanding do not come without work. That path may be narrow and steep, but do not forsake it, for it will lead to your higher nature."

She again held up the Υ. "This symbol represents the

choice between two paths." She pointed to the central stem. "This depicts the path of life. As you walk along that path, you will undoubtedly come to a fork, a parting of ways. The left side represents the way of earthly wisdom, the right the way of divine wisdom. As a being of free will, you have the power to choose." She placed the papyrus back in the codex. "Use it wisely."

From the corner of her eye, Aristea saw a figure standing at the far end of the grove. She glanced in that direction and saw Cleon, the eldest priest of Apollo's sanctuary, watching and waiting.

She turned back to her class. "That concludes our lesson for today. Tomorrow, we will begin on our mathematics curriculum."

As the pupils dispersed, Aristea walked through the grove, purposefully brushing against low-hanging leaves as she passed. She never missed an opportunity to feel the hand of nature.

She thought it odd that Cleon stood in the same spot and didn't bother to meet her halfway. She shrugged it off, attributing it to his age. His fifty-seven years were becoming more and more evident in his bent back and the silver strands that crowded out his jet-black hair. Even his dress told of an advanced age: though it was nearing summer, he covered his priestly robes with a fawn skin lest he catch a chill.

As she approached, she took silent stock of this man

who had been her trusted friend since she was ordained into the priesthood at age sixteen. His eyes betrayed concern, as if something had happened.

She spoke to him in a cheerful tone. "You have come a long way, dear Cleon. What brings you to our humble school?"

"Still teaching those girls, are you?"

"Of course." She looked over her shoulder to the platanus that served as her classroom. A couple of the older girls conversed beneath its shade. "It is only through education that they will become more than someone's wife or mother or daughter. And maybe one day women will no longer be invisible in our country."

"You hope for much."

"Things are changing, Cleon. We must give voice to women if we are to stand as a strong society against the oppressors."

"That is why I am here." He drew a deep, shaky breath. "I wanted to be the one to tell you."

Sensing his distress, she placed a hand on his shoulder. "Tell me what, old friend?"

"Theodosius has been named emperor of both sides of the Roman Empire. He has supreme power. That is not good news for us."

A chill traveled down Aristea's spine. While governing the eastern half of the empire, Theodosius had proven himself a ruthless leader. The destruction of the Serapeum the year prior was one of many atrocities committed by the emperor who waved the sword of a supreme being foreign to Aristea and her people.

The emperor also had ordered a retaliation against the Thessalonians for executing one of his governors, an action that resulted in a bloody clash and the loss of more than seven thousand lives. More recently, Theodosius had issued a number of decrees, all directed toward pagan places and methods of worship.

Though she felt the drumbeat of doom in the pit of her stomach, she stayed positive for the old priest's sake. "He will not harm us. We have done nothing worthy of his wrath."

Cleon leaned forward. "Hear my words, Aristea. Theodosius has issued a new law proscribing paganism. Regardless of how peaceful our rituals, we are hereby forbidden to engage in them. Blood sacrifices carry a penalty of death. So does prophesying, which in their eyes is a form of witchcraft."

"We'll do it in secret. No one has to know."

He shook his head. "They have their eye on Delphi. As the most important pagan sanctuary in all of Greece, it is under much scrutiny. What I mean to say is, we can no longer accept supplicants. No one will risk prison and torture to journey here anyway."

The revelation hit Aristea like a stone off a catapult. "But that will mean the end of Delphi. That cannot be."

A breeze came down from the mountaintop and

swept through the grove. Cleon wrapped the fawn skin more tightly around him and turned toward the uphill path. He glanced behind him. "Be careful what you teach those girls. You don't know who is listening."

She knew Cleon was right, but it irked her nonetheless. "With my last breath I will share with them what I know. It is my birthright and my sacred duty."

He smiled. "Your ancestress Themistoclea was just as foolhardy."

"Look after yourself, old friend."

Cleon walked along the path to Delphi. Aristea gazed toward the top of the mountain, where the Phaedriades rose like dogs' teeth toward a shimmering sky. For centuries her people had stood in the boulders' shadow and communed with the divine.

She swore no rabid emperor would take that right away from them.

Ten

"I'm sorry, Sarah." Daniel's face was as hard as the basalt of the mountains. "I should have told you sooner."

His announcement that he was returning to Saudi Arabia—alone—rattled her. She hadn't seen it coming. "I don't understand. I thought we were sailing this ship together."

"This isn't about you. I need to fly solo for a while, work some things out." He zipped up his backpack and slung it over one shoulder, then reached down for his army-green duffle. "My driver is waiting."

"I suppose you should get on then." Her voice was shaky.

He placed a cold hand on her face and stroked her cheek with his thumb. She pulled back, repulsed by the hypocrisy of it.

He stared at her with vacant eyes, then turned toward the door, swung it open, and let it slam behind him.

Sarah jolted awake. It took her a moment to realize she'd fallen asleep at the table in her cabin. She'd been reading the Pausanias volumes on her laptop until late and must have dozed off. She went to the sink and splashed cold water on her face, trying to sober herself from the crowbar-to-the-knees effect of the unwelcome dream.

It didn't do any good. She could feel in her gut something was wrong and made up her mind she would not let it go this time. She needed to talk to him.

She zipped up her fleece and made her way through the darkened grove to Daniel's cabin. The wan moonlight illuminated a mist of snow falling between the chestnut leaves and melting as it hit the ground. It seemed winter had come in earnest to the Theban hill country.

Sarah stopped in front of Daniel's door and knocked, steeling herself for whatever would come. Shivering, she cupped her hands and blew into them. There was no answer. She rapped again, calling his name this time.

Again, no answer.

She went to turn the doorknob but stopped herself, thinking it too invasive. Maybe it could wait until morning, after all.

She took the long way back to her cabin, past the car park. In the back of her mind, she knew the Rover wouldn't be there. And she was right.

For a long moment, she stood beneath the falling snowflakes, staring at the sole vehicle—Evan's Land Cruiser—in the car park. Daniel was gone.

Her face tingled with alarm. Could it be?

She glanced toward the monolithic building beyond the grove. She launched into a jog, then a full-on run, jumping over exposed roots and crunching fallen leaves as she hurried toward her destination.

By the time Sarah got to the lab door, she was breathless. Her hands trembled as she entered the combination and pushed the heavy metal door open. She turned on the lights, and the space was flooded in a shock of fluorescent white. Squinting, she looked around the harshly lit room. As her eyes adjusted, she was relieved to find everything as she had left it about eight hours prior, when she had finished studying the rhyton.

She turned to the vault. She punched in the combination and heard the familiar pneumatic sigh. She pushed it slowly and scanned the stacked trays full of artifacts. Her gaze stopped at the empty tray marked *Brass obelisk, Boeotia*.

She clenched her fists. How could he do this?

She shut the vault and went straight to the hooks by the front door, where the Land Cruiser keys were hanging. She pulled them down and scribbled Evan a quick note:

Had to take the Cruiser into town. Won't be long.
                    —Sarah

By the time she exited the lab, the snow had picked up. She expected it would be worse on the high mountain passes that enclosed Livadeia and the Herkyna River. All the more reason to make haste.

Eleven

The narrow road winding around Mount Helicon was treacherous enough by day. In darkness, and with the added disadvantage of a snowfall, it could be deadly.

As he made his way down the mountain to the town that lay in the valley, Daniel distracted himself by contemplating the moonlit landscape. The cliffs of Helicon were bare save for the occasional shrubs sprouting among the stones, mere whispers of fecundity in this otherwise parched stretch of earth. Against this rugged backcloth, modest houses emerged here and there, perhaps the homesteads of shepherds and other tenders of the land, testaments to man's persistence even in the most improbable places.

That had long been the way of the Greeks. Since Greek civilization rose from the Dark Ages in the eighth century BCE, clans had staked their claims upon a patch of barren earth and devised ways to draw milk from stones. In all of antiquity, there had not been a more clever and productive people. To that day, the Greeks had that capability but did not call upon it, choosing instead the treacherous road of entitlement based on an illustrious inheritance.

He glanced at the passenger's seat, where a hardcover copy of Pausanias' *Description of Greece* lay open. He'd acquired it earlier that day in a bookstore in Thebes, eager to have the text in the original Greek rather than an English translation. So far, its guidance had been invaluable. He just hoped its clues were accurate enough to lead him to the vicinity of the long-lost cave. Once there, the obelisk—in theory—would grant him access. He hoped it would be swift, so he could return to Thebes before anyone realized the object was gone.

In the distance, snow-dusted peaks glowed beneath the moonbeams. Mount Parnassus. The domain of Apollo and his half-brother Dionysus, who symbolized the two opposing forces of human nature, and the realm of the Muses. It was there Trophonius and his brother, Agamedes, began their ill-fated journey.

Daniel replayed Pausanias' words in his mind. Trophonius and Agademes had been commissioned with building the temple of Apollo at Delphi, antiquity's most important sanctuary. When they finished the iconic landmark, King Hyrieus of Livadeia was so impressed at their work that he hired the brothers to build a treasury for his palace.

They constructed a rock-solid chamber, complete with a secret entrance chute only the king knew about. Hyrieus rewarded them handsomely, but—as human nature would have it—they got greedy. They entered the secret passage under cover of night and pilfered the treasure little by little.

The king, of course, found out—and set an iron trap for the thieves. On one of their nocturnal forays, Agamedes got caught in the trap's jaws and could not extricate himself. He told his brother to leave him and save himself. Trophonius agreed but, before leaving, did the unthinkable: he cut off his brother's head so Agamedes would not, in a moment of weakness, divulge the truth.

His hands stained with Agamedes' blood and his heart marked by regret, Trophonius ran to the hills and hid in a cave, living out the rest of his tortured days in isolation and fear.

The story of Trophonius was a cautionary tale about betrayal and the torment it wreaked upon a man's spirit. Upon Trophonius' death, his cave became symbolic of that dark moment of the soul. A descent into the cave of Trophonius was a journey into oneself, with all the demons and turmoil that entailed.

Daniel took a hairpin turn a little too fast and heard the tires screech against the asphalt. The mountain road was devoid of streetlights, and the only illumination came from the moon, whose silhouette was soft behind a layer of clouds. In the valley beneath the pass, tiny dots of light indicated the city of Livadeia, whose white buildings were huddled in a tight cluster despite the expanse around them.

He bypassed the city and turned on a narrow road

through rocky foothills dotted with Aleppo pines. His destination—the headwaters of the Herkyna, from which he would ascend on foot to a grove above the river—was about ten kilometers away.

He pressed down on the gas pedal. As he followed the road uphill, a pair of eyes glowed white in his headlights. He stepped on the brake to avoid the animal that stood squarely in front of the Rover and swerved into the shoulder, sideswiping a pine tree as he brought the vehicle under control.

The animal skittered away. Daniel stopped the car and sank back into the driver's seat. He took his hands off the wheel and noted a slight shake. He closed them in tight fists and struck the wheel, frustrated by the panicked reaction so foreign to him yet now happening with increased frequency. He told himself that it was only the aftermath of the plane crash, that it was all in his head. With the back of his hand, he wiped a mist of sweat from his brow and steered the Rover back onto the road.

It was twenty-five past two when Daniel reached the headwaters of the Herkyna. The spring bubbled forth from a limestone rock, trickling into a narrow groove that widened as it carved its way down the mountain.

He parked in an inconspicuous spot, then continued on foot through a stand of pines to the Herkyna's source. Though he could not see it, he heard the hiss of water from the falls that fed the river. He reached inside his backpack for night-vision binoculars and scanned the olive grove climbing up the hillside, a green aberration between two bald crags rising above it.

He let Pausanias' description of a hollow cave from which the river sprang forth guide him and eventually came to a limestone womb that stood over the river's edge. He shone a flashlight inside the cave, registering a hollowed-out rock that led nowhere.

Referring to the ancient text, Daniel followed a path uphill through the olive grove. In the distance he saw the remains of the unfinished temple of Zeus the King—another clue. The oracle cave was said to be past the ruins and above the grove, marked by a circular wall of marble.

Pebbles crunched as he stepped over them with thick-soled hiking boots, somewhat hurriedly, profaning the otherwise silent space. He recognized the sharp green scent of mountain thyme, which grew wild in the cracks of the rocky slopes. In ancient times, he recalled, its perfume was thought to bring courage to those who inhaled it.

Inside the grove, the growth was so dense and high it gave the trees an eerie effect. Their branches seemed to reach like dark claws eager to consume the intruders in their embrace.

A shaft of moonlight announced the clearing. *Getting close*, Daniel thought. He had memorized the words of Pausanias: *And the oracle is above the grove on the mountain. And there is round it a circular wall of stone, the circumference of which is very small, and height rather less than two cubits. And there are some brazen pillars and girders that connect them, and through them are doors. And inside is a cavity in the earth, not natural but artificial and built with great skill.*

"An enclosure," he mumbled to himself, looking around. He was aware eighteen hundred years had passed since Pausanias' writing. In that time, the structure likely had crumbled to ruin.

He walked along the groin where the massif rose above the grove and, looking through the binoculars, shifted his gaze from the ground to the mountainside. Even after walking half a mile, he saw no openings, no fissures, no sign of any dilapidated wall.

He didn't expect it to be obvious. After all, it had eluded scientists and explorers for decades. But those who came before Daniel did not have what he did: the brass spike.

He shone his flashlight across the ground, scanning every square inch for clues. He stood still for a moment, watching the snow flurries dance in a light wind and land on the winter-scorched grasses.

There was one spot, about fifteen feet from where he stood, where the snow did not alight. Could there be an opening? Daniel walked over and noticed a dip in the ground. Kneeling, he felt around the brush and held his breath as his hand landed on something hard and smooth.

He parted the grasses to reveal a chunk of white marble that could easily be overlooked as a stone. It was a piece of the enclosure; he was certain of it. He felt gingerly around the area, searching for anything the stake could fit into. As he felt a second piece of marble with an indentation in its center, his heartbeat quickened.

He unzipped his pack and removed the brass obelisk, unwrapping it from the protective foam sheets. Though dulled by the patina of the ages, the object gleamed in the pale light of the gibbous moon. He stood and thrust the sharp end into the marble. When nothing happened, he turned to the right, then to the left. It didn't work.

The architects of the cave would not have made it that easy. He searched his memory for Pausanias' words, hoping for another clue. The chronicler of antiquity, who claimed to have experienced Trophonius' cave firsthand, described the cavity as a "bread oven"—likely a cylinder—four cubits wide and eight cubits deep.

There was intent to everything the ancient Greeks did, and those measurements may well have been ordained by mathematical principles. Daniel had read that, in his repentance, Trophonius had subscribed to the Pythagorean tenets and lived out his days seeking the esoteric wisdom purveyed by Pythagoras, whose philosophy revolved around the divinity of numbers.

The number most sacred to Pythagoras, Daniel recalled, was ten: the triangular number and metaphysical symbol signifying the order of the universe. Then he thought of the arrangement of the numbers adding to ten. *It's worth a shot*, he thought.

He turned the obelisk clockwise four times, then turned it in the opposite direction three times, then two, then one.

Daniel heard a low rumble and felt the ground move beneath his feet. He jumped back as he realized the earth was yawning open. He tried to escape to solid ground but was sucked into the chasm.

He landed on his side so hard it knocked the wind from his lungs. As he lay there, struggling for breath, his mind's eye filled with the familiar blinking red light. *It was just a fall*, he told himself in an attempt to stay calm. *Nothing to worry about.*

As his lungs refilled with air, he realized his flashlight had shattered. Crawling on all fours, he felt for his night-vision binoculars, but they were nowhere. Like his backpack, they likely lay on the ground above the cave floor.

Thoughts of doom infiltrated Daniel's mind. He sat on his knees and grasped his hair with both hands, trying to shake the sensation. He had two choices: to explore the innermost reaches of Trophonius' cave and see what was hidden there, or to find his way out of the cylindrical cavity.

He glanced up at the round mouth that marked the entrance to the cave and surveyed the structure's derelict masonry walls. Getting out without rope would be difficult but not impossible. For a moment, he considered abandoning his assignment and getting the hell out. But he had never aborted a mission and wasn't about to start.

He took a deep breath to steady his nerves and groped in the dark for the opening Pausanias had described. In the seam joining the cave floor and walls, there reportedly was a tight opening that led to the inner sanctum, where oracle seekers received their visions. The journey was said to be terrifying, for it involved a strong sense of self and of faith. Those who faltered in either regard emerged from the oracle of Trophonius shaken, bewildered, traumatized, and, on occasion, dead.

Daniel ran his hands across the cave walls, feeling for any clue. The stones used to build the cave had crumbled or had been covered by overgrown vegetation, making the task difficult. Eventually, his fingers ran across a small groove at the bottom of the structure, obscured by a tangle of roots.

This is it.

He ripped the roots apart until more of the opening was revealed. He felt a horizontal crack, like a torn seam, stretching between the earthen floor and the crumbled limestone wall. He kicked the crack, tentatively at first, then more decisively. It gave way.

The opening, he figured, was about two feet wide and six inches high—barely big enough for a man's lower limbs to fit into.

Pausanias' narrative was explicit. *On the descent between top and bottom is an opening two spans broad and one high. He who descends lies flat at the bottom of the cavity and, having in his hands cakes kneaded with honey, introduces into the opening first his feet and then his knees; and then all his body is sucked in, like a rapid and large river swallows up anyone who is sucked into its vortex.*

Though he heard a voice in his head telling him to stay away, Daniel decided to go for it. He lay on the floor on his back and pressed his feet into the hole, then pushed his legs in up to the knee, following Pausanias' prescribed technique.

This was the point when the chute supposedly swept a man into its belly, but nothing happened. In fact, Daniel was stuck, unable to move in or out of the opening. His feet dangled in a void he could not see. Whatever was behind the wall was hollow, like a shaft. He tried to shimmy deeper in, to no avail.

He sensed a faint vibration against his back and put a hand on the wall. It felt as if the structure was settling. The vibration turned into a tremor. Instinctively, he tried to wiggle out of the opening, but the aperture had too tight a clamp on his legs. He was trapped.

With a low rumble, a portion of the floor fell away, pulling him inside a shaft. It was a near-vertical drop in the pitch black that felt as if he were plummeting into an abyss. As he fell with mounting velocity, his heart pounded so hard he thought his arteries would burst. Hardly able to breathe, he gasped for air, but there was no oxygen to take in. He felt like a man about to die. He had known that sensation only once before, a time he had tried so desperately to erase from his memory.

He had no awareness of his body. The utter blackness was replaced by a blinking red light that, with every heartbeat, grew in circumference until it flooded his mind's eye.

A searing heat overtook his throat and traveled up to his head and down both arms. He felt something press down on his chest like a vise. He clutched at it with all his strength, tried to pull it apart. But the sensation was still there. It became tighter, suffocating him.

He landed with a thud that resonated in his ears and forced a primal scream from his throat. A second cry came, then another, until his lungs had no more air to give. His eyes rolled to the back of his head, and then there was nothing.

Twelve

*I*n the remains of night, Sarah retraced Pausanias' steps through the olive grove on the hills above Livadeia. But this wasn't an archaeologist's journey. It was a voyage driven by a need for clarity—and resolution.

Adrenaline surged through her as she imagined the confrontation with Daniel. It was the last thing she wanted, yet there was no longer a choice. By taking the obelisk without informing anyone—not even the partner he supposedly trusted implicitly—he had stepped so far over the boundaries that there was no return. No motivation in the world could justify such an action.

She willed the noxious thoughts out of her mind for the time being. It was difficult enough to locate an ancient cave without any emotional agitation; she needed her wits about her to guide her through the darkened landscape.

The Aleppo pines rustled in the evening breeze, releasing their green, bittersweet scent into the air. With a constant, telegraphic trill, a flock of nightjars serenaded the night. At the top of the grove, Sarah stopped and looked around. Midway up the massif rising above the hill country was a lone, whitewashed monastery wedged into the rock. She had no doubt it was still occupied. The Greeks had a history of building monastic habitations on difficult places, where the men of God could study without worldly distractions.

Panning a penlight across the desiccated grasses, she scanned the clearing for any sign of the cave. If Daniel had indeed been there before her, he likely had gained access using the brass stake. Sarah cringed at the notion of following him rather than walking beside him. As far as she was concerned, it was the beginning of the end.

At the tip of her light beam, she noticed something peculiar and did a double take. The ground was covered with pine branches in a tight arrangement that could not have occurred naturally. She walked closer to investigate.

It seemed as if someone had dragged the branches there, perhaps to cover something. Holding onto a low branch from the nearest tree, she stepped onto the area. Her foot sank into the branch structure, confirming her suspicion that there was no solid ground beneath.

She stepped harder onto the branches and watched them sink into the earth. She repeated the process until a hole was exposed. She squatted to get a closer look. Judging by the newly torn roots on the edges of the crater, it had recently been opened—likely that night.

There was no sign of entry—no obelisk, no tools, no rope. She shone a light inside. The chasm was as Pausanias had described it: cylindrical and manmade, rather akin to a bread oven. Her pulse quickened. One of antiquity's great mysteries had been revealed.

Sarah slipped her pack off her shoulders and searched quickly for a stretch of rope and a headlamp. She figured the distance to the bottom of the chasm was at least a dozen feet—too high to jump. Besides, she'd need a way out. She secured the rope to a nearby pine tree, tying the bitter end into a timber hitch. She threw the other end of the rope into the hole and quickly slid on it down to the bottom.

She held still for a moment, letting the space speak to her. The walls were a rudimentary masonry, rough-cut blocks of limestone that had been covered over by the roots of trees and bushes aboveground. She turned three hundred sixty degrees, scanning the structure from top to bottom.

Then she saw it: a fissure between the wall and the dirt floor. It looked as if the ground had crumbled away, perhaps under the weight of something. She looked closely. An object was wedged into the dirt. She parted the soil and recoiled when she saw a shattered torch she swore belonged to Daniel.

Could he be in there? The doubts and anger that had been rising inside her were instantly replaced by a deep concern. No matter what he had done and how distant they had grown, she could not bear the idea of him being hurt.

"Danny?" she called, softly at first and louder when she got no answer.

Sarah clawed at the dirt to create a larger opening. It was soft and moist, almost like quicksand. She considered Pausanias' explicit account—*and then all his body is sucked in, like a rapid and large river swallows up anyone who is sucked into its vortex*—and wondered if there was a spring nearby that caused that pull.

There was nothing to do but descend into Trophonius' hole. She braced herself in case the eyewitness account of Pausanias was true. He'd insisted oracle seekers were seized by a presence and dealt prophecies and insight in the most terrifying way. Presumably owing to drinking the waters of Lethe, the supplicants did not even remember what had happened in the dark recesses of that forest womb. A few did not survive the experience.

Then again, those early seekers did not have the benefit of climbing rope. Sarah glanced at the coils of rope stacked on the cave floor and figured there was an extra ten feet there; she hoped it would be enough. She tossed the end into the opening and, holding on to the rope, wedged herself in feetfirst.

Once she was past the narrow mouth, the rope tensed as she dropped into a cavernous space. She did not have enough rope to reach the bottom. Holding on tightly, she dangled in the void. The heavy scent of moist earth laced with the must of fungus hung in the air. A chill radiated from the damp soil. Water definitely ran nearby.

She tapped on the headlamp and scanned the space.

Though it was impossible to illuminate all the dark reaches, she could at least surmise the floor was another ten feet down.

"Danny? Are you here?" Her voice echoed inside the cavern.

As expected, there was no answer. She weighed her options. She could jump to the bottom and explore more closely, or she could come to the conclusion she was chasing ghosts and forgo the risk of entering a volatile space with no easy way out.

Her biceps burned as she held on to the taut rope. Her strength would not allow her to hang there much longer. She had to make a decision: jump down or begin the climb back up.

Sarah never had been one to dodge risk. She had always calculated it, knowing fully what she was entering into. In this case, there was not enough rope to reach the bottom, which meant she didn't have a good exit option. On top of that, there was only a minuscule possibility that something—or someone—was down there. The risk was great; the reward, dubious. And yet the pull of the unknown was too strong to ignore.

She pointed the light at the cavern wall. It was soft, black soil held together by elaborate root systems that could help her climb down. She swung back and forth on the rope until she gained enough momentum to reach the wall.

She grasped for a handhold to slow her forward motion, but it took several times before she could grab hold of something solid. She held on to a particularly large root and tied her rope to it for easy reach later.

She took a moment to survey the way down. The moist earth was too slippery to negotiate, but there were enough roots and rocks to support her descent. Looking over her shoulder to illuminate the route, she moved slowly down the earthen wall, feeling the cool, wet soil beneath her fingernails.

Sarah had only ten, maybe fifteen vertical feet to scale. It was nothing she hadn't done a hundred times during her career. Still, something about this terrain felt odd, almost sinister. She tried to shake the feeling, telling herself she'd been influenced by the texts of writers often given to hyperbole.

As the hole deepened, there were no more roots to hold on to. She dug her nails into the dirt and kicked for a toehold. Her foot hit something hard—a rock?—and she placed her weight on it. As she stepped to make her final bid for the cave floor, the mass moved. It was far lighter than she'd expected. Under her weight, it came out of the soil and tumbled down.

Losing her purchase, she fell and landed squarely on the object. She sat up and pointed her headlamp toward it. She lifted a hand to her mouth.

A skull.

She pointed the light toward the dirt in which the skull had been wedged and saw more half-buried bones: a broken tibia, a clavicle, portions of a rib cage.

It seemed as though the person had been injured on impact and rendered unable to escape. She panned the light around the cave. Aside from the remains, the space was empty. She scanned the ground for footprints or any sign of recent entry.

Her gaze stopped on two fresh tracks in the dirt. It looked like someone had been dragged. A shiver traveled down her spine, and the hairs on her neck stood on end.

She knew she should not linger. Before exiting, she took a final look around, concentrating on the spot where the skeletal remains lay. She held the light on the bones for a long moment and surmised from the pelvic structure the deceased was female. Odd, she thought. According to the recorded history, the seekers of Trophonius were all male. Could this woman have stumbled into the cave, and perished there, long after oracles had been silenced?

Sarah noticed something on one of the rocks wedged nearby. She twisted to release it from the soil. It was an ordinary potsherd, about three inches wide and two inches high. She pulled it out and brushed the dirt away with her hand.

Something had been haphazardly carved on the clay: perhaps the ill-fated woman's final, desperate attempt to communicate. She brushed more of the dirt away to expose the full engraving. The writing was late Hellenistic, the form of ancient Greek spoken and written in the early part of the Common Era, up to the passage into Byzantine Greek in the sixth century. Based on that, she surmised the deceased was likely not an oracle seeker, for the cave of Trophonius had been sealed around Roman times.

On top of the shard was a carved symbol, like an upside-down *U*. It seemed as if the person had tried to convey a design within that symbol, but the pottery had chipped in too many spots to distinguish a true pattern.

She studied the text. Though the surface had chipped and some of the letters were unclear, she recognized the words *house* and *new god*.

She turned the shard over. On the other side was a line carving of a mountain whose midline was riddled with holes. Were they caves? The windows of a building? Beneath the drawing were four faded letters—*MELÁ*—and an illegible word that started with the Greek letters *ΣΩΦ*.

She sat back and gathered her knees to her chest. The chill radiating from the damp soil made her shiver. Simplistic scribbles on a random piece of clay: there was no art in it, only a message meant to be found.

Sarah knew what she was about to do was unorthodox. Removing an object found in situ without the proper procedure went against all the rules of archaeology. But she also knew the message carved on that shard was a map pointing to the whereabouts of a long-buried object—and that object was what the looters were seeking.

With a plan formulating in her mind, she stood and tucked the object into a cargo pocket. She jumped up to reach a root about three feet above her head. She grabbed hold and used it for leverage, hoisting her body up a little at a time until she got to the rope. With one hand she held on to her nylon savior, and with the other she untied it from the root.

She gripped the rope tightly as the weight of her body caused her to swing into the void. Engaging every muscle in her upper body, she pulled herself up the length of rope toward the entrance shaft, perhaps a bit too hurriedly. She heard the rapid rise and fall of her breath and realized how exhausted and anxious she was. She forced herself to slow her pace so she could conserve energy for the task ahead.

A faint light from the main chamber of the cave finally came into view. Sarah made a final push for the top, low-crawling through the entrance shaft and propelling herself forward with her forearms. As her head brushed the top of the shaft, loose dirt fell into her eyes, stinging them.

When she emerged onto the top chamber, her muscles twitched in protest and her hands were scraped raw by the friction of the rope. She lay on her back, catching her breath before the next portion of the ascent. Some twelve feet above her, the round mouth leading into Trophonius' underground world was no longer dark. A column of white light entered the cave, heralding a new day.

A breeze blew down the hole, and she felt its cool sting on her sweat-dampened skin. Though she was exhausted, there was no time to linger. She grasped the rope and, grunting, climbed toward the light.

On the surface, the snow that had dusted the grasses the night before was beginning to melt. The sun had barely risen above the peaks of Mount Parnassus, suffusing the scene with golden light. It was cold, but Sarah barely noticed. Adrenaline still surged through her as she gathered the rope in a figure eight between her hand and elbow.

She reached into her trousers and pulled out the stone. It looked even more remarkable in the daylight. She ran a finger across the carving of the mountain peak and the letters beneath it: *Melá*. The word meant *black* in the Pontic Greek dialect. It also was the name of a mountain in the Pontus region, along the Black Sea in modern Turkey.

It was coming together. The words *house* and *new god* could well be a reference to the mystical monasteries built high on the cliffs of Melá as early as the fourth century, when Christianity took hold of the region. The idea of something being buried within their confines was both tantalizing and daunting. The monasteries had been rebuilt many times over the centuries, and an object from antiquity might not have survived the evolution. Still, there was a possibility—and for Sarah, that was enough.

She untied the bandana from her wrist and wrapped the stone, then stuffed it and the rope in her backpack. She slung the pack over both shoulders and turned to leave.

She had not taken two steps before a masked man emerged from behind a tree. From his balaclava to his trainers, he was dressed in all black, holding a knife in a gloved hand. She froze. Her gaze darted to the left, then the right, searching for an escape route.

A second man, similarly attired, stepped out from behind another tree.

Then a third.

She was outnumbered. And she knew what they wanted.

Thirteen

Delphi,
393 CE

Under the light of the crescent moon, Aristea approached the Castalian spring, dressed in her bathing clothes.

There was perfect silence in the forest. Not even the cicadas that trilled incessantly that time of year dared defile the sacred moment.

She removed the leather cord that bound her hair into an upswept twist and released silken black tresses down her back. She slipped off a privacy cloak made of sackcloth and stepped into the marble pool that held the Castalian waters.

The cold assaulted her skin like thousands of bee stings—just for a moment, and then it passed. As she stood in waist-deep water, the lightweight linen of her bathing gown floated around her, giving her the appearance of a lotus in bloom. She held her breath and dove under.

The moonbeams shimmered on the ripples of the water like naiads whose light flashed like a beacon, luring souls to their lagoons and marshes. Such beauty should have filled Aristea with joy, but instead it saddened her. She knew in her heart such ritual ablutions would cease thereafter, for that night she would deliver the last oracle.

The last oracle.

She repeated the words in her mind so she would believe them. For nearly two decades she'd held the agency of the high priestess at the sanctuary of Apollo and had served as the sun god's mouthpiece to mankind. Now her voice had been silenced, for none was there to hear it.

Cleon's prediction was right: no one came anymore to Delphi. An entire year had passed since Theodosius declared war on paganism. Who dared now to challenge his authority and seek the advice of the oracle? All the supplicants from Greece, Egypt, and Mesopotamia had scattered like ants in the rain, crouching beneath the emperor's iron fist.

Once the richest treasury in all of Greece, Delphi's coffers had run dry. There was barely enough money to buy oil for the sacred fires. Aristea and the priests were reduced to begging for their food. She didn't mind. Despite her renown throughout Greece and the demand for her services, she always had chosen the life of an ascetic, based on the recognition she was a bridge between the human and the divine.

Her head broke through the surface of the water. She smoothed her raven locks back and exited the water. With a linen sheet she dried off and slipped into the white, pleated gown of the prophetess.

She removed a torch from its iron holster and walked

to a small altar, where pearls of white and black barley had been formed into a pyramid-shaped pile. She touched the fire to the grain, and it ignited without hesitation.

The fire quickly burned down, leaving only white smoke, billowing in the direction of the wind. Aristea let it envelop her, reveled in its nutty scent. According to her religion, barley smoke cleansed souls so they could be pure before the gods. Pure for the rigors of judgment.

Her spirit one with the universe, she was ready for the ceremony. She picked up the white veil with which she typically covered her head during oracular rituals. She regarded it for a moment and put it aside. Instead, she picked up a wreath of laurel leaves and placed it on her head like a crown.

That night, Apollo's chosen was both oracle and petitioner.

The last prophecy she would deliver would be her own.

The sanctuary looked very different that night. Normally surrounded by torchlight so its brilliance can be seen from leagues away, now it was plunged in darkness. Only one fire burned: the eternal flame, deep in the heart of the sanctuary building. Set upon a tripod, the copper bowl that held the flame of Apollo had burned continuously since the sanctuary had been built a thousand years prior and would not be extinguished to appease a crusading despot.

Aristea stood at the altar of sacrifice, encircled by her family: Cleon, the patriarch of the Delphic priests, and the three *hosioi*, the holy men who performed the rites. Each of them wore a solemn expression, for they knew what they were about to do was forbidden.

Cleon placed an urn on the sacrifice stone. "Who brings forth the sacrificial beast?"

One of the *hosioi* stepped forward with a goat tied to a jute lead. Aristea bowed to the animal, then released it from its bonds and led it to the altar. She stepped back and watched as Cleon raised the urn over the animal's head and doused it with frigid spring water. The goat shivered, a tremor that began at its hooves and rippled up its body to its head: an auspicious sign.

Cleon removed a knife from a sheath hanging from his waist sash and held it between his hands as he uttered a prayer to the sun god: "On this seventh day of Bysios, as new growth springs forth from the melted snows, we implore the mighty Apollo to impart wisdom upon those who seek his counsel. O fairest and gentlest of gods, accept this humble sacrifice, and let your will be revealed in the organs of this poor beast that dies now in your name."

With a swift motion, the priest drove the knife into the goat's jugular vein. Even as the animal expired with great convulsions, Cleon sliced open its belly and pried the skin apart until the viscera spilled onto the stone. He studied the arrangement for a long while.

Finally he proclaimed, "The omens are favorable."

Without the usual pomp and with no light to guide

their steps, the holy men and the priestess proceeded inside the sanctuary. The *hosioi* took their place at the shrine of the eternal fire.

Cleon turned to Aristea. "Do you approach this rite with pure heart and without reservation?"

"I do."

He gave her a lingering glance. She read his apprehension in it. "Then let us proceed."

The two descended the thirteen steps to the temple's inner sanctum. Nowhere did Aristea feel more at peace than inside the stone womb that smelled of lilies from the Macedonian vales. She approached the most hallowed of symbols, the *omphalos*, the stone that marked Delphi's position at the center of the Earth. It was declared thus by Zeus himself. In the beginning of time, the god of gods had released two eagles—one from the West, the other from the East—and commanded them to meet at the Earth's navel. They collided above Delphi and fell into the ravine between the Phaedriades.

But the stone bore another, even more powerful mystery. Carved of black rock spewed by the great volcanic eruption at Thera, it was carved with twelve pentagons that came together to form the exalted dodecahedron, devised by the great mystic Pythagoras as the divine depiction of the universe. Within its vertices were found the formulae to answer many questions, including the one that had vexed Greeks for centuries: the cause of the

Theran catastrophe that had buried alive the enlightened inhabitants of the island, the Minoans.

For nearly eight hundred years, the secret had been handed down from priestess to priestess, along with the charge to preserve it. When Aristea was a child, her grandmother, Io, had explained it to her thus: "Before the gods were born, a great civilization existed in the islands of Greece. Many say the Minoans came from the celestial dust and had powers mortals could only dream of. But one day the Earth heaved with a great rumble and spewed fire and rock that buried these people alive and sank their island into the sea. And a great wave—taller than ten temples stacked atop each other—rose and crashed onto distant shores, swallowing up the rest of the Minoans and their cities in a terrible, swirling froth.

"For years, people blamed the wrath of the nascent gods—until Pythagoras of Samos came along. He could explain with mathematical precision what happened deep inside the Earth's belly—and warned that it could happen again. Based on that knowledge, Pythagoras spent the rest of his days devising ways to stop great quakes from rising again. Alas, he was unable to achieve this in his lifetime. As an old man, he inscribed his formulae onto the navel stone, that men of future generations might be able to continue the work he began and quell another great calamity.

"Yet he knew greed dwelled in men's hearts, so he

entrusted this great mystery to women. He told it to his tutor, our ancestress Themistoclea, and together they decided only her descendant priestesses would guard the *omphalos* and the powerful knowledge etched upon it."

Aristea kneeled before the stone and paid silent homage to Pythagoras and to the woman who had taught him ethics and humility and prudence.

She stood and took her place on the tripod of truth. Cleon handed her a laurel branch and the ceremonial bowl filled with water. Bowing, he backed away.

Aristea closed her eyes and inhaled the vapors issuing from the chasm on which her tripod sat. The fissure reached deep underground to the place where demons dwelled. It was one of those demons, the snake monster Python that once reigned over Delphi, that Apollo had defeated in his quest to replace darkness with light. Because it was pierced by Apollo's golden arrow, Python's rotting carcass emitted a sweet smell, a tribute to the god who had slayed it.

She felt the familiar lightness of being and surrendered to it. Apollo was in the room and would soon possess her. She regarded this awareness without assigning consequence to it. Her seeing powers depended on her ability to detach.

Cleon began to chant. In her mind's eye, she saw a swath of red silk billowing in harmony with his words. She placed a laurel leaf in her mouth and chewed. Her tongue registered a mild and pleasant bitterness followed by the tang of resin. She swirled the leaf until every taste receptor was coated with the flavor.

When her senses engaged fully, the silk shroud was lifted and she was rewarded with the first vision. She saw fire—great flames swirling toward the heavens, leaving clouds of black smoke in their wake. The smoke reeked of burning flesh. She smelled it as if she were there.

She felt herself choking and gasped for air.

The vision became even more vivid, and details came into focus. Behind the curtain of copper flames were fragments of stone. An altar broken in two. Columns crashing to the ground. A heap of ashes and ruins. A fragment of a pediment engraved with words she could not read behind the raging fire.

Suddenly the flames parted and the words she had come to regard with such reverence, the ones on which her spiritual training was founded, mocked her.

Γνῶθι σεαυτόν. *Know thyself.*

With a jolt she realized the house of Apollo burned. Everything swayed to and fro, like a ship caught in the fury of the sea.

A man with eyes like the ocean in winter glared at her, then held up the *omphalos* stone and hoisted it into a dark abyss.

"No," she heard herself cry out.

Everything swayed again, and her body slammed

against something hard. She opened her eyes in time to see her laurel wreath sail down the chasm.

It was so real. So very real.

She lay on her back on the *adyton* floor, her sinew and bones protesting. Next to her, the tripod of truth lay on its side, still rolling from the impact.

Cleon ran to her. He kneeled and took her shaking hand. "Tell me what you saw."

"They are coming, Cleon," she said, choking back tears. "They are coming to destroy us."

ourteen

aniel blinked away the fog that had settled onto his eyes. It was dark. From the corner of his eye he perceived a tiny amber light, like a candle flame. He lifted his head and, feeling a heinous pressure behind his eyes, let it fall back down.

He had no idea where he was. He felt cold and instinctively raised his hands to his chest. His shirt was soaked through, the front of it torn to shreds. What the hell had happened?

He rubbed his eyes and looked around. He was lying on a cot, and exposed masonry walls closed in around him. The space was small and inhospitable, like a prison. With great effort, he turned his head toward the light. On a wooden table, a kerosene lamp flickered in the draft from an open window.

Daniel searched his mind for a memory of what had taken place before he lost consciousness. Trophonius' cave. He recalled sliding on a chute into utter darkness, clawing at the earth around him for a handhold to slow the fast drop, the soil crumbling through his fingers. He replayed a sound track of guttural cries, so excruciating they hardly seemed his own.

Yet they were. He had lost it down there. It was the first time in his life he'd felt such raw, debilitating panic. Even on the morning of the plane crash, when he was certain he was going to die, he'd received his fate with a cool head.

He sat up. His head felt heavy, and his vision was blurry. Still, he had to get out of there—wherever *there* was. At the foot of the bed was a neatly folded, black hand-knit sweater and, on the floor beside it, his backpack. He unzipped the main compartment, where he had kept the brass obelisk. It was missing.

He heard a click, then a scraping sound as the door grazed the floor. A dark figure stood at the doorway. "You are awake," a man said in Greek. His voice was shaky, like he was a hundred years old.

Though he was fluent, at that moment Daniel could not recall a word of Greek. "What's it to you?"

The man walked toward him. Daniel still could not see his face. He only heard the sound of rustling fabric and something rattling in his hands.

The man stepped into the light and placed a cup and saucer on the table. "Some mountain tea," he said. "If you wish."

Daniel stared at the man with the unkempt gray beard and waist-long ponytail of silver hair covered by a skullcap of the same weave as the sweater. He wore the long black tunic and overcoat of a man of the cloth. The room wasn't a prison; it was a monk's cell.

With shaky hands, Daniel took the cup and let the warm liquid touch his lips. He drank the tea in one gulp and wiped his mouth with the back of his hand.

The monk sat on the bed. "My brothers, who are much younger than I, were in the forest for their evening meditation and heard shouts. They pulled you out of the cave. You would have died there."

Daniel sighed loudly and felt his shoulders relax. "I owe you my gratitude. But I must go." He tried to get up.

The monk put a hand on his shoulder. "Not yet. I have some questions."

Daniel glanced at the old man, taking notice of a cataract marking his right eye. He let him speak.

"The key that opens the cave entrance had been lost for nearly two millennia. How did you come upon it?"

"I work at an archaeological dig in Thebes. A shepherd found it at the bottom of the Herkyna and brought it to us. I was doing some research; that's all."

"And did your research yield anything?"

"If you're asking me if I saw anything down there, the answer's no." He looked down at his torn shirt. "Didn't exactly have time."

"Good. Some things aren't meant to be found." The monk steadied himself on the edge of the bed and stood. "You won't be getting that key back. Otherwise, you're free to go."

Daniel stood on shaky legs. "You can't do that. That object has been classified for scientific research."

"Your science means nothing. In this country, we bow to one supreme authority. Have no illusions: between spiritual and secular matters, the Orthodox church will prevail every time." The monk surveyed Daniel from the top down. "Do you believe in God, archaeologist?"

A gust blew through the narrow window, causing the kerosene flame to quiver. "I accept nothing on faith," he said.

"Accept this: whatever is down there is the work of the devil. It must never come to light."

"You should know someone is determined to dig it up. Someone whose intentions are not honorable."

He nodded. "There is a group resurrecting the heathen religions of the ancients, not far from here. They seek a pagan object they think will give them power."

"Who are they?"

"An American—a soldier of some sort—and his flock of lost souls. They and their rituals are anathema to the church."

"The object they seek . . . is it inside the cave?"

"No. It was once the property of the Orthodox church, but it has not been seen in fifteen hundred years. This American believes there is something in that cave that will lead him to the prize."

"And what do you believe?"

"Unlike you, I believe the past should stay buried."

"The inconvenient past, you mean."

"Even so." He took two steps backward and stood at the open doorway. "The cave of Trophonius will be sealed again tomorrow—and this time, it will not be reopened. The brass stake will be destroyed. You can tell that to your archaeologist friends."

The monk took his leave.

"Wait," Daniel called behind the monk. "What do they call you?"

"Father Athanasius. I am the abbot here."

"I am indebted to you and your brothers. I will repay your kindness."

"Do not think of us. Look after yourself. You seem to be in dire need of it." He made the sign of the cross in the air. "Go in peace, my son."

Daniel picked up the sweater at the foot of the bed and put it on. The heavy perfume of incense had permeated the fibers, but he was grateful for its warmth. He slung his pack over one shoulder. He was not in shape to hike out of that forest, nor to drive back to Thebes, but he had to do it before daybreak. He had a lot to think about and more to account for.

No sense in delaying the inevitable. He blew out the kerosene lamp and ducked through the cell's low door.

Fifteen

The masked assailant held up a knife. The blade glinted in the fragile sunlight. He took a step toward Sarah. His two accomplices followed his lead.

Sarah's limbs tingled as fear gripped her. She glanced around for anything she could use to defend herself but saw nothing. Her only option was to run.

Their shoulders hunched in attack mode, the three masked men rushed toward her.

The only clearing was to her left, the steep path that led down to the banks of the river. It was risky, but it was all she had. Hoping they didn't share her ability to negotiate such terrain, she made a run for it.

They ran after her. She led them down the most treacherous part of the route, scrambling over boulders and stepping over two-foot-high shrubs with the agility of a mountain goat. Two of the men fell behind, but one was gaining on her.

Sarah led him across the boulder field to the edge of a steep slope. She looked over her shoulder: he was on her heels. She surveyed the incline and figured it was about sixty degrees. It could not be negotiated in a hurry.

She heard the masked man's panting as he caught up. He reached for her backpack, throwing her off balance. She quickly regained her footing and slipped the pack off her shoulders, swinging it at him with all the strength she could muster.

The move caught him off guard and sent him tumbling down the cliffside. His cry of distress, more a growl than a scream, grew fainter as he rolled toward the river. As she strapped her pack on again, she saw him slam back-first against a boulder. He was not out, but she knew it would be nearly impossible for him to climb out and catch up to her.

Aware the others were gaining ground, she bolted along the cliff's edge running parallel to the river. The path was no more than a foot wide and the drop precipitous: she could not afford a single misstep.

In pace with her gait, she exhaled in short, controlled bursts of mist. She scanned the path ahead for an opportunity to evade them. Up ahead, rising above the hillside, was the massif into which the monastery was built. The exposed rock was sheer but textured enough that she could free-climb it.

Sarah glanced backward. The hooded assailants were no more than twenty feet behind her. She sprinted toward the crag. Her plan was to either lose them on the climb or seek refuge in the monastery.

Though she was winded from the long sprint, there

was no time to catch her breath. She launched up the limestone cliff, pushing her pace to the outer limits of safety. Her scraped hands were a handicap, but she did not let the sharp sting slow her down. She looked over her shoulder. They were climbing after her.

She hadn't had time to study the pitch before ascending, and that was to her detriment. Just ahead, a particularly smooth piece of rock made passage difficult. Though it meant losing valuable time, she had no choice but to climb around it.

Just above was a rudimentary staircase carved into the rock, obviously what the inhabitants of the monastery used to travel up and down. If she could make it there, she was certain she could evade them.

Aware of the risks of the terrain, she picked up the pace anyway. It was folly. She slipped and slid down several feet, giving her pursuers an advantage. Precariously perched on a slim piece of rock without an adequate foothold, she struggled to pull herself back up.

The leader, with the knife tucked into a sheath around his waist, was just behind her. Gritting her teeth, Sarah reached for a groove in the rock and wedged her fingers inside. With that secure handhold she ascended, albeit a few inches at a time.

The man grabbed hold of her foot. She kicked backward to shake him loose, but he only tightened his grip. With a sideways kick, she crushed his hand onto the rock, eliciting a grunt. He let go, and she seized the opportunity to scramble upward, if a little haphazardly.

Sarah gauged the distance to the staircase. It was probably fifty feet away: not close enough. She made a bid for it anyway.

She heard a rip and felt a fiery sensation on her calf. She looked down and saw her pursuer with knife in hand. The second man was now just behind him.

Blood trickled down her pant leg and dripped steadily onto the cliff. Judging by the throbbing of the injured muscle, it was a deep cut. The odds were stacking against her.

"Let the bag go," the leader shouted.

Though her body had tensed from the pain, she kept a calm face. "I don't think so."

Knife in one hand, the man inched up. His cohort caught up to him. Together they grabbed her ankles and pulled.

Losing her grip, Sarah tried kicking again, but she was too weakened by the injury.

The crack of gunfire echoed across the hillside, jolting her. Someone spoke in Greek. "Leave the girl. I won't hesitate to shoot."

Squinting in the sunlight, she looked up at a man in a long black garment and knit skullcap standing on the staircase leading to the monastery. One of the monks.

The leader shouted some obscenities at the monk, who in response pointed the barrel at the two masked men. A second gunshot released a bullet that ricocheted off the rock near the leader.

"I'm not finished with you," the man hissed at Sarah. "You will see me again. Count on it." Then he and his accomplice retreated down the cliff and disappeared into the brush.

Sarah struggled to hang on.

"Wait there." The monk scurried up the stairs and, a moment later, reemerged with a rope basket. He tossed it down to her.

Sarah had seen the contraption in photos. The basket, something like an oversized plaited-rope bag one might take to the grocer, was what monks had used since the middle ages to ascend and descend the cliffs on which their priories sat. Only in the past thirty years had the system, by then obsolete and rather dangerous, been replaced by the building of stairs.

When the cage was next to her, she grasped the coarse rope and parted the strands to gain entrance. As she slipped inside, the weight of her body pulled the basket down and closed the openings. "Let's hope this works," she muttered, tugging on the main pulley line to indicate she was ready.

As she was hoisted up, the squeak of rope rubbing on metal unnerved her—though not nearly as much as the end of the journey did. She was left dangling next to the staircase, a few hundred feet above a precipitous drop.

The old monk offered a cane. Even in a matter of life

and death, the man of God kept his vow to not touch a member of the opposite sex.

As the rope basket swung in the crosswinds that often whipped the hill country, Sarah steadied herself with great effort. Grabbing the cane, she staggered out of the cage onto one of the steps. Her hurt leg buckled, and she inadvertently kneeled in front of the monk.

She looked up at him. His skin was the color of caramel and carved in a spiderweb pattern, and one of his eyes was covered by the gray film of a cataract. A scraggly salt-and-pepper beard brushed his sternum. "Thank you," she said in Greek. "I know you didn't have to do that."

"My faith requires me to help the ailing." His tone was cold, making her question his sincerity. "Even those who snoop where they don't belong."

"I've done nothing wrong." She winced as she stood. "I was merely looking for someone . . . a friend who's gone missing."

He gestured toward the cliff. "Men like them don't hunt a girl who's gone for a walk in the woods. You have something they want." He glared at her. "Don't you?"

She said nothing. It was clear he knew the score.

The monk tapped the cane on the stone step. "That cave is cursed. And so is everything in it."

"You know about the body."

"I've done what is required of me. Now you leave." He started up the stairs.

"Father, please. A man has been murdered. Others, including me, are at risk of harm. I beg you: tell me what is buried at Melá."

He stopped but did not turn around. "The instrument of the pagans. To uncover it is to sin against God." He spoke over his shoulder. "You should forget what you have seen."

"I'm an archaeologist. I cannot forget."

"Another archaeologist." He scoffed.

She shifted her gaze toward the monastery building. Was Daniel there? "You've seen him, haven't you? Is he all right?"

He did not answer. He hobbled up the stairs and stood by the ramshackle wooden door that separated the forbidden realm of the Orthodox holy men from the rest of the world. He inserted an iron key into the lock, and the door creaked open. He glanced at Sarah. "You should not be concerned with what is buried at Melá but rather with the one who seeks it. He is committing the ultimate trespass—and should be silenced."

"It seems to me we are fighting the same war," Sarah said. "We can help each other."

He pointed with his cane toward the mountain range in the distance and spoke in ancient Greek. "If you want to know thine enemy, you must first know thyself."

There was only one place connected to that reference,

and it sat on the other side of Mount Parnassus. "Delphi," she said.

The monk crossed the threshold into the monastery and slammed the door.

Sixteen

Delphi,
393 CE

Aristea ambled along the forested trail above the sanctuary, alone but for the incessant *cri-cri-cri* of the cicadas. The summer sun filtered through the oak trees, casting soft shadows where she stepped. She regarded the shadows as spirits urging her forward on the path that was chosen for her so long ago—the path she now chose for herself.

A week had passed since the vision that shook her to her core, and she still could taste the black smoke in the back of her throat. She wanted to believe it was only a dream, the figment of a frightened mind, but she knew better: the oracle was never wrong.

She heard the snap of a twig and froze. Was someone there? Did an animal lurk behind the oaks? She listened actively. Another snap, this time closer. Then, voices.

It felt as if water from the mountain springs coursed through her veins. She hid behind an old tree trunk and listened.

"Look at all that." Judging by the man's accent, he was of Eastern origin. "A theater, a stadium, treasuries, a marketplace . . . It must be a prosperous city."

"Yes. The Delphians have enjoyed great fortune. They have lured people from all parts of the empire with promises of foretelling the future."

"The devil's work."

"It is time they learn that only God has the power to see the future. Their false prophets must be crushed."

"And what of all this treasure?"

"It must be confiscated . . . for God's work."

"For God's work."

The emperor's mercenaries. It was the moment Aristea had foreseen, the moment she feared.

The men continued talking, but their voices grew more distant until they could no longer be heard. A vision of smoke rising between the temple columns flashed before Aristea's eyes.

She had to warn the others.

She stole a furtive glance around the tree trunk and was relieved to see she was alone again. Urgency hastened her pace as she launched onto the downhill path toward the city. With great agility she sprang around rocks and exposed roots, never slowing her gait. She knew those woods like she knew her own body; over the thirty years of her life, the forest had become an extension of her.

For a moment, she considered it might be the last time she felt the cool soil of Mount Parnassus beneath her bare feet, the last time she felt safe in the forest's embrace.

A pang of agony ripped through her gut, and the hard truth was laid naked before her: all she'd ever known and cherished would soon crumble to ruin.

Panting, she arrived at the stoa of the Athenians. At the end of the long hall of fluted marble columns, near the platform displaying the prows and cables taken from the defeated Persian armada during the Battle of Marathon, Cleon and two *hosioi*, Nikias and Iason, were engaged in conversation.

As she ran toward them, her bare feet slapped against the marble floor. One by one, they stood. Cleon went to her, catching her as she collapsed to her knees.

"My lady, what draws the blood from your face and steals the breath from your lips?"

"I came across the emperor's men. They spoke of destruction and plundering." She grasped Cleon's arms with raptor-like grip. "They will be upon us at any moment. We must prepare."

He helped her to her feet and gestured to Nikias and Iason to approach. Cleon addressed the group. "The moment we have feared has come. Our enemies mean to extinguish the flame of Apollo. We must act quickly." He turned to Nikias and Iason. "Order the acolytes to remove from the sanctuary as many sacred objects as they can carry and start on the forest road to Thebes. No one knows that path; they will be safe there."

A grave look crossed Iason's youthful face. "What will become of us?"

Cleon placed a hand on his shoulder. "Hatred is a powerful thing, my young brother. It can wipe away the most fortified cities and crush entire generations. All we can do is hold true to our faith and hope it will lift us, like a wave lifts a ship."

"We will stay here and fight," Nikias said.

Iason waved a fist. "Fight to the end."

Aristea extended a hand into the middle of the circle. "Let us make a pact. Should we escape with our lives, we shall meet in the cave of Trophonius, on the other side of Mount Parnassus. When the imperial beasts have tasted enough blood and begin to retreat, we can again honor our rituals, even if in secret."

Each of the men placed a hand on hers. "To the cave of Trophonius," they said in unison and scattered to their tasks.

Cleon glanced at Aristea. She turned so he would not see her eyes had misted.

"Be brave, my lady. Whatever happens, know in your heart you have lived a pure life and have not strayed from your path. That is your freedom, and they cannot strip it from you."

"I do not fear for my life, Cleon. It is the injustice of one man imposing his will upon another that angers me. What god condones the use of such brutal force to gain disciples?"

"No god demands this. It is solely man's doing. They merely hide behind a holy name to glorify their greed and their ambition." He took her hands and held them gently.

"I have lived much longer than you, Aristea. I have seen anger and hatred corrupt men's souls. We must rise above it, for if we don't—"

"We risk the demise of peace." She squeezed his hands. "There cannot be peace on Earth if no peace exists in our own hearts."

"You have been blessed with the gift of wisdom. Your mother would be pleased at the woman you have become." The lines around Cleon's eyes deepened as he attempted a smile. "Now let us make haste. There is much to do."

Aristea stood at the entrance of the temple and watched the full moon rise above the peaks of Parnassus and cast its silver rays onto the Gulf of Corinth, far below Delphi.

The moon's face was larger than she'd ever seen it. She took it as a sign: the gods illuminated the path of the Delphians who had fled the city with the treasures of Apollo.

In her peripheral vision, she saw a cluster of lights and turned her gaze toward the Sacred Way. The lights traveled up the Way toward the temple, as if it were a procession of faithful marching toward the oracle and the promise of knowledge.

But this was no prelude to ceremony. She regarded the lights without emotion, for she knew they would come. She counted torches: two-score, maybe more; she could not be sure. She knew only that they were outnumbered.

Aristea went inside the temple, where Cleon, Nikias, and Iason tended to the sacred relics. They all turned to face her. No words were necessary.

She met them at the altar, and they all joined arms and bent their heads. Cleon led them in a soft hymn in tribute to the god of light, truth, order, and healing. They sang of Phoebus—the bright—Apollo being delivered to Mount Parnassus on the back of a winged horse to fight the serpent Python, in whose throat dwelled all the world's ills.

> With every fiery breath, the monster dimmed the sun,
> And men went entranced into the dark oblivion of evil.
> Then came Phoebus with his golden arrow
> And pierced the heart of darkness,
> And evil plunged into the bowels of the Earth.
> O men of honor, do not forget the gift you have been given
> By the one who shoots sunbeams from his fingertips
> And grants song to the birds and fragrance to the
>   wildflowers,
> Lest evil return from the arid depths—

A loud crack brought the hymn to an abrupt end. Aristea looked up and saw the temple door come crashing down. With the entrance breached, a hailstorm of stones the size of men's heads flew into the holy shrine. One hit a statue of Apollo and broke the torso in two. The alabaster fell to the ground and smashed to pieces.

Aristea and the men dropped to a prostrate position

and waited, huddled, for the barrage to stop. With every thud she shuddered, imagining the damage.

She could no longer stand it. She broke free of the group and crawled toward the entrance. She crouched by the broken doorway and waved a white veil.

A male voice shouted. The onslaught slowed, then halted.

Aristea stood on shaky legs and gazed into the court-yard. A wheeled cart with a ballista attached was pointed toward the temple. Behind the contraption was a gathering of men. In the torchlight, their faces were like brazen statues—hard, vacant, incapable of feeling.

Her lip trembled as she spoke. "We are people of peace. We are not breaking any laws of the empire." She swallowed hard. "Our treasuries have gold. Take all you want. Just leave our sanctuary standing."

One man stepped out in front. He wore chain mail across his chest and a bronze helmet, as if Apollo's priests were going to engage him in battle. "We need no permission to take your gold. That is the currency of the devil, and we have every intention of confiscating it for the work of God." He pointed toward the temple. "The fire of hell burns within that house. Under order of Theodosius the Great, rituals of the profane shall not be tolerated."

"But no one comes here anymore." Despite attempts to keep emotion at bay, Aristea's voice was shaky. "In accordance with the emperor's decrees, there are no rituals."

"And what are you doing here, then?"

"This is my home. I mean to protect it."

The soldier pointed to her. "If this is your home, then you answer to the devil." He glanced over his shoulder and barked a command to his men. He raised a gladius and released a cry.

"Please," Aristea pleaded. "We mean no harm—"

The man grabbed her by the elbow and dragged her inside. She glanced back and saw a legion of men enter the temple after their leader. It was an all-out siege.

He pushed Aristea to her knees in front of the tripod in which the eternal flame burned. Cleon and the others were seized by the other men and brought to kneel beside her. She glanced at Cleon. The serenity on his face gave her courage.

The soldier pointed to the flame and turned to Aristea. "Do you deny that this is the fire of hell?"

"I do not know what the fire of hell looks like," she said calmly. "I know only light."

He signaled to his men. With a war cry that echoed off the marble, they toppled the tripod and beat the flames with their capes until all that remained of the light of Apollo was the faint scent of burnt oil.

Leaving the prisoners unattended, they ran like rabid animals to the altar and down to the *adyton*. They would leave nothing standing.

Aristea turned to her brothers. "Remember our promise. We shall meet again. Now leave this place."

Ignoring Cleon's pleas, the priestess picked up the tripod and swung it with all her strength at one of the men. He fell unconscious. She did the same to another, and another, until the leader noticed and lunged at her.

She fought him with the tripod, but he quickly overpowered her and sent the brass vessel clattering across the hall.

He grabbed her by the hair. "You think you are a match for me, witch?" He pulled her head back. "Answer me!"

"What one man has built, another has no right to destroy." She spat on the floor. "You disgust me."

He struck her across the face with the back of his hand. The force made her fall to her side. As she raised her head, blood dripped onto the marble. Through blurred vision, she watched the emperor's men swing heavy iron axes at the columns, cracking them. Her face hot with anger, she swung a fist at her captor's groin and watched him dive, howling, to his knees.

She felt arms hoist her upright. She turned to face Cleon.

"Don't be a martyr," he said. "Save yourself."

She shook her head. "I will sooner go down in flames than abandon Apollo." Python-like arms gripped her from behind and squeezed the breath out of her lungs. "Run," she mouthed.

A cloud of white linen trailed Cleon as he ran toward the doorway. It was the last image she registered before she succumbed to darkness.

Seventeen

By the time Sarah returned to camp, the midday sun had burned off what little snow had fallen twenty-four hours prior. It was a windy but clear day, yet there was nothing sunny about her mood.

She drove up to the car park, noting the absence of the second vehicle. Perhaps it was better that Daniel wasn't there. If she saw him at that moment, she almost certainly would say something she would regret. On the other hand, she worried about him. That push and pull of emotions created a dissonance within her so maddening she knew it would not end well.

Limping, she walked to her cabin to change clothes. She winced as she peeled off her climbing trousers and had a first look at the wound on her leg. Beneath a bloody crust covering the length of her calf was a cut about four inches long. The skin had split open, revealing severed tissue. It needed stitches, but she had no time for that. She dug around her bag for the antiseptic and rope dressing she'd picked up at the chemist in Thebes on her way back to camp. It wasn't the best treatment for the situation at hand, but it would have to do.

After dressing the wound, she quickly put on a long-sleeved Capilene top and her black expedition trousers. She tucked the amulet fragment in the inside pocket. Though she didn't know what, or whose, the object was, she wanted to keep it close. She had a feeling its purpose would be revealed in due time.

She closed the blinds and reached into the bottom of her backpack to remove the find. She unfolded the bandana and, with fresh eyes, looked at the potsherd. With a finger she traced the curves of the mysterious object carved into one side.

If there was truth to the monk's words, those who sought the buried object were somehow associated with Delphi. Reconciling that clue and the beehive-like shape carved onto the shard, Sarah suspected the object was the long-lost original navel stone used by the Delphians in oracular ceremonies. The "instrument of the pagans": it made sense.

She turned the shard over and reread the four-letter word. She wondered if the object was hidden somewhere in or near Sumela, the old Orthodox monastery in Turkey's Trabzon region.

Perhaps a visit there would shed some light. But given the events of the past days, going to Sumela alone was like stepping into the lion's den. Logic told her she shouldn't even be considering such a move.

Sarah placed the object back in the bag and stepped

outside to gather her thoughts. She cupped her hand against the wind and lit a cigarette. The sun's saffron rays reached between the silver-green olive leaves, casting trembling shadows onto the yellow grasses. In the distance, the citadel of Kadmeia faded into the sky like an angel ascending.

She blew out a stream of menthol smoke. A blast of cold wind hissed across the hilltop, tousling her loose curls. She wrapped her arms around her chest to contain a shiver.

"Sarah."

Daniel's voice startled her. She turned to face him. Her chest tightened for a moment. She exhaled a trembling breath. She could not find the voice to greet him.

He took two steps toward her. Though she could not see his eyes behind dark aviators, she could tell by the lines in his forehead and the sallow tone of his skin he was in some kind of distress. He pointed to the cigarette in her hand. "I thought you'd quit."

"Where have you been, Danny?"

"It's a long story. I'm not sure you want to hear it."

Her gaze traveled down his body, confirming her suspicions about what had happened. His knuckles were bloody, and there was a slight tremble in his hands. His jeans were streaked with mud. But the most telling sign was the black jumper he had on: the knit was identical to the skullcap worn by the keeper of the monastery rising above the Herkyna River.

"Let me have a go." Her tone was calm and measured, if a touch frigid. "You've had a bit of a night prowl in the area around Livadeia. Perhaps even found the entrance to the forbidden cave. And somewhere along the way, you befriended a monk who dwells on a cliff high above the river." She took a long drag and inhaled the smoke. "Is that about it?"

"You followed me." He reached beneath his aviators and rubbed his eyes. "I suppose I haven't been completely honest, so I deserve that."

She read a change in his attitude. For the first time since they'd come to Thebes, he seemed willing to share the truth. "I think you ought to tell me what's going on."

He nodded. "I was asked to go on a recon to test the obelisk, see if it worked as a key."

"Asked by whom?"

"The chairman of the foundation. I cannot reveal his identity. I can only tell you he's a high-ranking official of the British government. And he has an agenda."

"What sort of agenda?"

"He believes the guy behind all these shenanigans heads up a major underground antiquities ring that has amassed significant relics, including something of grave interest to the crown. He's asked me to gather data that might lead to his capture."

"So you're acting as an informant."

"In a way, yes."

Her face tightened. She found it hard to believe a British official would trust a civilian with classified business. Something else was going on, and Daniel was either tight-lipped or unaware.

He grasped her arms and leaned in. "Listen, Sarah. I should not be telling you any of this. I'm risking—" He did not complete his thought. "I can see the distance between us, and I don't want it to grow any wider."

She pushed him away. "Too right there's distance. You've agreed to some sort of deal I knew nothing about, and you've been lying about it for months." She raised her voice. "This isn't what I signed up for."

"I'm sorry. I was only trying to protect you."

"If you truly saw me as an equal, you'd know there is no need to protect me."

"That's not fair, Sarah. I've always looked out—"

She put up a hand. "Stop doing me favors. I can fend for myself."

He pushed his hair back with both hands, revealing silver strands at the roots. With a sharp exhale, he let his hands drop. "What can I do to make this up to you?"

She gestured toward the lab. "For starters, you can return the obelisk to its rightful place."

"I can't. I don't have it."

"What?"

"The monks pulled me out of the cave. I was . . ." A

pained look crossed his face. "Never mind. The obelisk is in their possession now."

"You let them have it, just like that?"

"Jesus, Sarah. You think I'd just hand it to them? Father Athanasius, the abbot, confiscated it. He intends to seal the cave and destroy the key. There's something down there he's determined to keep hidden."

She decided to keep her own intel close to the vest. "Did he say what?"

"Something about a pagan object that'd been held by the church since the fourth century but has since vanished. He led me to believe there's a clue of some kind in Trophonius' cave." He paused, as if trying to recall something. "Athanasius mentioned a cult resurrecting ancient rituals. Apparently, the head of the cult wants that object in the worst way. I'm guessing he is the same guy who's been causing us grief."

She narrowed her eyes. "A cult. Neopagans?"

"That's what I'm thinking."

She looked toward Delphi, the center of the ancient world and site of the oracle of Apollo. It was all coming together.

"Sarah?"

She turned back to Daniel.

"Did you find the cave?"

She could not lie to him. "I did."

"Was anything down there?"

"The remains of a female. And some sort of map scrawled on a potsherd." She paused, wondering if she could trust him. In a way, showing him would be the ultimate test. "Wait here."

Sarah went into her cabin and removed the wrapped potsherd from her pack. She stepped back outside and unwrapped it in front of Daniel.

"Wow." He exhaled a long breath. "Who else knows?"

"Some men confronted me in the grove just outside the cave. I was able to lose them, but they'll be back. I think it's time to get out of here, maybe find a way to that object before they do."

He shook his head. "Bad idea. Too risky."

"That's never stopped us from doing what's right."

"Trust me about this, Sarah. We don't want to go up against these guys. I have it on good authority we'd pretty much be walking into a suicide mission."

"I suspect the object is buried at or near a monastery in Turkey. Maybe Father Athanasius and his monks will help us gain access."

"Are you serious? The monks have an innate distrust of scientists. And they are part of a powerful institution that's notoriously secretive. You're barking up the wrong tree. Besides, they've been trying to hide this relic for sixteen hundred years. What makes you think they have any interest in sharing it with the world now?"

"If this is what I think it is, it doesn't belong with the

church. It's a piece of human history that everyone has a right to. It should be turned over to the state."

"Stop being so idealistic. You and I both know the Greek church controls a load of relics. Always has. And that's the way the holy men like it. They're not going to cooperate with any archaeologist. They see us as the enemy. You want to go up against that, go right ahead. But I'd advise you to forget it, move on."

His reaction chilled her. How could he, of all the people, call her idealistic? How could he dismiss the moral responsibility they once shared? "So where does that leave us?"

"There's nothing more we can do. We should get out of here as soon as possible." He looked away and rubbed the thick dark stubble covering his jaw, talking less to her than to himself. "I want to be rid of this nightmare."

"Should have thought of that before you made a deal with the devil," she blurted out and felt more satisfaction than regret.

"Just so you know, I did it for you."

"This is absolute bollocks. I cannot hear it." She started toward her cabin.

He grabbed her elbow. "Don't walk away. Not now."

She sensed the desperation in his voice, but pride muscled its way into her consciousness and didn't allow her to take stock. "I have some thinking to do." She pulled free of his grip and walked on.

He called behind her. "Come back here, Sarah. We're not finished."

Sarah didn't answer or turn to face him. She hurried into her cabin and locked the door, ignoring the bangs on the other side. She crumpled onto the bed. The freight train of emotion that had been gathering steam for months crashed through the gate of her defenses. She could no longer stop it.

Eighteen

Daniel went into his own cabin and turned the dead bolt. He stood with his back to the door and exhaled. Things had gotten out of control—and it was all his fault.

He sat down at a table in the far corner of the room. He eyed the bottle of whiskey that had been his steady companion of late. He poured a finger into a shot glass and checked the clock on his phone. Four in the afternoon, UK time. He dialed the number.

Langham picked up on the first ring. "Madigan. It's about damned time."

The last thing he needed was this guy's attitude. "Lay off, James. Things have been pretty intense here."

"I don't give a toss. I will not be made to wait." He cleared his throat. "Now then. What have you found out?"

"The cave of Trophonius is real."

"Brilliant. What was inside?"

"Some sort of road map leading to the ancient object your collector friend is after." Daniel downed the shot of whiskey. "So I hear."

"What do you mean? Did you not see it?"

"No. It's hearsay. Do with that what you want."

A momentary silence. It was clear Langham was annoyed. "I see. And who exactly is giving you this information?"

Regardless of what had transpired, he would not betray Sarah. He skirted around the issue. "The abbot of a monastery near the cave knows the history. I had a chance encounter with him that did not end well. He confiscated the obelisk. I have no idea where it is."

"You're joking."

"Wish I was. At least I got some intel in exchange. The abbot knows who's after the relic: an American guy, former military. Apparently he's seeking this object for some ancient rituals he's reenacting."

"An American soldier. That is very interesting indeed. I will run this information over the network and see if we can connect it to any known collector's profile. In the meantime, there's something I must ask you to do."

"Is that so?" Daniel poured himself another shot.

"I want you to go to Cairo to meet with Ishaq Shammas—the London gallerist who was arrested three years ago for trafficking in stolen antiquities. We suspect he was the primary supplier for the buyer we're seeking but could never get him to talk before he was extradited to Egypt. He's fiercely loyal to his clients."

Daniel kept quiet, let Langham talk.

"You will introduce yourself as an independent anthropologist working on the Thebes project. You will not mention—or, if questioned, will deny—any connection to us. You will bring detailed photographs of the brass obelisk and tell him it grants entry to a long forgotten cave, inside which is an item of interest. When he is intrigued, and he will be, you will ask him to connect you with a broker who can appraise it. He will know what that means."

Daniel upended the glass. "You're crazy. He'll never talk to a complete stranger."

"Nonsense; you're the perfect envoy. You've worked in Egypt and you are fluent in Arabic. And you're a bit rough around the edges. No offense meant."

"None taken."

"Good." The sound of papers being shuffled came from the other end of the line. "I've taken the liberty of having a ticket booked for you. Flight 107 to Cairo leaves Athens late tonight."

Daniel's pulse pounded in his temples. "That was very thoughtful of you, James. Only I'm not going. My work for you is done."

"Need I remind you," Langham hissed, "how much you owe the crown?"

"No need. I've paid an inordinate price to square my debt to the crown. The way I see it, I owe you nothing."

"Do you really, Dr. Madigan? Perhaps you should think about this: Interpol can very easily find out you stole the obelisk from the ephorate archives and delivered it to an interested party. A national treasure, lost forever." He paused to let the message sink in. "The head of the foundation will be only too glad to testify against you—and your accomplice."

He could envision Langham's triumphant smirk. "You bastard."

"Have a safe flight." Langham clicked the phone off.

Daniel let the phone drop from his hand and pounded a fist on the table. A single promise made at a moment of desperation: that was all it had taken to be sucked into their game. Sarah was right: he had made a pact with the devil.

Images came and went from his mind like ghosts from another life. He envisioned himself on the chaotic streets of Cairo, the horns of choked traffic blaring all around him, faces glaring at him in distrust, small-time peddlers accosting him every two steps to sell him perfume or felucca rides in the Nile. He imagined the Egyptian prison, the filth and stench of it, the hard stares of convicts, the improbability of reasoning with a hyper-connected criminal who was probably still doing business from behind bars.

His thoughts turned to Sarah. Their partnership hung in the balance. If he went to Egypt now, there would be no return to her. The thought of losing her triggered an ache deep in his core.

He walked to the bathroom and looked in the mirror. The fluorescent lights were unkind. His skin was dry and devoid of color, his eyes dull and distant behind red eyelids. He was startled by how much he looked like his father, whom he hadn't seen since the old man had walked out on the family thirty years prior. It was the first time Daniel had noticed the resemblance, and it repulsed him.

He opened the medicine cabinet door and picked up one of two packets of Valium. He emptied the last two blue pills into his hand and tossed the box and blister pack into the trash bin. He walked to the table, popped the pills into his mouth, and chased them with a long swig of whiskey. He grimaced as his throat burned.

Without bothering to undress, he lay down on the bed and closed his eyes.

Every seat on the coach cabin of the EgyptAir 777 was taken. By Daniel's estimation, there were some four hundred people on board, all engaged in capsule versions of their lives within the seventeen inches allotted to them.

All but him.

He looked out the window at the black underbelly of the gathering clouds. A silver thread of lightning illuminated the distant horizon. He didn't realize how hard he was gripping the armrest until a gentle hand landed on his forearm.

"Danny, are you all right?"

He relaxed his grip and turned his gaze to the seat next to his. With her serene countenance and flaxen curls spilling over her shoulder, Sarah looked like an angel. He nodded. "Fine."

"It's just a storm, you know." She smiled. "We've been through worse."

The plane jolted. A woman in the back screamed. The seat belt light came on, followed by an announcement from the cockpit.

"Ladies and gentlemen," said the male voice with the thick Arabic accent. "We are experiencing turbulence due to some inclement weather. Remain in your seats with your seat belts fastened."

Sarah squeezed Daniel's hand and held it. Though the space between them was silent, he felt her strength and her loyalty. He wanted so badly to embrace her, to be healed by her.

He closed his eyes. *If she ever found out . . .*

A second, more violent jolt came. The lights in the cabin went out and the oxygen masks dropped, prompting a chorus of panicked screams that, within a moment no longer than a heartbeat, were drowned out by a deafening *cr-r-r-ack*.

The plane shook like it would break apart. Daniel looked across the cabin and out the windows on the opposite side of the aircraft. He tensed.

A single flame had broken through a seam on the wing. It quivered in the open air until it was extinguished and replaced by a stream of black smoke.

"We've been hit by lightning." Sarah's voice was calm. "He's going to have to land."

Daniel felt the invisible vise around his chest squeeze so hard he could not breathe. He clawed at his arms, his chest, his neck in an attempt to shake the sensation. Sarah was talking to him, but he could not hear her over his own panicked breath.

The sound of an explosion filled the cabin. Overhead bins opened and suitcases were sucked out by pressure from a breach in the aircraft. Four hundred people wailed in unison, their voices howled down in the wind tunnel that had overtaken the cabin.

Overhead, the craft cracked open. Seats with people still on them were ripped from the floor and tossed every which way. Sarah looked at Daniel, her blue eyes misty. "Nothing is forever."

Her seat came off its hinges and was swept into the void as he fell in the opposite direction. He closed his eyes and yelled her name, but his voice was claimed by the wind.

Gasping for breath, Daniel bolted upright. He felt around him in the dark and clutched the bedsheets. They were damp, just as they had been every other time that had happened. He rubbed his eyes and tried to reassure himself: *it was only a dream.*

He groped for his phone on the nightstand and

turned it on. The green digital characters announced nine at night. Below that were two texts: one, the ticket confirmation from the travel agent; the other, an address in Cairo from Langham's secretary.

Now wide awake, he lay back on the pillow and caught his breath. The images from his dream drifted into his mind, mere shadows of the violent visions that had haunted him in sleep. All that remained was the feeling of desperation, like the bitter taste after swallowing poison.

There was no doubt about it: he was damaged. He could not hold back the memories that came rushing toward him like a tsunami, drawing him into an abyss of darkness and torment. He needed Valium to stop the shakiness deep inside him—that and booze to make him sleep. In a profession that was rife with dangers, he couldn't avoid heights, high speed, or sudden threats— the triggers that thrust him into a steel capsule thirty thousand feet in the sky, nose-diving into the Atlantic, unable to run to safety.

He was no good to the project, no good to himself. He certainly was no good to Sarah. Though unspoken, his weakness stood between them like smoldering wreckage. If he hadn't already lost her, it was a matter of time before she would lose respect for him—or worse, pity him.

No way in hell he was going to let that happen.

He got out of bed and turned on the light. He was stunned to see long, bloody grooves cut into his skin, as if he'd been clawed by a rabid animal. The trace of dark brown residue under his fingernails was the final affirmation of what he had to do.

Daniel dragged a duffle bag out of the closet and stuffed his few clothes and possessions into it. He took the full box of Valium out of the medicine cabinet and threw it into his backpack, an unusual companion to his other essentials: camera, eleven-inch laptop, climbing rope and carabiners, lock-picking tools, a bulked-up Swiss Army knife.

He was good to go. He glanced at the pad of paper on the nightstand and considered leaving Sarah a note. Though she deserved something—an explanation, a declaration, an apology—no words would justify his abrupt departure. She would not understand and likely not forgive.

Perhaps it was better to say nothing.

He zipped up the duffle, slipped his phone and keys into his pocket, and left for Athens.

Nineteen

The rains of winter had not relented that evening. The rapid fire of drops hitting the metal roof of the lab were a meditation of sorts, softening the edges of Sarah's misery.

Unable to find peace after the confrontation with Daniel, she'd decided to distract herself with work. She'd gone to the lab with the intent of digging further into Trabzon and Sumela, but the turmoil within had not allowed her to concentrate. Like the aftermath of an earthquake, the altercation had left her shaken deep inside, where the light of temporal pleasures did not reach.

Shaken and confused. Had she been unfair to him? Had her own ego prevented her from looking at his side of things and caused her to condemn him too soon? Should she forgive him—yet again—and carry on as before? Surely, after all they'd been through, another chance was warranted.

No. He'd lied. Whatever his reasons for doing so, dishonesty was inexcusable. Their relationship had worked because of the unspoken trust between them. Besides, something about him was different. A sudden lack of confidence, perhaps; an inexplicable weakness.

Yes, it had to be finished. She would move forward alone. And yet, without him even the noblest of goals seemed hollow.

It was nearing eleven when the barrage slowed to a trickle, then stopped altogether. Sarah stepped outside. She closed her eyes and inhaled deeply, breathing in the petrichor—the scent of rain awakening dry earth and turning dust into soil. That fleeting moment was balm for the anxiety that had been building inside her since she'd last spoken to Daniel.

The sound of footsteps sucking at the mud jolted her out of her thoughts. Eyes wide, she stood rock still. "Danny, is that you?"

Evan stepped into the sliver of light coming from the half-open door. "What are you doing here so late?" His tone was barbed.

"I might ask you the same." Her gaze traveled to his hand. He was holding something wrapped in black fabric.

"I think it's best that you ask no questions right now." He walked inside the lab.

Sarah followed him. "What are you talking about?"

He held up the wrapped item. "This."

"Stop playing games, Evan. Tell me what *this* is."

He placed the item on the table and unwrapped it. It was the brass obelisk, the key to Trophonius' cave. His jaw was tight, his gaze harsh. "You and Daniel Madigan have some explaining to do."

A deep chill made her skin tingle. Had Daniel lied about the monk confiscating the object? Would he really go that far? The words came out strangled: "Where did you get that?"

"The trunk of the Land Rover." He took two steps toward her. "Perhaps you can tell me if there's a logical explanation."

She felt paralyzed. Telling the truth would mean the end of Daniel's career, perhaps worse. Leaving it out would be a lie by omission. She was caught between Scylla and Charybdis. "I can't say."

"Can't . . . or won't?" He repeated her own words.

Her thoughts began to settle, and she looked at the matter more clearly. Even if he were sneaking about, Daniel would never leave something like that in the boot of a car. Something was definitely off. She elected to keep silent.

"Have it your way." He turned back to the obelisk and rewrapped it. "I have reported this incident to the foundation and to the ministry of antiquities. They will decide whether or not to press charges." He glared at her through those thick black glasses. "In the meantime, you're fired. I want you out of here in an hour."

There was nothing she could say in her defense. She walked out into the cold, damp night. Her face tightened as she questioned what could possibly have happened.

She launched into a fast walk, but mounting adrenaline compelled her to run. Unable to see in the dark, she tripped on a root and fell to her side, her face landing in the mud. Sitting up, she noticed something peculiar: the same herringbone footprint she had seen at the museum on the night of the heist.

It was a fresh print. She fumbled in her pocket for a penlight and shone it on the ground, following the trail of prints to the lab. She pressed her hand to her mouth.

She turned off the light and sprang to her feet. She ran through the woods to Daniel's cabin.

By the time Sarah reached the clearing in the orchard, she was out of breath. One last push: she sprinted to the cabin and banged on the door with an open palm. A blast of cold wind whistled across the clearing, making her shiver.

"Danny, open up." She heard the desperation in her own voice.

There was no answer. She knocked again, harder this time. When he didn't come to the door, she turned the knob and was surprised it was unlocked. She called his name again. Nothing. She cracked the door open, looked over both shoulders, and went into the dark room.

"Danny, it's me."

She turned on the light. An open bottle of whiskey and a shot glass were the only items on the table near the door, where his computer normally sat. She recoiled at the pungent odor.

As she walked toward the bed, she noticed the empty

closet behind open doors. Her brow wrinkled as she looked more closely. His duffle bag and all his clothes were missing. Her gaze darted across the room, scanning for any trace of him. Other than the whiskey, there was nothing. He had gone—and wasn't coming back.

She sat on the edge of the bed, unsure what to make of the situation. She wanted to believe that there was some explanation, that he would be back at any moment, that he had not forsaken her. But the burning sensation in her abdomen warned her otherwise.

She put her hand on the bed to steady herself and noticed the sheets were damp. She looked down, and seeing faint streaks of blood on the crumpled bed linens, she gasped.

Sarah turned over every pillow and looked behind every piece of furniture for a note. Even if he had run off, she wanted reassurance he was all right. Considering their history, how could he not leave her with at least that?

She continued her search in the bathroom. There was nothing on the counter, nothing in the bathtub. Even the medicine cabinet was empty. She noticed something in her peripheral vision and did a double take.

In the trash bin was something all too familiar to her: a box of ten-milligram Valium—the strongest available—and a spent blister pack of pills.

"My God." Her eyes welled up.

Memories came rushing back: her mother dead in a bathtub, a similar box of pills sitting on the bathroom counter. It had been twenty-one years, but it was only recently that she'd come to terms with the loss that had made her feel so alone and abandoned.

Ironically, it was Daniel who'd helped her heal. Over the three years they'd known each other, he pushed her beyond what she perceived were her limits. But more than that, he'd never once let her down, calming her deepest fear: that everyone she loved would leave her.

She blinked, and tears rained down. How could he disappear in so cruel a manner? How could she have been so wrong about him? She took a deep breath and dismissed the self-pity. What did she not know?

The phone vibrating in her pocket startled her. She wiped her cheeks with her palm and reached for it. It was a blocked number. She picked up but didn't speak.

"Sarah Weston?"

She stayed silent.

"Heinrich Gerst here." He spoke with a heavy German accent. "I am with Interpol. I wish to speak to you about a Daniel Madigan."

She clicked the phone off. Though she normally made it a habit to cooperate with authorities, she knew her involvement in an investigation would incriminate Daniel. Whatever the reasons for his disappearance, she could not do that to him.

She had to get out of there. She skulked through the woods to the other side of the clearing and her cabin. She packed a few essentials, including her passport, into her backpack and left the bulk of her belongings in the cabin. Knowing they would use it to track her, she tossed her phone onto the bed.

She slipped on her threadbare oilskin coat and strapped on her pack, ready to descend to Thebes on foot. By the time anyone realized she'd left the camp, she would be long gone to Trabzon.

Twenty

Sumela Monastery, Anatolia,
393 CE

A rooster crowed, announcing morning. Aristea rose from the stone bunk and took two steps to a window that was no wider than the span of her shoulders. She wrapped her hands around the iron bars and regarded the dawn.

Clouds thick as cotton wool hung over the ravine, obscuring all but the spindly crowns of the evergreens. In the dead stillness of early morning, the trickle of water persisted: somewhere, a river flowed.

It was the seventh morning she'd woken to that view. She'd watched the square patch of Earth change as the hours passed: the clouds lifting to reveal rows of pines crowded together like Homeric armies, the misty peaks in the distance, the sky painted with strokes of ochre and vermillion as day turned to night.

Aristea had tried to meditate on the beauty beyond the bars that confined her, but her efforts were futile. The reality of her stone prison would not let her find peace.

A heavy knock made her jump. She pulled the woolen blanket from the bed and wrapped it around her. "Who's there?"

The wooden door opened with a lingering creak, and a man dressed in a gray woolen sheath entered. He wasn't the same mute fellow who had been bringing her food for seven days.

He placed a bowl with steaming contents on the edge of the bed. "In case you are hungry."

She was surprised to hear her own language. "You speak Greek."

"Yes. I am Athenian. My uncle and I have journeyed a long way to build this place."

She regarded him from head to foot. "Judging by your dress, you are not a traditional Athenian."

"If by traditional you mean pagan, you are correct. I am a Nicene Christian. A Christian monk." He placed a hand on his chest. "My name is Sophronios."

She wrapped the blanket more tightly about her. "What do you want of me? Why have I been brought here?"

Sophronios stepped into the pale light coming in from the window. He was a man her own age, with taut honey-toned skin and a short black beard growing beneath high cheekbones. Beneath a fitted hood that covered his hair were eyes that looked like autumn chestnuts in the morning light. "There will be an answer to your question in due time. But first, you should understand where you are, for it is quite a special place." He pointed out the window. "This is Melá Mountain. It is near the Black Sea in Anatolia. My uncle Barnabas and I were sent here by the virgin mother to build this holy house in her name."

"Who is this mother?" Aristea said. "Is she Greek?"

Sophronios shook his head. "You have much to learn. I speak of the holy mother of Christ. She died many years ago, but her divine presence still guides us. She appeared to my uncle and me in a vision." He looked up. A look of rapture brightened his face. "It was beautiful. She was bathed in light."

Aristea understood the concept of visions. Regardless of what, or whom, one believed in, guidance was received in the same way. "But why here? On this remote crag?"

"We were called upon to find an icon of the virgin, painted by one of the Christ's disciples, Saint Luke." He pointed to a barren ledge in the distance. "It appeared to us on that spot, and we knew this was the place. It was the impossible feat to bring up the stones and build on this steep cliffside. But with our lady's help, a miracle happened. Our monks moved in seven years ago"—he crossed himself—"God be praised."

Intuition told Aristea Sophronios was a gentle, if misguided, soul whom she needed not fear. But she could not reconcile this man's piety with the barbaric incident at the sanctuary of Apollo. Memory persisted, flooding her mind with images of fire and destruction by men who were all but holy. She decided no one—not even the kindly monk before her—could be trusted. "Again I ask you: why have I been brought here?"

Sophronios tapped his fingertips together. "The monastery is also a center of education. People come from all parts of the empire to learn about our religion. Some become monks and stay here to the end of their lives." He gave her a lingering glance. "It is very important to learn about Christianity . . . to embrace it."

So that was what this was about. "You want me to accept your ways."

He put up a hand. "Let us take it one step at a time."

"Don't waste your time, Sophronios. There is nothing about your religion that interests me. Just as you have given your life to your god, I have sworn allegiance to mine. I promise you that will not change."

"You cannot stay wicked forever—"

"Wicked?" Her eyes burned with indignity. "How can you condemn me when you know nothing about my soul?"

"I know this: women should not talk to men in that way."

"I am a priestess. I do not have to bow my head to you."

"Those are the ways of the past. Greece is now part of the Byzantine Empire. Polytheism is strictly forbidden. It is imperative to know the laws of God." Sophronios reached inside the folds of his heavy gray robes and pulled out a small codex bound with jute. He placed it on the bed next to the bowl. "When all is illuminated, you surely will repent and accept the new faith—for if you don't, the consequences could be dire."

Aristea recalled hearing the stories of non-repenters

being burned alive or publically stoned. "I will not convert to your faith. If that is your aim, then give me your consequences now." She took his hands and wrapped them around her throat. They were warm and soft, as if he hadn't done a day's work in his life. She looked dead into his bewildered eyes. "Do it."

His face flushed. He jerked his hands away and hastened to the door. He glanced back at her but quickly diverted his gaze. The iron ring handle rattled as he shut the door behind him.

Aristea sat at the edge of the bed. She knew the display was overly theatrical. She wanted to call Sophronios' bluff, to see what he was made of.

His heart was not like the others'. Not only could he not hurt her, but he might one day be her ally.

Twenty-one

The pine needles quivered as winter's frosty breath blasted across the hills of New York's North Country. The sun was high, a brilliant ball of white fire obscured behind a dense haze that had not lifted in days.

Stephen Bellamy walked along a trail through an alley of white pines, his Doberman by his side. It was a meditation of sorts. Every day he walked for two hours, getting to know every blemish on the old-growth trees on the hundred and twenty acres of his property. It was a mantra left over from his military days: always know your surroundings, because your enemy does.

A machine rumbled in the distance, profaning the stillness of midday. Singha stood dead still, her ears perked, and barked a warning.

"Settle down, girl." Bellamy stroked her nape.

The rumble turned into a growl as the ATV came into view. Bellamy recognized the rider: Tom Sorenson, his aide. He could tell from Sorenson's relaxed shoulders it was good news.

Sorenson parked the ATV in a clearing beyond the trail and let the engine idle. "You really ought to carry a phone, Colonel," he shouted.

"Nonsense, boy. I don't care to be found." He smirked. "You got some news for me?"

Sorenson turned off the engine and walked to his boss. "We have the key to Trophonius' cave. It took some coercing. The monks were determined to keep it to themselves."

"How many casualties?"

"Four, maybe five." He made a downward motion with his hand. "Dove off the cliff. You know, ritual suicide."

"Happens." He adjusted his black wraparound sunglasses. "Tell me, what did our boys find in the cave?"

"That's the problem. They found nothing. Only some skeletal remains."

"Impossible," he barked. "Have them scour every inch."

"Already have, sir. The map was not there. What we do know is that Sarah Weston and Daniel Madigan—separately, not together—have been in the cave before us. We suspect one of them has it."

Bellamy scratched the back of his head. It was a complication he had not counted on. Those two-bit archaeologists were becoming real thorns in his side. But after all that life had thrown at him, this was nothing he couldn't handle. "Getting to them might be tricky. Do we know who's backing them?"

"She's a free agent; he's a Rutgers field scientist. But this is not a university assignment. As far as I can tell, they're working independently. Their only support is each other.

But we're working on that." Sorenson winked. "We've framed Madigan with some incriminating evidence that will land him squarely in the hands of the authorities."

Bellamy grinned. The authorities, including Evan Rigas, were on his payroll, which meant Madigan was as good as captured. But that gave Bellamy only a 50 percent chance of recovering the map. "And Weston?"

"Poor principled Sarah Weston. How shocking that her partner is embroiled in something so scandalous." Sorenson shook his head. "He isn't the man she thought he was. She will want nothing more to do with him, so she will go it alone. Alone and vulnerable—just as we like."

"Good thinking, boy. That's why I pay you: to find solutions."

Sorenson looked at his watch. "I'll be speaking to our man in Thebes in a few minutes to get an update. I expect everything to go smoothly from here on out."

Bellamy patted him on the back. "Well, it's about time. Now leave us be. Singha is anxious to finish her walk."

"Yes, sir, Colonel." Sorenson got back on the ATV. He revved the engine twice, then wove the vehicle through the woods with the swiftness of a deer.

With a satisfied grin, Bellamy inhaled deeply to admit the sharp scent of pine resin. He heard a squawk overhead and looked up to see a bald eagle gliding across the leaden sky. Its wingspan stretching to a man's full height, it was a near-perfect specimen, a symbol of strength, rarity, and fearsome beauty. It reminded him of America and of the oath he made long ago to protect it.

That pact had been broken forever.

It was not his doing. Betrayal of the worst kind would cause any man to forsake something once sacrosanct. It was going on twenty-two years since the dishonorable discharge he did not deserve, and he still felt the pain deep in his gut. It was fuel for the machine he set in motion two decades prior: the plan for retribution against those who had stripped him of his dignity and caused him to live in the shadows.

The day of his vindication drew nigh.

Bellamy patted Singha on the ribs. "Let's go, girl. We have a lot to do."

Twenty-two

Daniel slouched in the backseat of the taxi transporting him from Cairo International Airport to the accommodation Langham's people had arranged, some nondescript chain hotel on the banks of the Nile. He rubbed his eyes to break through the fog lingering from the flight, during which he was heavily medicated. It was the only way he could get through it.

Using a hand crank, he opened the window to get some air. The stinking fumes hovering over the city assaulted his face like a dragon's breath. Cairo was as grimy and crowded as it was ten years ago, when he was on assignment in the Valley of Kings. The streets were choked with emission-belching buses, the ubiquitous dark-blue-and-white taxis, an inordinate number of Mercedes-Benz sedans, and bicycle vendors improbably balancing over-sized trays of bread on their heads. As the traffic slowed to a crawl, pedestrians flooded the streets, some crossing, others walking between slow-moving cars for the sport of it. Women dressed in western clothing with hijabs wrapped around their heads wove through the traffic on mopeds, ignoring the lewd remarks from the salivating men stuck inside their vehicles.

The traffic was habitually thick in that part of town, but that day it was particularly heinous. The taxi driver laid on the horn and shouted some obscenities at another driver, who reciprocated, even though neither of them was at fault for the traffic.

Daniel craned his neck to see what the holdup was but saw nothing but parked cars. "What's happening, friend?" he asked the driver in Arabic.

"Some protest." He spat out the window. "Radical hoodlums who hate the president." He squinted at Daniel through the rearview mirror. "Where you from?"

"Here and there." He knew the remark would not translate in Arabic. "I mean, I work all over."

"What kind of work?"

"Too many questions."

"Sorry. Just making conversation. Looks like we'll be here awhile."

The incessant blaring of horns, along with a cacophony of twangy Egyptian pop playing on too many car stereos, rattled Daniel's nerves. "How far is Tora from here?"

"Tora? The prison? What kind of trouble are you in, man?" The driver chuckled. "It's far. South end of the city."

"Tell you what." Daniel pulled out a bundle of money from his pocket and counted out double the fare. "I'll get off here. Show up at the Novotel in three hours to take me to the south end, and I'll make it worth your while."

The driver counted out the bills, a hint of greediness in the act. He put his elbow on the back of the seat and turned around. "I'll be there. Who do I ask for?"

Daniel strapped on his backpack and exited the car. He leaned into the passenger window. "I'll find you."

The sandstone gates of Tora Prison took on an ochre hue in the late afternoon sun. Daniel was not surprised to see a row of tanks, painted desert khaki, stationed outside. Soldiers dressed in sand-colored fatigues and helmets surrounded the tanks, guns at the ready. A helicopter roared overhead, likely patrolling the grounds to ensure the prisoners stayed in line.

The taxi stopped at the guard station, and the driver produced papers. The guard eyed Daniel. "What is your business here?"

"I am here to see one of the inmates," he said in flawless Arabic. With his golden-brown skin, shoulder-grazing mahogany hair, and five-day facial growth, he did not look out of place there. "Ishaq Shammas."

"Passport," the guard barked.

Daniel gave him what he asked for and watched him disappear into the guard house.

It was almost twenty minutes before he came back out and signaled to two armed soldiers. He bent down and peered at the passenger through the driver's window. "Step out of the car. The men will show you inside."

Daniel exited the taxi and walked toward the soldiers. One pointed a gun at him; the other searched his backpack. Daniel had already emptied out the bag in anticipation of this. He was carrying only a map, a bottle of water, his passport, and a set of printed photos he had shot earlier that day as decoys—streetscapes and landmarks around downtown Cairo, locals he paid to pose, and antiquities at the Egyptian Museum, into which he mingled the photos he intended to show Shammas.

The soldier thumbed through the photos and was satisfied there was nothing suspicious. He waved Daniel into a tent and ordered him to strip down to his boxers. He searched his pockets and shoes for anything suspect, then patted down his hair and body. His gaze lingered on the scratches on Daniel's arms and chest. "What happened here, pretty boy?"

"What can I say? She was a wild one."

The guard chuckled and threw Daniel's clothes at him. "Get dressed."

They walked across the courtyard in single file, the visitor between the two guards. A blast of dry heat blew in from the desert, bringing with it the scent of raw sewage. The smell became more pervasive as they walked inside Tora Istikbal, one of the prisons within the complex. Prisoners were held there before being sentenced and transferred to either the general or maximum security facility. Word had it some of the inmates had been on lockdown there for years, removed every so often to be interrogated and tortured as they waited to be tried.

Though the cells were not yet visible, Daniel could tell the conditions were bordering on inhumane. They walked down a dark corridor that reeked of mildew, their heavy footfalls echoing off the concrete floor and walls. A ceiling-mounted light fixture flickered on and off, revealing stains from a variety of bodily fluids.

One of the soldiers stopped at a thick iron door and unlocked three dead bolts. The soldier said something, but it was hard to hear over the drone of chatter punctuated by loud guffaws. He pointed his gun toward a corridor on the left.

The cells, made of iron bars and encased in diamond mesh safety fencing, were lined up in two rows and held sixty, maybe seventy prisoners each. Most hung together in packs, oblivious to the visitor. Daniel caught the gaze of one man who sat alone against the wire cage, observing in silence. He looked away but could sense the prisoner's glare following him before feeling a wad of phlegm land on his arm. He seethed but acted as if nothing had happened. He didn't want trouble.

The soldier stopped at one of the cells and yelled out to a prisoner. A man in his late fifties or early sixties emerged from the crowd and walked toward them.

Though all prisoners were dressed in grimy prison whites—long-sleeved shirts and long pants—and wore the same snarl on their faces, Shammas stood out. With a full head of wavy white hair, high cheekbones, gray-green eyes, and a distinguished air, he had the look of someone moneyed Europeans would trust.

The soldier nodded toward the visitor. "This man is here to see you. Remember: try anything and it's back to detention." He turned to Daniel. "Make it quick."

Daniel bowed slightly at Shammas and pulled up a stool next to the cage. Shammas sat on a chair on the other side of the hard wire mesh. He crossed his legs and wrists.

He regarded his visitor for a long moment, then spoke in English with an accent that revealed his British education. "American, no?"

"What difference does it make?"

Shammas shrugged. "Suit yourself."

"Mr. Shammas, I'm an anthropologist. My name is Daniel Madigan."

Shammas' nostrils flared slightly. "What can I do for you, Mr. Madigan?"

Daniel looked over his shoulder. The soldiers stood behind him but seemed disinterested in the conversation. They likely didn't understand English, anyway. He turned to Shammas. "I work in Thebes—with the Greeks but not for them. I'm an independent consultant." He put weight on the word *independent.* "I have come across an interesting object." He pulled the photos out of his backpack. "If I may?"

Narrowing his gaze on Daniel, Shammas nodded.

Daniel slipped the photos of the brass obelisk through the iron bars.

As he scanned them, Shammas' face gave nothing away.

"Do you know what that object is, sir?"

No change in his expression, Shammas looked up. "No."

"Perhaps the years in prison have dulled your memory. Let me refresh you." Daniel leaned forward. "This is the key that grants access to the cave of Trophonius—and to an old, forgotten inscription that lies within."

Shammas shifted in his seat. His gaze darted toward the guards, then the other inmates. "What sort of inscription?"

"It's a map leading to something. That's all I'll say."

He handed the photos back to Daniel. "I see. And where is this map now?"

"I'm not at liberty to say." Daniel placed the stack of photos inside his back pocket. "Let me get to the point. I suspect the cave contents are of value to one of your clients."

He raised an eyebrow. "I wish I could help you, Mr. Madigan, but sadly I am no longer in the antiquities business. I do not have clients."

"Don't misunderstand me, Mr. Shammas. I am not here digging for information, nor do I intend to put you in a compromised position. I am merely hoping you can put me in touch with the right broker." He paused, ensuring he had Shammas' full attention. "I'm looking for an appraisal."

Shammas' poker face cracked. The aloof glare in his

eyes was replaced by an alert, viper-like gleam. "Perhaps something can be arranged."

Daniel felt the butt of the soldier's gun between his shoulder blades and heard him bark, "Time's up!"

Shammas spoke behind his teeth. "Irwin Post, Marylebone, London."

Daniel stood and spoke in Arabic. "May Allah hasten your release." He smiled and followed the soldiers out.

Twenty-three

In late February's embrace, the evergreen blanket swaddling Mount Melá appeared gray beneath the low-drifting cloud cover. A sprinkling of fresh snow rested on the boughs of the pine trees growing out of the steep cliffs, some three thousand feet above sea level.

Above the tree line, cut into the bare rock, the Sumela monastery was an aberration, the only habitable structure in a dense mountain wilderness that stretched miles into the horizon. Its construction was simple—a row of vertical towers with three levels of windows topped with an arched breezeway—but its location made it a feat of engineering, particularly in the fourth century, when it was first built. Though the monastery had since been destroyed many times and for many reasons, the original intent of sequestering holy men above the fray and as close to the heavens as possible was so strong it justified the pains of rebuilding.

Sarah stepped out of the dusty white dolmuş, the shared taxi she'd taken from Maçka. A gale blowing in through the mountain pass pressed against her, as if to push her away. Her hair whipping behind her, she leaned into the frigid wind and marched forward. She had a long road ahead.

It had taken the better part of two days to get there. Reluctant to fly lest she get detained, she had chosen to travel overland by a seemingly endless combination of trains, buses, and taxis. While waiting for the next conveyance at one stop, in northeastern Greece near the Turkish border, she had picked up a newspaper and scanned the headlines.

She still tasted bitter bile when recalling the story about the holy men plunging to their death on the hills outside Livadeia. With a sensationalism typical of the Greek press, the writer had painted the incident as ritual suicide, quoting cops who confirmed there was no evidence of violence or forced entry.

Sarah knew different. The brass obelisk in Evan's possession confirmed it. It was never in Daniel's jeep; it was brutally stolen from the monks and delivered to Evan, who clearly was on the take, to frame Daniel with the crime.

It seemed no one could be trusted, least of all the officials. She had to avoid the authorities at any cost—and stay a step ahead of this heinous enemy.

What she regretted most was her parting with Daniel. Had she not allowed ego to seep into her consciousness, she might not have exploded in the way she did; and had she reacted differently, he might not have run off.

Wherever he had gone, one thing was certain: Interpol were after him, and it would be only a matter of time before they'd have their man. And she could not even warn him. The way he left, so abruptly and stealthily, she could not begin to know where to look for him. She was determined to not let the encounter in Thebes be their last. She would find him—but first, she needed the advantage. She was the only one who knew where to look for the object. She intended to track it down and deliver the information to proper custody.

Sarah was the only soul on the high forest trail leading up to the monastery. Winter kept most of the casual visitors at bay, and the day's fog, thick as steamplant emissions, discouraged the rest. Through the mist, pine boughs reached for her like the fingers of Dionysian creatures frozen in an ethereal pose of rapture. She felt strangely protected by them, the sentries of this isolated mountain kingdom.

As the thicket of trees thinned, the crag on which the monastery was built came into view. A set of stone steps carved into the cliffside led up to an arched opening through which one entered the monastery complex.

Sarah stood in the courtyard, breathing in the icy air that signaled more snows. She smelled the vague scent of wood smoke as someone, somewhere, endeavored to keep warm.

No one but a few caretakers lived there. The monks had long since gone, taking their religious treasures with them. The faded frescoes depicting the mother and child, cherubim, and saints, painted onto the rock walls of the monastic compound, were the only reminders of the painstaking effort that had gone into exalting the virgin to whom the monastery was dedicated.

That it was deserted suited Sarah just fine. The answers she sought would be found in solitude, if at all. The library of Sumela, housed in a small building within the compound, contained archives dating back to the fourth century. The Sumela scribes had kept record of every ecumenical event and dedication, every changing of the guard in the church's leadership, and the threats and invasions that rocked the establishment.

She didn't expect that the object she sought was still within the confines of the monastery. Like all other treasures, including the famous icon of the Panagia Sumela—a depiction of the Virgin Mary supposedly painted by the evangelist Saint Luke—had been spirited away, some to a purpose-built church in northern Greece, others to smaller chapels throughout Anatolia.

She opened the door to the library and nodded to the attendant. The woman was dressed in a coat dress, stockings rolled down below her knees, and a kerchief wrapped tightly around her head, all in mourning black. Her vacant eyes suggested she was only there to collect a day's wage. Sarah greeted her in Greek, but the attendant replied in Turkish. A stranger to the language, Sarah understood the universal language of rubbing together a thumb and forefinger. She gave the woman twenty euros and gestured toward the books. The woman tucked the twenty in her bosom and waved her in.

The small room containing the archives was crammed with rows of metal shelves and lit more as a crypt than a library. Stuffed on the shelves helter-skelter, books were badly in need of restoration. Some tomes were bound by needle and thread, others held together by frayed paper spines, most yellowed and tattered by time.

Sarah drew a deep breath. Finding any information about the whereabouts of objects stored at the original monastery was going to be a monumental task. She claimed a table near the stacks and went to work.

The bare lightbulb hanging overhead swung to and fro in the draft coming in from an open window. The cold prickling Sarah's ears roused her from her meditative focus. She looked up. The small window near the ceiling was not open but broken, the victim of a vandal's rock. She was surprised to see it was dark outside.

The caretaker shrieked a few Turkish words. Sarah glanced over her shoulder at her. The woman in black gestured with an open palm toward the door. It was time to go.

"Just a few more minutes," Sarah said. "Please."

The woman held up two fingers and returned to her knitting.

Sarah was too close to stop now. She had begun the search with a codex bearing the name of Sophronios, a monk who had cofounded the monastery in the fourth century. In Greek, the name began with ΣΩΦ, the letters inscribed on the potsherd.

The codex contained a combination of the monk's theological views and accounts of his daily activities. In the entries dated 393, he recounted his efforts to convert a female prisoner to Christianity, seemingly to no avail.

She calls herself a holy woman yet speaks of God as if he were an oppressor, not the benevolent, radiant, merciful being He is. It has become the mission of this humble servant to move her soul, for with faith nothing is impossible.

As the entries progressed, Sarah could read the frustration in his writing, particularly in this passage:

She refuses spiritual nourishment, engaging only in conversation about the ideas of the sage men. She does not eat. She barely sleeps. For long hours she gazes at the horizon, singing the hymns of the godless. May God forgive me for my inability to pierce the darkness.

The more Sarah read, the more convinced she was that the woman in Sophronios' texts was the same as the female who perished in the cave. *Holy woman.* Perhaps she was a pagan, a priestess who refused to abandon her beliefs and was persecuted for it. The year—393—was a dark period in pagan history, when non-Christians were driven from their temples and often killed.

It also was when the sanctuary at Delphi was destroyed. There had to be a connection.

Behind her, Sarah heard the impatient sigh of the caretaker and knew time was running out. She reached into the zippered compartment inside her coat and pulled out all the money she had. She kept just enough to pay for transportation back to Greece and put the rest in her pocket.

She walked over to the woman and kneeled in front of her. She spoke in Greek, hoping the woman understood. "Lady, I am an archaeologist. There is something in these books that can help me with my research. Please allow me to stay here overnight."

The old woman chuckled, revealing a row of badly damaged and missing teeth, and dismissed the request with a wave of her hand. She spoke in broken Greek laced with Turkish words. "No one can stay here overnight." She nodded toward a back room where a cot had been set up. "Only workers and patrons of the church."

Sarah pulled the bundle of cash out of her pocket. "A donation for the church." She put it into the woman's palm and placed her own hand on top. "It would please me if you would accept it."

The caretaker fanned the cash. Her expression brightened when she realized it amounted to roughly five hundred euros. "This will help with the restoration." She crossed herself. "Praise God."

Sarah took that as permission. She stood and helped her companion rise from her seat. The woman placed the money in a metal box, presumably for donations, and walked with it to the back room.

Sarah returned to another promising document she'd located earlier. It was a stack of unbound papers, handwritten on parchment with a rusty brown ink she suspected was made from nut gall. Headings were in red, likely cinnabar. Over the years, the ink had undergone chemical changes and had partially eaten through the paper. The pages had to be handled with utmost care, which slowed down her research process.

Judging by the materials, the more compact letter formation, and the use of *koine* Greek—the common Greek dialect prevalent in the Byzantine Empire and in early Christian writing—this document was produced sometime in the sixth or seventh century. Exactly the period she was interested in: it was during that time the original monastery was sacked by the Hagarenes who had invaded from the south, pillaging and setting fire to Christian holy sites.

Reading ancient Greek was rigorous. Though Sarah was highly skilled in linguistics, the language was so intricate and nuanced—the verbs alone had multiple moods and voices, as well as a complicated conjugation system—that translating long-form text took an inordinate amount of time.

The rhythmic clinking of metal against glass came from the kitchen. Since childhood, Sarah had associated that sound with Sunday morning. Her thoughts traveled to Wiltshire and the home of her youth, where her father insisted on cooking Sunday breakfast. Sir Richard would shoo away the housekeeper and take over the kitchen. No one was allowed in. The only hints of what was coming were the smell of eggs and bacon frying and the pleasant ring of a spoon against a porcelain mug as he made Sarah's favorite, hot chocolate.

She felt a dull ache. So much had happened since then: the bitter divorce, her mother's shocking death, the strained relationship with her father, her choice to run from the privilege that had cost her so much. In the interest of self-preservation, she'd consciously pushed away memories, even happy ones, but there was no escaping the past.

The caretaker placed a glass of milk tea and a couple of pistachio biscuits on the table. Sarah accepted them gladly. It was the only food she'd had in twenty-four hours.

The woman waved and retired for the night. It was just past eight o'clock. Sarah had a few hours to finish translating the eight-page passage she'd identified earlier as a potential lead. What had piqued her interest was this:

The barbarians with their swords and torches of fire trampled over the land, burning trees and slashing the throats of animals just to see the red of their blood. They had

set their sights on the holy virgin's sanctuary and would not
stop until its walls were shattered, stone by stone.

Somewhere in that dark chapter, she hoped, was a clue as to what happened to the original sanctuary treasures after the monastery's epic fall in the seventh century.

The sun shimmered high in the sky. Sarah sat back and rubbed her eyes. It had taken sixteen hours of working without rest, but she had done it.

She picked up the stack of papers containing her translation, a sloppy document rife with strikethroughs and notes, and began reading.

In the year of our Lord 644 the unthinkable came to pass. The house our fathers built to exalt the holy icon of the Virgin Mother, drawn by His Holiness Saint Luke who sat at the right hand of Christ, was set alight and brought to ruin. The barbarians from the hinterlands had come, armed with all their anger and wickedness, determined to extinguish our faith.

Like phantoms they came in the dark of night. With their sickle swords they slaughtered our brothers in their sleep, leaving no one alive. They fouled the altar and the holy of holies and threw great torches of fire onto the sacred vestments.

Fire engulfed the mountain and burned without submission for six days. On the seventh day, God sent a torrential rain that doused the flames and restored natural order to the land. But the harm had been done. The trees on the high peaks stood lifeless and ashen. The pines no longer perfumed the air. There were no more leaves to rustle in the breeze or to sparkle on a dewy morning. Like the smoke from the mouth of a demon, death's vulgar breath lingered everywhere.

Our beloved monastery of the Panagia Sumela was no more. The stones that with such pains had been carried to the high place lay in ruin, stained with the blood of martyrs and smoldering to the heavens. Those who witnessed the carnage from afar speak of a wail heard among the fallen stones: a woman's lament, fragile as the song of the mourning dove, calling to the sunrise.

Even in such despair, there was hope. By the grace of God, we had been warned. The shepherds were informed by their brethren to the south of an evil force approaching: men with eyes of fire, like demons hungry for the flesh of innocents. They laid to waste all life in their path and would not stop until every God-fearing man, woman, and child was slaughtered.

With heavy hearts our brothers prepared for the onslaught. By order of the emperor, they removed every icon and every treasure from the holy of holies and from the tunnels beneath the sanctuary and transported them by barge across the sea. As destiny would have it, the pagan marbles claimed from the heathen temples of Greece were left behind to fall to the barbarians' torches.

Out of the devastation came resurrection. The four hundred monks who had fallen in service to God were replaced by holy men numbering in the hundreds and hailing from all *parts of the empire. The ruins of Sumela, a terrible reminder of the dark period that had befallen us, were taken away to Mysia and given new life as building stones in the project begun by the great Emperor Justinian. The monastery of the virgin was remade high on Mount Melá, larger and stronger than before.*

Let it be known to all who read this that faith prevailed and, so long as there are disciples, will do so unto the ages of ages.

Sarah's pulse quickened. The passage about the pagan objects left to burn and carried off to Mysia with the rest of the ruins was exactly the clue she needed. She had only to identify the project begun by Justinian, whose reign was a full century before the carnage. The prolific emperor had built much of the city of Constantinople and had ordered the construction of bridges across Turkey, including several in the western province of Mysia.

One of those bridges was the location she sought. And she was determined to find it.

Twenty-four

Melá Mountain, Anatolia,
393 CE

The rhythmic clop of donkeys' hooves on rock had haunted Aristea's ears for the better part of the morning. There were six animals in total, five with native riders—village men, she supposed, who had been hired to escort her to a destination that had not been revealed to her.

At the command of one of the men, the donkeys turned down a steep path and staggered down the cliff-side. Aristea leaned back and held on to the saddle to minimize the jostling. It seemed impossible the beasts could negotiate the near-vertical trail without tumbling down the mountain, yet they were as well adapted as they were resigned to their rugged surroundings.

The rider leading the caravan reached the bottom of the path quickly and dismounted his donkey. Without waiting for the others, he ducked inside the black mouth of a cave, one of many in the vicinity.

"That is where he waits," the man behind her said in broken Greek. "The inquisitor."

Aristea was not in the mood for banter. It was the twelfth day of her captivity and the first day she was allowed out of the stony confines of her prison cell. She wanted only to fill her eyes with green and to feel on her cheeks the fresh breeze that smelled of pine and mountain tea.

Since the visit from Sophronios, no one had come to see her except the mute deliverer of millet. Now, it seemed, the purpose for her internment would be divulged by one "inquisitor." She contemplated the weight of the moniker as she dismounted and was escorted inside the cave.

Upon entering the dark womb, a chill touched her skin. Aristea and the villagers walked single file along a narrow corridor until they came to a wider passage. Wielding a torch, the caravan leader stepped out of the shadows.

"Walk this way." He swung the torch round to illuminate a chamber.

Aristea blinked to adjust her eyes to the darkness. The room seemed to be filled with objects. As they drew closer, she recognized alabaster statues of gods, marble busts of wise men, pediments with frescoes, implements of gold, magnificent painted vessels of every sort . . . The treasures of her land, stripped from their sacred homes, silent witnesses to this new age of injustice and tyranny.

In the depths of the chamber, a man was seated. His back was straight and his fingers were interlaced upon a book on his lap. His dress—a long pleated tunic with an oxblood-colored robe fastened at the shoulder and draped across his chest—identified him as a Roman.

"Approach," he said. His expression was no warmer

than the stone surrounding them.

One of the villagers prodded Aristea with a stick, indicating she should step forward. She took two steps toward the Roman. In a small act of defiance, she kept a comfortable distance.

The man looked down his aquiline nose at Aristea. "You may address me as Senator *clarissimus* Arcadius."

"Senator." She bowed slightly. "I am Aristea of Delphi."

"The city whose name you uttered is no more. It has been seized by the great emperor's army. A basilica is being built on the ruins of your iniquitous house." In his smirk she read delight. "Thus your identity is of no consequence."

Aristea had feared this would come to pass, but hearing it brought reality into sharp focus. A knot rose to her throat. "How can your emperor, who claims to be so righteous, condone such a crime?"

"You dare speak of a crime? The offense is yours. And you will be judged for it."

"I have done nothing to be judged by. My people and I have followed the emperor's decrees to the letter."

"Is that so?" He tapped his lips with a finger. "Then perhaps you can explain to me why your vulgar altar was smeared with fresh blood."

For a moment, the breath was trapped inside Aristea's lungs. She recalled the sacrifice of the goat on the night of the last oracle, mere days before the siege. There was nothing she could say in her defense.

"The decrees are clear." Arcadius lifted the book on his lap and opened it to a marked page. The cover read, *Codex Theodosianus*. "'Let superstition cease. Let the madness of sacrifices be exterminated; for if anyone should dare to celebrate sacrifices in violation of the law of our father, the deified emperor, and of this decree of Our Clemency, let an appropriate punishment and sentence immediately be inflicted on him.'" He closed the book. "There is but one true God. Have you come to accept this?"

She looked down.

He stood and pointed to her. "Then you are guilty of the highest crime against the creator."

Aristea knew he wanted to intimidate her, to watch her crouch in a corner and whimper. Instead, she stood straighter and lengthened her neck, as if she were about to orate. "As a Hellene, I believe in debate—the ability to come to a logical conclusion through reason. Tell me, then, Senator: what makes your god superior to mine?"

"I will not engage in the ways of the heretics. The one true God is accepted on faith, not reason."

She raised an eyebrow. "Are you saying you cannot justify through discourse the supremacy of your god?"

"Silence, brazen woman!" His voice boomed across the stone chamber. "You will be judged against the emperor's decree: 'The perverse pronouncements of augurs and seers must fall silent. The universal curiosity about divination must be silent forever. Whosoever refuses obedience to this command shall suffer the penalty of death and be laid low by the avenging sword.' Behold, then, your punishment."

Aristea tapped her sternum. "I am a being of free will and spirit. Inflict your punishment. I am not afraid of your avenging sword, for this body is merely a fleeting habitation for my soul, which shall exist forever."

"Then so be it. But know death will not come swiftly. You will suffer terribly to repay your multiple offenses"—he paused—"unless you choose to cooperate with the state. Come with me."

She followed him to the dark rear of the chamber. He called to one of the men to bring forth a torch. The light followed his outstretched hand. "Do you recognize this?"

The copper glow illuminated a stash of gold coins. Her gaze traveled beyond the gold to a bust of Apollo with the nose broken off. Beyond that lay the spoils from the battle of Marathon and—she gasped—the sacred *omphalos* stone. She turned away so he would not see the bewilderment in her eyes.

"Quite a trove, isn't it? Yet much is missing." He commanded, "Look at me."

She met Arcadius' hard blue eyes, and an unfamiliar feeling infected her soul. She never before had wished harm upon anyone. Unwilling to say something caustic, she remained silent.

Hands clasped behind his back, he paced. "By the time our men reached the temple, the treasures had been removed. I suspect your fellow barbarians are hiding them somewhere." He stopped and stared at her. "Is this true?"

"I know nothing."

"I think you do." He ran a hand across the navel stone. "The emperor is adamant about gathering up all the treasure of the infidels and making it the property of the church."

"What does the church want with pagan objects it claims to despise?"

"Simply to keep them out of public view, where they cannot tempt anyone into idolatrous worship. Such trappings are dangerous, for they can poison the mind and soul of innocents." He took a step toward her. "If you tell me where the treasures are hidden, I am willing to forgo the charges of subversion that have been brought against you. You will be set free."

"I told you once: I do not know."

"It seems you need some encouragement to bring forth a recollection." Arcadius glanced at the village men. "I must take my leave. My men will continue the interrogation."

"Do not trouble yourself. I have nothing to say."

"Perhaps after they finish their work, you will." He took a piece of silk draped on an altar and wiped his hands with it. He crumpled it and threw it onto the floor.

The act of disrespect offended Aristea. The man

before her was not worthy of touching revered objects. He was neither honorable nor truthful. The church wasn't gathering temple treasures to snuff out the tendency toward pagan worship; it was amassing wealth. So much gold and invaluable art could build up the church's treasuries to unprecedented levels. It was the most despicable of acts.

Arcadius swung the hanging end of his mantle over his shoulder, raised his chin, and walked away. The slap of his leather sandals echoed inside the stone womb.

When the sound diminished, she felt another prod from the man with the long stick. She pivoted on her heel and faced him. "Leave me be. I have nothing to say."

"I command you, in the name of the almighty God, to reveal the location of the heretical objects." He spoke in a Pontian Greek dialect. "Speak, or suffer the consequences."

"I do not fear you. Do what you will."

Two other men approached. The three walked in step toward Aristea. She inched backward. She did not like the animal-like glint in their eyes.

"Do you choose deception and defiance over righteousness?" He held up the stick.

Aristea's body tensed. She clenched her fists, ready to retaliate should they attack. "I choose my right to cultivate the garden of my soul as I see fit. What to one man is deception is to another loyalty."

"Loyalty can exist only within the context of the

empire and the church. All other loyalties are forbidden."
He struck the ground with the rod. "Where, then, does
your loyalty lie?"

She knew it was folly to answer, but silence consti-
tuted the highest betrayal. Her voice trembled as she sang
the words of a paean typically uttered to avert evil as men
entered battle.

Ships' prows gather, block the sun.
Arrows rain upon Athens' sacred shores,
Striving to bring death to the deathless.

"Be silent!" The back of the Pontian's hand, heavy as
a bear's paw, struck her mouth.

She stumbled backward but did not fall.

The sea trumpet sounds, calling to the dolphin.
With victory on its back, it glides through golden-crested
    waves.

"Enough!" He pushed Aristea to the ground. Like
sharks to blood, the others gathered round their leader. He
said something to them in a dialect she did not understand.

Two of the five men squatted beside her and pinned
her arms down. She struggled to break free of their grip
but did not possess the physical strength.

"Repent and denounce the perverse ways of the heretics, or prepare to pay with your blood," the Pontian said.

Her lower lip trembled. "What god condones such
tyranny? In what divine tribunal is free thought a crime?"

He squatted beside her. "Men who walk alone are a

threat to the established order. But a woman who thinks this way is an abomination." Saliva trickled from the side of his snarled mouth. "It seems you need to learn your place."

At the Pontian's nod, the two men tightened their hold on her arms. Two others stepped out of the shadows and stood over her. The Pontian placed his hairy paws on the straps of her gown and ripped the fabric apart.

Aristea screamed. To the virgin priestess of Apollo, it was an insult higher than any foul word or the bloodiest strike to the body.

The Pontian straddled her and bent over her, and she smelled his putrid sweat. Even in the dim light, she could see the hunger in his bloodshot eyes. A sharp pain tore through her abdomen, as if she'd been impaled onto a spit. She tried once more to writhe free, but it was for naught: she was pinned to the ground.

She shouted for help. The trespasser covered her mouth with a hand until her pleas were muffled. She squeezed her eyes shut and let tears of indignity roll down her temples. Her most sacred vow had been desecrated with the same wanton disregard that had brought down the gods' temples and had claimed innocent lives by the thousands.

O fairest son of Zeus, he whose arrows of truth slayed evil, when will the torment end?

There was no answer, no sign from Olympus. The world had fallen into darkness.

Twenty-five

The moon's round face rose above Cairo's illuminated skyline, its silver reflection shimmering in the waters of the Nile. Daniel sat at a balcony three stories above the river with his laptop and a bottle of Auld Stag, trolling for information on Irwin Post.

Post, a Scotsman who'd been living in London for three decades, acquired rare art and antiquities for galleries, which in turn were sold for lucrative margins to private collectors. He had dealt with everything from Qin Dynasty pottery to Egyptian New Kingdom canopic jars and, as far as Daniel could tell, had a flawless track record—and a profile to match. He had been quoted in the press, from the *Financial Times* to the BBC, about the illicit antiquities trade, each time presented as the watchdog against such activity.

Daniel took a swig of the whiskey straight from the bottle. He frowned at the taste, more akin to turpentine than the blended scotch it purported to be. He logged in to the Rutgers indexes and databases, to which he had privileged access, and searched for more information. The only thing of note was a trade journal article about

Post coming under fire for selling Iraqi antiquities to museums in the late nineties, when much of the country was being looted. To clear his name, Post had produced rigorous documentation proving the objects had come from long-held private collections or were deaccessioned museum pieces. The authorities had eventually accepted this proof, and the case went no farther.

Post either was legit or had a watertight authentication network. Or, more likely, there was money to be made on both sides, so certain things were overlooked.

Daniel picked up his phone and checked for any communication from Sarah. His abrupt departure surely had embittered her, so it should not have been a surprise that she had not tried to reach out. Though they had parted ways before, he'd always known they would reunite. This time, he wasn't so sure.

The phone vibrated in his hands. It was the third time that night Langham had called. This time, Daniel picked up. "You don't give up, do you?"

"You ought to know better than to ask. How did it go at Tora?"

"I got a dealer's name. A chap in London named Irwin Post."

"Brilliant. That will make the final step easier." He cleared his throat. "I want you to call Post and tell him you have the map and wish to make an exchange."

"Let me guess: the map for the firman."

"You do catch on quickly."

Daniel's face burned. "This is what you intended all along. It was never meant to be an information-gathering mission. You needed someone to do your dirty work."

"Now, now, Madigan. We had no idea what lay inside that cave. Your mission sort of . . . evolved."

"Listen here, James. I'm out. This is not what I agreed to, and I don't particularly care for your strong-arming tactics."

"No; you listen. The Greek lot have been promised access to the firman in exchange for the obelisk, which now sits squarely in Rigas' hands."

"Not true. The monks—"

"The monks are all dead." His voice rose a notch. "The stakes are being raised, Madigan. It is imperative you carry on with the mission. Without that firman, Britain may well lose the right to the marbles, and that would not only be humiliating for the crown; it would be disastrous for humanity. As someone who has vowed to preserve archaeological treasures, surely you realize those relics would suffer in the hands of the Greeks."

"In the hands of the Greeks is where they rightfully belong. It's their heritage, and they have a right to it. Who are you to question that?" He huffed. "We clearly have a difference of principle. But it's my fault I got sucked into your sordid game. Good-bye, James."

"We are not finished, Madigan." Langham's voice bellowed across the line. "Interpol is after you—and after

Weston's daughter. After all that's transpired, you will end up in prison. I will make sure of it."

"Do your worst." Daniel hung up and blocked Langham's number.

He slipped the phone into his pocket and walked inside. The room was lit softly by the moonbeams; any artificial illumination seemed superfluous. He glanced at the wall and saw a bearded man with a detached gaze staring at him. He tensed, ready to strike. It took him a moment to realize he was looking at his own reflection in a mirror. Of all the life-or-death predicaments and dangerous characters he had encountered during his career, this frightened him most.

Turning his gaze to the sky, he clenched his teeth. *No more.* He walked back to the balcony, picked up the bottle of Auld Stag, and went into the bathroom. He poured the contents down the toilet and dropped the bottle into the trash bin. He looked through his wash bag for his other crutch so he could deliver it to the same fate.

A knock interrupted his search. He ignored it, hoping the person would go away. Another knock came, louder this time.

"Not now," Daniel said, a touch too angrily.

A male voice announced, "Engineering. Very important."

Daniel went to the door and looked through the keyhole at a slight Egyptian man dressed in a faded blue maintenance uniform with the hotel logo. He cracked the door open.

"Sorry, sir, we've had a disruption to water service on this floor," the worker said. "May I come in to turn on a valve? Only one moment."

Daniel let him in and watched him make his way to the bathroom. He was on guard until the man turned on the faucet and nothing came out. He decided to let him do his work and began to pack his things.

When finished, he texted Sarah. *Flying into Athens from Cairo tonight. Need to see you.*

The alarm clock blared. Arabic popular music at full volume assaulted his ears, and he walked to the night-stand to turn the alarm off.

As he searched for the off button, he felt a sharp sting between his shoulder blades, followed by a numb sensation. He turned around and saw the Egyptian put something away in his tool box.

Daniel reached for the man, but his arms felt heavy and uncoordinated. He tried to say something but the words came out slurred. White spots crowded his vision, and the room looked distorted. His breathing became labored. He dropped to his knees, then crumpled onto the floor.

He heard his assailant pick up the phone and say in Arabic, "Send up the paramedics." Then he slipped out the door.

Daniel fought to keep his eyes open. Behind the fog that shrouded his vision, he saw three men dressed in dark green uniforms with fluorescent-yellow stripes—paramedics, presumably—enter the room and lift his limp body onto a gurney. One barked at the others in Sa'idi Arabic, the dialect of the south, spurring them to move quickly.

With Daniel strapped to the gurney, they hurried down the corridor and into the elevator. Daniel saw the distorted faces of people stepping aside as the paramedics rushed him out of the lobby and loaded him into an ambulance.

He lay there helpless as the blue lights swelled and waned in synch with the two-tone siren. On the outside, the emergency vehicle looked the part. Inside, two of the three rescue workers were smoking and shooting the breeze, uninterested in their human cargo.

He had been betrayed.

Too numb to summon any strength, Daniel lay in a near-catatonic state as the ambulance blasted through the freeway and finally turned off on the exit marked *Heliopolis*.

They were going to the airport.

The vehicle had not yet come to a full stop at the tarmac when two of the men threw open the door and jumped out of the vehicle to lower the ramp.

Holding a syringe, the third bent over the victim. "Have a good trip," he said and plunged the needle into Daniel's arm.

Twenty-six

The parched, waist-high grasses on the banks of the Gönen Çayi rustled as Sarah carved a path to the river's edge. She could see her destination through the tangles of wild oak branches leaning into the river: two megaliths of ancient masonry, the vestiges of a once-great bridge built in the Byzantine Empire.

She was certain this was the location. Though Justinian had launched many bridge projects during his sixth-century reign, the Aesepus Bridge was the only one whose construction continued into the seventh century. Around the time of Sumela's destruction, the bridge builders were remaking demolished parts of the pillars and the road they supported. To make them stronger, they reinforced the structures with fill.

Sarah sat on the rock next to the bridge ruins and studied the pier fragments jutting from the water like Neolithic henge. They were solidly built of brick and granite blocks held together with sand-and-shell mortar. On the top of each pier were the famous hollow chambers employed in several bridges in the region, a building technique the Romans perfected as early as the fourth and fifth centuries.

Over the years, much of the bridge—all the arches and one of the piers—had succumbed to neglect and vandalism and was eventually abandoned. The question was: what had happened to the derelict stones and slabs? Were they carried away for other building projects, or did they sink into the riverbed?

Sarah was betting on the latter.

The Gönen Çayi flowed around the piers in its journey northwest to the Sea of Marmara. Tiny whitecaps, the product of winter winds streaming down from the mountains, agitated the surface and animated this long-forgotten piece of history.

Sarah stood and slipped off her coat and shoes. With the brisk gust needling her skin, she considered the madness of what she was about to do.

There was no time for misgivings. The answers lay somewhere beneath the river's surface, and she was determined to find them. She stepped into the river, letting her bare feet gauge the temperature. The water was warmer than expected but still frigid enough to limit her time below.

She stepped around the rocks that lined the river's edge and lowered herself in. When the water washed over her midriff, her body tightened. She took a deep breath and held it, then submerged.

The water was moving but clear. The pylons on which the bridge piers were built drilled into the seabed a good forty feet below the surface. She swam to the one closest to the western shore. It was the foundation of a pier that had been bolstered several times over the years and finally crumbled in the nineteenth century. That part of the structure, she estimated, was the weak link.

Her hair floating like golden sea anemones around her face, Sarah hovered over the broken pylon and looked into the interior. Shattered stones, marble fragments, and pieces of clay mixed in a gray mortar stew had been pushed into the center of the structure. Her gaze darted to the other pylons. The same substance had been used to reinforce or seal the base of all three piers.

Feeling the familiar pressure in her chest, she surfaced and swallowed a lungful of cold air. She took a moment to normalize her breathing and dove back down, this time exploring the base of the center pier.

Swimming slowly around it, she noted the fill was darker and more textured. She took a closer look. One of the marble chunks—a shard no more than three inches wide—appeared to have been carved or possibly fluted, a sign that it might have come from a temple. It was more than she had hoped for.

She continued her reconnaissance on the other sides of the structure, looking for anything unusual. A dark, textured surface caught her eye.

Her fingers tingled, and sensation had all but disappeared from her lips. Too excited about a potential discovery, she pushed on. Whatever the toll on her body, she did not care. She stared at the object as if it were manna for the starving.

Though much of the object was wedged into the fill, she could see enough to determine its mass was a modified cone, not unlike the beehive shape on the potsherd. The stone was the color of coal and vaguely porous, like volcanic rock. But it had undoubtedly been shaped by human hands. Not only was the surface meticulously rounded; it was marked by a relief of characters and forms that were linked together.

Sarah let out a small puff of air. As the bubbles raced toward the surface, she ran her fingertips across the stone, following the raised forms toward the top of the object: two eagles with outstretched talons, holding a branch in their beaks.

Her fingers explored further, stopping on a groove cut into the surface. Only part of the carving—a straight, horizontal line—was visible. She released another puff and was suddenly aware she had no more time. As her pulse hammered against her temples, she reached into the fill as far as her hand would go and felt more of the carved shape: a vertical line . . . another horizontal line . . .

Eyes bulging, she pulled her hand away. Her suspicions had been confirmed.

Sarah ascended toward the light. Her head burst through the surface, and she gasped for air. The sunbeams breaking through the clouds assaulted her eyes, disorienting her. Her head bobbed in and out of the river as she tried to stay afloat. She swallowed water, aspirating some.

Coughing and sputtering, she swam to the riverbank and held on to a low oak branch, unable to summon the strength to pull herself out of the water. She stayed in that position for several minutes trying to regain her composure.

By the time she felt strong enough to crawl onto the bank, her teeth were chattering and her body was quaking. She lay on the grass, curled in the fetal position, to warm herself.

She felt utterly spent. It was a small price to pay for such a discovery. Her instincts had been correct: the object in the fill bolstering the Aesepus Bridge was the original *omphalos* stone that marked Delphi as the navel of the Earth and was central to the oracular rituals that so profoundly shaped the ancient world.

The pagan rituals of which the monk spoke were likely a reconstruction of the oracle of Delphi. The ancient *omphalos*, which had been lost centuries ago without a trace, was central to the art of prophecy and perhaps even enabled the visions of the priestesses delivering the word of Apollo. Possession of the stone surely would influence such rituals today, legitimizing both the process and the outcome.

Sarah could only imagine what sinister intent was behind the cult leader's relentless hunt for the stone. She knew only it had to be kept out of his reach at all costs.

Still shaking, she sat up and crawled to her backpack. She pulled out some dry clothes and quickly changed into them. There was no time to waste. She had to get back to Greece.

It was well after midnight when she got to the border. Her eyes stinging and head pounding, Sarah leaned against a wall as she queued to cross over into Greece. There must have been fifty, sixty people waiting—remarkable, considering the hour.

The one passport control officer did not seem to be in any hurry. He checked each person's papers manually and barked a litany of questions before deeming a passport ready to receive a stamp. Entry was granted with a series of thumps as the rubber stamp slammed ceremoniously against the passport and each accompanying immigration paper.

It didn't help that half the people queueing carried vast amounts of baggage, much of it in cartons sealed with miles of tape and tied several times over with rope. Each time one of those boxes had to be opened and checked, it added half an hour to the process. One woman, dressed in the widow's black uniform, carried a dog in a chicken-wire cage. Judging by its incessant barking, the animal was not terribly happy about its accommodations.

Sarah closed her eyes and thought about a conversation

she'd had earlier that night. Desperate to track down Daniel, she suspected he might have returned to Saudi Arabia or even the States. When she arrived in Istanbul on her way to the border, she had rung up Jackson Barnes, Daniel's advisor and the head of anthropology at Rutgers University.

The exchange had taken an unexpected turn. She could not get it out of her mind.

"Dr. Barnes, Sarah Weston here . . . Daniel Madigan must have spoken of me." She looked through the Plexiglas of the public phone booth to ensure she wasn't being followed.

"Yes, yes, of course." There was a pause. "Is Danny with you now?"

She sighed. He obviously didn't know more than she did. "I'm afraid not. I don't know where he is, actually." She was careful not to say too much.

"I've been looking for him myself." His voice took on a somber tone. "I have some news for him."

"I normally wouldn't ask for personal information, but I'm rather worried about him. Can you share that news with me?"

"I know he trusts you . . ." She could hear him breathing uneasily. "All right. It's his father. He's been killed in a car accident."

"Dear God." The blood drained from her cheeks. "When did it happen?"

"Only last night. There will be a service on Tuesday . . . I thought he might want to know."

Though Daniel hadn't spoken to his father in years, she knew this would be a blow. No one knew the depth of Daniel's sensitivity better than she did. Losing a parent, even an estranged one, could be devastating if one was in a fragile frame of mind. Given what she'd found in his cabin in Thebes, she suspected he wouldn't handle it well. "Of course. If I see him, I shall have him ring you. But I must be honest, Dr. Barnes."

"Jack."

"Jack." Emotion leached into her voice. "I don't know if he's coming back."

"If he does get in touch, where can I reach you?"

"Don't worry. I will reach you." Sarah regarded the busy Istanbul street and caught a glimpse of a twenty-four-hour DHL office.

She hung up. Ultimately, her plan was to report the Aesepus Bridge find to the antiquities authorities via an institution like Rutgers that could provide neutral over-sight to the excavation process. Sending the potsherd to Jack Barnes was the beginning of that process. Besides, she could not risk having it confiscated.

Sarah was next up in the queue. The unshaven immigration officer with the downturned mouth waved her over. She placed her passport on the counter. He looked through the stamped pages before turning to her photo.

He held it up and shifted his gaze between the photo and the real deal, comparing the two faces. Frowning, he leafed through some papers on his desk.

He stood. "Just a minute," he said with a heavy accent.

Her body tensed as he disappeared with her passport into a back room. She sensed trouble. She considered making a run for the Greek side, but she knew the border was heavily guarded. She had no choice but to wait.

A few minutes later, the officer reemerged. "Come with me," he said.

Heart racing, she did as told. On the other side of the door were two gray-suited men. The taller, thinner of the two produced a badge.

Sarah held her breath as she read the identification written in bold capital letters: INTERPOL.

"Dr. Weston," he said. "I believe we've spoken. I'm Heinrich Gerst. I'd like you to come with me."

Twenty-seven

Gerst parked the black Mercedes-Benz sedan on a sidewalk in downtown Athens. Parking was at a premium in the capital, where roads were built hundreds of years ago for pedestrians and had never been modernized. In a city built wholly on ancient ruins, any construction was a time-intensive and expensive proposition and, therefore, avoided in favor of workarounds.

Speaking in German into his mobile phone, he opened the rear door for Sarah. He clicked the phone off. "We are going to Solonos Street. Eight blocks from here."

Sarah nodded and followed Gerst. His associate walked behind her. Though they had made it clear earlier she wasn't under arrest, she definitely was monitored, lest she try anything foolish.

Maintaining a rapid pace, they walked in tight single file past swarms of pedestrians crowding the sidewalk. Acropolis Hill, the monolith on which the Parthenon was built some twenty-five hundred years earlier, stood over the city with all its gravitas, reminding all passersby of the former glory of the Athenian Empire.

Sarah imagined Pericles, the statesman who called for

the building of this grand citadel, standing on that very hill and addressing his fellow Athenians. Though he was known as the father of democracy and a great general who led his men on successful military excursions, Pericles considered the Acropolis his crowning life achievement: he had spared no expense in commissioning not only the monuments but also the art within them, most notably the marble statues that decorated the interiors, metopes, and friezes.

The Parthenon's devastation, and the subsequent selling off of the marbles, was one of the tragedies of modern history. The Ottoman Turks, who had occupied Greece for nearly four hundred years between the fifteenth and nineteenth centuries, had seen fit to use the Parthenon as a munitions storage facility during the Venetian siege of 1687. When a mortar shell hit the temple, the gunpowder exploded and blew the roof off, sending priceless works of art crashing to the ground and causing irreparable damage to one of antiquity's greatest treasures.

But the biggest blow came at the turn of the nineteenth century, when the Sultan of the Ottoman Empire decided to sell a good deal of the marbles to Thomas Bruce, seventh Earl of Elgin and British ambassador to Ottoman Greece. Under a dark cloud of controversy that remained to that day, the marbles were transported to England and became the prize collection of the British Museum. Though she understood the politics, Sarah had always felt ashamed that her countrymen insisted on holding on to these relics instead of returning them to the nation of their origin, where they belonged.

Gerst stopped at the glass-and-iron door marked number twenty-three and rang up to the third floor. Sarah questioned the location. Interpol's National Central Bureau was based at the Greek police headquarters. Was this not official Interpol business?

A loud buzzer sounded, and the door clicked open. The building, probably of early 1900s vintage, was dark as a tomb and smelled musty, like an old grandmother's house that had not been opened in years. Gerst pushed a button to turn on the staircase light and led the way up the gray-veined marble treads to an office labeled Costantinos Argyros, Attorney.

A female assistant met them at the door and waved them into a living room that was the antithesis of the building. The black marble floor was so highly polished that it looked wet, the cream leather furnishings were spotless, and bright light filtered through sheer white curtains. A pleasant, almost imperceptible, lavender scent embroidered the air.

The woman took her leave and came back a few minutes later with five glasses of café frappé and a bowl of sweets individually wrapped in gold foil. If cutbacks were universal in Greece, Sarah thought, it certainly wasn't apparent here.

Twenty minutes later, a blue-suited, middle-aged man walked in with an air of authority. He was trim but for a paunch that made the buttons of his white shirt strain at the midsection. His thinning hair was combed straight back, revealing a wide, unwrinkled forehead and V-shaped brows. He offered Sarah his hand.

"Dr. Weston, Demetrios Floros, head of Interpol Athens." He pronounced every vowel and consonant distinctly. "I have heard a great deal about you."

She smiled, but her heart wasn't in it. "Pleasure." She glanced at the five glasses of iced coffee. "Who else is joining us?"

He ignored the question and gestured for her to sit. "Dr. Weston, I will get right to the point. Our officers have been tracking an antiquities theft ring with arms throughout the world. There are many layers to these criminal organizations, as you no doubt know. This necessitates our collaboration with various intelligence agencies"—he paused and reached into his jacket pocket—"and sometimes with civilians."

Floros held up an iPhone. From the scuffed-up rubber case, she recognized it as her own. "It seems you forgot this in Thebes." He tapped the screen several times. "We had to break your security code. I hope you don't mind."

As if she had a choice. "I have nothing to hide."

He smiled. "I'm not accusing you of hiding anything, Dr. Weston. I merely want to point out a text message sent to your phone the night before last." He held up the phone in front of her.

Sarah read Daniel's message: *Flying into Athens from Cairo tonight. Need to see you.* Her shoulders relaxed. He had returned after all.

Floros placed the phone on the coffee table and leaned forward. "I need you to answer this question truthfully. Have you spoken to Daniel Madigan?"

She glanced at him, then at the other two Interpol agents. They all wore the same grave expression. "No," she said. "I have not."

Floros inhaled sharply. He seemed unhappy with her answer.

"I don't understand. Why are you after him?"

"We are not after him, Dr. Weston," Floros said. "We are trying to protect him."

She felt like the only one not in on some elaborate plot. "Protect him from what? Or whom?" She raised her voice a notch. "I demand to know what this is all about."

"There is someone who can answer your questions better—someone I believe you know." Floros turned to his left.

A male figure emerged from the shadows of the long hallway.

Sarah stood, her gaze riveted on the ice-blue eyes she'd known for thirty-seven years.

"Hello, darling," he said. "It's been a long time."

Twenty-eight

Sir Richard Weston walked up to his daughter and regarded her with the haughty glare perfected by the upper class. "Have you nothing to say? Not even a hello?"

Sarah took a deep breath to steady herself. She didn't know what was more shocking: seeing her father for the first time in almost two years, or realizing he played a part in this increasingly surreal game. She glanced at Floros, then at Sir Richard. "I want some answers."

"I will leave you two to talk," Floros said. "I have a meeting at headquarters." With the wave of a hand, he summoned Gerst and his assistant and they all left the room.

As soon as the door closed behind them, Sarah turned to her father. "Where's Danny?"

"It's complicated, darling."

"I've got all the time in the world. I no longer have a job or a partner. I certainly haven't got a family. So, please: tell me your complicated story."

"Very well." Sir Richard sat and gestured for Sarah to do the same. "Some time ago, a prominent dealer was arrested in London for trafficking in illicit antiquities. One of the items he'd sold to an unspecified collector was of grave importance to Her Majesty's government." He paused. "Sarah, we are talking about the original Turkish firman proving that Lord Elgin had been legally granted rights to remove the Parthenon marbles and transport them to England."

Sarah raised an eyebrow. "That firman hasn't been seen since 1809. The entire world presumes it lost."

"Yet we've been tracking it for three decades. The document surfaced in the 1980s in a bank safety deposit box owned by an Athenian woman. She died with no heirs, and the box went unclaimed for two years. When the bank staff opened it and found the firman, they called the Center for the Acropolis Studies, and it became minor news. But before anything could come of it, a next of kin surfaced—an estranged brother, apparently—and claimed it. We contacted him and offered to purchase the letter, but he ignored every attempt."

"Is the brother still living?"

"No, he died some time ago. His estate was divided amongst three heirs, and we lost the document's scent. This is the closest we've come to locating it since." He leaned forward. "I'm sure you can understand why it's so important we get our hands on it."

Of course she could understand. The original document would silence the Greeks' claims, vociferous of late, to the marbles and placate the critics who'd been crying foul for decades. It could neatly put an end to this argument once and for all.

Or not.

"How can you be so sure of what it says?" she asked. "There has always been some controversy as to what rights Lord Elgin was granted. For all we know, this firman could prove he had permission only to study and reproduce the Parthenon art—not take it away."

Sir Richard's thin lips curled into a smile. "Either way, that document is of great value to Britain."

He didn't need to say more. She turned the conversation. "What does any of this have to do with Danny—and with me?"

"Fair enough. Let's start with Madigan. His assignment in Thebes had nothing to do with the university. He was working for us."

She'd heard that story before. "Working for you how?"

"Even after we arrested this dealer, Ishaq Shammas, and extradited him, the thefts continued. It became apparent his network was still in motion. According to the dealer's computer records, the mysterious collector who had bought the firman also was after a brass obelisk and willing to pay any price for it. Through Interpol and the Thurlow Foundation, we knew such an object had been found near Thebes. We also knew the director of the ephorate was not trustworthy. We needed someone on the inside—someone who had our interests at heart—to monitor the activity and report back to the head of Joint Intelligence."

"And who better than a scientist on official business?"

"Exactly right." When she huffed, he placed a hand on her shoulder. "Be a big girl, darling."

She jerked away. "Don't patronize me."

"Hear my words, Sarah. He would have never agreed to any of this if it weren't for you."

She bit her lip and turned away. It was what Daniel had tried to explain—and what she had categorically dismissed—when she'd last seen him. She'd refused to accept she had anything to do with Daniel's decision to work for the government, for a man should take sole responsibility for his actions. Yet she knew the truth was more complicated than that. Some part of her didn't want to hear it for fear it would add to her guilt.

"It was last November, after the plane went down," Sir Richard continued. "He came to me with information about the Ashworths, demanding their arrest. He feared for your life in Jerusalem. I was on a diplomatic mission, so I put him in touch with James Langham, the head of Joint Intelligence. Langham also happened to be chairman of the Thurlow Foundation, which was a strategic appointment to protect the crown's cultural interests. At any rate, Langham made Madigan a deal he could not refuse: our intervention in Jerusalem in exchange for his cooperation in Thebes. Madigan was desperate to save your life, so he accepted."

She snapped her head toward him. "You took

advantage of a desperate man for your own means? You and your cohorts are more despicable than I thought."

"Madigan got what he wanted, and so did we. I see nothing despicable about that."

"Of course you don't. You never do." She stood. "I've heard enough."

As she walked toward the door, he came after her. "I know you're angry, darling, but I need you to hear what I'm about to say."

Sarah took hold of the doorknob. She wanted to bolt out, to get lost in the grimy streets of Athens, to run until the cord to Sir Richard and his circle of power were severed for good. But she also needed to hear the whole truth, no matter how painful it might be. She let go of the knob and turned to face her father.

He took two steps toward her. "Listen to me, Sarah. I need your help. I fear Madigan is in serious trouble."

Twenty-nine

Stephen Bellamy stood on the rooftop terrace of the main house at his Delphi compound, admiring the view. Below the dense canopy of pines and orchards that populated his property, the barren slopes of the Phaedriades rose from the lavender mist. At the foot of the mountain, the still waters of the Gulf of Corinth lay hidden within a necklace of peaks dissolving into the horizon. It was a scene straight out of a Homeric epic, a forbidding land that gave away nothing, the ultimate battleground where heroes were tested and men's cunning prevailed over brute force.

The stories from mythology stirred him. He could relate to the ancient warriors who put honor above all else and fought to the death for the ideals that mattered— ethnic purity, autonomy, the right to worship and express themselves as they damn well pleased. It pained him that his own country did not recognize those qualities in him. He was determined to prove his mettle and regain the respect that had evaporated on that ill-fated February day.

It was 1990. He was stationed in Seoul as part of the United States Forces Korea but was often in the field, training his men to be battle-ready should tensions in the region flare up again. On one of those occasions, Bellamy's men were conducting exercises in the north along the DMZ.

The colonel personally led his men on drills through the uplands. He still remembered the icy fingers of winter on his skin as he tore through snow fields, in places three feet deep. He didn't mind. He'd always regarded tough terrain as a welcome challenge, a privilege even.

When they reached a peak and looked down the ridge toward the valley below, they saw a makeshift cabin just inside the North-South border. Smoke rose from a chimney: someone was in there.

Bellamy signaled to his men to follow him down the mountain. As they fell into position to cover him, he approached the structure and looked inside the frosted window. Six men huddled around a table, discussing something in Korean.

Though he didn't speak the language, he understood every word. It was only natural after eight years in the godforsaken country.

Wind hissed in his ears, raising fresh snow that whipped his face like a thousand needles. He didn't flinch. He put his ear to the wall and listened.

What he heard astonished him. Ignoring the mounting flurries, he stood in the same spot for almost an hour and heard the entire, surreal exchange, allowing for the possibility he'd misunderstood.

There was no mistake about it. The men were discussing a seismic weapon. It was clear the North Koreans were in bed with the Russians, and together they were developing a sinister technology that could amount to the ultimate terrorist weapon: an earthquake so powerful it could tear a nation apart, decimating its population and plunging it into economic ruin.

And responsibility would lie with the blameless, for it would be deemed an act of God. It was the perfect scheme.

The wind blew up again, this time howling with fury. One of the Koreans looked out the window. Bellamy's reflexes were not fast enough.

"Somebody's there!" The conspirator shrieked.

A shot shattered the window, and a burst of glass shards exploded onto the snow.

One of Bellamy's men fired back.

"Hold your fire!" His order could not be heard over the wind or seen through the raging snowstorm. His ears rang with the staccato blasts of machine-gun fire. One of the shots—he could not tell if it was from the enemy or friendly fire—grazed his shoulder. As he reached for his own weapon, he watched his own blood pour down his arm and spill onto the bright new snow.

The cabin went quiet. His men stopped firing in response. Bellamy had no illusions about it: the North Koreans were not down and out. He stole a quick glance through the jagged glass teeth of the splintered window and saw one of the men sprawled onto the table and another on the floor. A third crouched under the table, reloading a weapon with shaky hands. He was no soldier.

Though the Koreans were armed, they were no match for his troops. Convinced his men could take them all down and put an end to their malicious conspiracy, he signaled to his men to fire.

It was a mistake that would haunt him for the rest of his life.

A square-jawed blond man with eyes the color of a glacier stepped out of the shadows of the cabin, holding a shoulder-launched weapon.

"Jesus," Bellamy cried, crouching only a split second before the blast.

Hyperventilating, he looked across the snowfield and watched the missile detonate in a massive fireball. In slow motion, body parts flew through the air and pools of blood splayed onto the snow. No one had been spared. The only evidence of what had happened was the smell of charred human flesh, an odor that had stayed with him to that day.

The blond man came through the front door of the cabin and pointed an automatic at Bellamy. Three other men, equally armed, exited the cabin and stood behind their leader. He spoke to his captive in Russian, then repeated the words in English. "You. Put down your weapon and stand up."

"Russian scum," Bellamy muttered through clenched teeth. He did as told.

The leader barked some orders in Russian, and two of his cohorts rushed to Bellamy. They handcuffed and hooded him, then pushed him to his knees. He felt the business end of a weapon graze the back of his head. He heard the click of a trigger.

Gunfire exploded all around him, so loud he could not hear his own screams for mercy. He fell to his side, shaking like a fish out of water. He was certain he was dying.

The salvo stopped, but the bursts of fire echoed across the mountains, mocking him anew. He lay in a fetal position, his world dark beneath a black hood, waiting for death to come.

It never did. But in the nightmarish years that followed, he often wished his life had been taken on that bitter winter morning.

"Colonel."

Bellamy turned to face Sorenson standing at the threshold of the French doors that separated the salon and the terrace. "What's with the sourpuss, Tom?"

"Colonel, I can't hold off Zafrani any longer. He says he wants answers by this weekend—or he will put a hold on the wired funds."

"Damned Syrians have no concept of patience." He brushed past his aide as he went back inside. He walked to a burled ash humidor box sitting on a shelf and removed a Montecristo. He lopped one end off with a guillotine and wedged the other between his teeth. "You let him know we'll be ready."

"But, sir, we don't have—"

"Silence, boy. You let me worry about that." He scanned the dumped-out contents of his captive's back-pack, neatly arranged on a table in the center of the room. He paced the perimeter of the table and looked more closely at each object. Based on the climbing tools and rope, he surmised Daniel Madigan could hold his own in the backcountry. Still, he didn't see that as a threat—mostly due to a small packet that spoke volumes.

Bellamy picked up the blister pack of Valium, then tossed it back onto the table. He shook his head. "That boy ain't right. This is going to be easier than I thought."

He reached inside his pocket for a lighter and lit the cigar, twirling it as the flame turned the tip red hot. He rolled the smoke around his mouth before exhaling it. The Cubans, he thought, weren't good at many things, but they sure could turn tobacco into poetry.

He glanced out the French doors at the acres of chestnuts, oaks, and pines spread across his property. His gaze traveled to the barren mountaintops beyond. On the other side of that mountain, his destiny would soon un-fold. He smiled as he let the thought settle.

"Tom, get word to Isidor. Tell him to be on the

lookout for a blonde English woman. It's only a matter of time before Sarah Weston takes the bait." He spoke over his shoulder. "Oh, and Tom?"

"Sir."

He turned his focus back to the woods. The sprawling no man's land was the perfect place to go hunting.

"Get me the MK12 and the 6P62." He smirked. "It's time to have a little fun."

Thirty

Sarah wandered the back streets of Omonia, the square in the heart of downtown Athens. She needed time to process what she'd just heard and a distraction to keep from doing something she'd regret.

She glanced furtively at the faces around her: Bangladeshi men, dressed in sarongs and tank tops, chewing paan as they sat idly on stoops of shuttered buildings; homeless waifs lying on filthy blankets on the sidewalk, staring vacantly at passersby and on occasion summoning the energy to extend an open palm; an emaciated young woman dressed in a cheap, skin-tight micromini, standing against a corrugated metal construction wall, cigarette in hand, soliciting business.

She couldn't believe how Omonia Square had changed in the years since she'd visited Athens. Apart from the die-hard souvlaki stands and tobacco kiosks, businesses had gone under, leaving behind boarded-up buildings that eventually became magnets for posters and political graffiti. The apartments, once desirable real estate, had been left to decay and converted to low-rent immigrant quarters, many with no heat or running water.

The Greeks had all fled to other neighborhoods, handing the spiritual keys to their Omonia over to poor, jobless foreign settlers—some legal, some not—and letting them turn this former hub into a cesspool of debauchery.

Sarah stopped by the temporary wall, behind which was an abandoned construction site now strewn with garbage. She took a cigarette out of her jacket pocket and fumbled for a lighter. The streetwalker walked up to her, offering a light. Sarah accepted it, noting the multiple needle marks on the woman's arms. She met her gaze and realized she was probably no older than sixteen. The girl flashed a smile, a heartbreaking playfulness in it. Sarah nodded her thanks and walked on.

The bleakness of the surroundings reflected Sarah's mood. Since the conversation with her father, she wanted to be anonymous and invisible, to be lost in the underbelly of misery. It had been nearly two years since they had spectacularly parted. She'd refused to walk in his shadow; he'd disinherited her. It really was that simple, that final.

And yet, because of Daniel, it wasn't. Daniel had known Sir Richard long before he'd met Sarah, which made for a complicated triangle. Even after Sarah and her father had fallen out, Daniel did not lose contact with Sir Richard. It was an odd symbiosis—the two men couldn't have been more different, both in background and worldview—but they had a mutual respect that meant they always had each other's back. Some sort of men's code, she supposed.

She hadn't fought it. If anything, she'd secretly hoped it would be the catalyst to bring her and her father back together. But she wanted him to reenter her orbit on her terms—not as the mighty Lord Weston, aloof and doling out orders, but as a present and loving parent.

In a stroke of supreme irony, she got her reunion. It was definitely not what she had in mind.

Sarah took a drag and exhaled slowly, breathing her angst into a plume of smoke. Gazing absently at a small gathering of Muslims kneeling on carpets and bowing to the East, she replayed the conversation in her mind.

"What sort of trouble?" she'd asked in response to her father's proclamation about Daniel.

Sir Richard's mouth stiffened. "First let me say there were conversations between Langham and Madigan I knew nothing about. Langham tends to act quickly and decisively, which is why he is so good at his job. But this time, I fear he's gone too far."

Already he was trying to shift blame. So typical, Sarah thought. She'd spent a lifetime watching her aristocrat father declare his righteousness at the expense of others, sparing no one, least of all his own family. She braced herself for whatever bomb he was about to drop.

"The original deal was simple: Madigan would pose as a consultant and collect information on the obelisk—what it was, why this collector wanted it, that sort of thing. He also was meant to keep an eye on Evangelos

Rigas, whom we suspected of corruption. We now know it was worse than we thought: Rigas and several others up the food chain had been promised access to the firman in exchange for the obelisk and, more to the point, what it unlocked. As you know, the Greeks would do anything to get their hands on that document."

Sarah recalled the twin footprints at the Cadmeia crime scene and outside the expedition lab. "Did Danny know about Evan's implication?"

"Yes." Exhaling, he ran a hand across his neatly parted, if thinning, golden-brown hair. "But he didn't know the extent of it until he was in Cairo."

She put a hand up. "You have to break that down for me. What's in Cairo?"

"Ishaq Shammas, the antiquities dealer. He's serving a sentence in Tora."

"Danny was sent to the prison? To do what?"

"To tell Shammas he was in possession of a message found within the cave of Trophonius."

She shook her head. "That's a lie."

"A bluff. It was part of Langham's plan. Since Shammas is the only person known to be affiliated with this organization, Madigan was to ask Shammas who could appraise the find."

"But that's code for 'I want to sell.'"

"Or exchange. The ultimate goal was to exchange the map for the firman."

She was incredulous. "And Danny knew this?"

"Not until the very end, at which point he refused to go along. He gave Langham a right bollocking and cut him off."

She exhaled her relief. "Thank God."

"Not so fast, darling. This is where it gets sticky." Sir Richard's face went pale, and the corner of his mouth turned down. It took him a moment to utter the words: "No one's heard from Madigan since. My fear is that he has been abducted."

"Being incommunicado to being abducted is a big leap."

"Not really. When Madigan didn't answer calls, Langham asked me to intervene. My staff rang through to the hotel where he was staying and were told Madigan was taken away in an ambulance last night."

Her mind's eye was flooded with the images of the box of Valium, the bloodied sheets, the spent whiskey bottle. She recalled the Valium had come from an English chemist. "He was taking some medication. What do you know about his condition?"

Sir Richard cocked his head. "He hadn't talked to you about it?"

"He went out of his way to hide it from me."

"He probably did not want you to think him weak." He sighed. "He suffered from anxiety, some sort of post-traumatic stress related to the plane crash."

Sarah closed her eyes and hung her head. How could

she not have known? She blamed herself for not seeing Daniel's plight and supporting him when he most needed her. But more than that, she blamed her father for knowing—and pushing Daniel anyway.

"I don't suspect his disappearance had anything to do with his mental state," Sir Richard continued. "I've had my staff call every hospital and medical facility in Cairo, but Daniel Madigan hadn't been admitted at any. Worse yet, we tracked down the number plates and they weren't registered to an ambulance company at all. They belonged to some sort of warehouse." He paused. "And there's another item of concern. The abductors likely also have his personal belongings. His phone could easily connect him to us."

Sarah clenched her fists to keep from slapping him. She should have known his interest lay more in protecting his own hide than in rescuing his so-called friend. She would have walked away then had it not been for Daniel's plight. She bit her tongue for her partner's sake. "I suspect you haven't come to me for a confession, so tell me what it is you want."

"Fair enough." He reached into his jacket pocket and pulled out a folded sheet of paper. "Since Madigan's disappearance, Interpol have received a cryptic message from an unknown sender. I need you to tell me what it means."

Sarah felt mist on her face and looked up at the angry pewter sky. The drops descended with more urgency, swelling to a full-on rain. The moist air smelled of urine and dust. A homeless man sitting on the sidewalk made a tent out of his cardboard ground sheet and cowered beneath it, but the bowing Muslims persisted despite the storm.

Rain trickled down Sarah's cheeks like tears. She pushed a few wet tendrils of hair away from her face and kept walking, the words of the message muscling all other thoughts out of her mind.

> *Where eagles soar and the earth's fangs rise toward the sky,*
> *Where the eternal springs have withered*
> *And the air no longer smells of sweet earth,*
> *The mortal son of Dionysus awaits sacrifice.*
> *Let whosoever holds the key to his redemption bring it forth*
> *On the seventh night after the new moon of elaphebolion*
> *Following nine years of spiritual famine.*

Sarah knew exactly what it meant.

And she knew she was the one who held the key.

Thirty-one

Sumela Monastery,
393 CE

*A*ristea heard the crunch of stones and felt her head sway. She slowly blinked awake and saw the arid ground moving beneath her. The gray hide of a donkey's hind legs came into focus. She had been draped, facedown, like a sack of wheat onto the saddle. Without protest, the beast carried its load up the mountain.

She stroked the animal's ribs and commanded it to halt. The donkey stopped tenuously on the uphill path, and she reached for the saddle knob. With an effort that retold the extent of her injuries, she righted herself on the saddle. She clicked her tongue to urge the donkey onward.

She looked down and shuddered. The white vestment of her priesthood had been torn to shreds and fouled with blood. In an attempt to regain her modesty, she pulled together the tatters of linen as best she could.

She felt a throbbing sensation on her inner thigh and parted the linen to investigate. A bright-red, open wound surrounded by charred skin wept clear liquid. She had been burned.

There was a gap in her recollection. Though she liked to remember everything and learn from it, she was grateful for this lapse. Her last memory of the encounter in the cave was of the Pontian retreating with a satisfied sneer and one of the other men taking his place atop her. At that point, she must have passed out.

Stabs of pain in her pelvis caused her to fold forward and lay her head onto the beast's wiry mane. Nothing could offer her comfort. But the harm that had been inflicted upon her body did not compare with the greater calamity: the theft of precious objects from Apollo's sanctuary, and from so many others throughout Greece, in the name of religious hegemony.

Aristea cringed at the recall of the Roman senator's impure hands on the sacred *omphalos*. No mortal had the right to touch the navel stone that held the universal secrets divined by the sage Pythagoras, the gods' gift to the Earth. As a Delphic oracle-priestess in the line of the great Themistoclea, Aristea feared she'd failed her ancestor and the age-old promise to safeguard Pythagoras' formulae for the future of mankind.

Liberating the navel stone on her own, with no allies and on such difficult terrain, was impossible. Yet she could not let it be lost forever. She vowed to record its location so that, one day, others would come for it. She would ink it with her own blood if she had to.

The donkey rounded a bend, and the monastery

came into view. Beneath a mist of cloud, the hive of monks' cells and study halls hung from a precipitous cliff. She wanted to be repulsed by it, for it was built by the emperor who had quashed human liberties and requisitioned so much slaughter, but even after all that had happened to her, she could not find the hatred in her soul.

Aristea glanced behind her at the valley cut into the mountains and dreamed of her escape. She longed to be lost in the green embrace of nature, away from the false righteousness of senators and the grubby paws of cretins posing as judges. Alas, her moment would have to wait. Two of the men from the cave rode behind her, well farther down the path. The distance between her and them, she imagined, was occupied by their guilt.

At the path's end, the donkey lurched onto the courtyard to deliver its human cargo to the old monks in attendance. Aristea steadied herself to dismount, but her knees gave out and she crumpled onto the cobblestones. The monks scurried to her side, murmuring among themselves as if they weren't sure how to help her.

She looked up at the sun, imploring her patron god for strength. At a small square window beneath the roof eaves, Sophronios looked down at the commotion, then disappeared.

"Leave me be," she told the old men. She turned a shoulder to them and staggered to her feet. The pain was such that she saw double, yet she wanted no hypocrite's help.

From behind the wall of monks came a familiar voice. "Step aside."

She looked over her shoulder and saw the crowd part. Sophronios pushed his way through. He met her gaze and held up a woolen mantle. "I will see to this prisoner," he said.

Aristea let Sophronios drape the mantle over her shoulders and guide her away from the whispering monks to the dim corridor that led to her holding cell. He twisted the iron ring and pushed the door open.

She shuffled to the window and stood with her back to him. She did not want him to know how vulnerable she felt.

He closed the door. "What happened to you?"

Memories of the heinous act crashed through the gates of her consciousness. Her eyes filled with tears.

He asked again: "Who hurt you?"

Did he really not know? She took a deep breath to control the flood of emotion that threatened to overtake her. "Leave me." Her voice was so feeble she scarcely recognized it. "Please."

The monk said nothing else. The door creaked open, then slammed shut.

Finally alone, Aristea collapsed onto the stone bed. Her shoulders quaked with the silent sobs of martyrdom.

A series of knocks roused Aristea from deep sleep. Unsure where she was, she surveyed her dark surroundings. The scent of damp stone reminded her she was in the prison cell at Sumela.

"Who's there?" she croaked.

Sophronios came through the door and walked to her bedside. He placed a crust of bread and a bowl of something that smelled of boiled potatoes on the table next to her. He lit an oil lamp, and the room was suffused in amber light.

He pulled some folded clothes from under his arm and placed them on the foot of the bed. "A monk's tunic. It may be big, but it is clean."

Aristea winced as she sat up.

"How do you feel?" There was genuine concern in his voice.

The cool night air made her shiver. She wrapped the mantle tightly around her. "I hurt."

"I was informed of what happened." He shook his head. "I am sorry."

"No apology will ever restore the dignity of my oath. Your people have violated that which was most sacrosanct. No matter what god you believe in, such a crime is unforgivable."

Sophronios lowered his gaze. "You are right. I have prayed to the holy virgin to ease your suffering."

"Maybe your virgin will tell you the only way to ease my pain is to let me go."

He held up both hands. "Do not speak such blasphemy. Voices carry across these chambers."

She didn't bother to lower her voice. "I have nothing to hide."

He kneeled next to her. "I will help you," he whispered. "Such brutality will not happen again. I have told my brothers I accept responsibility for your soul. No one can come to this cell without my consent."

"Not even the emperor's butchers?"

"The emperor bows to the bishop. The church is stronger than the state." A bell tolled. Sophronios looked out the window. The sun's first rays glowed behind the mountain range. "It is time for morning prayers. I must go. I will be back later for your catechism."

The priestess sighed. Sophronios was offering his protection, but like everything else in that dismal place, it came at a price.

Thirty-two

Sarah arrived in Arachova just after the sun had completed its descent behind the crowded peaks of Mount Parnassus. In the fading light, the village clinging to the mountainside seemed like a distant memory, a postscript to a love letter.

Sarah parallel parked her hired Fiat in a tight spot along the main road and stepped out into the brisk air of the Parnassus high country. Diffuse saffron light spilled from the street lamps: fog had begun to roll in from the east. She raised her coat collar and crossed the street.

Standing beneath the eaves of a three-story apartment building, she unfolded the piece of paper on which she'd scribbled some notes earlier that day.

I Folia
Address?? Basement, no sign, in alley beneath
the clock tower
Lydia - surname unknown

Though it wasn't much, it was the most promising lead she had. Lydia, whose surname no one seemed to know, as if she were an urban myth, supposedly had information about the mysterious cult that had installed itself in Delphi. One of Sarah's sources—a lawyer who sat on the governing council of the Greek-god-worshipping sect Ellinais—even suggested Lydia was one of the Delphic cult's founding members.

"She's a little crazy," the lawyer had said, "but she'll give you an earful—if you can find her."

Several calls later, Sarah learned Lydia was last seen waitressing at I Folia, a traditional music club that operated only in winter, when Arachova's population swelled due to a nearby ski resort.

If Lydia's identity was hard to ascertain, the cult's practices and *raison d'être* were pure enigma. No doubt, a handful of neopagan groups had begun to proliferate in Greece. Strangled by the economic crisis and out of faith, a few had turned to the pagan methods of ancient worship. They were called Hellenic Reconstructionists, and their goal was to revive the religion of the dodecatheon—the twelve gods of Mount Olympus. They were the bane of the all-powerful Greek Orthodox establishment, whose holy men openly blasted the neopagans' godless ways.

But something told Sarah these people had far more sinister intent. It was why they—unlike other, similar groups—did not worship openly and why their leadership remained a tightly guarded mystery.

Sarah crumpled the paper and stuffed it into her pocket.

She ducked behind the building and followed a path uphill toward the eighteenth-century clock tower, which stood on a lone crag above the red-barrel-tile rooftops.

As the town climbed up the mountain, the roads turned to alleys paved with centuries-old cobblestones. She walked among rows of *petrina*—buildings made of local stone and decorated with ironwork balconies—whose chimneys released puffs of white smoke into the gathering fog. Her footfall reverberated on the empty alley, reminding her how alone she was.

Sarah ducked inside a pastry shop. The smell of sugar made her think of Christmases past. Her mother had always insisted on a huge buffet of sweets after Christmas lunch. Though the tradition had long since faded, that cloying scent always triggered the memory—and a sense of comfort.

Behind the case jammed with cakes and honey sweets, a woman scrubbed a pan. Sarah asked her for directions.

The woman wiped her hands on her apron. "Right at the top of the alley, then take the steps up to Eleutherias Street. You will see a red awning. Across the street is a *petrino* with a small basement. It's easy to miss. They like it that way. Keeps the tourists out."

Sarah nodded her thanks. "By any chance, do you know a local woman named Lydia?"

"Only one Lydia in this town. She lives not far from here, in the house with the black shutters that are closed winter and summer. What do you want with her?"

"I have a message from a friend."

The shopkeeper scoffed. "She doesn't have any friends." She leaned on the counter, only too eager to offer gossip. "She's not well, you know. She lost her child years ago and has been hiding since."

Sarah filed away the new information. She thanked the woman and walked out.

The wind howled through the alley. Hair whipping behind her and eyes watering from the cold, she leaned into the wind and continued uphill.

I Folia—which meant *the nest*—was indeed hard to find. With no windows and a door that appeared shuttered, the tiny basement could have been a storage room. Sarah walked down the steps and put her ear to the door. The faint sound of music came from inside. She was at the right place.

She opened the door and was immediately greeted by a wall of cigarette smoke. She stood at the entranceway, sussing out the place. It couldn't have been bigger than a thousand square feet. Sconces cast shadowy light on the exposed stone walls and granted dubious visibility to the room. At a traditional club known as a *rebetadiko*, people didn't come to see, anyway. They came to listen.

A few people—mostly men—sat at the small round tables, sipping from squat glasses, cigarette packets at the ready. Their attention was on a small stage at the far end of the room, on which two men sat cross-legged on tall stools, balancing instruments on their knees. One played the guitar, the other the bouzouki. Together they delivered the slow, soulful melodies known as *rebetika*—traditional Greek folk music from the turn of the twentieth century that had been kept alive by a culture loath to let go of its past, yet funneled underground lest it be touched by the grimy hands of commercialization.

Sarah spotted a sole female server at the bar, placing drinks on a deep aluminum tray. She was a waif of a woman, dressed in an ankle-length floral dress about two sizes too big, a brown wooly cardigan, and boots. Though there was no one near her, her lips moved, as if she were talking to herself.

Sarah watched her deliver the drinks to a table and return the tray to the bar. The woman stood idle, gazing at the stage and rocking back and forth.

Sarah approached her. She spoke in Greek, addressing the woman in the plural, a sign of respect. "Are you Lydia?"

The woman took a step back. The trembling bronze light accentuated the deep shadows beneath her cheekbones and the chestnut brows framing hazel eyes in which dwelled a naked madness. "How do you know my name?" Her voice was as fragile as the nightjar's trill.

Sarah did not answer, instead offering the code she was sure Lydia would understand. "After nine years of spiritual famine, the seventh night after the new moon of *elaphebolion* draws near."

She looked over both shoulders. "Let's talk outside." She called to the barman: "I'm going on my break."

Sarah followed Lydia out the door. They stood shoulder to shoulder in the pit of the basement.

Lydia pushed a shock of frizzy brown hair away from her face. "Did Delphinios send you?"

"Let's just say I have been summoned to Delphi for this occasion. Is Delphinios the cult leader?"

"So you don't know him." Disappointment darkened her gaze.

"No. But I understand you do."

Her smile was bittersweet. She looked up the stairs and spoke into the wind. "We haven't spoken in a long time. But I know he's coming for me." As if she'd just remembered something, she jerked her head toward Sarah. "Why am I telling you this? Who are you?"

"My name is Sarah. I've spent many years studying pagan rituals. I'm here to learn from this cult, but first I need to know what I'm getting into." She softened her gaze. "That's why I've come to you. I'm hoping you can tell me more about this Delphinios."

She shrugged. "We were lovers in the early aughts. He was American but knew everything about Greek mythology—the history of my people. He worshipped Apollo and believed he was the god's reincarnation. He had just begun to form the cult when I got pregnant with his child. I thought he'd be upset, but he was delighted. He said I was his goddess, destined to be the mother of a divine being. I was in love with him and wanted to believe what he believed."

Lydia shifted awfully quickly from a defensive stance to a willingness to share intimate details—a possible sign of mental illness, Sarah thought. She wondered how much of what she was hearing was reliable but pressed for answers anyway. "So you were part of this cult?"

"Oh, yes. I helped form it. I searched all over Greece for recruits. There are more neopagans than anyone realizes. They were looking for a way to organize, and Delphinios was a very charismatic leader. They saw his vision. After a while, people—Greeks and foreigners—started coming to us." She paused to push away the unkempt hair that kept falling over her eye. "A couple of years later, we began holding ceremonies. They were small at first, but as Delphinios gathered the artifacts, we added bathing rituals, burnt offerings, sacrifices . . ."

"What was your role in all this?"

"I was the priestess"— she smiled wistfully—"the human form of Gaia, as Delphinios liked to say. That was before Isidor came."

"Isidor?"

"The high priest. His knowledge of Apollo and ancient Greece was extraordinary. Eventually, my role diminished and Isidor took the lead. And then . . ." Her eyes misted, and she looked down.

Sarah put a hand on Lydia's bony shoulder. Like a tiny bird away from its nest, the woman was trembling. Sarah felt strangely close to her, perhaps because she, too, had known loss. "If you'd like to talk, I'm willing to listen."

Lydia reached inside her bosom and pulled out a locket hanging from a long chain. She opened it and showed Sarah a photo of her with a young girl. "Delphinios took her from me six years ago. He believed she was a special child with a higher purpose, so he was going to hide her from the world." Her voice cracked. "He said he'd come for me when he was ready, and we could be a family again."

The hairs on the back of Sarah's neck stood on end. A mother's hope was so inextinguishable, she could not fathom the truth: she had been used.

The barman swung open the door and gestured wildly at Lydia. "Get back inside. People are waiting."

She shrank at the admonition. Without a good-bye or even a glance at Sarah, she scurried in.

Sarah let a moment pass and entered the room. The haunting melody of an *amanes*, a song with distinct oriental sounds harkening back to the Ottoman occupation of Greece, had the audience rapt. Sarah stood in the shadows until she caught Lydia's gaze. When the woman glanced her way, Sarah lifted a hand.

It was more a sign of solidarity than a good-bye. Sarah didn't know why, but she felt for this frightened, lost woman. There was no doubt in her mind: they would see each other again.

Thirty-three

The message sent to Interpol was unambiguous in its reference to Delphi. The eternal springs of Castalia sat in a ravine between "the earth's fangs"—the Phaedriades, twin rocks that encircled Apollo's sanctuary, built into the rocky belly of Mount Parnassus. "The air no longer smells of sweet earth" surely referred to the sacred *pneuma*, the ethylene vapors the priestess Pythia supposedly inhaled before prophesying. Ethylene, a sweet-smelling gas, likely rose from a volcanic fault during ancient times. That fault was no longer active, so any trace of the gas had disappeared.

The most promising clue was the reference to a concrete date: *On the seventh night after the new moon of elaphebolion following nine years of spiritual famine.* In the sixth and fifth centuries BCE, the Greeks kept a calendar that began with the new moon after the summer solstice. The calendar, whose purpose was to mark the nation's festivals of sport, culture, and worship, contained twelve months, each named loosely for the festival it marked. *Elaphebolion*, named for the deer-hunting practices of the Dionysia festival, would have fallen between March and

April, depending on the lunar cycles.

The reference to the seventh day was significant, as well: the seventh of each month was dedicated to Apollo and marked with ceremonies, and sometimes sacrifices, celebrating the god's birthday.

The clues led to a date that was nearing. It was March 4, two days after the moon's first sliver had appeared in Delphi's indigo sky. If the message were to be taken literally, the cycle of rituals had begun; in another five days, the bearer of the key would be called forth.

Sarah pondered the facts while sitting at a *kafeneio* at the edge of town, away from the busy restaurants and bars on the main strip. After nightfall, the place was frequented by elderly Greek men who sat idle at small round tables, canes by their sides, nursing shots of watered-down ouzo.

She was the only woman there, but her presence went mostly unnoticed. Most of the men carried on playing backgammon, shouting obscenities when the dice didn't favor them. A pair of octogenarians talked openly about her, probably unaware the blonde English woman was fluent in Greek.

"Women have no shame these days. What is she doing in a men's house?"

"She's a tourist. She doesn't know."

"Where do you think she's from? Russia?"

"Maybe. She's pretty."

"Bah! Too skinny."

And on it went. Sarah acted as if she didn't hear a word of it. She wanted to be alone, invisible. It was what she needed to focus on her work, but there was more than that. She felt profoundly detached from people with ordinary lives—people who got married and had mortgages and went on summer holidays—like a ghost among the living.

The waiter, a wide-eyed chap from somewhere in the Balkans, came around the corner, a handled aluminum tray dangling from his finger.

"Double Greek coffee, no sugar." He spoke English with a thick accent. Albanian, she figured. "That'll keep you up all night." He winked.

"Maybe." She gave a weak smile and handed him five euros. "What goes on late at night in Delphi?"

He raised a thick, black eyebrow and pointed a thumb over his shoulder. "I have a motorcycle. I could show you."

"No, thanks." She blew on the surface of the coffee until the skin that had formed receded, revealing the black liquid beneath. She took a sip.

He counted out some coins and offered them to her. She waved them away. "Nothing goes on in Delphi at night. It's a ghost town. Eleven o'clock, everyone sleeps. You should go to Athens. I have some friends who could show you around."

"Thanks," she said, "but I'm fine here."

He shrugged. "As you like." He walked away.

Sarah took another sip of the strong coffee, fortifying herself for the night ahead. The streets of modern Delphi might be dead still by midnight, but beyond the city limits, when the moon was highest, something sinister was unfolding.

She sat back on the metal chair and gazed at the sky. The silver crescent was waxing, indicating the third day of the lunar cycle. She considered what she was about to do: reconnoiter the sanctuary of Apollo in the dark of night, hoping to find evidence of a practicing cult and its leader, the American known as Delphinios. She would study their movements and, when the moment came, come forth with information leading to the navel stone in exchange for Daniel's release. Every way she looked at it, it was folly.

She thought of the exchange with her father in Athens. He had handed her a pair of earrings embedded with a tracking device so that Interpol officers could pinpoint her coordinates.

"You've helped enough already." Staring at him coldly, she tossed the earrings onto the table. "I will do this my own way."

Though at that moment she needed all the support she could muster, she felt good about her actions. For the first time in her life, she had not allowed her father to rattle her. Unlike him, she was driven only by a need to do the right thing and was strong enough to walk that road alone, without any crutches.

She drained the coffee cup to the mud-like sediment and gathered her things. She slung her backpack over one shoulder and launched into the dimly lit street. Taking the long way to the ruins, she figured, would be about an hour's walk. No matter. She had all the time in the world.

And no time at all.

In the hours before dawn, Sarah sat beneath a platanus tree on the foothills of the Phaedriades, leaning against the cracked bark of its ancient trunk. The lushly leafed branches of the old specimen bent toward the earth, providing good disguise.

From that spot she had a good view of the sanctuary, some hundred meters below. In the wan light of the waxing moon, the broken columns looked like apparitions, stone sentries from another world, guarding what was left of their civilization.

Nothing stirred that night; not a nocturnal creature, not an insect, not even the wind that tore through the slopes of Parnassus on its way down to the valley. It had been a long time since she'd experienced such stillness. She tried to embrace it, to feel it in the depths of her heart, but it was for naught.

Steeped in the eternal stillness of the mountain, she felt at once protected and exposed, forced to be honest with herself. She admitted something circumstances hadn't allowed her to accept before that quiet moment: she was truly afraid. Not afraid of what would unfold that night in ancient Delphi or how she would pull off the mission she'd been charged with. She feared for Daniel.

He had been in jams before—chased, shot at, beaten, imprisoned—and had always managed to come out on top. But this time was different. He was vulnerable in a way she'd never seen in him. She agonized over the potentially lethal combination of benzodiazepines and alcohol with which he was toying, and the demons he insisted on fighting alone.

If he was indeed abducted, he was in bona fide trouble. It was difficult enough to fight against a powerful enemy with every wit intact, but nearly impossible to do so when compromised. His captor could easily detect a weakness and use it against him.

She touched the Tibetan prayer strand Daniel had given her and rolled the yak bone beads between her fingers. She closed her eyes and sent him a silent message: *I've got your back.* Whether he knew it or not, she would put everything on the line for him.

A light flickered downhill. Then another and another, all in a row, flames trembling like soldiers being marched to an uncertain fate. Sarah tensed. Though she'd known in theory she could encounter some sort of ceremony, watching it unfold was appalling. She struggled to reconcile her contempt for the defilement of an ancient place with her mandate to stay back and keep quiet.

The posse traveled a short distance up the mountain before stopping at the forecourt of the sanctuary and arranging in a semicircle. Sarah picked up her night-vision binoculars and trained them on the group. She counted about twenty heads, both male and female. They wore long white tunics, consistent with the costume of the ancients, draped at the shoulders and cinched at the waist. Long veils covered the backs of the women's heads but not their faces. The men wore simple headbands—except for one, presumably the high priest, who was crowned by a laurel wreath. All carried branches of laurel in one hand, a burning torch in the other.

The priest stepped out of the semicircle and approached a tripod perched within the temple. He walked to it and poured a liquid, possibly oil, into the vessel, moving his hand in a spiral pattern to cover the entire surface. When he finished, he extended his hands and raised his face to the sky. She could hear the faint whispers of a chant—an offering, she assumed, to the sun god.

He placed his torch on the bowl of the tripod and took a step back as it erupted into a flame several feet high. The other worshippers, hands crossed at the breast and faces glowing like molten gold in the firelight, began to chant a somber melody.

Sarah zoomed in on the illuminated faces. Though the image was grainy and detail was scant, her impression was that this was a multinational group. Whoever was behind this elaborate setup was open-minded enough to recognize polytheism wasn't an exclusively Greek ideal.

She trained her binoculars on the priest. In the style of the ancients, his black hair was cropped close to the head yet extended into tightly curled strands that rested upon broad shoulders. A short black beard followed the sharp angles of his jaw. From a distance and in artificial light, he looked like one of the marble statues that crowded the archaeological museum at Delphi.

As the flame in the tripod diminished to a low, slow burn, the priest stepped down to a flat-topped stone structure. He dipped the laurel branch in a bowl that sat at the edge of the structure and swept it across the stones, presumably anointing them with it.

From the dark edge of the Sacred Way, a cloaked figure approached. Sarah could not tell whether the person was male or female. The visitor walked slowly, with head bent toward the earth, holding something. She tried to zoom in but had already pushed the lens to the limit.

It wasn't until she heard a feeble bleat that she realized what it was. She felt nauseated at the thought of a living thing being slain to appease a deity. As an archaeologist, she had encountered the concept of sacrifice countless times and had accepted it as part of ancient ritual worship. But in modern, and presumably more enlightened, times, the act was no sacrament; it was wanton slaughter.

After a few minutes of chanting and gesticulating toward some unseen force, the priest circled the stone structure three times and stopped in front of the hooded figure. He accepted the small animal—a lamb or a goat, Sarah could not tell—and placed it on the flat surface.

The priest raised his arm over his head, and the object in his hand glinted in the firelight. The animal bleated more loudly, a final plea to be spared from the cruel blade. Sarah put down the binoculars and looked away, unable to watch the taking of a life.

In a moment, there was silence—complete, reverential, unbearable silence. She looked up. The men and women of Apollo engaged in a dance unaccompanied by music. Their bodies moved in unison as they orbited the altar, their arms flailing overhead and their gowns billowing as they pirouetted at the four points of the compass. In the copper glow of the ebbing fire, they looked like wraiths from the underworld.

The dancing stopped, and each disciple approached the tripod holding an oil lamp. With heads bowed, they accepted the fire—presumably the flame of knowledge— from the high priest. Then, one by one they fell into a line and followed the priest down the Sacred Way. Two acolytes stayed behind to extinguish the fire and erase any traces of the ritual.

Sarah used a strap to fasten the binoculars onto her head and ducked through the thicket of platanus and pine as she descended, following a wide arc to stay out of view of the sanctuary. The night-vision lenses allowed her to step with relative confidence over the rocky terrain, so she pushed the pace, her hurried steps in stark contrast with the slow, measured gait of the group following the snaking path downhill.

She reached a vantage point above the way and crouched behind a boulder, watching the procession of light approach from the opposite direction. The tap of the priest's staff and the rhythmic swish of fabric were the only sounds fouling the stillness of the mountain.

As they walked past, she could see their faces more clearly. The priest was hypervigilant, his gaze darting across the rocky landscape. He was younger than he had appeared at a distance—somewhere in his thirties, she figured.

Behind him was the hooded visitor, followed by seven men and seven women, each face marked by the same expression of trance—or stupor. Despite the ancient directive, *Know thyself*, that had long been the mantra at Delphi, the modern-day adherents seemed less like self-actualized souls and more like sheep responding to the bell of a faceless master.

Sarah watched the priest lead them around a bend she hadn't noticed before. She craned her neck for a closer look. The procession stopped. A low murmur among the disciples escalated into a cadenced chant. Among the classical Greek utterances, she could make out the phrase

"By the grace of the god"; the rest was unintelligible.

Through the wall of disciples, she could no longer see the priest. She surveyed the vegetation around her and zeroed in on an old platanus with twisted branches. She skulked up the trunk and onto a thick branch and wrapped her limbs around it.

The priest was nowhere. If this was indeed an oracular ceremony, he and the visitor had probably withdrawn into a secret chamber, perhaps an improvisation of the *adyton*—the room within the sanctuary in which the Pythia of ancient times delivered her prophecies—that had long since been decimated.

It was a long while before the priest and visitor emerged from the crags. Somewhere back there was a place of worship; she could not tell what or where, but it wouldn't be difficult to find out once the crowd had dispersed. She lay on the branch, motionless, and waited.

The priest sent his adherents away, and they all disappeared down the hill. The visitor lowered his hood—he appeared to be of Arabic descent—and bowed at the priest. He offered him a bundle and backed away, retreating in a different direction.

The holy man stood alone. Sarah studied his face. There was a sadness in his dark eyes she found oddly disconnected to the scene that had just unfolded. She found herself staring at him, drawn into his melancholy gaze. Was this Lydia's Isidor?

He pulled out a small golden bell from the folds of his robe. He rang it once, releasing a delicate chime that echoed across the mountain like the chirp of a bird.

Another figure wrapped in a thick blanket from head to toe emerged from the shadows, shuffling across the dry brush. Sarah felt a sharp pang in her gut at the sight of the modern-day Pythia. She imagined the woman beneath the woolen covers—drugged, exhausted, exploited—and silently cursed the men who'd put her in that spiritual prison.

The priest put his arm around her hunched form and led her down the mountain. It was a scene both tender and revolting: the perpetrator and the victim in an embrace, walking in step toward a shared reality.

They disappeared around a bend. Sarah checked the time: it was going on five o'clock. Soon the sun would peek through the distant mountains, heralding the advent of a new day. She let herself hang from the tree limb, then jumped and landed with a soft thump.

She checked her surroundings—all clear—and crept down to the area from which the Pythia had emerged. Her heart knocked against her rib cage, protesting what she was about to do. It was risky, but she needed answers.

In the dead quiet, she could hear her own breath rise and fall as she searched for evidence of an oracular chamber. Nothing was obvious. Her gaze traveled up the Sacred Way to the sanctuary. Her intuition told her the

Pythia's new lair was located directly beneath the spot where the *adyton* once was. At the height of the oracle's power, priests supposedly used a network of tunnels that connected the *adyton* with antechambers. Because archaeologists had tried to find the network to no avail, it had long been assumed that either it never existed or it had been destroyed in earthquakes.

And yet something was there, deep within the thicket and crags, invisible to the untrained eye. Sarah was determined to find it.

She ducked into a wooded area and walked until she came to a dead end. It had to be the place. Her eyes registered every square inch of the landscape, looking for an entry in the jumble of boulders and gnarled tree branches.

She squinted as something caught her eye. Someone who hadn't spent as much time as she had on cliffs and in caves would never have seen it: a fissure behind a massive boulder, just big enough for one slender-bodied person to enter.

Sarah held her breath as she considered her options. She had no idea what—or who—she would find inside. She could easily be walking into a trap.

She thought of the message and of Daniel. Time was running out for him. She had only four days to save his life. She closed her eyes and inhaled deeply. It calmed her racing heart long enough for her to access the courage she needed.

She found a handhold in the boulder, which was at

least a foot taller than she was, and used it to hoist herself to the top. She slid down the other side and landed in front of the fissure. She slipped her hand inside. The rock's surface was smoother than she'd expected—an indication, she thought, that the passage was carved out rather than natural.

She wedged her body into the opening and shimmied inside. It was as she had thought: the entrance was narrow as to not invite suspicion, but the passage itself was wide enough to accommodate a single person.

She walked gingerly over the loose gravel of the tunnel floor and steadied herself against the cold, hard rock. The feeling was akin to holding the hand of a cadaver. The pitch-black, tubular passage closed in around her, and she had a flashback to the cave of Trophonius. She willed it out of her mind so she could focus on the task at hand. At that moment, any distraction could be deadly.

The narrow corridor opened up. A vaguely sweet scent laced the stuffy air. As she approached the antechamber at the mouth of the tunnel, the odor became more pervasive. It had the sweetness of overripe fruit with the tang of musk.

Sarah's eyes widened as she realized she smelled pure ethylene. She knew the gas in small doses could cause trance and hallucination followed by amnesia; in large doses, it could cause brain damage and even death. So it was with the priestesses of antiquity. Some had mild reactions, whereas others had flailed violently as they spoke in tongues. In every case, the latter died.

Through her night-vision binoculars, the antechamber resembled a gray tomb. She entered anyway. At the far end there was an opening. She followed it, certain of what she would find there.

She was spot-on. The chamber on the other side, a space no bigger than six feet square, was the Pythia's lair. Nothing was there except five spent torches surrounding a tripod.

Sarah looked down. Laurel leaves—some intact, some crushed—littered the ground. And there it was: a crack, probably a foot wide, directly beneath the priestess' seat. The smell of ethylene was thick, and it made her lightheaded. She walked toward the crack and confirmed the gas was emanating from the earth.

Impossible, she thought. Some of the world's most highly regarded archaeologists and geologists had searched for years for evidence of ethylene, and none had found any. It had long been accepted that the chasm in the earth that had allowed the delivery of the vapors had closed, perhaps due to an earthquake or other natural event.

Even ancient historians corroborated the theory. According to recorded fact, the oracle of Delphi had been crippled because the vapors had ceased. Without the trance, the Pythia could dispense no oracle. And without an oracle, there was no reason for anyone to make the pilgrimage to the cliffs of Mt. Parnassus. The coffers of the Delphians had dried up and the city's power had waned, leaving the way free for the Byzantines to annihilate the operation.

How could ethylene possibly flow forth again? She searched her mind for an answer but came up with nothing. The inhalation of the gas distorted her thoughts and impaired her ability to make sound decisions. She removed her binoculars and rubbed her stinging eyes. A choking sensation seized her throat, and she let out a violent cough. She needed to get out of there.

She turned around, only vaguely aware she could see nothing in the utter blackness. Driven by instinct, she reached for a wall—anything that could steady her long enough to put the binoculars back on. Her hands landed on something firm but warm. It twitched and contracted at her touch.

Sarah froze.

Strong hands grasped her upper arms, and her knees weakened. An accented baritone voice boomed across the stone womb: "What is it you seek?"

Thirty-four

A gray fog shrouded Daniel's eyes as he woke. He grimaced. It felt as if an ice pick had been driven through his brain.

Still queasy from whatever drug had been injected into him, he summoned all his strength to roll onto his side and sit up. He looked around. He was in a windowless room, lying on a futon sprawled out on the floor. A small table with a tall glass of water was next to him. He salivated with desire for the liquid and licked his parched lips. He did not dare touch it. He smelled the cedar of the plank siding that lined the walls. It reminded him of mountains and gave him comfort.

He rubbed the back of his neck in a futile attempt to calm the pain. He absently regarded his own appearance: a crumpled, untucked khaki button-down, coarse with dried sweat, hung loosely over ripped jeans streaked with dirt. It looked like he had either been in a struggle or been dragged through the woods. He had no recollection of any of it.

The last thing he remembered was his hotel room in Cairo. He recalled texting Sarah moments before the "engineering" worker knocked and his world went black. He felt in his pockets for his phone and looked around for any sign of his belongings. Of course it had all been taken.

He wondered if Langham had caught wind of his absence, and if it would even matter. To Langham's kind, people like Daniel were expendable, good only while they were offering something. The moment they were caught, all bets were off.

No, Langham, or even his buddy Richard Weston, was not coming to his rescue. Wherever he was, and who-ever his captor was, he'd have to rely on his own wits to escape. For the first time in his life, he wondered if he had it in him.

A suspicion crossed his mind, and he looked around the room. There it was, in a corner of the ceiling: a small glossy black eye registering his every move. He observed the heavy metal door with the combination entry. His opponent had a singular advantage. All Daniel could do was sit and wait. Since they knew he had come to, the wait probably wouldn't be long.

His hunch was right. About ten minutes later, the pneumatic door sighed open and a barrel-chested man with curly black hair and a thick moustache entered the room.

The man looked Daniel up and down. "You come with me," he said in a raspy voice and an accent Daniel couldn't place.

Daniel leaned on one arm and hoisted himself off the

floor with some effort. His body felt creaky and compressed; at that moment, his physical reality was that of a man twice his age. He gritted his teeth and showed no pain.

The emissary held the door open, and the two men locked gazes for a fleeting moment. Daniel saw ruthlessness in his foe's expression and shot him a hard glare in return.

"To the end of the corridor and up the stairs."

Daniel didn't turn to acknowledge the command. He walked with a stiff gait down the dark hallway, also paneled in cedar. *Up the stairs.* They must have held him in some sort of basement.

Or sub-basement. The twelve or so steps up led to another windowless space. He squinted as his eyes were assaulted by the fluorescent lighting overhead. He furtively surveyed his surroundings, searching for any opportunity to flee. The place was tight as a vault.

"Stop." The raspy voice ricocheted off the narrow halls.

Daniel did as told. He heard a click and looked over his shoulder. The burly guy pushed open a door hidden within the paneling. Daniel hadn't noticed it as he walked by. The disguise was remarkable. He wondered how many other surprises the facility concealed.

He walked into the dark room. A series of lights came on, illuminating in bursts the four corners of the room. Daniel felt a chill ripple down his spine as he realized all four walls were lined with display cases: glass shelves with glass fronts and mirrored backs, each holding a collection of guns. There must have been two hundred specimens, from pistols to Uzis. An eerie blue light illuminated the weapons, as if they were objects to be admired, like art rendered in cold, hard steel.

He turned to his escort. "What the hell is this?"

The man was expressionless. Without taking his eyes off Daniel, he tipped his head in the direction of the ceiling. "It's showtime."

Daniel looked up to see a small projector. In front of him, an image began to materialize. The pixels, at first loosely arranged, came together in a tight configuration to reveal a man's form. It was a hologram.

"Hello, Daniel Madigan." He was American. "Welcome."

Daniel tensed. "Am I, now?"

He chuckled. Both the image and the sound were so realistic, it was hard to believe it was an illusion. "Course you are, son. Anyone who has something of value to me is welcome in my home."

Daniel's eyes narrowed. "And where is home? Hard to tell when you're kept in a dungeon."

He let out a loud belly laugh. "You sure got a sense of humor, boy. Let's just say some things are best left to unfold."

Daniel studied the man's rotund face, the ruddy skin cut by the channels of time. That and his gray, wiry, and windblown hair suggested an advanced age—he was in his seventies, Daniel figured—but his robust demeanor and razor-sharp glare suggested he was a foe to be reckoned with.

Something about him looked familiar, and Daniel searched his memory for a recollection. He couldn't place him. "Whatever you say, pal."

"I detect an accent. Where are you from, Daniel?"

He wanted to say, *None of your business*. But another glance at the walls of weapons convinced him to keep his mouth shut. "Tennessee."

"Beautiful country, Tennessee. Let me guess: you're from the mountains. Little town called Briceville, near the coal mines."

"That's right." Daniel clenched his teeth and exhaled sharply through his nose. "I'd like to know who I'm talking to."

He smirked. "Just call me sir."

Was he kidding? "What do you want with me, sir?"

"For now, I just want you to shut up. I'm asking the questions." He rubbed a fleshy cheek. "Tell me something, son. Was Johnny Madigan your daddy?"

The guy obviously had done his homework. "What's that to you?"

Sir ignored the question. "Johnny and I were in basic training together, back in the day. Only he didn't have what it takes to stay in the Army. Too lazy, and a wicked booze habit to boot. But I'm not telling you anything you don't know, am I?"

Daniel spoke behind clenched teeth. "Just get to the point."

"I saw old Johnny again not that long ago. We met up

at a bar in some small town up in hillbilly country, had a few drinks." He reached back and pulled out a folded newspaper from his jeans' back pocket. He unfolded it and read aloud. "On February 21, about one in the morning, a man drove off the road, plunging his car down a barren cliffside." He tossed the paper onto a table. "Let me summarize: all that was left of the victim was a pile of bone and mangled flesh and a bloodied ID card that read: John Patrick Madigan, born April 11, 1948."

The lingering nausea stirred his gut, and Daniel fought back the urge to retch. Was it true or an elaborate ruse to weaken him?

"Poor Johnny Madigan. Just couldn't help himself. He was wasted on the local moonshine." He sneered. "Like father, like son, I guess."

Daniel clenched his fists. If the real man were standing before him, he would have struck him senseless, consequences be damned. A bead of sweat formed on his forehead, so hot was his anger. "Why should I believe you?"

"Because I'm the maker of your fate, boy." Sir's voice thundered. "On your knees."

Daniel felt the burly guy's hand clamp his shoulder and bear down, pushing him to the floor. Even after forcing Daniel to kneel, he did not release his steel grip. Daniel's left side buckled, but he was determined not to let the pain show in his face.

"That's better," the American said. "Now let me tell

you the reason you're here. My friend Ishaq Shammas tells me you are the keeper of an age-old secret I've been trying to get my hands on for a mighty long time. Know what I'm referring to?"

"I might."

The holographic likeness paced in front of Daniel. After a long pause, he stopped and faced his visitor again, his deep-set blue eyes glinting with anticipation. "For more than ten years, I've followed leads that have taken me to dead ends. And now I'm so close. So let me cut to the chase. The map you told Shammas about . . . where is it?"

Daniel's lips curled into a snarl. "I believe I owe you nothing."

"That right? Well, I beg to differ." A glance at his henchman yielded a blow to the back of Daniel's head.

Daniel landed headfirst on the polished wood floor. His vision faltered like a lightbulb shorting out, and he thought he might lose consciousness. Thick hands grabbed the back of his shirt and hoisted him upright. The room spun.

"Has Ayberk changed your mind, or do you need more convincing?"

Daniel put the name and the accent together to figure out the strongman was Turkish. Not that it mattered. "Do your worst, pal. I'm prepared to take the information six feet under."

A hint of static crackled across the hologram. Sir's expression turned steely. He picked up an iPad and swiped. "Does this person look familiar?" He turned the tablet toward his captive.

It was a snap of Sarah sitting against a rock wall, knees curled to her chest, tousled hair spilling around her bent head. The camera flash bounced off her black climbing suit. The photo was taken at night—or inside a cavern.

Daniel felt her distress more than his own. But he knew any association between the two of them would put Sarah in grave danger.

Sir narrowed his eyes and smirked, and Daniel knew what was coming. "Sarah Weston, PhD, thirty-seven years old, field archaeologist, educated at Cambridge University, daughter of British aristocrat Richard Weston and American actress Alexis Sinclair, now deceased. Last assignment: Saudi Arabia, working in an expedition headed by none other than yourself. So I would say you *do* know her, and judging by the look on your pathetic face"—he leaned forward and smiled—"you're in love with her."

Daniel felt an inner tremble and his hands shook with rage. If the opportunity to kill this psychopath presented itself, he wasn't sure he'd pass it up. The emotion unsettled him, made him direct his anger inward.

"What's the matter, Danny boy?" It was what Johnny Madigan called his son when he was a boy. "Worried about your girlfriend? Well, you should be. My intelligence tells me one of you has the information I seek. So I have decided to extend the same hospitality to both of you." His face collapsed into the expressionless stare of an assassin. "Let's see which one of you cracks first."

The hologram dissolved, but the brutal presence lingered. Daniel knew he was being watched—and manipulated.

"Let's go," Ayberk barked.

Daniel cast a final glance around the munitions room before following the Turk out the door. He took mental inventory: an M2 Browning machine gun, a variety of AK assault rifles, a grenade launcher, likely Chinese. Some of the firearms were Army issue and not easy for a private collector to get a hold of. He harbored no illusions about his captor's sinister intent.

Ayberk wrapped a fleshy paw around Daniel's arm. "I said, let's go."

As he turned to leave, Daniel noticed a gap in the otherwise perfectly arranged case. Two of the guns were missing.

Thirty-five

The caverns beneath Delphi's springs radiated a wet chill. Shivering, Sarah vaguely recalled the high priest hoisting her over his shoulder and carrying her down a dark passage to the depths of the cave. Impaired by the ethylene, she was too weak to fight him and, though conscious, too disoriented to imprint the route.

Despite a heroic attempt to stay awake, she'd ended up sleeping off the effects of the drug—for how long, she didn't know. In the dark, she felt around the tomb-like space and touched the ceiling from a seated position. She ran her hand across the stone and pulled back when the sharp edges tore her palm. She sucked the open wound, tasting warm blood laced with the salt of perspiration.

Unable to stand, she crawled on all fours, occasionally extending a hand to assess her surroundings. She surmised she was in a chamber that measured no more than five feet deep, three feet across, and at most four feet high. She sat back, leaning on the rough stone. She could hear her breath rise and fall, and the sound made her keenly aware of the passage of time. Time she could ill afford to lose.

A pale light flickered like a bolt of lightning. She froze and stared at the spot, letting her eyes adjust. The light illuminated a tubelike passage no wider than a drain pipe. The fire of adrenaline was lit in her gut.

The light grew brighter. She smelled the familiar charred-earth scent of a hemp wick burning in a pool of oil.

Someone was approaching.

Her breaths grew more rapid, and she instinctively shrank into a corner. There was nowhere to hide.

In the dead stillness, her ears amplified every sound—the rustling of fabric, the shuffling of feet, her own agitated heartbeat.

The white light of a lantern flooded the cell. She raised a hand to guard her eyes from the shock of sudden radiance. When her eyes adjusted, she lowered her hand and saw the kneeling white-gowned figure framed in a pale halo.

Sarah squinted for a better look. Before her was a girl, likely prepubescent and so thin her bones showed in startling detail. A wreath of twigs encircled uncombed light brown hair that reached to the middle of her back.

"What is your name?" Her voice was high-pitched, fragile.

"I'm Sarah. What's yours?"

"They call me Phoebe, in honor of Apollo. Phoebus was one of the god's names. It means bright."

"It's beautiful. Who named you?"

"My father." A faint smile crossed Phoebe's lips and she looked off, as if daydreaming. "He is Apollo's manifestation on Earth."

Sarah was disgusted that a child had been led to believe this. She kept her thoughts to herself. "And your mother?"

The smile was wiped away. "I don't remember my mother. She left me years ago."

The girl obviously had been fed carefully constructed lies. "And what do you do here, Phoebe?"

"I speak the words of Apollo. I am his chosen."

Sarah recalled the hunched figure walking out of the oracular tunnel in Isidor's arms. Realizing it was Phoebe turned her stomach. These people had conscripted a young girl to the role of priestess, forcing her to inhale ethylene and deliver ersatz prophecies to men who'd likely paid a mint to witness the modern-day oracle. It was inconceivable.

Despite her rising anger, Sarah kept a straight face. "Do you go to school at all?"

"My father doesn't want me to go to school. He says I'm too special." Phoebe's gaze darted from wall to wall. "Isidor has taught me to read. He brings me books sometimes. I'm not supposed to talk about it."

"There's nothing wrong with books, Phoebe. Knowledge sets us free."

"I know things books can't teach you." She offered her palms to Sarah. "I'll show you."

Sarah placed her hands lightly on the girl's palms.

Phoebe's eyes moved behind closed lids. The two remained in that position for a long moment before Phoebe's brow furrowed and eyes blinked open. The girl pulled her hands away.

"What have you seen?" Sarah asked.

A shuffling sound came from the chute beyond the chamber. Phoebe snapped her head toward it. "He mustn't find me here. I've got to go." She cast a glance at Sarah, blew out the flame of the kerosene lantern, and scurried out of the chamber.

The sound grew closer. This time, Sarah felt no anxiety about the impending encounter. Her mind dwelled on the young waif who had been lied to and abused yet knew nothing of it. The outrage she felt over the despicable situation, and an inexplicable need to protect that child, fortified her for whatever happened next.

Once again, light flickered beyond the chamber, casting long shadows onto the cave wall. Sarah sat with her knees to her chest and waited. Within seconds, a man dressed in long white robes entered. She recognized him straightaway.

With his honey-colored skin, deep-set brown eyes, and long, straight nose culminating in an arrow-like tip, the high priest looked like one of the iconic saints painted onto the rock of the monasteries in Trabzon. In his eyes was a combination of serenity and fierce intelligence that Sarah found slightly disconcerting.

"Sarah Weston," he said with a heavy Greek accent.

"I'm Isidor. I am happy to see you're feeling better."

It unsettled her to hear him call her by name. She sensed that wasn't all he knew. "Thank you for your concern, Isidor. Now, please show me the way out."

He smiled. "Follow me."

Crawling at first, then standing upright as the tunnel widened, she followed Isidor through a subterranean network that easily spanned a quarter of a mile. At the far side of the tunnel, Isidor stopped and pointed to an opening. "I'd like to show you something." He gestured for her to enter. "Please."

Sarah ducked inside. Isidor followed. He held up his lantern and illuminated a fragment of limestone carved with *E*—the Greek letter epsilon.

A look of surprise crossed Sarah's face. She was certain she was looking at a piece of the original pediment that capped the temple. Another object from antiquity presumed lost, hidden underground to satisfy the whims of a collector who valued his own indulgence above the right of humanity to understand its past.

Isidor lowered the lantern, and shadows trembled across the stone. "Do you know what this means?"

There were as many theories about the sacred symbol's meaning as there were philosophers in antiquity. Even the Pythians in the golden age of Delphi couldn't agree on its significance and had endless debates about it. She was familiar with Plutarch's essay on the subject, but even that was inconclusive. She shook her head. "No one knows the true meaning of epsilon."

The intensity of his gaze held her captive. "You disappoint me, Dr. Weston. I was hoping you'd be a worthier adversary."

"Listen. I don't know what sort of game you're playing, but I want no part of it. I'm not here to entertain you or your pagan friends."

"Then what are you doing here? Aside from spying, I mean."

She didn't answer. He probably knew her story anyway.

"Let me guess. You are looking for your American friend." He pursed his lips. "I don't think he'll survive the night."

The urgency of Daniel's plight gave Sarah a new burst of strength. "Let him go. He doesn't have what you want."

He turned to her. In the demilight, his facial bones seemed chiseled by the hand of an ancient sculptor. "Your friend's release isn't up to me. It's up to you."

"I will do nothing until I see him."

She had expected a negotiation. Instead, Isidor shifted his gaze to the stone fragment. He ran his hand across the linear grooves that formed the letter. "The one who devised this symbol is immortal. Even after thousands of years, mankind cannot comprehend his teachings, though it is all in plain sight."

The distraction irritated her. "What does this have to

do with the matter at hand?"

"A long time ago, someone buried a message in the cave of Trophonius."

She stayed silent, expressionless.

"That message may lead to one of antiquity's greatest mysteries. The original *omphalos* stone has been missing since Delphi fell into Roman hands in the fourth century. It is said that the newly minted Christians, who were obsessed with snuffing out paganism, carried the stone and other temple treasures to Anatolia. They also took a prisoner: the last priestess of Delphi. According to legend, she escaped captivity and returned to Greece but did not survive. It is thought she left behind a map outlining the location of the stone." He took a step forward, standing so close she could feel his warm breath as he spoke softly. "I need to know if you have that map."

She studied Isidor's face. She didn't see the fire of a zealot or the madness of a killer in his melancholy brown eyes. There was more to his story. "Even if I had, why would I tell you?"

"Because what is carved on the *omphalos* stone is . . . a vital truth from antiquity that can easily be misused. It cannot fall into the wrong hands."

She laughed. "Let me weigh the facts: you have stolen important antiquities. You condone the sacrifice of animals in the most brutal way. You intoxicate and manipulate a child for your own means. And you have abducted a man." Her face flushed with rage. "The way I see it, Isidor, you—and whoever is behind all this—are not worthy of that information."

Isidor lifted the lantern to illuminate his face. His expression was serene, unfazed. "Look at me, Sarah. I am not the enemy."

The light on his gauzy white gown brought into focus a detail Sarah had not noticed before. Her gaze followed the strip of black leather hanging around his neck down to its end, which was tucked beneath the fabric. As the light rendered the gown diaphanous, she noticed the amulet resting on his heart. It was a configuration of six dots in a distinct pattern.

Certain he wouldn't stop her, she reached for the chain and pulled the amulet out of his gown. She held the small marble object, warm with his body heat, in her palm. It was the other half of the amulet she'd found outside the museum at Thebes. For the first time, she realized nothing was as it seemed.

Sarah looked up at the man in priest's attire. "So that's the answer."

Thirty-six

Mount Melá,
393 CE

As the early morning breeze whistled through the orchards beneath the monastery, a single saffron-hued leaf sailed through the mist before landing on a carpet of russet and gold. The scent of burning pine, familiar and comforting, anointed the air. Autumn had settled in earnest on Mount Melá.

Though she remained captive, Aristea found a glimmer of joy in the daily morning walks with Sophronios. It had been his idea to deliver her lessons in the embrace of nature: anything to convince her to believe his book of lies. She had no use for his rhetoric but appreciated his gentle manner and his acquiescence to debate. He was unlike his brethren, who insisted on cramming their ideals down the throats of dissenters, waving the banner of harmony through homogeneity.

She stole a glance at Sophronios, who walked silently next to her, clutching his tattered codex of teachings. "You seem distracted this day, Brother Sophronios. What thoughts weigh on your mind?"

He continued to look straight ahead. "No more than the ordinary."

She sensed he held something back. She felt a curious urge to probe further but, for the sake of propriety, let it go. "Perhaps we should forgo today's lesson, then."

He stopped abruptly and turned to her, surprised. "That is impossible. I cannot forsake my duty in the name of the Lord and the holy mother."

In a way, Aristea felt pity for the monk. For all his dogma and his allegiance to the conventions of the church, he had no true foundation for liberating his soul. It was, perhaps, why he needed to hide in the misty realm of Sumela, away from earthly desires and anything that could shatter his fragile sense of virtue. But he had been nothing but kind to her, so she forgave his inability to veer from the prescribed order. "As you wish." She continued walking. "What does your duty require of me today?"

"Today we will speak of heaven and hell." He fumbled with his holy book. "It is a story of darkness and light. We mortals have the power to choose between the two. Yet we do not always choose wisely."

"Tell me, Sophronios: what is your heaven?"

"Ah, the kingdom of the age to come." He turned his gaze skyward. "It is a place where souls reside in pure love and bliss. Where there is no want nor conflict nor vice. None of the sins of our earthly bodies exist anymore. There is only the divine union, absolute and everlasting."

"And, pray tell, how do you reach this place?"

"By submitting to God's will and following divine law during your earthly life. If you do this, upon your death you will be granted a seat in paradise for all eternity." He stopped and glanced at her, seemingly for emphasis. "It is what all mortals should strive for."

A gust tousled her long black locks. She pushed the hair away from her face so he could see the conviction in her eyes. "This paradise you speak of exists within us. It is here and now; it is not a reward after death. These tales of a distant kingdom that can be reached only after our bodies perish were made for those who cannot access that state in life."

"How can one reach such an exalted state when all life is suffering? Humanity is given to so many ills . . . desire, greed, cruelty to its own kind. Only by dedicating our lives to God can we transcend our mortal weakness."

Aristea had a ready answer but paused to revel in the moment. The dialogue with Sophronios was the highlight of her otherwise miserable days. Though they disagreed on all points, she respected a man who, though wholly given to his faith, allowed another to articulate an opposing view without judgment or confrontation. In that regard, they were not so different.

"Forgive my protest, Brother Sophronios," she said. "Humanity is defined by its struggles, not doomed by them. It is in the way we endure those struggles that we transcend our lower nature and enter a higher realm." She reached down and picked up a dry, russet leaf. "This leaf has fallen from its mother and withered. Yet the tree does not mourn the loss. While barren, it stands tall, ready to bear the burden of winter, for it knows that through hardship comes renewal." She crumbled the leaf and let the pieces fall from her hand. "We are one with nature, Sophronios. Our travails are the same as the tree's or the wolf's or the lowliest insect's. I submit to you that every lesson worth learning can be found in these woods, these mountains . . . not in the book you clutch with such fervor."

"Who among us can endure struggles like the insect does? None but the most enlightened." His hooded head swayed in the wind. "Do not be fooled by the beliefs of your ancestors, priestess. Human nature is bound to the influence of temptation and sin. Unless tempered, it corrupts men's hearts."

"Human nature is not something to be despised. With all its flaws, it is many-colored, complicated, and deep. Why scorn something as beautiful as free will? Why suppress the human spirit?" She knew her words would be perceived as harsh but spoke them anyway. "Following a canon created to temper human nature leads not to salvation but to spiritual slavery."

His face tightened. Angst settled into the folds of his forehead. For the first time, he seemed frustrated by his inability to break through her iron-clad defenses.

"I should have been more tactful," she said. "Forgive me."

"It isn't that." He exhaled. "I must be truthful, for it is the only way I know. My superiors are questioning me about your conversion. They are less patient than I." His gaze lingered on hers, something he rarely allowed. "I vowed to protect you, but I do not know how much longer I will be able to do so."

She nodded. "I understand. I do not want you to endanger your favor with the church. I am prepared to accept the consequences." She turned on her heel and followed the path back to the monastery. Her heart hammered against her rib cage. She interpreted it as a warning. Longing to be alone, she began to run.

"Aristea!" Sophronios called behind her.

She did not stop. She ran uphill until she reached the arched entrance into the stony realm of the lower cells. At that moment, her only refuge was her prison.

That night, sleep eluded Aristea. She spent long hours gazing out the window, her slim, dark fingers wrapped around the iron bars that held her against her will.

She could not shake Sophronios' words from her consciousness. He'd made it plain that the day of her persecution drew nigh. Looking deep within her heart, she'd always known it. She had just lulled herself into a sense of false security, reluctant to accept that she was being sheltered by the enemy. How could she, a creature of exceptional logic and clarity, allow herself such delusion?

In the stars smattered across the midnight sky, she searched for her ancestors, mighty women who spoke the truth at any cost and who would have sooner died than betray the mysteries of their order. It gave her comfort to know she would soon be among them.

A faint sound made her turn abruptly toward the door. She held her breath and listened. *Footsteps.*

She walked to the door and placed her ear on the splintered wood. The footfalls grew louder . . . louder . . . and then stopped. Fabric rustled. Metal clinked.

They had come for her. She curled her fingers into fists to stop her hands from trembling.

Metal scraped against the keyhole. The key engaged, and two clicks resonated as if they were cracks of thunder.

Aristea stood her ground. *Let them come.*

The door opened slowly, and the familiar visage was illuminated by the moonbeams. Sophronios started, clearly not having expected to find her awake. He hurried inside and shut the door.

She took a step back. "You should not be here."

"I took the risk," he whispered. "I have come to warn you. The archbishop of Byzantium has sent a council to question the converts. Those who do not answer satisfactorily will be taken away—" He pursed his lips and looked toward the window.

"Do not fret about me, Sophronios. If this is my fate,

so be it."

He peeled off his hood garment and exposed shoulder-length raven hair. She was shocked to see him remove the symbol of his piety. He held up a bolt of fabric.

In the dark, it took her a moment to realize it was a folded monk's habit. "What is the meaning of this?"

"This I do with all my heart." He lifted a corner of the folded garment and exposed a blade. Its sharp edge gleamed in the moonlight. "There is a boat waiting at the edge of the Black Sea. If you hurry, you can reach it before dawn."

Her eyes misted. "But your oath . . ."

"My oath compels me to help the innocent. If it is a sin to be devoted unconditionally to one's faith, then I am as guilty as you." He held up the blade. "Do not judge me, as I do not judge you."

Aristea turned to the window and stared at the face of the moon. It was scarred but resplendent with light, casting its favor upon the treetops and the exposed basalt crags. It would be full only for a short time, allowing the tides to swell, the eagle owls to take wing, and the wolves to release their haunting howls, before relinquishing its radiance to darkness.

She knew what she had to do.

She turned to Sophronios and nodded. He took two steps toward her, standing so close she could smell the sweet wine lingering on his breath. He placed a gentle hand on her hair and pulled a strand into his palm. She closed her eyes.

"God forgive me," he whispered.

There was a slow ripping sound as the blade cut through the strand close to her ear. She exhaled a trembling breath. One more mark of her virginity, sacrificed. She let her head drop back into his hand, indicating her full knowledge and consent. It was a small trade for freedom.

With a tenderness that mitigated the violence of the act, Sophronios separated another tress with his fingers. As he sheared off her locks strand by strand, her head and his hands moved together in a kind of dance, forming a curious union.

The cutting stopped. She opened her eyes and saw the pile of cut hair, like a lifeless black fleece, on the stone floor. It was done.

"Put this on." Sophronios held up the monk's habit. "There isn't much time."

She slipped the habit over her head, then allowed him to help her with the hood garment. She pulled it down over her eyes to disguise her feminine features.

"All the doors are unlocked. Take the back trail down the mountain. The moon will guide your steps."

She nodded. "I will not forget this."

His chestnut eyes were clouded with tears. "May the holy mother keep you."

Aristea put up a hand. He lifted his hand to hers until

the tips of their fingers touched. In another time, another life, she could have loved him.

She pulled her hand away and hastened out of the room. She wiped a tear with her palm and launched down the corridor of her deliverance.

Thirty-seven

"Wake up."

A foot struck Daniel's hip, shaking him out of a fitful slumber. He had no idea what time it was, whether it was day or night. He rubbed his eyes and turned to face a dirty-blond thirtysomething with intense blue eyes peering through round tortoise glasses.

"Congratulations. You are being moved to the presidential suite." An ironic tone colored his Jersey accent.

Daniel sat up. "And you are?"

He clasped his hands in front of his crotch. "I'm Tom. I'll be your tour guide."

Daniel took stock of the dubious company. He seemed more likely to quote from Chaucer than to kick ass. "Whatever you say, man. Lead the way."

Tom opened the door and waved Daniel through with an open palm. "Please. After you."

Daniel launched down the dimly lit corridor. The clicking of Tom's hard-soled loafers on wood mirrored the pace of his own steps, reminding Daniel his escort was only a heartbeat behind him.

"Turn right."

Daniel turned onto an equally shadowy but even longer hallway. How big was this basement? He made a mental breadcrumb trail as they turned again and again, weaving through the labyrinthine network beneath the house. Whoever built this had money to spend—and something to hide.

"Here we are." Tom stopped and pushed a door open.

Daniel entered first. The room was octagonal with contemporary art hanging on all sides. In the middle sat a black leather sofa and a pair of white Barcelona chairs illuminated by a sunbeam. His gaze followed the beam up to a pyramid-shaped skylight. Seeing the outside for the first time in days, he was overcome by a sense of optimism.

"I hope you will be comfortable here." Tom's arrogant voice grated at Daniel's nerves. He couldn't wait to be rid of the guy. "In a few hours, the colonel will decide what to do with you."

"Colonel, huh? When did he serve?"

"I regret I cannot answer your questions." Tom turned on his heel and walked to the door. He hesitated, then turned around. "Oh, and do try to behave." He pointed to another shiny black orb before walking out and double-bolting the door behind him.

Alone again, Daniel stood in the middle of the room beneath the shaft of light. The warmth on his face bolstered him. He felt a hungry longing to reach for the light, devour it.

He looked up. Through the prism of the pyramid, he saw distorted images of the landscape above. It was dense with pine trees, the kind with long, slender needles and the silver-green hue of moss: the evergreens of an arid land. From the bough nearest the skylight hung a cluster of pinecones, distinctively elongated and teardrop-shaped, tightly closed, and green as spring.

Aleppo pines, the same variety that grew in the mountains of central Greece. That small snapshot through a three-by-three skylight was enough to give him a sense of place. He was convinced he had been brought back to Greece, stashed somewhere in the highlands. And she was out there, too.

Sarah. He closed his eyes and searched his memory. The photo of her, curled up inside a rocky warren, still disconcerted him—but it also gave him a clue. The characteristics of the rock were telling: a rough gray limestone eroded to reveal the reddish hue of the stone below. It was the unmistakable lithic composition of Mount Parnassus and the same stone the sanctuary of Delphi was built of.

Daniel felt the sharp stab of guilt over abandoning her with no apology, no explanation. How could he have let things get that far? Why did he not level with her from the start? He cursed his pride that prevented him from reaching out for her help. Now, it seemed, his missteps over the past three months would cost him dearly. Even if they did survive this, which looked less likely by the minute, the cord that bound them might be irreparably severed.

He peered up at the skylight again. It looked like some sort of Plexiglas, too strong to breach. His gaze traveled to the base of the structure, which was concealed by a rounded, bulging crown molding. He found the shape odd and wondered if the molding was more than decorative.

He glanced around the room for anything that would give credence to his suspicions. He tried the light switches—there was one for each wall—in various combinations, but they corresponded only to the lights above the art. He scanned the wood floor for any planks that might be removable, but nothing was obvious. He walked to the center of the room and sat on the sofa.

He looked closely at the tufting of the Barcelona chairs. All the buttons were the same—except for one.

Adrenaline surged through his body. He cast a furtive glance at the black orb at the corner of the ceiling. They were watching.

He sank into the glove leather and waited. Night could not fall soon enough.

Thirty-eight

Sarah reached inside the small pocket sewn into her trousers and pulled out the amulet she'd collected in Thebes. She fitted the two severed pieces together to form the ancient mystical symbol of the tetractys: dots arranged in four rows—four, then three, then two, then one—to form a triangle representing the perfect number, ten, the number of the universe.

"You're a Pythagorean, aren't you?" she asked.

Isidor did not answer. His gaze, now darkened, was fixed on the second amulet. "How did you come to have this?"

"It was outside the Thebes museum on the night of the break-in. Perhaps you can tell me who this belonged to."

"One of my brothers. He was posing as a guard at the museum. His mission was to protect the key to Trophonius' cave. That night . . . it was no break-in."

She tilted her head. "What do you mean?"

"He had finished his shift and left for the night, but he'd forgotten something and went back. He texted me a photo of someone sneaking out of the museum with a long object wrapped in cloth. I heard nothing more from him. He must have confronted the perpetrator and—"

He sighed and looked away.

That explained why the amulet was lying outside. There must have been a struggle that culminated in murder. The body was likely dragged inside—hence the bloody footprints pointing into the building—and the scene was made to look like a heist to throw the cops off the scent.

Sarah had known Evan was in bed with the enemy but didn't fathom he could go that far. The revelation made her shiver. "What about his phone? Surely it contained evidence that pointed to you."

"No phone number is registered to me. It would take the police a long time and much effort to trace his texts to real people. They'd never go to the trouble." He stared at her for a long moment. "What are you thinking?"

She was thinking the trace wasn't impossible but didn't voice her concerns. "I just find it remarkable your friend put his life on the line to protect a secret."

"Our oath is unto death."

Sarah knew this was true of disciples of the philosopher's famously secretive cult. What she didn't understand was why a neo-Pythagorean would be associated with an organization whose currency was stolen goods, human hostages, and wanton extermination. Though she'd never come across anyone who belonged to the cult, she'd heard the stories. Pythagoreans were supposedly enlightened beings who practiced asceticism and valued logic and reason above all else. Their religion was based on universal truths derived from number theories, and their ultimate goal was harmony of self and cosmos.

She wondered if Isidor was the authentic article or was posing to siphon information from her. The only way to know was to test him. "Tell me something, Isidor. Who is Delphinios? Why is he reenacting the oracle?"

He rubbed his short black beard and drew a deep breath. "He is a wealthy man, an American. He once had ties to the US government. He was very powerful, but then . . ." His jaw tightened. "Look, it's a complicated story."

"I'm good at complicated."

The corner of his mouth lifted. He paused, obviously careful about what he said. "He has an agenda. This authentic re-creation of the oracle is his way of gathering sensitive information and using it for his own means. The supplicants are high-ranking government officials from other nations who have been handpicked and invited here, supposedly to hear a prophecy.

"Only the prophecy is all smoke and mirrors. The classified information is passed from one source to another through the oracle—which means it cannot be traced to any official or covert source. If it wasn't so sinister, it would be genius."

Sarah felt a chill deep in her core. In her mind, Delphinios was simply a madman with a fetishistic pathos for antiquity who would stop at nothing to gather the treasures required to play out his fantasy. This was a twist she had not foreseen.

Questions rushed to the forefront of her mind, each vying for pole position. The most persistent had to do with the child priestess. "Does the Pythia deliver this information?"

"No. Her job is to inhale the vapors so she can fall into a believable trance and utter incomprehensible gibberish."

Sarah was sickened by that revelation. The girl's exploitation was a whole other issue, one she didn't plan to let go. "Then it comes from—"

"The high priest. I pretend to translate her utterances. But I have a prepared script. Delphinios tells me what to say."

"And this is something your religion condones?"

"Considering what's at stake, yes. I'm here to gather intelligence on behalf of the brotherhood. What Delphinios plans to use for destruction, we plan to use for good."

"I don't understand. What destruction? What are these grand plans of his?"

He shook his head. "I can't say. I can only tell you that if he succeeds, the entire world will be thrown into turmoil. It will be disaster on a grand scale. That's why he can never get a hold of the last piece of the puzzle—the *omphalos* stone." Isidor grasped her wrists and drew her closer. "We're out of time, Sarah. If you know where it is, I beg you to tell me."

"You first: what is inscribed on that stone?"

"Do not ask this of me. I cannot turn my back on my oath."

She didn't flinch. "I have sworn an oath, too, Isidor: to protect the treasures of antiquity and preserve them for the benefit of mankind, now and in the future. We could be locked in a showdown of wills forever—or we could agree to cooperate."

He let go of her wrists. "It's a lost Pythagorean formula. That's all I can say."

The encounter at the Aesepus Bridge was vivid in Sarah's mind. She could still feel the relief on the stone: the two eagles holding a laurel branch in their beaks perched above a net of interconnected geometric shapes. She hadn't recognized a mathematical formula. But then, she imagined, antiquity's greatest mystic wouldn't have made it that easy.

A low rumble, like distant thunder, sounded. Isidor placed a hand on the cave wall, his fingers vibrating. "It's coming."

Before she had a chance to question it, the ground beneath them shook. It lasted only seconds, but she'd been in earthquakes before—though being trapped beneath the Earth's surface added a new twist—and knew the pattern.

Another rumble came, this time louder. Hairline cracks formed in the stone.

Isidor snapped his head toward her. "We've got to get out of here." The ground moved again. "Now."

He grabbed her wrist and pulled her out of the chamber just as pieces of stone dislodged and came raining down. In his haste, he hadn't bothered to take the lantern, so they ran through the dark tunnel, where visibility was nil.

As the limestone around them quaked, Sarah felt as if the walls were closing in on her. She lost her footing, and her shoulder scraped against the craggy stone. She felt an initial sharp sting, but the sensation was dulled by the adrenaline rushing through her body.

A major tremor knocked them off their feet. Bigger chunks of stone fell from the ceiling. She crouched instinctively and lifted her arms over her head.

"Get up," Isidor yelled, hoisting her upright.

Stumbling, they ran as the tunnel disintegrated into a rock shower. She heard a dull thud, followed by a grunt, and suspected Isidor had been hurt by the onslaught of debris. Injury or no, he ran as fast as the shaking ground allowed.

He turned left, then stopped abruptly. "The exit is closed."

Sarah reached in front of her and felt a pile of fallen rocks. She turned toward him. Though she couldn't see his face, she heard his panicked breaths. She grasped his arms. "Listen to me, Isidor. When Plutarch wrote of this tunnel, he mentioned two exits. Where is the other?"

"Another exit . . . I . . . I don't know."

"I do." A tiny voice came from behind them.

"Phoebe." Isidor's voice suggested agitation. "You shouldn't be here."

"I've come to help you." Phoebe's voice was delicate but calm. "This way."

Sarah followed the swish of fabric down another passage. The girl was light on her feet, producing no sound of footfall. It was almost as if they were following a ghost.

The tremors quieted.

"In here." Her voice issued from the left now, perhaps from another chamber. "You must climb."

Phoebe led them, single file, up a series of steps carved into the rock like a ladder. The three stayed close to one another—so close Sarah could smell sandalwood and frankincense every time Phoebe swung her head. When they could climb no more, Phoebe spoke over her shoulder. "Wait."

A moment later, the ceiling cracked open and a shaft of gold pierced the blackness.

Sarah squinted. When her eyes adjusted, she saw the lower part of Phoebe's slender form slip through the crack and disappear. She tried to follow suit, but her shoulders were too broad to fit through the opening.

"Let me help." Isidor stood next to her on one of the stone rungs, and she saw the blood smeared across his face and matted on his cropped black beard. The top of his white gown was splattered with red.

He grunted as he pushed the stone out of the way, creating a wider opening. He spotted Sarah as she lifted herself out of the cave. Finally on terra firma, her knees collapsed and she slumped to her side, gulping the fresh air.

Isidor kneeled next to Sarah and put a trembling hand

on her shoulder. "This was not a random earthquake. It's part of his plan."

She sat up. The two-inch-long gash on his forehead still wept, but she sensed that wasn't why he appeared so shaken. "Are you saying the tremor was controlled?"

He nodded. "He is behind it. He needs but one thing to destroy us all—the formula inscribed on the stone." He leaned in. "If you tell him where it is, you will hasten the endgame."

She pulled away. "And if I don't, he'll kill Daniel."

"I will be completely transparent: the formula determines the precise depth at which catastrophic seismicity occurs. Pythagoras had spent years trying to figure out what brought about the Minoan Eruption and the massive earthquake that preceded it. At the twilight of his life, he solved the problem and handed the formula to the priestess at Delphi—his teacher. The knowledge was meant to keep a disaster of that scale from happening again." In his deep brown eyes was a profound sadness. "But it could also be used to trigger such a disaster. Delphinios already has the tectonic weapon; he just needs to know where to point it. If a megathrust earthquake wiped out the Minoans, it can certainly devastate the Americans."

He stood and offered her a hand. "I know I am asking you to make the ultimate sacrifice, but consider how much is at stake."

Sarah let him help her up. She wanted to regard

Isidor as an ally, but in this elaborate web of deception, she trusted only herself. "My mind is made up. Regardless of the stakes, I won't put his life on the line. I will do this my way."

"I pray you will be successful, for all our sakes." He gazed at Phoebe, who was sitting on a rock nearby. The girl's hair, a long swathe of golden brown curls, tangled and coated with the Earth's dust, billowed in a rogue gust. He turned back to Sarah. "Now, go. I will tell Delphinios you escaped."

Isidor walked to Phoebe and helped her to her feet. As they both walked toward the woods, Phoebe turned to Sarah. The breeze tousled the girl's hair, revealing a tiny face as pale as chalk and hazel eyes tarnished with an anguish no child should know.

Sarah's mission had just gotten more complicated.

Thirty-nine

Daniel had waited for hours, his gaze fixed on the pyramid-shaped skylight, his only window to the outside world. He had watched the light turn from bright and clear to the burnished gold of halcyon afternoons. Now, as dusk cast long shadows on the mountain peaks, the pine branches looked like old men's fingers clawing at an unattainable heaven.

The day had been uneventful until the tremor. It did not last long—maybe fifteen minutes, tops—but it was violent enough to shake the pinecones from the Aleppos. He watched them fall onto the Plexiglas skylight and could tell from the steady drop pattern that it was not a typical earthquake. There was no warning by way of a foreshock and no real aftershock; just a main shock that produced even vibrations.

In his prison room, the walls had rattled and lights had flickered on and off. Nothing fell; nothing cracked. The place was a fortress.

It had been a few hours since the last tremor, which was good news. The more time that went by, the less the chance of an aftershock—though in a seismic region like

Greece, nothing was predictable, much less guaranteed.

He worried about Sarah. She obviously was imprisoned in some sort of cave, or possibly underground—the worst place to be during a quake. He reminded himself she was the most competent person he knew, both intellectually and physically able to get herself out of jams. But he knew something she didn't: their opponent would employ ruthless tactics to obtain the information she alone held. Daniel was more determined than ever to get out of that hellhole and go to her aid.

He rubbed his forehead, then his cheek, absently noting the beard that had settled in earnest upon his face. The growth needling his fingertips reminded him how far he was from his true self, from Sarah, from the life he so passionately loved.

He lifted his gaze to the skylight. Night's indigo veil had descended upon the landscape. With scant illumination from the moon, the pine branches were hidden in darkness. The time was right to implement his plan.

Daniel's heart pounded in his temples as he went over the steps in his mind. His window was narrow; there could be no mistakes. If his execution wasn't flawless, he could pay with his life.

He cast a furtive glance at the ceiling-mounted camera. Though he didn't know which security system they used, he knew enough about this type of equipment to speculate their visibility would be greatly compromised if the room were dark. It was a risky wager, but it was all he had.

He moved over to the Barcelona chair, in front of which sat a water bottle. He cracked it open and took a long swig. He picked up the smart panel on the table and touched the section marked *Lights*. He touched *All Off* and lay back, pretending to turn in. He let a few seconds pass before casually moving his hand to the singular button on the chair seat.

He closed his eyes and pleaded, *Let this work*.

He exerted light pressure on the button and felt his finger sink slowly until there was a click. He heard a creak and looked up at the skylight, watching it lift upward. The crown molding separated from the wall, releasing a rope ladder.

Jackpot.

A shrill alarm punctured the silence. Daniel wasted no time. He bolted toward the ladder and climbed the rungs to the Plexiglas structure. Air wafted in from the crack, a curious combination of fresh pine and gunpowder.

His heart hammered double-time, reminding him he had seconds to escape. They would be on his trail in no time.

He pushed the Plexiglas upward, and it gave way easily. With a grunt he hoisted himself up and, clawing at the cold earth, crawled out of the opening.

He was free.

forty

By the time Sarah reached Arachova, daylight was waning. The Greeks called it the *wolflight*—the hour suspended between day and night, when nocturnal beasts began to prowl.

The village clung precariously to the mountainside, a haphazard arrangement of old stone houses with broken barrel-tile roofs and a few modern buildings wedged in between. A single, narrow road—no stop signs, no traffic lights—meandered through town; the rest of the access was on foot, via cobbled paths and steps cut into the mountain.

On one side of the road rose the slopes of Parnassus, a necklace of massifs that sprawled toward a misty horizon. The exposed limestone crags were cast into sharp focus by the shadows that had descended on twilight's back. Dark clouds obscured the nearest peaks. Sarah felt the impending rain in the cold, moist air.

Conscious of her blonde mane in a place populated solely by dark-haired villagers, she walked through the cobbled streets with her head bent, avoiding the curious stares. For the first time, she noticed the state of her clothes: her black top and slim expedition pants were covered with white smears, as if she'd rolled through flour. Her hands were scraped, quite raw in places. She realized they were staring at her not because she was a foreigner but because she looked as if she'd been through war.

A gust of wind swept up through the mountain pass. She hunched her shoulders and wrapped her arms around herself. A diminutive old woman dressed all in black in a housedress, tights, and a kerchief tied around her gray hair, called to Sarah from a balcony.

Sarah nodded and walked on, but the woman signaled to her to stop and scurried inside. A moment later, she came out her front door holding a shawl. She held it up and extended a palm-down wave, which meant *Come here*.

Sarah shook her head and said, "Please, no," in Greek, but the woman wasn't having any of it. She dashed toward the bereft visitor and draped a colorful shawl around Sarah's shoulders.

"I crocheted this when I was a girl, like you. Now I'm a widow and don't wear such things."

Sarah smiled. She recalled the unspoken mandate of Greek women from the old country: when they lost their husbands, they were required to wear black for the rest of their days, marking themselves as perpetual mourners and signifying their house had closed.

She also knew it was an insult to a Greek, particularly a villager, to turn down a gift. She pulled the shawl across her chest to indicate acceptance. Then she said, "I'm looking for a woman named Lydia. Do you know which is her house?"

The old woman waved toward the high point of the village. "She lives in her father's old house up the hill. All the way to the top, second set of steps. The windows are always shuttered." She shook her head in pity. "She's all alone, poor girl."

Sarah placed a gentle hand on the woman's shoulder. "I know. Thank you for your kindness." She pulled the shawl over her head and carried on up the hill.

A light rain on her face triggered the familiar stab of dread. It would be hard enough to get to Delphinios without the complication of weather. She exhaled sharply and shook off her apprehension.

On the high point of town, just beneath the peaks still dusted with the last winter snow, sat a cluster of *archontika*—the gracious old villas of the merchant class—looking down on the village commons. It seemed no one cared for these structures anymore. The stone walls had cracked, roof tiles were black with decades' worth of mildew, and no boxes of geraniums hung from the windows.

The drizzle fell with greater urgency. Sarah sized up the black clouds boiling overhead. There was no escaping the storm. She hurried up the second set of steps leading to the once-grand neighborhood and stopped in front of the two-story house with the boarded-up black shutters.

The rain pelted her face as she surveyed the façade. Oddly, not a single window was open to the light. The house and its inhabitant sent a very direct message: stay away.

Sarah walked up two steps to the landing and stood in front of the wooden door. The blue plaque with the white street number dangled from a single screw, swaying as the wind hit it. She knocked.

For a long while, there was nothing. Sarah had the odd feeling Lydia was standing on the other side of the door, listening. She placed her palm on the door and leaned in. "Lydia, it's Sarah Weston." The rain pelting the overhang drowned her voice. She knocked again and spoke louder. "If you can hear me, open the door."

Still nothing. She looked over her shoulder at the deserted street and the darkening sky beyond. She was running out of time. Lydia was her only hope for getting to Delphinios—and to Daniel.

She hit the door with an open palm and yelled to be heard over the driving rain. "Lydia, please. Open the door." When her plea wasn't rewarded, she rested her face on the splintered wood and spoke more softly. "I've seen your daughter."

Finally, there was a click. Sarah took a step back as the door creaked open. Half of Lydia's face came into view. Her eye was practically popping from its socket. "What did you say?"

"Phoebe. I've seen Phoebe."

Lydia whimpered. Tears streamed down her cheek. She didn't bother to wipe them.

"May I come in?"

Lydia left the door cracked and disappeared inside. Sarah pushed it open and entered the musty room, blinking to adjust to the dimness.

Lydia stood in the far corner, stoking the fire in a fireplace. The wood floor creaked as Sarah walked past mounds of clothes piled on the floor and a host of baby things—a walker, a feeding chair, storybooks, toys. The place was frozen in time.

Lydia wore the same clothes she did when she and Sarah first met. Sarah was sure she hadn't changed—or combed her hair—since. She put a hand on Lydia's shoulder and felt the woman shudder.

She turned to Sarah. Her face glowed with the copper light of the dying flames. "Where is she?"

"Delphi. She is the oracle."

Lydia dropped her face into both hands. Her shoulders shook.

Sarah put an arm around her. "Lydia, I need you to hear me. We must help each other. I promise to help you get Phoebe back if you help me get to Delphinios. I need to know where he lives."

Lydia started. "No. You can't go there. It's too dangerous. The . . . the guns . . ."

"He's holding my partner hostage." She leaned in and

stared into the woman's glistening eyes. "He will kill him before the night is over."

Lydia looked away. "What is she like?"

Sarah sighed. Her urgency was insignificant compared to a mother's renewed hope. "She looks to be eleven, maybe twelve. She's tall for her years, almost as tall as Isidor, and thin—very thin. She's lovely, Lydia. She has your eyes."

"Who looks after her?"

"Isidor is her guardian. He won't harm her." Sarah hesitated, unsure whether to tell her the whole truth. Lydia was already in a fragile state; too much information could push her over the edge. Or force her to act. She decided there was too much at stake to tread lightly. "But every time there is a ceremony, she is forced into a trance."

Lydia eyed Sarah. "Trance? How is that possible?"

"She inhales ethylene, which comes from underground. Just like the oracles of old."

She put a hand to her mouth. "So he's done it. He's opened the chasm."

"Tell me what you mean."

"When we first came to the ancient site, there were no vapors. The crack had been sealed for centuries. Delphinios' dream was to reinstate Apollo's cult and the oracular ceremonies. But without the gas, it couldn't be done. So he devised an elaborate plan to make ethylene flow forth again."

"Did it have anything to do with earthquakes?"

Lydia took a step back. "I'm not supposed to talk about it."

"Who are you being loyal to, Lydia? The man who tricked you and abandoned you?" Sarah spoke more sharply than she'd intended. She took a moment to get her nerves in check. "I'm sorry. I know you made a promise, and I wouldn't ask you to break it if it weren't a matter of life and death." She reached for Lydia's hand. Her bony fingers, cold and dry as a cadaver's, trembled in Sarah's grip. "I will not betray you. I swear."

Lydia pulled her hand away and wrapped her arms around her chest. "I overheard a conversation . . . but I don't really understand it, so I'm not sure I can explain it."

"It's all right. Just try."

"This was years ago at his house up the mountain. He was talking to a visitor whom he called *machednik*."

The Russian word for *commander* or *chief*. Sarah kept quiet, reluctant to rend a moment that was as fragile as a spiderweb.

"Delphinios was talking about the fault beneath Delphi, how it had not moved in years. But he was going to change that using"—a perplexed look crossed her face—"the power of water?"

"Go on."

"From what I gathered, he wanted to inject water into the earth." She shook her head. "It all seemed very strange."

It wasn't strange. The technology to pump wastewater into deep underground wells existed. Hydrofracking—hydraulic fracturing—was a technique to extract natural gas from deep fields blocked by shale deposits. By injecting water into the wells via horizontal veins, the shale was loosened and gas flowed forth.

That was one part. The other was the disposal of the process' byproduct—chemical-laden wastewater—into holes deep inside the planet's core. It was a rather controversial technique, fraught with risk of contaminating groundwater—and causing earthquake clusters.

And yet it was viewed as a necessary practice to draw upon previously trapped natural gas resources. Greece, whose relations with Europe had grown increasingly strained due to the nation's vast debt, had launched into exploration of its own resources by allowing local energy companies, backed by Russian and Chinese investment, to pan for hydrocarbon and mineral deposits beneath the sea. Fracking could easily be part of that exploration.

Though everything hadn't yet come into focus, Sarah gathered Delphinios was in bed with the Russians. Somehow, he must have been involved in pumping water into holes beneath the earth or sea—sites that communicated with the fault to bring about minor tremors. If he indeed had a tectonic weapon, this was a good way to test it—or perfect it. The release of ethylene gas, the product of shifting plates deep beneath Mount Parnassus, was just a bonus.

The fire went out, and a chill settled into the room. Lydia shivered. "Perhaps I've said too much."

"You're doing the right thing. Do you have any more recollection of that conversation?"

"There is one thing." She gazed at the spent fire. "I remember him telling the *machednik* that if all went well with this experiment, the Americans would regret what they did to him."

So Delphi was an experiment, an elaborate ruse for a revenge mission. "What did the Americans do to him?"

"I am not sure. He didn't talk much about his past. He didn't even want me to know his real name. But one day I went snooping and found some photos of him dressed in fatigues, together with some other soldiers. It seemed like he was in the military."

"Was there a name patch on his jacket? Think."

"Yes." Her brow furrowed as she tried to recall. "Bellamy, I think."

"Listen, Lydia: I have every reason to believe this man is dangerous. I need you to help me get to him. Where is his house?"

Lydia nodded toward the north. "On top of the mountain. But there is a lot of security. You'll never get in. Unless . . ." She shook her head. "No. It's folly."

"Tell me anyway."

"There is an area under the fence where the dogs always used to dig. It was big enough for a slim person to squeeze through. But I'm not sure it's still there. It's been a long time . . ."

"I'm willing to take the chance. Just tell me where to go. I need to get there straightaway."

Lydia's eyes sparkled. "Come with me."

Sarah followed Lydia through a network of narrow paths surrounded by stacks of boxes and random hoarded stuff. The smell of dust was pervasive, indicating nothing had been moved in years. They exited through a back door to a concrete stoop surrounded by an overgrown patch of earth that once was a garden. The rain was raging, and veins of silver lightning cracked the gloomy sky.

Lydia walked to a covered object and pulled back the canvas to reveal a BMW motorcycle of seventies vintage. "It was my father's. It still works."

"Brilliant. May I?" With Lydia's nod, Sarah straddled the seat, kicked the pedal into neutral, and started the engine. It sputtered and choked. On the second try, she revved the throttle until the engine came to life with a growl.

Lydia hopped on behind Sarah. "You'll never find the place alone. I'm going with you."

Sarah was unsure about the company. She didn't want to endanger anyone else; besides, she could be a lot stealthier if she flew solo. But Lydia was right: she needed her. "Fine. But only to show me the point of entry. I will go in alone. Do I have your word?"

Lydia nodded and slipped her arms around Sarah's

waist. Sarah steered the bike onto the street. Once she hit asphalt, she twisted the throttle gently. She knew it was a mistake to drive a motorcycle, particularly an old one, hard before becoming familiar with its quirks. Before it could reward her with performance, she had to engage in a dance.

Night had fallen in earnest. An accumulation of clouds, barely illuminated by the meager light of the waxing moon, was suspended low in the sky, a warning that the rain wouldn't end anytime soon. In the darkness and driving rain, the motorcycle's headlight was too weak. Sarah tried not to think about the cliff plunging a good mile down from one side of the narrow mountain road.

As she leaned into a curve, the raindrops felt like icy needles on her face, making her aware her clothes were soaked through. She should've been shivering, but she felt nothing but the hard beat of her own pulse.

Lydia leaned in and shouted in Sarah's ear. "Do you see that light up there?"

Sarah looked up and registered a cluster of white pin lights flickering in the blackness like stars.

"That's his house," Lydia continued.

More like a compound, Sarah thought. She estimated it was about twenty kilometers away. She turned her head toward Lydia. "Hang on." She shifted gears and twisted the throttle for a new burst of speed. With her passenger's hands clasped tightly around her waist, Sarah leaned into the handlebars and gunned for the summit.

forty-one

Harbor of Avlis, central Greece,
393 CE

Almost a fortnight passed before the boat docked in the harbor outside Thebes. Aristea regarded the land beyond the bow with such deep reverence she could have worshipped the very soil. It was her land, comely and clement, a place she thought she'd never see again.

The journey across the Black Sea and through the Hellespont to her beloved Aegean Sea had been treacherous. Autumn brought cruel storms that raised the waves like great swelling monsters threatening to swallow intruders into their dark bellies. Behind leaden clouds, Zeus released lightning bolts from his fingertips without mercy. Silver streaks ripped open the sky and clawed at the heaving waters yet somehow spared the little wooden boat carrying provisions and scant human cargo.

She considered it a sign. The gods had the power, and every opportunity, to sabotage her passage back to Greece. That they didn't meant there was purpose to her voyage. Her life had been spared not for its own sake but so that knowledge she alone held would not be forgotten.

The captain, a surly, hardened soul with a habit of murmuring to himself, tied the boat at the dock and began removing sacks of grain that had doubled as ballast. Aristea lowered the hood over her eyes and climbed out of the stern. She touched the captain's head in blessing, the expected recompense from monks who'd taken a vow of poverty, and went on her way.

The port city of Avlis buzzed like a beehive as boat people yelled back and forth and travelers jostled for position near the front of the queue. Sacks of foodstuffs and jars full of unguents, wine, and oil came and went, tossed from hand to hand by shirtless laborers. The rhythmic clang of iron tools emanated from the shipyard adjacent to the harbor, where great vessels were constructed for the Greek naval fleet.

In that chaos, she would be lost, her identity never questioned. For all bystanders knew, the person within the robes was an Orthodox monk, not a fugitive pagan priestess. The disguise provided by Sophronios was genius. Without it, she would never have made it past the woods around Sumela.

Anxiety clawed at her core as she considered the consequences when the church fathers detected her absence from the monastery. How would Sophronios, her custodian, explain it? Would he be blamed—and punished? Would his god spare him knowing Sophronios served justice, or would he strike him down for aiding a nonbeliever?

She didn't comprehend the new religion enough to know how tolerant or vindictive the deity was. She only hoped this god would forgive a man whose actions were motivated by the purest kind of love.

Aristea crossed the port gate and stood at the crossroads leading to Thebes on one side and to Athens on the other. The road to Thebes would continue on to the mountains of central Greece and to the underground cave that would shelter her and her brothers in secrecy. It was a journey of about two weeks, she reckoned. She thought of the great distances suppliants had traveled to hear the oracle of Delphi and considered the irony of making a similar voyage. How life had changed.

She drew a deep breath and launched onto the Thebes road.

forty-two

The light on the security-room console blinked red, indicating there had been a breach. Stephen Bellamy regarded it calmly, shifting his gaze to the computer screen marked *Basement Access*. A silver-hued figure slithered beneath the skylight and stumbled upright, checking the surroundings for a directional clue.

The escape was flawless, just as Bellamy had planned it.

The colonel smirked and sucked on a Churchill stump. In the smoke of spent tobacco he could taste the venom of malice. It was a luxury he allowed himself only once in a while, just enough to dodge the laws of the righteous. No material thing, no carnal pleasure delivered the rapture he felt when facing a man whose wits were no match for his own and dealing out the just punishment. Elimination of the weak: it was his duty and his privilege.

"Go on and run, Danny boy," he mumbled behind the cigar clenched between his teeth. "The colonel is coming for you."

His mobile phone vibrated against his hip. He picked up after the first ring. "Isidor. Is everything in place for tonight?"

"She's gone, sir. The girl escaped."

The cigar fell out of Bellamy's mouth as he roared, "What? How?"

"The earthquake. Falling rocks trapped me inside the tunnel. I could not run after her."

"You idiot! Do you know what this means? The entire plan pivoted on her. Now I have to change everything at the eleventh hour because of your incompetence."

Bellamy tapped the phone off and tossed it onto the table. He huffed. The plan he had so carefully woven was beginning to unravel. It was flawless: he'd wear down Madigan with his special tactics, then tie him up like a pig and take him to Delphi to be sacrificed to the gods. As the screws got turned on her boyfriend, that virtuous little wench Sarah Weston surely would rather come forth with the information than watch him burn in the sacrificial pyre.

Little did she know, with her escape she sealed Madigan's fate.

He hit a button on the console. Tom's voice came over the speaker. "Sir."

"Tommy, get the Renegade ready. Make sure all the toys are loaded on."

"Yes, Colonel."

"There's one other thing: Sarah Weston is on the move. I want you to mobilize a massive manhunt. This time, she cannot get away."

"I'll take care of it."

Bellamy took one last look at the security screen that showed Madigan running through the thick woods. He synced the screen on his wrist to deliver the same image and walked over to the arms cabinet, where he kept the weapons chosen for the occasion. He unlocked it and removed an MK12 sniper rifle and a tricked out 6P62, a cherished gift from his Russian comrades. He inspected both to make sure they were loaded.

He licked his lips and reveled in the lingering taste of Cuban tobacco. The familiar cold steel of the guns against his arms was comforting. He smiled. "Okay, Danny boy. Let's do this."

forty-three

A burst of pewter light filtered through the cloud veil obscuring the sky. The thunderclap came almost immediately, indicating the strike was within a hairbreadth. Seconds later, it happened again—and again, a succession that fueled Daniel's anxiety as he ran through a stand of tall pines.

His visibility hampered by the relentless downpour and his ability to navigate by the stars completely effaced, he had no idea where he was going. He looked over his shoulder at the house and realized he was heading downhill. That could give him an advantage: even if the path were to dead-end into a ravine, he could use his free-climbing skills to get away.

If only he could silence the demons that made his pulse race and his skin burn. He was walking a knife's edge between lucidity and disorientation, fighting against the rip current of his subconscious to keep his thoughts nailed on Sarah and not his own plight. He was hyperaware of his breath—a rapid pattern bordering on hyperventilation—and the fact he was drenched. To counter the sensation, he ran faster, as if the forward motion would flush the agony out of his system.

Another bolt of lightning illuminated the thicket and gave Daniel a split second of light to judge direction. At the far left, there seemed to be a clearing. He wasn't sure if his eyes cheated him or his mind was slipping into paranoia mode, but he thought he saw a dark speck in the distance. He ran in the opposite direction, letting the thick old trunks of the Aleppo pines shield him.

Where the ground wasn't covered with pine needles, it was slippery as a greased pig. The patches of slick mud slowed him down and forced him to think about every step. The last thing he wanted was to go sliding with no control in unknown terrain.

A crack of thunder jolted Daniel. The rain hissed in his ears as the water came down in sheets. He stopped for a moment to catch his breath. With his forearm, he pushed the dripping strands of hair away from his face.

And then he saw it: a bright, round light in the near distance, growing larger as it headed toward him. It was either a powerful torch or a vehicle headlight. His heart hammered.

As he ran away from the approaching light, he heard the roar of an engine and realized they were on his tracks. He headed into the thickest part of the stand, hoping a vehicle couldn't negotiate the path, and looked over his shoulder. He could make out the dark outline of an all-terrain vehicle. It was gaining ground—fast.

Daniel sprinted through the forest, barely noticing the branches that whipped his skin raw. The headlight was so near that it cast a ghostly pallor onto the trees, making them seem like frozen soldiers from a prehistoric army. There was nowhere for him to hide: they could see his every move.

Suddenly, the engine idled. Daniel looked behind him again and saw the light was no longer moving. The ATV couldn't make it through the thick woods. He allowed himself the luxury of thinking he had a reprieve, until he heard the crack of gunfire.

A single shot, intended for him. With the blast lingering in his ears, he scrambled to the nearest trunk and crouched behind it. A second shot rang, this time closer. His pursuer was on foot. Unwilling to be a sitting duck, Daniel moved from tree to tree, dodging the bullets released from what he believed was a sniper rifle.

Daniel had no illusions about his opponent's marksmanship. He knew he was missing on purpose; the shots were intended to intimidate and disorient him—at least for now.

"Come on out, Danny boy." The colonel's voice was spiked. "Come on out and play."

Daniel scanned the surroundings. Directly ahead, the forest was dense and the trees seemed to angle down. The path led sharply downhill. It was a gamble, but he had nothing left to bet on.

With his back against the peeling bark of an Aleppo trunk, he stood slowly and took a deep breath to steady his racing heartbeat. It was no use: his body was in full fight-or-flight mode.

He darted toward the cluster of trees and zigzagged between the trunks. The rifle cracked again, and a bullet ripped toward him, hitting a tree. The colonel was no longer toying with him; he wanted blood.

Daniel ignored the gunfire and kept running, jumping over pine roots and ducking branches as he made his way out of the thicket. His breath, rapid and erratic from a cocktail of fear and exhaustion, was a disconcerting reminder that time was running out.

The colonel shouted, "You think you can run from me, boy? Ain't no place for you to hide. I know every inch of these woods."

As Daniel gulped the air, he tasted the rain, something like cold, liquid metal. The sounds around him were suddenly amplified: the snapping of branches and the crackling of fallen pine needles exploded in his ears like fireworks.

Then the next shot came, so loud it caused him to stumble. He felt a sharp sting in his shoulder and clenched his teeth. The sensation intensified into a burn that radiated down his arm and buckled his knees. As he tried to get on his feet, he slipped on a patch of mud and went sliding. He clawed at the slick ground, to no avail. A jumble of pines, shadowy and ominous, rushed past as he tumbled toward an uncertain fate.

The familiar fog descended on his mind. The red light blinked in a corner of his memory, threatening to ensnare him in its greedy veil. He had the urge to shout, to wail, to rip something apart with his hands—anything to dislodge the sensation.

Sarah's face flashed in his mind. What good was he to her now? A wave of anger crashed down on Daniel's consciousness, sobered him.

His torso struck something that broke his fall. He struggled to focus, to get a clear grasp of his situation. He'd hit a fallen tree whose trunk appeared split in two. Thick branches were scattered about. A lightning strike? The earthquake? He couldn't round up his wits enough to make a determination, and that scared him more than any smoldering weapon.

With great effort, he tried to prop himself upright but fell to his knees. His shoulder felt as if it had been branded, and the strength in his left arm had diminished. He had never felt so weak, so close to the end.

One after another, negative thoughts invaded his awareness like an alien army: the terror of free fall from thirty thousand feet, the brutal duplicity of the British, his father's alleged fatal accident. He forced himself to concentrate on Sarah. She needed him. He had to get himself together for her sake.

The steel barrel of a gun pressed against the back of his head.

"Well, well, Danny boy. Looks like you're in a bit of a quandary." The colonel's voice had the lilt of victory. "You good at math, boy? Listen up. There are two of us, but only one is going to make it out of these woods alive. How many dead men does that make?"

Click. Daniel shuddered as his opponent released the safety.

forty-four

espite the cold rain pummeling his skin, Daniel's face flushed. He could feel the blood surging through his carotids. It was checkmate.

"Say your prayers," ordered the smug voice. He pulled the trigger.

Daniel crumpled to his side and rolled onto his back. He was shaking, unsure if he was alive or dead.

The colonel stood over him. "I've seen men with what you have a thousand times, son." He tapped his temple. "It's the mark of a weak mind." He held up the MK12. "Mock execution. It's one of our more charming tactics to induce a useful anxiety in our enemies. But you don't need help from me, do you?"

Daniel released a series of sharp exhales as he tried to come to grips with the fact that he was alive. Then he realized the blinking red light was extinguished. He leered at his assassin and choked out the words: "Is this the way you serve your country, Colonel? By using torture and corruption? You have no right to call yourself an American."

"My country abandoned me, boy. But that's none of your business. If I were you, I'd be more concerned about my own predicament. And you've sure got one." He kicked Daniel in the ribs. "Your girlfriend has run away. She was your one hope of salvation. We gave her a chance to save your pathetic life, but she deserted you. And who can blame her, after what you did? Lying to her . . . walking out." He shook his head. "Just like your old man."

Daniel clenched his fists. "You piece of trash . . . Who are you to judge me?"

The colonel reached behind him and produced an automatic weapon. "No more fun and games, Danny boy. This badass baby's loaded." He held the gun in front of him, the firing end pointed at Daniel. "Now tell me what you know about the map, or I promise both you and Weston are going to hell tonight."

Daniel looked past the colonel's shoulder at the house on top of the hill. An amber light trembled inside one of the windows. He knew that glow: it was the unmistakable mark of fire. Using his peripheral vision, he scanned the fallen branches and considered his next move. Perhaps it wasn't checkmate after all.

"Everything you need to know is sewn into the lining of my backpack. But better get it fast"—Daniel nodded in the direction of the house—"before it burns."

The colonel glanced back and did a double take. "What the—?"

With a motion so swift it sent a searing pain down his arm, Daniel grabbed one of the heaviest branches and, gritting his teeth, swung it at the colonel's knees. It knocked the man off his feet and pinned him to the ground just long enough for Daniel to stagger upright and run down a steep patch of hillside.

The automatic weapon roared with a rapid succession of shots that echoed off the limestone monolith. He heard the colonel call behind him. "You've sealed your fate, Madigan. Run all you want. I will have your hide in the end."

Daniel heard more shots, then the distant rumble of the ATV engine, but didn't look back. The pitch was getting sharper, too vertical to gain purchase. Knowing the terrain was unsuitable for a vehicle buoyed him—until he reached a ledge above a sheer drop. He halted, attempting to assess the rock face beneath him. A bolt of lightning gave him a split-second visual; it was all he needed. The angle was about sixty degrees, and the face was layered limestone. In normal times, he would not have hesitated to tackle that, but a shoulder injury all but ruled out a free-climb.

Through the rain's constant trickle he heard a curious sound, like the cry of an animal. He listened more intently. It was indeed an animal, or rather a pack of them. Wolves? As the sound grew louder, he realized he was hearing the frantic barks of dogs. He turned back to the precipice.

"You can do this," he whispered to the weaker part of himself.

The snarls were louder as the pack closed in. Daniel sat on the ledge and lowered himself to a toehold. The chalky dust that covered the limestone had turned into a paste in the downpour. Every micromove mattered. He felt the lime under his fingernails as he dug in to the rock.

"Steady . . . steady."

He had descended no more than twenty feet when the black dogs halted at the ledge, barking at him with a fury. The whites of their eyes and their bared teeth glinted in the darkness. There were six of them, likely Doberman pinschers.

One launched down the rock face, and the others followed. The pitch was steep enough to keep them from moving quickly but not so forbidding it stopped them.

Eyes wide, Daniel looked around. There was a ledge beneath him, but he'd have to jump a good ten feet to land there. The good news was, the dogs wouldn't be able to follow.

As they drew nearer, piercing the night with their bloodthirsty growls, Daniel let go of his handhold—and his fear. He landed on his side and rolled twice to the edge of the ledge. The pain was so crushing he could hardly breathe. Clutching his wounded shoulder, he groaned through clenched teeth.

He looked up at the sextet of animals howling in frustration: they wouldn't taste flesh tonight.

The rain had slowed to a drizzle. Daniel shifted his

gaze downhill. Perhaps two hundred feet beneath the ledge, a white pin light traveled in a straight line. He squinted. Could it be?

Following the light trajectory, he realized it was traveling on flat ground, steadily heading uphill. Emotion choked him, making him forget about the violent spasms in his shoulder and ribs. He could think of nothing but the black ribbon beneath him, so close he could smell the asphalt.

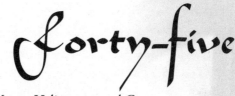

forty-five

Mount Helicon, central Greece,
393 CE

A hand shook Aristea's shoulder with a hint of aggression. She jerked awake and rubbed her eyes. She had fallen asleep on the roadside, leaning against a chestnut tree on the mountain pass to Livadeia.

"Ah, you are awake. I thought you had died, brother."

She turned toward the voice. A hooded monk, wearing a gray linen tunic and goatskin coat cinched at the waist with a jute rope belt, stood over her.

"Where do you come from?" His accent identified him as Macedonian.

Aristea did not speak for fear her voice would betray her. She bowed her head and placed a hand on her mouth.

"You have taken a vow of silence, have you?"

Avoiding his gaze, she nodded.

"Then I shall leave you be." He took two steps and turned back. "Before I go on my way, may I offer you some sustenance?"

Aristea was famished. It had been days since she'd had a proper meal, subsisting mainly on what she could pluck from the earth or what was given to her by passers-by. She nodded again, perhaps too eagerly.

The monk reached inside the wool bag that was slung across his chest and pulled out a small clay pot. "Must pudding. I have made it with my hands." He pointed toward the north. "We grow grapes at our monastery near the waterfalls."

Aristea accepted the pot and scooped out the thick pudding with her fingers. The sweetness of the grape must spiced with cardamom and cinnamon reminded her of ambrosia. She licked her fingers.

"You seem hungry. You must have traveled for many days." He reached back inside his bag and pulled out a piece of bread. "Take this. It will sustain you on your journey."

She accepted the bread and bowed in thanks.

The monk lingered a while longer, staring at her. Had he suspected something? She pulled her knees to her chest and shifted her gaze to the ground.

Finally he spoke. "Forgive my indiscretion, but I don't see a cross. Do you wear it beneath your robes?"

She said nothing. Answering in the affirmative might prompt the monk to ask to see it. Conversely, a negative reply might initiate trouble.

"Perhaps you have lost it." His tone revealed a vague skepticism.

She raised a hand to shield her eyes, indicating she did not wish to address the matter. The habit's ample sleeve fell to her elbow, exposing a slender wrist and fore-arm. She lowered her arm, immediately regretting the swiftness of movement that seemed like she was trying to hide something.

"Go in peace, brother." From the corner of her eye, she saw him make the sign of the cross in the air. "May the Lord bless your journey."

At last he walked on, following the path down into the valley. She was grateful he traveled in the opposite direction, for she wanted no one to haunt her steps. She cringed when she considered the encounter on the road-side might not be her last. As much as she longed to be invisible, there was nowhere to hide.

Nowhere, except the cave of Trophonius.

She tore a hunk of the dense brown bread with her teeth and tucked the rest under her arm. She would ration it, for she knew not how long it would take to reach the cave. She sensed she was close: so close she could feel the cool baptismal waters of the Herkyna and smell the moist earth fed by the river. She looked up at the sun, marking its passage toward the west. Though day was waning, Apollo's presence was evident in the bright fingers reaching through the clouds and caressing the mountaintops.

She closed her eyes. Even if all else were stripped away, that moment would remain with her, giving her strength to the end.

Beneath a night sky thick with storm clouds, the woods at the edge of Mount Helicon seemed a dark, hostile place. The autumn wind whistled through the thinning canopy of oaks and chestnuts, forcing the few remaining leaves into an aerial death march.

Aristea remembered her mother reciting the central Greece accounts of Pausanias, in which the chronicler had described that very place. If his famous insight held true, beyond the grove was a clearing that led down the mountain into the valley of Livadeia and the banks of the Herkyna.

Her heart beat a little faster. She had arrived at last. Apollo had guided her steps to the threshold of darkness, where the curtain of pain and misery was lifted, leaving only light.

If she made haste, she could descend into the cave of Trophonius before daybreak. She picked up the pace, ignoring the blisters and cuts that had afflicted her feet during the long days and nights of her journey.

The ground was lined with fallen foliage. The sounds of nature—the hissing of the wind, the soft crunch as the leaves yielded beneath her feet—were almost hypnotic. She concentrated on the music of the mountain mingling with the cadence of her footfall and, for the first time, allowed herself to believe she might make it.

She thought of her fellow Delphians. It was, perhaps, a fool's hope to believe their plan would come to pass exactly as they'd dreamt it—yet that hope had sustained her through imprisonment and rape and the witnessing of the worst side of humanity.

A cloud passed over the waxing moon, casting a silver streak on Aristea's path. She could see the clearing and the pines beyond. The Herkyna was within reach.

Air whooshed past, causing her robes to flutter. She looked about for anything out of the ordinary—and saw it: a long, slim object lodged into the trunk of an old oak. It wasn't until the second arrow flew past that she realized she was not alone.

Her mouth went dry, and a fire burned in the pit of her stomach. She had been betrayed. The kindly monk on the roadside must have realized she was not who she pretended to be. It wasn't unfathomable that word from Sumela had reached the shores of Greece. The monastic community could well have been informed a female prisoner had escaped, even that she hid beneath a monk's robes for survival.

However it happened, she had been found.

Aristea wasted no time. She bolted through the grove, weaving in and out of the tree trunks to throw off their aim.

Once more, angry clouds gathered in solidarity, obscuring the moon and veiling the fugitive in shadow. The priestess had the advantage—for now.

forty-six

Lydia leaned into Sarah's ear and raised her voice to be heard over the rumble of the motorcycle engine. "This is it. The path is just up ahead."

Sarah nodded. Braced by the icy air and drenched to the bone, she was fully alert and aware of her strength. At that moment, she felt as if there was no challenge she couldn't meet.

Her gaze darted along the shoulder of the road, searching for a good place to pull over. She saw a light in her peripheral vision and checked the rearview mirror. A blue flash blinked, approaching from the distance.

She turned to the left and parked the bike between a tree and the craggy mountainside. Motioning to Lydia to be still, she turned off the headlight and shut down the engine.

The blue light neared, now joined by the wail of a siren. Two more vehicles followed.

"The fire brigade," Lydia whispered. "Something has happened."

"We'll have to go on foot from here." Sarah looked up. "Bit of a steep pitch." She turned to Lydia. "You sure you want to do this?"

"I know my way around. I can help you."

Sarah was uncertain. Even if the woman's frail constitution concealed a hidden strength, her obsession with Delphinios could be a hindrance. But she had no time to argue. "All right. Go on ahead. I've got your back."

The emergency vehicles passed, and the road was once again deserted. Farther up the hill, Sarah could see the stalled lights flashing. Hunching, she followed Lydia along the shoulder to a stair-like path carved into the mountain. It appeared manmade.

Lydia turned to Sarah and smiled. "Shortcut."

Grateful for the distraction of the fire engines and for the finally dissipating storm, Sarah ascended the path with vigor. She was pleased at the agility of her companion. Lydia had tied her long skirt in a knot between her legs and her sodden cardigan around her waist. Even her great clumps of hair, so frizzy that the rain had failed to mat it down, did not seem to faze her.

Though she was breathing heavily, Lydia didn't stop. A curious determination seemed to drive her. Sarah knew why. A woman's cracked heart always harbored hope, and the glimmer of possibility was a powerful motivator. She could read Lydia's mind even if she spoke nothing of it. She'd waited years to be with him. She no doubt expected it to be different this time. Sarah cringed at the thought of what awaited Lydia. She wanted to protect her from the heartache, but she knew it was futile: one didn't learn without firsthand experience.

About midway up the face, they reached a ledge that separated the barren rock from the tree line. Aleppo pines hugged the mountainside, thicker as the elevation escalated. It was harder terrain to traverse, but it could also provide much-needed cover.

Lydia grunted as she tried to lift herself onto the protruding shelf. Panting, she turned to Sarah. "I can't do it."

"We'll do it together. Hold tight. I'll go up first and help you."

Lydia nodded. One of her feet slipped as she struggled to hold on to the rock.

Sarah kicked into a toehold and climbed around her as quickly as she could. She placed her elbows on the ledge and pulled herself up.

She could see Lydia's wide eyes below. Sarah lay on her stomach at the edge and reached an arm down. "Hold on to my hand."

Lydia looked disoriented. She jerked her head to and fro, then turned to look behind her.

Sarah remained calm to counteract her companion's panic. "Don't look down. Stay with me."

Lydia's lip quivered. "I can't hang on."

"Yes, you can." Sarah swallowed hard. "Focus on my hand. Can you do that?"

Sobbing quietly, she nodded.

"Slowly. You can do it."

As she reached up, Lydia's foot faltered, dislodging small rocks and hurtling them into the precipice. She slid down by a couple of feet.

Sarah held her breath as she watched Lydia's hand slip out of reach. She looked around and noticed a fallen pine branch, about four inches in diameter with two smaller branches extending from it. The perfect handle, she thought. She crawled on all fours to the branch and dragged it back, then offered it to Lydia.

The woman held on but was practically deadweight, obviously too exhausted and frightened to help herself. Sarah grunted as she pulled with both hands. She prayed Lydia wouldn't panic, hurtling them both down the mountain.

"A few more inches," Sarah choked out. "We've got this." She reached under Lydia's arms and clasped her wrists against Lydia's back for one final pull. They both landed flat on the ledge, gasping for breath.

Sarah sat up first. She wiped her mouth with the back of her hand and placed a palm on Lydia's shoulder. "All right?"

Lydia sat up and fell into Sarah's embrace. She was shaking, whimpering. "You are so brave. How can I thank you?"

Sarah gently pushed her away. "By staying here and keeping yourself safe. I will carry on up the mountain—alone."

"I want to—"

"No, Lydia. You haven't the strength. I don't want anything to happen." She thought of Daniel—their last encounter, her failure to see his trouble and help him—and managed a bitter smile. "There's enough on my conscience already."

The women gazed at each other for a long moment, a silent understanding between them.

Sarah stood. "I'll be back." She looked up, haphazardly mapping out a plan of attack.

"Sarah?"

She glanced behind her.

"I want you to do something for me." She wiped a tear and unclasped her locket. She handed it to Sarah. "If something happens . . . will you give this to Phoebe?"

A knot rose to Sarah's throat, but she didn't show emotion. It would've made things worse. She took the locket. "You have my word."

It was a difficult climb to the ridge just below the summit. Had the slope been bare, it would've been too steep to ascend without equipment. Sarah was grateful for the pines, whose roots and trunks provided some measure of footing.

Her mouth dry and breath clipped, she rested against a tree trunk and looked up at the white smoke rising from the summit. Though she couldn't see Bellamy's house yet, she could see the water bursting from the fire hoses. The pyre was still raging.

Thoughts assaulted her mind: What had transpired?

Was it arson or an accident? Would the ceremony, set for the wee hours of that night, be aborted? And, most importantly, was Daniel safe?

Sarah considered what she was about to do. Finding Bellamy, let alone delivering the intelligence that would liberate Daniel, in the midst of the chaos would be near impossible. Logic told her to flee, to abandon this foolhardy mission. She likely couldn't save him anyway. But her instinct—the part she trusted most—urged her toward the summit. She had to go all in, for his sake.

She inched forward. The scent of charred wood and sap permeated the air. The fire must have spread to the pines. Sarah took short, measured breaths to avoid inhaling the smoke, which grew progressively thicker.

With one big push that rendered her breathless, she made it to a clearing from which the scene was visible. The house was more like a compound of buildings. Sarah's heart sank as she digested the enormity of the disaster. The entire left side of the house was engulfed in flames that a dozen firefighters were struggling to get under control. Nearby trees were blazing or reduced to cinders.

She closed her eyes and silently called to Daniel. His face, serene and smiling, crossed her mind's eye. She was certain he was alive.

"Sarah."

Sarah started. Heart thumping, she turned around. Lydia stood behind her, pale as a ghost. Her clothes, wet with rain and sweat, clung to her bony frame. "For God's sake, what are you doing here? I asked you—"

"I fear for my dearest's safety. I must go to him. He needs me."

Sarah bit her lip so she wouldn't scream. Her plan was a hairbreadth away from falling to ruin. She wanted to shake Lydia. Instead, she took a deep breath. "This is not the time or the place. Do you really want to risk your life in this way?"

"You're risking yours . . . for a man."

Sarah searched for a watertight comeback, but Lydia was right. It was hypocritical. "I can't force you. I can only point out how dangerous this is for someone who's not trained."

Lydia started to speak, but Sarah turned her head and raised a hand. She'd heard savage barks.

Eyes wide, she turned to Lydia. "Does he have bad dogs?"

The woman nodded.

"Follow me—now." Sarah launched down the mountainside. She glanced to and fro, searching for a tree to climb. She ran frantically and, for the first time in her life, feared her heart might give out.

She glanced back. Lydia was losing ground, and the shadows of the four-legged beasts approached. "Run," she commanded, but her voice came out feeble, choked.

Lydia screamed.

Sarah stopped and saw her companion had fallen.

There was a window of seconds before the dogs would be upon them. She ran back and grabbed Lydia's wrist, raised her to her feet, and pulled her along.

The barks were deafening, as if there were dozens of dogs.

Sarah checked over her shoulder. Sharp canines glinted in the moon's platinum glow. The pack was closing in.

With her head still turned away, she felt an arm grip around her torso, breaking her stride.

"Quick! Up here!"

Sarah was so bewildered, it took a moment to realize what was happening. As if in a dream, she watched Daniel climb a few feet up a tree and offer her a hand. She took it and let him guide her to one of the high branches. Then he did the same for Lydia.

The woman took his hand and struggled up the tree trunk.

"Don't let go," he shouted over the frenzied howls beneath them. "Don't let go!"

Sarah watched in horror as one of the dogs snatched Lydia's long skirt and Daniel fought to hang on to her.

There was a long ripping sound, followed by a blood-chilling scream. Sarah yelled down to Lydia. "Don't panic! You're safe."

But the woman shook her head and let go of Daniel's hand. He reached down to regain a grip, but it was too late.

Sarah's heart pounded in her throat. Over and over she shrieked, "No!"

Daniel climbed up to her. He put one arm around her back and buried the fingers of his other hand in her hair, turning her head away from the grisly scene.

A cacophony of wails, rips, and growls echoed off the mountainside. Sarah clutched onto Daniel's shirt and buried her face in his neck to muffle her hysterical screams. As she released pent-up sobs, her body quaked in his arms. He gripped her tightly and whispered words to calm her, but no amount of comfort could console her.

Lydia's screams trailed off until they were heard no more.

forty-seven

Sarah stood at the roadside with only a vague idea of how she'd gotten there. She recalled moving from tree to tree while the dogs were distracted, then jumping onto terra firma and sliding down a steep cliff to the ridge.

They had managed to elude the beasts, but their guttural growls rang in Sarah's ears all the way down the mountain and haunted her even as she stood in safety. She had survived, but she felt guilty for it.

She felt a gentle hand on her shoulder. "Sarah."

She turned to Daniel.

"I'm sorry."

She blinked back fresh tears. She took his sentiment as a condolence, for he owed her no apology. If anything, she owed him one. But she had no words at that moment. She slipped into his embrace and squeezed his shoulder.

His arm shuddered, and he grunted slightly.

She pulled back. "You're hurt."

"I'll be all right."

"Nonsense, Danny. Give us a look." She turned him around and lifted up his shirt, following a streak of dried blood to the left trapezius muscle. She gasped. The skin looked as if it had been hacked with a dull handsaw, and blood was smeared across his back.

He spoke over his shoulder. "Sniper rifle. I think the bullet was intended for my heart."

She exhaled. "You're very lucky; it just grazed you. Still, we'll need to see to that."

He turned to face her. "We? Is there still a we?"

His comment was like a bucketful of cold water. "Why do you think I'm here? Sightseeing?"

Daniel nodded. "Just making sure. I've had a lot of conflict lately, inside and outside. Feel like I don't know who's my friend anymore." He exhaled sharply, as if expelling bad karma. "Now, let's get on out of here, try to put this nightmare behind us."

He started to walk toward the motorcycle.

She didn't move. "Danny."

He turned around. It was the first time she noticed how worn out he looked. His skin had a pallor consistent with suffering a gunshot wound and bleeding heavily. His clothes were filthy, and he sported a full beard. It was obvious he'd been through a lot; she couldn't ask more of him, but she needed to tell him the truth.

"I can't leave now." She pulled Lydia's gold pendant out of her pocket and let it dangle from her hand. "I've made a promise."

Daniel walked back to her. He took the locket in his palm and opened it. He winced and snapped it shut.

"Who was she?"

"Her name was Lydia. She was the lover of the man who imprisoned you and masterminded a new oracle at Delphi. Years ago, she helped him gather disciples for his pagan cult, even bore his child. Then, when he no longer had use for her, he kicked her out."

"And the kid?"

"He took her from her mother when she was six. He enslaved the child and drugged her, raising her to be a latter-day Pythia delivering oracles that would further some sinister political agenda. Apparently, he's a former military man with a real vendetta for the Americans."

"That's right. He was a colonel back in the time of the Cold War."

"You're a Navy man. Does the name Bellamy mean anything to you?"

A wrinkle formed between Daniel's brows. "Yes. There was an Army Colonel Bellamy . . . Stephen Bellamy, I believe. I recall he was captured by the Russians. I'm fuzzy on the details, but I'm pretty sure he was dishonorably discharged. Something about leaking classified information to the enemy." He looked deep into Sarah's eyes. "You think he's that guy?"

"It's consistent with what I've heard. Bellamy has something up his sleeve that will destroy the Americans; perhaps it's his way of seeking revenge."

"You know he's after the original *omphalos* stone."

She nodded. "Apparently, it holds a mathematical formula inscribed by Pythagoras, which is vital to his plan."

"I almost hate to ask this: do you know where that stone is?"

"I followed the clues on the map to the Sumela Monastery, where it was taken in the fourth century. It has since been moved, and now it's underwater near the Baltic Sea. It's part of a bridge pillar erected by the Romans. I dove down . . . I felt an inscription but couldn't decipher it. I found out later that it's the formula to determine the core-mantle boundary at which catastrophic seismicity, such as the quake that tore apart Thera, occurs."

Daniel shook his head. "How do you know all this?"

"The priest, Isidor, is a Pythagorean undercover. The formula is a long-held secret his tribe means to keep hidden."

He pushed his hair away from his forehead. "Jesus."

"It gets worse. Bellamy plans to use the formula to generate a megathrust earthquake that will have a devastating effect on America. He's already begun his experiments. This afternoon's earthquake was manmade. There will be others."

He put his hands up. "You're blowing my mind."

"It's true. He is using the oracle to gather America's enemies one by one and transfer information about the making of the perfect tectonic weapon. We're talking about a terrorist act the scale of which the world has never known. And he's this close"—she held her thumb and forefinger half an inch apart—"to making it happen. All he needs is the stone—or the map that leads to it. That's why I have to go back to Delphi tonight."

"Wait. What?"

"I'm going to stage my capture. If I'm right about the ceremony he's about to conduct, there will be a sacrifice tonight."

Daniel's eyes grew wider. "You don't mean—"

She raised a palm. "Don't worry. I have a plan."

"My God, Sarah. Don't do this. You have no idea what this guy is capable of."

"I have to. I can't turn my back on that child."

Daniel bent his head and rubbed his eyes, his hands slightly trembling.

She touched his arm. "Danny, I can't ask you—"

The roar of a helicopter diverted her attention. They looked up simultaneously. The flashing red taillight rose like a phoenix from the ashes.

"Hide," Daniel commanded. He grabbed her hand and pulled her into a roadside ditch. They rolled down, their bodies landing with a splash on two feet of muddy water. He lay on top of her and whispered in her ear, "Don't move."

As the copter thundered overhead, Sarah held dead still. With her head on Daniel's chest, she could hear his heart gallop in unison with her own. After an eternal moment, the sound dissipated. She looked up and saw the copter bank toward Delphi.

Daniel sat up and offered her a hand. "Looks like we have some work to do."

She gave him a weak smile. "We?"

He swept away a mud-soaked tendril that had fallen over her eye. "I'm with you, lady. Always have been."

forty-eight

By the time Sarah and Daniel arrived in Delphi, the pyre of Apollo had been lit. The flames churning inside the sacred tripod bathed the sanctuary's ruined columns in amber light and trembling shadows, a silent drumroll heralding the ritual that would ensue that night.

The self-appointed guardians of Delphi hadn't yet gathered. Somewhere, Sarah imagined, Bellamy's spiritual soldiers were slathering themselves with unguents and suppressing their natures with mood-altering concoctions in preparation for the spectacle of spectacles.

Sarah could not shake a sense of foreboding. In order for her plan to work, she needed the full cooperation of Daniel and Isidor. Each of them would have to execute flawlessly, or the entire operation would crumble. She had yet to get Isidor's buy-in, and though she was confident he would be onboard, she wondered if he had what it took to carry off something that precise.

She shook off her doubts and turned to Daniel. "The coast is clear. We can follow that path"—she pointed to a footpath through the forest running parallel to the Sacred Way—"down to the spring."

"Lead on," he said and followed her downhill to the Castalian Spring, where sooner or later the high priest would come to pay respects to the god before beginning the ritual.

Sarah and Daniel descended into the spring basin through a patch of laurel trees, said to have been planted there by Apollo himself as a tribute to Daphne, the object of his forbidden love, who was turned into a laurel by her father to thwart Apollo's advances. Heartbroken, Apollo had embraced the branches and vowed to use them from that day forward in his sacraments. According to all historical accounts, supplicants held these branches in tribute to the sun god, and the Pythia sucked upon them before delivering her oracles.

The spring itself had long since dried up. An empty marble pool now served as a hollow reminder of Delphi's glory days. Sarah and Daniel stood at the pool's edge, surveying the surroundings.

There was a reverential silence to the place. The air was embroidered with the delicate scent of almond blossoms carried downwind from the orchards above Delphi. It reminded Sarah of spring and renewal, and it gave her hope.

The crackle of branches nearby jolted her. She turned to Daniel. "We ought to make ourselves invisible." She gestured toward a tombstone-shaped niche cut into the rock. "Over there."

They walked across broken pieces of marble and up a

short flight of ancient stone steps to the dark niche. They climbed inside and sat at opposite sides of the opening so they could survey either direction.

Sarah saw the shadow first: the figure of a man approaching a bronze cauldron at the far end of the bath structure. He bent over it and splashed water on his face. As his hair dripped into the vessel, he gazed into its throat and murmured in rhythmic fashion.

She recognized Isidor's voice. She glanced at Daniel. His face tensed as he listened.

The whispered words had the cadence of iambic pentameter verse, the ancient method of oracle delivery. "The time is right for war on foes of old. The trench is filled with water, lo! But deeper we must go to cause a slide to sea. Old summit crumbles, water swells; the seed removed for good. Minoans mourn the gift they left; canaries sing the song of death. Your fate awaits; go forth and dominate."

The night's revelation, which Isidor had been instructed to deliver to the supplicant. Sarah gave Daniel the signal she was ready to make a move and bounded out of the hole.

Isidor jumped. "Who's there?"

"Sarah Weston."

The man went silent. Sarah approached. "We meet again." She peered over her shoulder and saw Daniel step out of the shadows. "This is my partner, Daniel Madigan."

Isidor glanced at Daniel, then at Sarah. "You are not

safe here. The colonel has men all over the mountain looking for you."

"Let's just say we're turning ourselves in," she said.

"First things first." Daniel stepped forward. "That little chanty you were mumbling earlier . . . does it mean what I think it does?"

Isidor shifted his gaze to the bronze vessel. He ran his hand across the water, causing a ripple that traveled from one side to the other. "It's my burden, not yours."

"I beg to differ. Terrorism is our collective problem." Daniel raised his voice a notch. "Let me see if I've got this straight based on what you said. Old Summit—Cumbre Vieja in Spanish—is a volatile volcano in the Canary Islands. Everybody agrees the big eruption is coming, and some say it might cause a megatsunami that will wipe out the East Coast of the United States.

"Now, scientists believe, and rightly so, it's not very likely a single eruption of that magnitude will take place. It will happen in waves. Unless—"

Sarah cut him off. "There's a massive earthquake at the exact point of the subduction zone that will trigger an eruption and cause a flank collapse of the volcano. A landslide of that size could indeed cause walls of water as high as a thousand meters, maybe more."

"And that wave," Daniel added, "could travel across the sea and crash down on American shores. A major loss of life and property and a deadly blow to a major world economy. Tell me something, Isidor: who's coming to hear that oracle tonight?"

Isidor gazed at Sarah, who nodded to encourage him. "Abdul al-Zafrani, Syrian commander and a high-ranking member of IS. He's working with the Russians."

"The Russians certainly have the technology to pump water into deep wells," Sarah offered, "and it's no secret they've developed some manner of a tectonic weapon. But I don't get one thing. Why is the colonel collaborating with the Russians, after what they did to him?"

Isidor smirked. "You don't know the entire story, do you?"

"I'd sure like to," Daniel said.

"Colonel Bellamy was held hostage for almost four years. He was tortured pretty badly, almost to the breaking point. But he held fast to his allegiance to his country. He genuinely believed the Pentagon would negotiate his release. There was some attempt at diplomacy, but nothing came of it. He remained in Russian capture and was eventually classified as a POW . . . practically forgotten, a blot on the map of global prisoners.

"At some point, I don't know when, something changed in him. Instead of waiting for liberation, he gave up and began to sympathize with the enemy. He became one of them." Isidor looked down, as if in shame. "An accomplice."

Daniel and Sarah exchanged glances. It was obvious they had the same question, but only Sarah asked it. "And how is it you know so much?"

He hesitated. His dark eyes were heavy with a distant pain. "I watched it happen. I'm his son."

forty-nine

In the lingering drizzle and gusts, the helicopter landed with a jolt. Bellamy removed his headphones and let the rumble of the rotors fill his ears. Since his military days, that sound had made him feel alive.

He checked his watch: 3:10. The ceremony would begin in less than an hour. In the years since he'd founded the cult, tonight's ritual was the first he would personally attend. It was that important.

He signaled to the pilot to cut the engine and stepped out the door, ducking as he passed beneath the blades. He stood away from the commotion and dialed Tom.

"Is our guest here?"

"Zafrani just landed at the airstrip. He should be arriving at the site in twenty minutes."

"Good." Bellamy shoved a stick of gum into his mouth and tasted the bite of spicy cinnamon. "What about Weston?"

"Our security cameras picked up a motorcycle parked by the road below the house. We think it belonged to that Lydia woman."

Even Bellamy shuddered when he heard her name. Before leaving the compound, he had had a visual of the massacre of his once lover. The scene was more gruesome than anything he'd seen on the battlefield. He pushed it out of his mind. "And?"

"Right after the copter took off, the motorcycle was gone. We told the local authorities we suspected it belonged to an arsonist and asked them to locate it pronto. Ten minutes ago, I got word it was abandoned in a ditch a couple of miles south of Delphi." Tom grinned. "The cops found blood, mud, and two long blonde hairs."

"Good work, Tommy. Spread the word among cult members. I want everyone alerted to the possibility she's here."

"What about Madigan? Do you think he's with her?"

Bellamy cackled. "If he is, so much the better. They can die together. Tell Isidor I want them captured. I will deal with them personally."

"Sir . . ." Tom hesitated. "About Isidor. I received a call earlier from Evan Rigas."

"What did that idiot want?"

"The police finally traced the texts on the museum guard's phone. They led to a phone number registered to a Panos Konstantis, who had died years ago. His widow had never disengaged his number, letting her son use it instead. Authorities followed that man for three or four weeks but came up with nothing—until last night, when he went into a basement in Piraeus and took part in some initiation rite for some shady group." Tom paused. "He was a Pythagorean."

"Cut to the chase, Tom. What's that have to do with Isidor?"

"The man the cops were following turned out to be an undersecretary for the leftist party. His arrest would have brought much embarrassment, so he chose the lesser of two evils: to expose the associate to whom he had secretly entrusted the phone."

"Are you saying—?"

"I'm sorry, Colonel. I thought you should know."

"There must be some mistake. Isidor has been by my side for years. He doesn't have associates." The possibility clung to the back of his mind, but he pushed it away. He had more pressing matters to tend to. "I'll deal with this later. Now let's get things moving. Time's wasting."

"But Colonel, what if—?"

"Do as I say, Tom." Bellamy hung up and raised his face skyward. The cool mist from the remains of the storm tickled his lips. It tasted of anticipation. Of revenge. He had waited a long while for this. Nothing—not even the suspicion of disloyalty—could stop him now.

The clouds had begun to part, revealing a smattering of stars. The conditions couldn't have been better for the theater about to unfold on the slopes of Mt. Parnassus.

He smirked. "Let the games begin."

Fifty

The confession blindsided Sarah. She glanced at Daniel. She'd seen that skeptical look before and knew what he was thinking: this guy can't be trusted. She allowed for the possibility that he was right.

She turned to Isidor. "All that talk about the Pythagoreans, about the preservation of the formula . . . Was that all for show?"

"Would I have let you go if it was for show? Would I have told you the truth about Lydia . . . and about Phoebe?"

It hadn't sunk in until that moment. "Phoebe is your half-sister. It's why you're protecting her."

"Phoebe was conceived and bred as the reincarnation of the original Pythia, who was a child virgin devoted to Apollo. At least that's how he's presenting it to his seekers."

Daniel glared at him. "And what will he do with her when this charade is over?"

"Send her back to her mother, I suppose."

"Her mother is no longer living," Sarah said. "Aside from you, that girl has no one."

"And all because of some sick mission to even the score." Daniel shook his head. "That man should be behind bars."

"My father is not the man he used to be. He's been blinded by his need to get revenge."

"But he's still your father," Sarah said. "Do you have the courage to stand against him?"

"I do. I swear it." The hard look in Isidor's eyes suggested he was telling the truth. "Come this way."

Like a white handkerchief waving good-bye to a lover, Isidor's robes billowed behind him as he stepped swiftly through the jumble of old trees. As she and Daniel followed close behind, Sarah's gaze darted around the forest, scanning for threats. She could see Daniel was doing the same.

Though wounded and spent, her partner seemed to be his old self: vigilant, strong, principled. She still worried. In the mind of a PTSD sufferer, anything could be a trigger at any time. With so many dangers lurking and so much ruthlessness and deception surrounding them, she wondered if his strength would hold. Just one more complicating factor in a lineup of many.

Isidor emerged from the trees onto a rocky path. He ascended it to the top of the spring and stopped. When the others caught up, Isidor pointed out to the void. Though barely visible, something was there. Sarah squinted for a better look, but it was hard to tell in the dark.

"A foil screen," Daniel said. "So Bellamy is planning a hologram—a large-scale one, by the looks of it."

"He has an entire audio-visual crew working on the other side of the mountain," Isidor said. "They're using a 3-D projection system and some pretty sophisticated technology to deliver a lifelike image of Apollo descending from the clouds."

Before Sarah had the chance to ask a question, Isidor put a hand up. "Be silent."

Isidor pushed a button on a bracelet-like wrist device and spoke into it. "Everything is ready." He adjusted a clear earpiece Sarah hadn't noticed before. As he listened, he shifted his gaze to the ground. A few seconds later, he looked up at Sarah. "I understand. We'll be on the lookout." He paused again to listen. "Tell the colonel not to worry. I'll take care of it."

Isidor removed the earpiece and cast a dark gaze at Sarah. His face was a shade paler than before.

"They know we're here," Sarah said.

"Yes. They've ordered your capture."

She'd foreseen that complication. She'd known all along that going back to Delphi was a step into the wolf's lair. But she couldn't run in the other direction, not with so much at stake.

Isidor looked over both shoulders. "I have a friend at the monastery of Profitis Ilias. It isn't far from here. There is a back way to get there, but you must hurry."

Sarah stopped doubting Isidor's sincerity. He had the perfect opportunity to deliver her to Delphinios, as commanded; instead, he chose to help her. Knowing she had an ally in him emboldened her for the riskiest move she'd ever made. "I'm not running. I'm turning myself in."

"No, Sarah," Daniel said. "It's madness."

"He's right," Isidor said. "I can't guarantee your safety."

She glanced at the two men, both of whom wore grave expressions. "Let me worry about my safety. Here's what we're going to do."

Fifty-one

The faint sound of chanting hung in the misty night air. The ceremony was about to begin.

Daniel watched Sarah emerge from the back of the spring, dressed in a flowing white gown, her soft blonde curls spilling over her shoulders. It was the first time he'd seen her look so feminine. She was so ravishing he had to look away.

She offered her wrists to Isidor, who bound them loosely with a length of jute. She slipped her thin wrists in and out of the binds and nodded her approval.

As Isidor briefed her on the events about to take place, Sarah looked confident, determined. The plan called for flawless execution not only on her part, but also on that of Isidor and Daniel. If one of the three engines malfunctioned, the operation would fail. Daniel shuddered at the thought of the consequences should that happen.

Isidor put one hand on Sarah's shoulder, the other on Daniel's. "Are you ready?"

Sarah nodded. "Ready."

Daniel kept his eyes fixed on Sarah. "Let's do this."

Isidor lifted a finger to his mouth and adjusted his

earpiece. He pushed a button and spoke into the micro-phone on his wrist. "I have the hostage. All systems go." He averted his gaze and paused as he listened to further instructions. "Okay . . . yes. Ten minutes." He motioned to Sarah with his head. "Let's go."

"Give us a minute?" Daniel said.

Isidor nodded and walked away.

Daniel turned to Sarah, whose blue eyes shone in the silver light. She was so fierce and yet so vulnerable. If he'd ever doubted his feelings for her, that moment solidified them. "Promise me you'll be careful. There's no room for error."

"I'll be all right, Danny. Just look after yourself."

"Listen, Sarah . . . I know I haven't been myself lately, and maybe I've let you down . . ." Her wrists still bound in jute, she took his hands. A warmth surged through him, giving him the nerve to continue. "Just want to say, I've got your back. That's all."

"I've never doubted it. If I did, I wouldn't consider doing what I'm about to do."

His eyes misted. He needed to say it, in case he never got another chance. "Forgive me, Sarah."

"Forgive you? What for? For risking everything, even putting your sanity on the line, so you could save my life? For being true to your word, even to your own detriment? You're the most honorable man I know." She squeezed his hands. "We'll get through this together, okay?"

"Let's just get through tonight." He touched his forehead to hers for the count of two heartbeats, then let go of her hands. She gave him a lingering glance, slipped a diaphanous white veil over her head, and walked toward Isidor.

Fifty-two

Cave of Trophonius,
393 CE

The darkness, boundless and profound, was an invisible weight pressing down on Aristea. For hours she had sat in the same position, her shivering back against the cool earthen wall, too steeped in shock and agony to move.

The longer she sat in that frigid womb, the more her body temperature dropped. She had to do something to save herself. She clenched her chattering teeth and ripped off the other sleeve. She shredded it and tied the strips tightly around her shin to secure the bone as best she could.

With an effort that made her heart protest, she clawed at the soil and dragged herself across the cave floor. Her immobile leg was deadweight behind her. Attempting to engage it would have made the already intense pain unbearable and worsened the injury besides.

Pressure mounted inside her head. She propped herself with one hand and reached out with the other, feeling for anything that would give her a clue as to the size and constitution of her surroundings. It was for naught: she felt only the moist air.

Exhausted, Aristea collapsed onto the ground,

finding comfort in the smell of damp earth, the coolness of the soil against her cheek. She closed her eyes.

As her heartbeat slowed and her strained breath quieted, perfect silence engulfed the cave. The priestess lay motionless in the dark, her mind surrendering to a meditative state. In her mind's eye, images waxed and waned without reason, without awareness. She let it happen, knowing she was making the ground fertile for Trophonius to sow his seeds.

In time, a force seized her. She gave into it completely. In that semiconscious state, she perceived a different world, one where Mount Olympus was covered in frost and wars were fought for religious dominion, not for the preservation of human rights. A world where the great philosophers crouched in indignity while new orators spoke of oppression instead of ideas.

The words that reverberated in the space between her ears were unmistakable: *Don't let them forget.*

She opened her eyes to blackness and had a revelation: the cave of Trophonius would be her tomb. It could be long years, centuries even, before someone found her remains—and the message she was compelled to leave behind. Perhaps by then, the world would have become a more enlightened place. Perhaps people would no longer harm each other for the advancement of their own race or creed. Perhaps they would cherish vital information left behind by their ancestors, such as the mathematical innovations of Pythagoras, and use it for the good of all.

The pain no longer significant, Aristea crawled on her belly like a serpent, propelling herself forward by the elbows. She groped for something she could use to scrawl a missive and rejoiced when her hand came across a broken pot, likely from a past supplicant's offering to Trophonius.

She felt for the biggest piece as well as a smaller, sharp one. With these in hand, she dragged her body until she came to the edge of the cave. Breathless and perspiring despite the cold, she leaned against the wall and in the utter darkness scratched at the potsherd. However haphazardly, she would reveal the *omphalos'* location—and the name of the man who had saved her—so that neither would be forgotten.

Fifty-three

With her head lowered in submission and her wrists tied, Sarah walked behind Isidor in the procession toward the temple. Behind them was a long column of acolytes dressed in white linen vestments, each holding a candle lantern and murmuring a monotone chant.

Other than the high priest, no one knew who she was. As far as the neo-Delphians were concerned, she was a nymph of the forest to be offered to Apollo. In the past, Isidor had explained, young women had been selected at random and presented at the altar on a bed of flowers. If it pleased the god, the woman would be venerated during the ceremony and set free after.

If it didn't, she would be sacrificed.

The men and women of the cult had no idea that Sarah's destiny had been preordained. Nor did they seem to care. Prior to marching along the Sacred Way, they all had partaken of the "golden elixir," as Isidor called it. Whatever was in it had turned their mood pleasantly numb and their eyes glassy. It was important, apparently, that the acolytes follow and obey without questioning their master's motives.

Holding a lit torch in one hand and a cauldron of incense in the other, Isidor glided along the path like an apparition, vapors streaming behind him and embroidering the air with the sweet scent of cedar and anise. Sarah had put all her trust in him. A single misstep on his part would cost her life. She hoped he was the man she believed him to be.

At the entrance of the sanctuary, the procession stopped and Isidor alone entered the temple. He placed the incense on the marble remains of the grand portico. Sarah visualized the columns that once marked the sacred entryway and supported a pediment carved with the phrase *Know Thyself*. In her mind, she repeated the words like a mantra.

Isidor walked to the center of the temple and walked once around the tripod before lowering the torch into the vessel's belly. Tongues of fire leapt several feet into the air, then calmed down to a steady flame. Isidor lowered his head and chanted a hymn in ancient Greek. That part wasn't an act: he seemed genuinely caught in the moment of worship, of offering fire to the spirits that controlled men's destinies.

To calm the nervousness, Sarah let her mind wander to her comfort zone, where voices from the distant past echoed. So much had changed in twenty-five hundred years, yet the stones of antiquity still stood, albeit battered, as testaments to an early humanity that was as brutal as it was enlightened.

Seeking divine guidance amid fear was a concept as old as time, but it was among those stones that the notion was first integrated into political and military strategy. The prophecies handed down by the priestesses of Delphi didn't only mollify the anxious masses; they steered decisions that shifted boundaries, toppled regimes, and brought forth the demise of nations. When the stakes were no less than world-altering, the sacrificial blood that watered the crags was a necessary device in obtaining truth.

A cold gust, moist with the aftermath of rain, blew through the Phaedriades, pressing the veil against Sarah's face. Isidor glanced at her and blinked slowly, indicating it was time. A chill pricked her skin.

As the adherents lifted their palms to the sky and chanted, he approached her. His face was like the stones of antiquity, yielding nothing. He offered Sarah a hand, and she took it, letting him lead her to the altar of wildflowers.

She stepped onto a square slab, about two feet off the ground, that was the foundation of a long-since ruined building. The platform had been strewn with laurel branches, dwarf iris, and tiny purple blossoms of mountain thyme. She inhaled the sharp, resiny scent and recalled the ancient Greeks' penchant for burning thyme incense to elicit courage.

If ever there was a time for courage, it was now. Sarah sat on the stone and, like a demure maiden, wrapped her arms around her torso. The singing continued until Isidor raised his hands to quiet the voices. He turned toward the Sacred Way, where a second procession ascended toward the temple.

As the flickering flames drew nearer, it was dead quiet. There was no sound, no movement to profane the sacred moment. Sarah saw the faces of three lower priests leading the supplicant: a cloaked figure carrying a wooden box about two feet wide, like a miniature coffin.

The hooded stranger stopped in front of Isidor and placed the box at the priest's feet. Before the visitor had a chance to rise, Isidor placed a hand on his head. "Be humbled, honorable seeker, disciples of Apollo, for this night is sacred beyond any other." He panned his gaze across the gathered neopagans, making eye contact with each. "It marks the birth of the sun god, the day that light and harmony came unto the world. Any oracle given on this night is to be received with reverence—and most of all, to be accepted without questioning."

He let go of the visitor's head and raised his voice an octave. "O, hear us, mighty sun god, as we implore your beauty and wisdom. Accept our modest offerings"—he waved an open palm toward Sarah—"for they are meant to please you. Regard those who search for truth and, if they are worthy, shine your light upon them so they can see."

Isidor nodded to one of the adherents holding a small lyre. The man plucked at the strings and released a sweet melody that reverberated against the ancient stones.

Isidor turned to the visitor. "Reveal yourself to Apollo, kind stranger."

The supplicant lowered his hood. His hair was wrapped in a tight black turban, and a thick black beard engulfed his jaw. The golden torchlight made his dark eyes glisten. He cast a hungry glance at Sarah, who averted her gaze.

"O, seeker of truth," Isidor continued, "what is your sacrifice?"

The man gestured to a goat tied to a cypress tree nearby. The animal shuffled its forelegs, as if it knew what would come next.

Isidor closed his eyes and murmured something incomprehensible before proclaiming, "The god deems you worthy of sacrifice. This you shall do to gain entrance to his sacred sanctuary."

He turned to the other priests and raised his hands to the sky. The chanting swelled, staccato bursts echoing off the mountain. A priest dipped laurel leaves into a bowl of liquid and sprinkled the temple floor. Another brought an urn and placed it on the sacrifice stone, directly in front of the platform on which Sarah sat.

At Isidor's signal, the visitor untied the goat and walked it to the altar. He took a step back and watched as the high priest poured spring water onto the animal's head. As the cold shower overwhelmed it, the goat trembled from its hooves up.

With arms outstretched, the priest looked toward the moon: "On this auspicious eve, as the snows give way to new life, we celebrate the return of Apollo from the land of the Hyperboreans and honor his presence. Mighty Apollo, fairest and gentlest of gods, shine your light upon those who implore you for guidance. Accept the flesh of this poor beast and let its stricken body become a conduit for your will."

An acolyte approached and offered Isidor a sheathed knife. The priest exposed the blade a little at a time, making theater of the act. He lifted the knife above his head and drove it into the goat's throat. The animal bleated and convulsed as its blood spilled onto the stone.

Though she'd known it was coming, Sarah felt as if she would retch.

Isidor searched the fallen viscera for a sign. He stopped, stabbed the knife into the liver, and proclaimed in a voice so loud it echoed off the mountain: "The omens are unfavorable. The god is not pleased."

A murmur fell over the gathered. The supplicant glared at the high priest, his stance suggestive of an animal in attack mode.

Only Sarah was not surprised. She knew this was part of Delphinios' plan to unnerve his guest before delivering the show of shows.

Isidor clutched his hair with both hands and revealed clenched teeth. He dropped to his knees, then grunted and jerked like a man possessed.

Sarah bit her lip. *No margin for error.*

In a fiendish voice, Isidor uttered a string of unintelligible words. The supplicant stared at him wide-eyed and took small steps backward. He looked around, as if searching for a clue as to what to do next.

A deep rumble shook the mountain. A puff of smoke shot up from the earth, then another.

"What is this?" Sweat glistened on the visitor's brow. "I demand to know what is going on here!"

The smoke grew more profuse until it clouded the mountainside. The priest ran his bloody hands along his face and down his white vestment. He stood, slumped and spent, heaving as he caught his breath. He choked out the words, "The spirit of Apollo is among us."

A thunderclap sounded, and a high-definition, three-dimensional image materialized in the gorge beyond the sanctuary, eliciting a collective gasp. A youth with golden curls tumbling down his neck, faint but radiant behind a layer of blue fog, spoke to the assembly in a hushed tone. "Let whosoever has faith drop to his knees."

Isidor kneeled first, and one by one the other neopagans followed suit. The supplicant was the last to obey the order.

Sarah did not move.

The likeness of Apollo pointed at the crowd. The resolution and the movement were so realistic that it would have intrigued even Sarah had she not known it was a hologram. "Is there one among you who doubts the gods can rip mountains asunder and raise fury in the seas?" He paused. They were still as the columns of antiquity. "Be cautioned, mortals: the wrath of the gods has been triggered. Only blood will appease them now." He shifted his gaze to the altar of flowers.

All heads turned toward Sarah. An adrenaline surge flushed her cheeks.

"Lift the veil," he whispered.

Isidor rose and walked to the altar. With shaking hands he lifted Sarah's veil until her face was revealed. As he regarded her eyes for a split second, his forehead tightened. He stepped aside and faced the apparition.

The youth wore a serene expression. He closed his eyes and smiled. "A beauty fit for a god. Release her spirit to me. Only then will I reveal the supreme and abiding truth."

Isidor walked to the altar of sacrifice, where the entrails of the goat were still strewn. With his back to the assembly, he placed one hand on the liver and the other on the knife that was wedged in it. He looked up at Sarah.

Sarah released a whimper and slumped forward. Her shoulders shook as she pretended to weep softly.

She felt the warmth radiate from Isidor's body as he stood inches away from her.

"Apollo has chosen you. Go in peace to your fate."

Sarah raised her gaze to her would-be executioner.

His bloodied left fist was pressed against his torso. He held out his right arm and pointed the blade toward her. She held her breath.

"As Apollo is my witness, I offer this soul to the four winds that will carry it to the heart of Olympus, where it will dwell forever. May it bring the god of light pleasure, and may he shine his favor upon mortals this sacred eve."

Isidor bent over Sarah and engaged the practiced gesture: he thrust his left hand toward her midsection, quickly slipping the animal's liver inside the fold of her gown. With his right hand, he drove the knife into the juicy organ, twisting and tearing to produce the maximum amount of blood.

As Sarah wailed and convulsed, Isidor removed the knife triumphantly and turned to the assembly with outstretched arms. Blood dripped from his hands to the soil.

The smoke grew more profuse, and the hologram faded to nothing.

"Apollo has sent us a sign." Isidor's deep voice carried across the chasm. "Let us not forsake it." He turned to the supplicant. "The god has agreed to grant you an oracle under one condition: it must be followed to the letter. Do this not, and face the gods' wrath."

The supplicant nodded, though the look in his eyes suggested he wanted out of there. He clearly was bewildered by the intensity of what he'd just witnessed.

As if on cue, the sacred fire inside the temple hearth

subsided, and the ancient site was once again cast in darkness. Sarah ceased to move and closed her eyes. She lay on her side, tomb-still. With shallow, imperceptible breaths, she inhaled the scent of thyme and was surprised it overpowered the pungent odor of the blood smeared across her body.

She heard the rustle of Isidor's robes as he approached the pedestal. A whisper of fabric descended upon her face, then her body. "The Pythia awaits," he said. "Let us make haste."

Feet shuffled across the rocky soil, crushing bits of limestone. The faithful uttered soft incantations to the beat of a frame drum. The voices grew fainter until they were heard no more.

She opened her eyes. The temple had been darkened, save for the embers of the eternal flame. Everyone had gone. She lay still a while longer, ensuring there were no surprises.

The first part of the plan had been executed flawlessly. But the trickiest part was still ahead.

Fifty-four

From a rented studio in a rundown five-story apartment complex on the edge of Delphi town, Bellamy watched the most important night of his life unfold.

Isidor had just entered the *adyton*, his hands and vestment stained with the blood of Sarah Weston. Bellamy sneered. At last, the detestable woman who'd challenged him every step of the way lay in a bloody, lifeless heap. Bellamy wished he could say the same of her partner.

Madigan was still at large, but without Weston, he was nothing. Bellamy was certain of it.

He trained his eyes on the screen corresponding with camera three, positioned just above the cubicle of the supplicant. Zafrani walked in and stopped in front of a wall separating him from the priestess of the temple, deliverer of Apollo's word and men's fates.

The Syrian's gaze was shifty. He kept wiping his brow with a kerchief, as if he worried what would happen next. *Good*, Bellamy thought. *Fear is a beautiful thing*.

Shortly after Zafrani was in position, Phoebe entered. Her youthful alabaster face and tumbling brown hair were hidden behind the hood of an oxblood cloak.

She took her position on the tripod of truth, whose legs represented the present, past, and future. The perch was positioned over a crack in the Earth for maximum access to the sweet vapors.

Isidor handed Phoebe a bowl of water and a laurel branch. The girl was silent, stock-still.

Five torches burned behind her. Trembling shadows danced on the stone walls. Bellamy marveled at the re-creation of the scene exactly as described by Plutarch. All was in place; the only thing missing was the *omphalos*, the stone that marked Delphi's position at the center of the Earth. The stone holding the secret that would destroy his enemies.

Isidor approached the supplicant. "Ask your question, and all will be revealed."

Zafrani's jaw tightened. Through a small window carved into the wall, he gazed at the priestess, poised as a living statue. He inhaled sharply. "O pure and sage Oracle, O great priestess of Apollo, are the omens favorable for exterminating the tyrants who rule the world with an iron fist?"

Phoebe sucked on a laurel leaf, then another. She shifted her gaze toward the bowl of water and looked into it for a long while. She was resurrecting an ancient rite, in which the Pythia stared at the sacred water from the spring of Kassotis to allow the vision of Apollo's will to manifest itself. Bellamy was delighted to see his rigorous instruction over the course of six years was paying dividends. His youngest child was the very manifestation of the priestess who once ruled the oracle of Delphi: pure, graceful, obedient, divine.

Phoebe looked up. In her vacant gaze Bellamy could see she was already high. She spoke in the language of the gods, incomprehensible to mere mortals. Her voice was hoarse as a man's, belying her delicate beauty.

Isidor interpreted: "Dwellers of the ancient kingdom, sons of the Sumerians and the Hittites, hear now the word of Apollo, son of Zeus."

Her eyes grew wider, and her voice rose a notch. And the priest said, "I hear the thunder of crumbling mountains, the roar of the raging sea. Poseidon's wrath has been provoked, and it cannot be reversed."

Phoebe shifted in her seat, as if unable to find comfort. Her body trembled as she spoke, causing ripples to disturb the holy water. The gases had taken effect, precisely as planned.

Isidor decoded her unintelligible utterings for the benefit of the seeker. "Old summit crumbles, water swells; the seed removed for good. Minoans mourn the gift they left; canaries sing the song of death."

Bellamy licked his lips. He could taste victory.

Zafrani asked again. "O sage one, unveil the secret that will crush our enemies and release our people from bondage."

More words, followed by a guttural gasp, left the

priestess' throat. Her eyes rolled back into her head, and her mouth dropped open. The branch fell from her hands.

Isidor continued. "Warriors of the Levant, take heed: evil stirs among your allies. He who hails from the infidel's lands will betray you before the deed is done."

Zafrani sprang to his feet. "What do you say?"

Bellamy stood. Tom was right: Isidor was a traitor.

Her chest heaving, her head fallen to one side, Phoebe shrieked out three words. The priest pointed to the seeker and spoke in a commanding voice. "Abandon or perish."

The priestess slumped on the tripod. The bowl tumbled to the ground, and the seeing water dispersed.

Isidor kept his gaze trained on Zafrani. "Your fate is bound to the Earth. It cannot be undone."

"Jesus Christ." Bellamy felt cold blood trickle through his veins. He yelled for his aide.

Tom Sorenson rushed to the doorway. "Sir. Is everything all right?"

"Start the earthquake sequence. Now." The colonel strapped on a holster. "I'm going in."

Fifty-five

By the time Sarah snuck into the tunnel, the atmosphere in the *adyton* was charged. The whites of his eyes glowing in the firelight and his nostrils flaring like a bull's, the Syrian visitor stood squarely in front of Isidor, staring him down. Obviously he didn't like what he'd heard.

"What is the meaning of this?" Zafrani hissed.

"That is the word of Apollo." Isidor's voice was calm. "Go now in peace."

He spoke through clenched teeth. "I was assured I'd be given specific instructions, so you'd better ask your god again." He pushed Isidor aside and grabbed one of the torches. "Or I will set fire to this place."

As he uttered the words, the ground shook. Zafrani swung the torch but missed the priest.

"You were warned to heed Apollo's oracle to the letter," Isidor said. "Now you have angered the god—and you must pay."

Zafrani came at Isidor, but the priest was too agile. He dodged the Syrian, leading him around in a circle.

Another, deeper vibration caused the cave walls to crack. Bits of limestone dislodged and crumbled to the ground. As the earthquake tore at the earth, the fissure from which the gases flowed grew wider. The Delphic tripod faltered and toppled, sending the dazed girl to the ground. She was inches away from the cleft.

Ignoring the tremor that threatened to knock her off her feet, Sarah ran to Phoebe and dragged her away from danger.

Uttering a string of obscenities in Arabic, Zafrani threw the torch to the ground and staggered toward the tunnel.

From the dark opening came a voice, loud enough to be heard over the rumble. "And where do you think you're going?"

Clutching Phoebe, Sarah turned toward the sound.

A stout, gray-haired man entered, his handgun pointed at Zafrani. *Bellamy.*

The colonel glanced at Sarah, then glared at Isidor. "Well, well. Betrayed by my own blood. I expected more of you, Isidor. I should have known you're no better than your conniving Greek mother."

Isidor stared down his father.

Bellamy spat and turned to the Syrian visitor. "Pay no mind to what you've heard this impostor say. The traitor he speaks of is himself. The plan will go off flawlessly as soon as we get our hands on the formula. My men are retrieving it as we speak. Forty-eight hours; no more."

Zafrani stared at him coldly. "Whatever you say, boss."

"You don't seem convinced, my friend. Perhaps you're unaware of what I'm capable of." He raised the gun to Zafrani's forehead.

A fresh tremor forced Bellamy to lose his balance. As he tried to steady himself on a wall, Zafrani took the opportunity to make a run for it. Bellamy fired after him, the gunshots exploding like a series of thunderclaps in the narrow confines of the oracular cave.

Sarah bent over Phoebe and raised her hands over the child's head. What had happened to Daniel? According to the plan, he should have been there already. The cave continued to shake violently, threatening to crumble around them.

"Sarah," Isidor cried, "watch out!"

She looked up just in time to avoid a slab of stone crashing down from the ceiling. To her horror, the fissure, the weak point, opened like a great maw and swallowed the tripod.

Bellamy stood and stumbled toward them, staying on the periphery of the crumbling structure.

Isidor yelled over the clamor. "Save yourself, Sarah. This is between me and him."

The colonel pointed the gun at her. "Oh, I don't think so, son. There won't be any survivors tonight. It's the least I could do to reward your performance." He leered at Sarah and spat, "Get away from my daughter."

Sarah stood. "How dare you pose as her father? You've only ever used her"—she pointed to Isidor—"and everyone else in your orbit. And all to commit treason."

Bellamy shot at the wall next to Sarah. "Treason is

only real if you believe in God and country, Dr. Weston. They both left me a long time ago." He turned the weapon toward Isidor. "As for you, deserter, get ready to pay. This is my last bullet. I saved it for you."

Sarah screamed as the gun fired. Isidor doubled over, clutching his midsection. He dropped to his knees and fell to his side. The wall behind him was spattered with blood.

Shaking, Sarah turned away, sheltering Phoebe in her arms. With surprising strength, the girl pushed out of Sarah's grasp and staggered upright.

Phoebe's eyes were glassy, but her gaze was fierce. "I've waited all my life to be with my father." Her voice was barely audible above the rumble of the heaving earth. "My mother said he had the strength of a lion and the wisdom of our ancestors. A great man, worthy of sacrifice." Rocks crumbled around her, as if she stood on the brink between heaven and hell. She faltered but did not fall. "Many times I wanted to run from this place, to be free. What kept me here was a sense of duty to a man I thought was real."

Sarah winced at the raw display of lost innocence. She swallowed hard. In her peripheral vision she saw Daniel standing in the dark folds of the tunnel entrance. But even the relief at the sight of him couldn't brighten the darkness of that moment.

"Well, I'm sorry to disappoint you, honey," Bellamy said. "It's good that you learn now: the world is full of letdowns and betrayals. You can't even rely on your own people to save you. There is no family, no divine law. We walk alone. We make our own fate."

Phoebe stood straighter. "I don't believe it."

"That's right, sweetheart." Daniel stepped out of the shadows. "Don't believe it."

"Well, look who's here: the righteous hillbilly." Spittle dripped from Bellamy's mouth. "Not very smart, are you, boy? You just keep coming back for more." He bared his teeth. "Come over here and let's finish this."

Daniel's gaze was riveted on Bellamy. "Sarah, get the kid out of here."

"Danny . . ." Her blood ran cold at the thought of leaving him alone with that monster.

He glanced at her. His amber eyes burned with determination. "Leave us. We have some business to see to."

With a primal yell, Bellamy lunged at Daniel. Daniel blocked the advance with his forearms and held him back.

Sarah was paralyzed, unable to decide between staying and helping her partner, or moving the child out of harm's way.

Phoebe decided for her. As another tremor dislodged more rocks and threatened to seal the entrance, she grabbed Sarah's wrist and pulled her toward the tunnel.

Hand in hand, they stumbled over fallen chunks of limestone as they made their way out. The thick dust stung Sarah's eyes, blurred her vision, and caused her to cough violently.

As they approached the mouth, the ceiling collapsed. Sarah wrapped one arm around Phoebe's waist and, holding the girl tightly, dove toward the exit. Together they tumbled twice on the wet ground before a tree broke their momentum.

Her ribs aching from the impact, Sarah rolled to her side and looked toward the tunnel. The entrance was sealed almost completely shut. She shouted his name and heard her voice echo in the void of the gorge.

Water dripped into her eyes from the ends of her hair. It was raining. A hand touched her shoulder, and she looked up. Phoebe was kneeling beside her.

"Do not fret." The girl's eyes were distant. Oddly, the words put Sarah at ease. "They will both live. I saw it in the water."

Sarah lowered her head into her palms, trying to find the strength to believe.

When she looked up again, the girl was gone.

Fifty-six

Daniel's biceps burned as he struggled to hold back his opponent. Bellamy may have been almost thirty years his senior, but he was strong as iron. Their bodies were so close that Daniel could see the sweat beads forming on the colonel's furrowed forehead.

From the corner of his eye, Daniel thought he saw Isidor stir. That split second of broken concentration cost him.

Bellamy pushed him away and landed a right hook to his jaw. Daniel stumbled on a pile of rocks and fell backward. The colonel pinned him down with a knee to the sternum and wrapped a hand around his throat. "Did you come here to kill me, boy?" He shouted, "Answer me!"

"No. You answer me." Daniel clenched his teeth. "Did you kill my father?"

Bellamy sneered. "Your daddy killed himself. I bought him rounds of moonshine, but I didn't make him drink it. A man has to take ownership of his own flaws." He pressed hard on Daniel's ribs. "Ain't that right?"

Daniel's eye twitched. "Son of a bitch. Killing you would be more than you deserve."

"You can't kill a dead man, son. I died a long time

ago. A long, painful death at the hand of the enemy. Know what that feels like, Danny boy?"

Daniel didn't answer.

"Well, let me tell you: it's some kind of hell. My captors had orders to destroy me. At first, they just made me watch other men being tortured. Men stripped naked and sprayed so hard with high-power hoses they were thrashing like cockroaches. Others tied to a chair and having their teeth sawed or their tongues crushed with pliers. Their wails replayed in my mind, kept me up at night.

"Then it was my turn. A Russian doctor roused me in the middle of the night and marched me into a chamber with a respirator tank. He told me to get in." Bellamy's face twisted into a look of disgust.

Part of Daniel wanted to punish the monster, but the empathetic part, the one he couldn't suppress even though he was seething, needed to hear him out.

The colonel leaned in. "Now I'm guessing you've never been tortured, so I'm going to tell you what it's like inside one of those tanks. You can't touch anything; you can't move. You hear nothing but the respirator's motor, this constant, low-pitch hum. You're floating in blackness with no sensation whatsoever—for seventy-two hours. You scream and cry like a woman, just to remind yourself you're alive. Know what happens to the mind of a man when there's sensory deprivation?" He crept his fingers up to Daniel's jaw and squeezed hard. "It snaps."

As a scientist, Daniel knew Bellamy was right: sensory deprivation caused abnormally high stress levels in subjects, a type of anxiety that couldn't be shaken when stimulus was restored. Some intelligence entities used techniques like that to brainwash prisoners into sharing privileged information—or buy into enemy propaganda.

Daniel clawed at Bellamy's fingers to dislodge them, but it only made his opponent bear down harder.

"I'm not finished, son," the colonel said. "Now listen carefully, 'cause there's going to be a test. After I was released from the tank, my captors put me inside a bright room—I'm talking blinding—and pumped me full of hype about America's imperialistic plans to control the world. I remember being tied up and listening to stories and watching films about American abandonment of its own citizens in favor of advancing a covert agenda."

"For God's sake, man. You were an army officer." Daniel choked out the words. "How could you believe such things?"

"'Cause they were true, that's how. It happened to me. I waited and waited to be freed, but no one came. After a while, I realized nobody gave a damn about me. I was written off, as if I never existed at all. I ask you, Madigan: is it worth being loyal to a country that wouldn't hesitate to betray you?"

"We had a saying in the Navy: not self but country. It's never about any one of us. You have to trust the greater purpose, even die for it. If you don't, you're lost."

Bellamy relaxed his grip and stood. "On your feet, boy."

Daniel obeyed.

Bellamy's eyes were wild, his chest heaving. He'd stepped over the edge of reason; there was no bringing him back.

"I don't like your holier-than-thou attitude, Madigan. I'm prepared to eliminate you here and now." He cracked his knuckles. "But I'm feeling generous, so I'm going to offer you one chance to redeem yourself. We have intercepted a DHL shipment sent by Sarah Weston to a Jackson Barnes in New Jersey. Want to guess what was in that box?"

Daniel winced at the notion of his advisor being pulled into this mess.

"Now we know the *omphalos* stone is in Turkey. But we as ordinary citizens can't get permits to dig it up . . . unless we have an eminent archaeologist on board. I'm proposing to hire you to head up our little operation. You don't even have to get your hands dirty; just lend your name. You do that for me, and I'll spare your life. You have my word."

Daniel shook his head and gave a sideways smile. "Colonel, my name's all I've got. And I'm not willing to sell it to you. I'd rather die."

An aftershock ripped through the cave. Daniel looked down and watched the ground crumble beneath his feet. In a heartbeat, he slid downward. As a cloud of red dust obscured his vision, he clawed for purchase but all the rock within reach had come loose. A chunk hit him just above the brow, knocking him onto his back on a thin ledge.

In the darkness, Daniel saw the shadow of a falling mass and heard Bellamy's profanities as the man landed next to him with a thud. Daniel felt the rock give and realized the ledge couldn't support both their weight. As hot blood streamed into his eye, he saw the flickering light.

Never again, he told himself. *Never again.*

Daniel struggled to sit upright. He felt lightheaded, nauseated. Grateful the tremor had stopped, he groped for a handhold until he found solid rock. Grunting, he tried to pull himself upward.

"Where do you think you're going, soldier?" Bellamy said. "You can't abandon a superior officer."

Without replying, Daniel edged upward.

"A man is down, goddamn it. Deserter! You're just like the rest of them."

Daniel's breath was clipped, and his eyes stung with a cocktail of blood and perspiration, but he pressed on. His physical struggle was nothing compared to his mental one. He fought against the riptide of memories: slamming headfirst onto a cockpit wall, sheets of blood obscuring his vision, straining to break free from an airplane seat to get himself to safety. And he wrestled with what to do with Bellamy.

Daniel had been trained, as a Navy Diver and as a man, to never leave the wounded behind. But this was different. Bellamy was a menace to society, a clear and present danger.

Daniel stopped. In the fog of his mind, he saw scenes from his life, as if the end drew near. He heard the voice of his mother insisting he go to college and pledging to work nights and weekends cleaning houses to pay his tuition. And the surprisingly gentle nature of his naval commander, who taught him it was worth paying the physical and emotional toll for greatness.

And Sarah: the woman who, without fanfare or ambition, followed her convictions, even if it meant being vilified for it. Who stood tall in the face of injustice but never raised a hand in judgment.

A single word came to his mind: honor.

He looked back at the shadowy outline of Bellamy. The colonel dragged himself in a way that suggested he'd lost use of his legs. He wouldn't be able to climb out unassisted.

Gritting his teeth and praying he wouldn't regret it, he climbed down and stretched a hand toward Bellamy.

"I didn't think you had it in you, boy. Once in a while, a man gets pleasantly surprised." The colonel wrapped his hand around Daniel's wrist.

Grunting, Daniel pulled the man up.

"I can't move my leg. I think something's broken."

"Get on my back and hang on. And pray for no more tremors."

Bellamy struggled to grab hold of Daniel's shoulders and, unable to balance his weight, hung there like a two-hundred-pound log. Sweat trickled down Daniel's face and neck as he pulled the two of them up an inch at a time. He felt his hold slipping under the stress of the extra weight.

His heart protested against the effort. As he strained, the tendons of his neck came close to snapping. He huffed and stopped to gather his strength. He was unsure he could carry on.

Suddenly, the cave was flooded with a white beam from above. Daniel looked up, squinting beneath the artificial light.

"Can you hear me?" a male voice said in Greek.

Daniel answered in the affirmative.

"We're from mountain rescue. We're coming down. Can you hang on a few more minutes?"

Daniel fought to maintain a grip. "I don't know. I'll try."

The rescue worker pointed the lights into the crevasse, and for the first time, Daniel could see how deep it was. The chasm reached so far down he couldn't see the bottom. The quake had left behind torn, jagged rock, like giant, fossilized teeth. Losing his grip wasn't an option.

He watched the workers gun the carabiners into the rock and pass the rope through. Though they appeared competent, he knew from experience it would take a good ten minutes, maybe more, to rig the rope system.

Daniel felt his fingers slide. Gritting his teeth, he struggled to maintain a handhold.

"There's not enough room here for two." With one hand, Bellamy reached for a hold on the rock. He smiled sideways and abruptly let go of Daniel's back, throwing him off-balance and sending him on a downward slide.

This was the end; Daniel was sure of it.

A limestone outcropping slowed him enough to gain tentative purchase on the rock. He hung there with one hand, his feet dangling in the void.

He looked up. Sarah kneeled on the edge of the chasm, her hands covering her mouth. His glance darted toward Bellamy, who clung to the rock twenty feet above.

One of the rescue workers, not waiting to be fully roped, clipped in and dropped to Daniel. "Steady," he said. "This is going to be tricky."

Daniel knew that already.

"Try not to move." The rescuer reached around his waist and fastened a belt, then clipped the belt to his rope. With one point of security, he passed the ends of the belt between Daniel's legs to make a makeshift sit harness.

Though it was not an ideal situation, Daniel could work with it. He grabbed the rope with his other hand and let go of the rock. He nodded to the rescuer. "Let's do this."

As they ascended to the cave floor, Daniel glanced at Bellamy, still stuck on the rock and awaiting his own rescue. The colonel's frigid expression turned into a snarl. At that moment, Daniel knew there was no redemption in that soul. He carried on climbing, vowing to never look into those eyes again.

When they reached the top, Daniel watched Isidor being carried out on a stretcher. The remaining rescue workers had tied a second stretcher to the rope frame and were lowering it to Bellamy.

As he unclipped from the rope, Sarah approached. Her white gown was ripped and covered in blood, and her skin and hair were coated with ochre dust. Still, she was radiant.

She lifted her hand to his face and wiped the blood from his brow. He placed his hand on hers and squeezed. They exchanged a lingering glance, both at a loss for what to say. It was all right: no words were needed.

The workers hoisted Bellamy's immobilized body strapped onto the rescue litter. Quickly they unclipped the apparatus and prepared to carry the stretcher out of the dilapidated cave.

A police officer informed Bellamy he was under arrest and read him a list of rights. Bellamy was quiet but smug. Daniel could read his mind: he was sure he could bribe his way out of this crime, as he'd done countless times before. He wasn't aware that while he was deploying holograms and inducing seismicity on the ancient ruins of Delphi, Daniel was communicating with Interpol. He'd called Heinrich Gerst on his private line, compliments of Sarah, and blown the disgraced colonel's cover, setting the wheels in motion for the seizing of his assets and his extradition to the United States. There would be no more chances for Colonel Stephen Bellamy.

As he was being carried out of the cave, Bellamy called to Daniel. "Hey, Danny boy. I'll see you—and your father—in hell."

"You're already there, cowboy," Daniel said softly. He didn't care to be heard. "You're already there."

Sarah turned to him. "Danny . . . Isidor is barely clinging to life. He needs a transfusion, but I heard the paramedics say he has a rare blood type. They're going to chopper him to Athens and hope for the best."

"What about Phoebe? Can't she help him?"

She shook her head. "Phoebe's gone missing."

"Any idea where she could've gone?"

"I'd assumed she'd gone to call mountain rescue. But she never reappeared." Sarah snapped her fingers. "That's it. Mountain rescue is based in Arachova. It's where her mother lived."

He put his hand on the small of her back. "Come on. We have to move fast."

Fifty-seven

Sarah and Daniel stepped out of the police car that had transported them to Arachova. The sun was beginning its ascent over the mountains, painting magenta plumes onto the steely post-storm sky and promising to disperse the fog that had settled upon the village.

Sarah led the way up the hill to Lydia's house. Phoebe had almost certainly retreated to the house she grew up in, looking for her mother. Sarah dreaded having to tell the girl the truth.

The front door was ajar. Sarah pushed it open and peeked inside. All was dark inside the shuttered house. There was a musty smell, like water had intruded, laced with the vague scent of wood fire.

She was there.

With Daniel behind her, she walked toward the living room. Phoebe was sitting in front of the fireplace, stoking a meager fire, unaware anyone had intruded. Sarah approached and called her name.

Phoebe jumped. "Go away!" Her voice quivered. "My mother isn't home."

"We mean you no harm, sweetheart," Daniel said.

Sarah noticed an oil lamp on the table and some matches nearby. She lit it and held it next to her own face so the girl would recognize her. "We come as friends," she said softly. "We're here to help you, like you helped us."

Phoebe relaxed. "What happened to my father?"

"He's been arrested," Daniel said. "He's hurt many people, including you. He needs help."

"Does my mother know?"

Sarah had practiced what she would say, but anxiety still gnawed at her. "Phoebe, your mother . . ." Emotion claimed her voice. She paused to regain her composure. "Your mother has died. I'm sorry."

"No." The girl whimpered. "You're lying."

Sarah glanced at Daniel. He looked down, obviously disturbed by the memory. "We were there," she continued. "We were with her when . . ." She couldn't get the rest of the words out. As she pulled the chain out of her pocket, tears formed in her eyes. She wiped them with her palm and walked closer to the child.

Sarah held out the pendant. "She wanted me to give you this."

Shaking like an aspen leaf in autumn, Phoebe accepted the object. She studied it for a moment, then opened the locket. "Mommy," she whispered and stroked the tiny photo.

Sarah placed a hand over her mouth to contain her own sobs. She wanted to say something to soothe the little girl, but all that had happened over the last couple of months crashed onto the shore of her soul like a tsunami. She'd faced evil before, but never had she witnessed the brazen stripping of a child's innocence.

She put her arms around Phoebe's shoulders. The child looked at her with melancholy but tearless eyes and collapsed into her arms. Sarah wanted to hold her for as long as it took to make it all better, but no amount of time could take that pain away.

Sarah felt Daniel's presence behind them. Phoebe released Sarah and gazed at him.

"You're not alone, you know," he told the girl.

"But I have no family. No one even knows who I am."

"You do have family," Sarah said. "Isidor is your half-brother. Your father's first child, from a marriage that dissolved long ago."

Phoebe took a step back, pallor washing over her face.

"I know it's a lot to take in, but it's the truth." Sarah clutched the girl's hands and squeezed. "Phoebe, Isidor needs you."

Her gaze trailed off. "That explains everything . . . my vision . . ." She looked at Daniel, then at Sarah. "I saw him drowning in a whirlpool. Then I put my hand in the water and it was calm. I could see his face . . ."

"He's fighting for his life. He needs a blood transfusion and the hospital will be hard-pressed to find a match. Only a close relative can help him."

The look in her eyes suggested she already knew.

"Tell me what to do."

"There is a police officer outside," Daniel said. "If you agree, he can take you right now to the helicopter that's flying Isidor to Athens. There's very little time."

"All these years, Isidor has never left my side," the girl said. "He's protected me like an angel. I'll give all I have."

"You're sage beyond your years, Phoebe," Sarah said. "It would have pleased your mother."

Daniel extended a hand. "Come with me, little lady."

The girl gave Sarah a quick hug. "We will meet again."

Sarah smiled. "I know."

The three walked out of the dark womb that was Lydia's house. As Daniel helped Phoebe into the backseat of the police car, Sarah looked back at the ramshackle edifice, the shuttered windows like closed eyes refusing to admit the harsh light of reality. A wisp of gray smoke escaped from the chimney and drifted toward the low-hanging clouds, becoming one with the fog.

Daniel placed a gentle hand on her shoulder. "We should go."

She nodded and ducked into the car. The officer turned on the blue lights and blared the monotone siren. Gravel crunched beneath the tires as he sped away, leaving a small gathering of curious Arachovites in a haze of red dust.

As the sun shimmered above the peaks of Mount Parnassus, a rooster called to it, welcoming the dawn.

Epilogue

Through a diving mask, the waters of the Gönen Çayi appeared halcyon and pristine, as if nothing had disturbed them in centuries. A beam of light broke through the surface, illuminating the way to the long-forgotten object.

Sarah inhaled through a regulator and glanced behind her at Daniel, who had just entered the water and was swimming to her side. Like her, he was outfitted in a black wet suit with full breathing apparatus. They were going to be down there for a while.

Daniel gave Sarah the thumbs-up, and she led the way to the spot she'd reconnoitered not so long ago. With smooth, barely perceptible strokes of her fins, she swam down to the base of the old Roman bridge. The last time she was there, she didn't have the benefit of scuba gear, so she stayed down only long enough to confirm the location of the stone. She was excited to spend more time with the artifact—and to have Daniel's input, which she'd profoundly missed.

Her pressure gauge recorded forty feet as they neared the base of the pylons' foundation. Sarah pinpointed the site—the base of the pier nearest the west bank—and descended for a closer look. She hovered near the spot, but the object wasn't readily visible, possibly buried as the riverbed shifted with the currents.

She pushed aside the silt, raising a plume of sand mud that made the water murky. As the sediment settled, the familiar blackened umber stone came into view. Sarah ran a hand across its porous surface and felt the grain and tiny depressions that distinguished it as the most primitive material of the universe, belched up from the bowels of the planet through a massive explosion.

Daniel shone a light on the surface and moved it across the markings on the stone. The inscribed pattern, eroded from centuries of being buried underwater, was a series of geometric shapes linked together with obvious intent. The carver was not simply amusing the eye; he was telling a story.

When Sarah had first seen the stone, she hadn't realized its meaning. Now, with exposure to the Pythagoreans' long-held theory, she could see there was profound truth in Isidor's claim. The symbols clearly were part of a mathematical equation. But deciphering it would be nearly impossible, as only a part of the stone was visible. The rest was wedged into the foundation structure. Getting to it would mean destroying the ruins of the bridge pylons, something for which they weren't likely to be granted permits.

Sarah unclipped the underwater camera from her belt

and began recording the find from various angles. That photographic record could help build a case for further study, or even excavation, of the artifact.

As she photographed, she imagined the hands that carved the intricate network of symbols with the mystical meaning. She thought of Pythagoras' legendary encampment in Delphi, his consulting with the priests of a center of waning influence and with the priestess who had the power to revive it, and suddenly she knew his intent.

As Greece's power diminished like a raindrop on hot stone and a fog settled over her once-enlightened inhabitants, Pythagoras had offered the ultimate, if dangerous, knowledge: if the Greeks knew the mysteries of planetary forces, they could harness them for ethnopolitical supremacy.

But it was not to be. In Pythagoras' day, the Greeks quarreled and divided. Desperate to subdue their rising enemies, they'd grown weary of nuanced philosophical thought and wanted quick, easy fixes. Though Pythagoras taught "domination through innovation," no one was listening. They were far too consumed with the barbarians at the gate to engage in that kind of reflection.

Perhaps it was just as well. Men, then and now, were incapable of wielding such power without straying from the knife's edge between humanity and human nature.

Daniel tapped the depth gauge on his wrist and pointed up. They were running low on air and had to surface. Sarah clipped the camera onto her belt and gave him the thumbs-up. As they ascended, the sunbeam breaking through the surface of the river shimmered into the depths, illuminating the shadows. She felt the sun's warmth on her cheeks and was overcome by a peaceful sensation.

She surfaced first and floated there, waiting for Daniel. The green fringes of the Gönen Çayi were dotted with red-and-white wildflowers trembling in the spring breeze. All was profoundly quiet.

Daniel emerged from the water and removed his regulator. "You're getting pretty good at this." He winked. "Diving, I mean."

They swam to the riverbank and exited the water, shedding their oxygen tanks and fins. Sarah caught a glimpse of movement in the distance. She did a double take and saw Isidor in a wheelchair, which Phoebe was pushing.

Sarah smiled. They'd arrived just in time. She peeled the black dive hood off her head and shook out her hair. Phoebe parked the wheelchair at the riverbank and ran into Sarah's arms.

Daniel shook Isidor's hand. "You're looking good. What are the doctors saying?"

"I'm lucky to be alive. The bullet exited through my spine, and I'm partially paralyzed from the waist down— for now, anyway." He smiled at his sister. "We're working on that."

"I've told him he has to get better to walk me to school in the fall," Phoebe said.

Sarah squatted next to Isidor's chair. "Well, here's something that will motivate you to walk again." She unclipped the digital camera and clicked through some of the photos.

"Remarkable. The symbols are clearer than I thought." Isidor squinted at the tiny screen. "But it's hard to tell there's a formula here."

"It's a partial representation," Sarah said. "The rest of the stone is hidden in the fill. The only way to get the full picture is to excavate it."

"Is that likely to happen?"

Daniel interjected. "We're looking at a stratigraphical layer, one of several. In other words, an artifact within an artifact. I'm not sure the Turkish government will allow an excavation. But we will try."

Isidor glanced at Daniel, then at Sarah. "Say they grant the permits. Then what?"

"Then an underwater archaeology team goes in and retrieves the artifacts," Daniel said. "It has to be done layer by layer. It's a slow process. Getting to the stone could take years."

"And deciphering the formula could take years after that," Sarah added. "At the end of the day, everyone will come out with a theory and no one will agree. It's the way the game is played."

"Even so, it makes me nervous." Isidor's gaze wandered toward the water. "In a way, some things are best kept a mystery."

Sarah put her hand on his. "We shouldn't fear the truth, Isidor. This knowledge wasn't meant to destroy. It was cautionary. A philosopher's charge was to present ideas, to lay the groundwork for others. In this case, enlightened men and women, whether in Pythagoras' time or some distant future, could use the knowledge to prevent disasters of a catastrophic scale, not cause them. The true strength of nations lies in innovation, not in war."

Isidor nodded and squeezed her hand. "It is exactly what the Pythagoreans believe. Only you have more faith in mankind than we do."

"When you study the ancient world, you can't help but have such faith. For thousands of years, civilized people have demonstrated enormous power—both good and bad. But we've persisted in spite of ourselves, haven't we?"

"Touché."

"Never argue with a woman wielding a shovel," Daniel said.

They all laughed.

"Take care of yourself," Sarah told Isidor, standing. "The next time I see you, I want you to be out of this chair."

As Phoebe and Isidor got ready to depart, Daniel placed a hand on Sarah's back and whispered in her ear. "I think we ought to give Phoebe an assignment."

She took a step back and regarded him with surprise. "Are you sure?"

He winked. "You bet."

Sarah studied Daniel's demeanor and saw only cool self-assurance. This was the Daniel she knew. She felt an overwhelming desire to hold him.

Phoebe approached. "I don't want to say good-bye."

"We don't either, sweetheart," Daniel said. He glanced at Sarah, and she nodded for him to go on. "We were thinking . . . maybe you'd like to join us on a dig next summer."

The girl's mouth dropped open. "Are you serious?"

"Now, Phoebe," Sarah said, assuming a faux didactic tone, "it's very hard work. You may have to climb rocks, descend into caves, and generally toil in very harsh conditions." She smiled.

"I accept!" Phoebe hugged Sarah, then Daniel.

Sarah caught a glimpse of Isidor. He'd sat back in his wheelchair, beaming with contentment. Everything about that moment felt so right.

"Until then, little lady," Daniel said. "You take care of your brother. Family's everything."

Phoebe nodded and returned to Isidor. She pushed his wheelchair toward the street, where a taxi was waiting.

Sarah turned to Daniel. "That was quite a thing you did. She needed someone to believe in her. You've given her that."

His amber eyes glimmered in the sun. "Everybody needs that chance. And God knows she deserves it."

She slipped her arms around his waist. "You're a hell of a man, Daniel Madigan."

He gave a sideways smile. "You trying to tell me you love me?"

She pulled him closer. "You're good at deductive reasoning. Here's some data for you to analyze." She kissed him with an exquisite hunger. Everything they'd been through over the past three months made that moment that much sweeter. She pulled back slightly and smiled. "So what's your theory, Doctor?"

"A hypothesis is starting to come together"—he winked—"but, clearly, I'm going to need more data."